THE HEADMASTER RITUAL

THE
HEADMASTER
RITUAL

Taylor Antrim

HOUGHTON MIFFLIN COMPANY

Boston · New York ·

Visit our Web site: www.houghtonmifflinbooks.com.

Library of Congress Cataloging-in-Publication Data

Antrim, Taylor.
  The headmaster ritual / Taylor Antrim.
    p.   cm.
  ISBN-13: 978-0-618-75682-7
  ISBN-10: 0-618-75682-5
  1. Teachers — Fiction. 2. School principals — Fiction.
3. Private schools — New England — Fiction. 4. Domestic
fiction. I. Title.

  PS3601.N58H43 2007
  813'.6 — dc22   2006023566

Book design by Melissa Lotfy

Printed in the United States of America

MP 10 9 8 7 6 5 4 3 2

For Liz

ACKNOWLEDGMENTS

For guidance and encouragement, thanks to Deborah Eisenberg, John Casey, Ann Beattie, Chris Tilghman, Laura Dave, Sean McConnell, Colin Mort, Callie Wright, and Jenny Hollowell. For help with matters Hollywood and real estate, thanks to Dana Fox and Chris Rice. A special thanks to my agent, Joe Veltre, and to my editor, Webster Younce, for the warm welcome and much-needed help down the homestretch. Thanks to my family for love and enthusiasm. And, most of all, thanks to Liz, my best reader, best friend, and everything else.

THE HEADMASTER RITUAL

July

D YER MARTIN CURLED his fingers through the chainlink and stared at the empty field of shrub. Riverside County sunlight found shards of glass among scattered rocks and twinkled in his direction. Tufts of foot-high desert grass waved gentle hellos in the Santa Ana's hot breath.

Jim Simon, Dyer's boss at Virgenes Development Corporation, had ordered him to take a look at the twenty-five acres he'd claimed for the company, to look at the stalled housing developments that surrounded it, to crouch down and sniff the chromium VI– and perchlorate-saturated soil. So Dyer had taken the 91 east, driving through a desert landscape of malls with empty parking lots, vacant glass-and-steel office parks, and windmill farms stretching to the Santa Ana mountains. Off the freeway exit just west of Perris, Dyer passed Palm Crest, a checkerboard of exposed foundations and roofless homes.

"That's a slice of wasteland you bought us," Jim Simon had said with something like satisfaction, guiding Dyer out the glass office doors and into the parking lot, squeezing his shoulder in a kind, fatherly way. They both stood beside Dyer's car, and Dyer enjoyed the weight and warmth of Simon's hand. "But don't worry," Simon had said, smiling and letting him go. "This is why we have lawyers."

From the time Dyer came on as a junior associate, Jim Simon had told him to be aggressive and creative in exploring opportunities — and to liaise only with him, not any other partner at Virgenes. So on a week when Simon was golfing in Maui, a broker named Jimmy Veltramo rung his extension, and Dyer took the call. Veltramo had described the Inland Empire plot's proximity to Palm Crest, a community of luxury homes, median price 500K, average owner age 29.9, average income high 80s. There was a dearth of shopping in the area, Veltramo said; perfect opportunity for a commercial developer like Virgenes. Timing was a problem; Dyer didn't want to call Simon on his vacation, and Veltramo needed a letter of intent signed by Friday, or he'd take the offer to another company. LOIs were standard practice — and nonbinding; Simon signed them all the time. A signature would pull the property off the market for thirty days. Veltramo could courier the LOI right then; Dyer could always let the period expire without a deal.

But Dyer hadn't caught the clause nestled in a block of type on the back side of page three. The $500,000 Veltramo required for failure to negotiate a purchase and sale agreement. Nor had he checked a Phase 1 environmental report on the land. Nor had he checked the zoning. Now there was half a million due on a zoned-residential plot with groundwater contamination in the middle of nowhere.

A bad blunder, a job-ending blunder. Dyer stood at the chain-link fence that surrounded the property, his ulcer throbbing deep within him, his mouth dry and sour, and he felt the guilt and embarrassment he'd been carrying around all week. He counted the things he could call his own — a dirt-colored Honda, a suitcase's worth of clothes, the rising knowledge that he had never really wanted to work in real estate for his girlfriend's father anyway.

Escape would be natural, a matter of Dyer's patrimony, of DNA, of blood-borne instinct. And there was his Honda, parked behind him, the driver's door ajar, the key-in-ignition tone pinging.

But Dyer was determined to stay in California and make it up to Jim Simon. He told himself that he loved Alice and didn't want to lose her.

Dyer put a foot in the chainlink and began to climb. The spiked top raked his thigh, tearing his suit pants as he swung a leg over. His knees buckled on the hard-packed sand. Stepping over bent lengths of rebar and miniature, thorny cacti, Dyer began to walk the boundary. The air wobbled with heat. Jim Simon had said wasteland, and yet with a little optimism, Dyer thought, with an eye for potential, you could imagine the sturdy geometry of a multi-level parking garage out here, or a retirement community of fountains and palm groves.

He blinked hard, then blinked again, playing peekaboo with the view. The visions kept coming: a twenty-five-screen cineplex, *blink,* a petting zoo.

He knew his ideas were impractical — there wasn't another person for miles. And yet to Dyer they felt like guy wires streaming off his body, digging into the earth, steadying him. A black snake, like a discarded bicycle tube, lay down the fence line. He felt behind him for the fence, for its reassuring grid of hot steel.

Dyer took a long breath, more visions flaring within him. He thought of Alice at her desk, lit by her laptop screen — her thick auburn hair, her gently curving upper lip, her little belly, those things that made his heart race. Sunlight blinded him, bulleting off a broken bottle of Miller Lite. He felt his hot ulcer prodding him in the stomach. He felt the half-million dollars clinging to his back. He felt the wires fray and snap.

FALL TERM

1

September

WE WERE SUPPOSED to meet this morning?" asked Dyer, standing in the shaded portico of Headmaster Wolfe's residence, the humid Massachusetts air on him like a quilt.

"Agreed," said Edward Wolfe with his hand on the door's brass knob. He moved out of the way. "Come in."

Dyer dipped his head and passed inside. The air had a still, musty smell, as if the windows hadn't been opened all summer. The hardwood floor in the wide foyer was bare except for a coarse straw mat and an Oriental rug rolled up like a sausage along the wall. Muddy running shoes sat on a radiator; a loose stack of mail covered a table by the door. An ornately framed portrait—old, Dyer thought, the paint webbed with cracks—of a black-suited couple in twin wooden chairs was propped against the wall. In its place hung a framed sheet of yellow paper with a typed list of names. Curious, Dyer took a closer look. Halfway down the page, he stopped: "Edward Wolfe; Boston, MA; Harvard; SDS."

Dyer felt Wolfe at his side and realized the headmaster had him by a good half inch. His jaw was block-shaped beneath coarse gray stubble, his lips, fish-white and thin. Body heat came off him in waves, mingled with a clean, soapy smell. Dyer told himself to look at Wolfe directly, to find his eyes in their deep-set sockets.

Even though Roberta O'Brien, dean of faculty, had offered him the job, even though he'd signed tax forms, even though there'd been a welcome letter for him in his Bailey House faculty apartment, this morning could still be some sort of final interview, a chance for Wolfe to make up his own mind. In late July during his interview with O'Brien, she'd said that Britton's headmaster had left a tenured post in Harvard's History Department to run the school. "He was looking for a more institutional role. To bring a progressive approach to the classroom," she'd said. "So he wants young, less traditionally trained teachers, candidates with higher academic degrees, not graduates of education programs." Dyer, with no prior teaching experience, with his Oxford M.Phil. in History, was "just the sort of candidate he's looking for," she'd said.

A reassuring memory — but Headmaster Wolfe had never met Dyer. And there had to have been more qualified candidates vying for the position. Lots of them. A teaching post at Britton was something of a coup, and they could probably get a replacement for Dyer, even with classes only a week away. Dyer straightened his back, rising on the balls of his feet.

"Nineteen sixty-eight," said Wolfe, nodding at the framed page of names on the wall. "An enemies list from Hoover's COINTEL-PRO files. An old friend of mine at the Justice Department copied the original for me."

"You were SDS?" asked Dyer.

"Don't kick our founders," said Wolfe, nodding toward the narrow-faced puritans at Dyer's knee.

Dyer stumbled back a step.

"Warner and Constance Britton. Suppose I'll have to find another place for them eventually," said Wolfe. "Maybe the john." The headmaster's clothes were casual, a little ragged: an old Harvard sweatshirt stained yellow at the neck, felt letters puckering from loose thread. Jeans belted with a length of rope. The getup calmed Dyer a little. On his walk this morning, the Britton School had appeared dauntingly correct; now, its headmaster didn't. Dyer tried to smile. Wolfe tipped his head toward a living room. "Shall we?"

Dyer followed him down a short hallway, along a threadbare Oriental rug, its red faded to rust, through an open doorway into the living room. The room was formal and grand, with crown molding, a plaster school crest in the ceiling, and a carved stone hearth. The windows went up above Dyer's head, the antique glass in their leaded panes distorting the view, letting in a weak, gridded light. It was a little cooler here, thanks to an air-conditioning unit gurgling in one window. Wolfe made for a shabby, squat armchair that seemed out of place in the room, settling down with a contented sigh, rocking his head back. He sank lower in the chair until he lay nearly flat, his legs straight out, one crossed over the other.

An oil portrait, the room's only wall decoration, hung directly above Wolfe's head. It took Dyer a moment to recognize the man in it as a younger, shaggier-haired, black-bearded Wolfe, sitting in the same armchair. In the painting he wore a thick tie and a brown jacket with wing-wide lapels. Surrounding him were swirls and licks of red and orange, as if Wolfe was the source of an enormous fire. His hands curled over the arms of the chair like catchers' mitts.

If Wolfe noticed Dyer staring — if he read Dyer's mind (narcissism? any other interpretation?) — the headmaster didn't let on. Wolfe gestured toward the navy corduroy sofa in the middle of the room, the cushions worn to a shiny indigo, another piece, like the armchair, that could have been dragged in from a yard sale.

Wolfe spread his arms. "Welcome to Britton," he said.

"Thank you," Dyer said, breathing out with real relief, lowering himself, a long way down, into the sofa. Change funneled out of his pockets into the cushions.

Wolfe dug at the chair's frayed stitching with a thumbnail. "You come to us from California," he said.

"L.A.," said Dyer. "I drove out last week." He thought of eastern Colorado, the prairie empty to the horizon, the white lane blinking beside the car like a reset clock. "I wanted to say how excited I am to be joining you here."

"Why's that?"

Dyer had to think. "I've always wanted to teach. I can't imagine a better place. Britton's reputation—"

Wolfe waved that away. "Our reputation's a handicap."

Dyer waited; no elaboration came. The Britton School was the oldest, most selective prep school in the country. Dyer had noted the 8 percent admit rate on the website. He'd focused on the other number, that staggering 92, the rowdy group of rejects he'd surely have been in, had he ever applied. The country's current president, at least two senators he knew of, the secretary of state: all Britton alumni. On Dyer's walk around the school grounds that morning, sweating, waving gnats out of his face, he'd passed brick and white wooden buildings with names and dates carved into stone plaques. Thomas Ramm Hall, 1924. Jordan Eccleson Hall, 1819. Holbert Weiss Hall, 1880. The neat, crisscrossing paths, the terraced lawns, the school's museum stillness, delivered the impressions Dyer had been expecting—prestige, privilege; both intimidating. But there was also this: a hushed refuge, a ringed enclave of quiet. A fresh start.

"I understand you were working real estate."

"It was sort of an experiment."

Wolfe leaned forward expectantly, but Dyer didn't want to talk about Virgenes, so he shrugged like a teenager, then tried to think of some way to change the subject. What he did want to talk about, he realized, was Alice. *I was trying to make a relationship work.* But he couldn't say it. Not to his new employer, a man he hardly knew.

Dyer suddenly wanted to call Alice, hear how her screenplay was coming. They hadn't broken up, not officially. After he'd accepted Dean O'Brien's job offer, they had agreed to defer the question, though Dyer knew this stalling was just to save their last weeks together. Which hadn't worked: "You knew that LOI was a mistake," Alice had told him one night, lying in bed. "You signed it on purpose."

"I didn't," Dyer said.

"Everyone acts out," she said. "It's just a question of scale."

"Your dad said to be aggressive. I was being aggressive," he said.

"You're being aggressive right now," she said.

Dyer told himself he was still young, younger than his father had been when he left his mother — and Dyer and Alice weren't married. There was no comparison, in fact. Taking the Britton job meant following a career path he'd always wanted (as opposed to, say, real estate). It also meant accepting responsibility for his future, holding himself accountable — two things his father had never done.

"You're probably wondering why I chose you for this job," Wolfe said, breaking the silence.

Well, yes. But Dyer answered quickly: "Roberta O'Brien told me you wanted someone without traditional training. That you didn't care about an education degree."

"Here's what I care about," said Wolfe. He took a newspaper that lay folded on the floor and tossed it to the couch.

Dyer read the headline: "U.S. Intelligence Agencies Fear Imminent North Korean Nuclear Test." He said, "I heard about it on the radio this morning."

"What do you think?"

Dyer hesitated. What was the right answer here? "We've been calling their bluff for a long time."

" 'We'?"

"The U.S."

"The most heavily nuclear-armed country in the world." Wolfe raised his eyebrows at Dyer.

Dyer looked back down at the paper, searching for something else to say. "I suppose it serves them to be provocative."

"Why, do you think?"

A few seconds slipped by. "What do you mean?"

"Put it this way: Don't capitalist nations tend inevitably toward war?"

Christ, thought Dyer.

"No?"

At Oxford, Dyer had taken a term's tutorial with Howard Phelps, a conservative economist at St. John's College. They'd done a study of the American New Left in the sixties and seventies, including the Students for a Democratic Society, the Port Huron Statement, the Progressive Labor Maoists, the Weathermen. In a series of essays, Dyer had described the New Left as naïve apologists for third world dictatorships, drawn more to revolutionary violence than coherent political ideology. He'd written that, historically, even those exploited by capitalism had more to hope for than the communist poor. Dyer certainly wouldn't be rehashing those arguments to an ex-member of the SDS. Wolfe would know, anyway, about his tutorial with Phelps. His name was on Dyer's transcript, included with his original application for the position.

"Historically speaking," Dyer finally said. "It's a good point."

Wolfe nodded toward the paper again: "Meaning you don't think we're headed for war right now?"

Dyer managed a nervous shrug. Footsteps crossed the hall outside the room. A thin boy with short wavy hair, carrying a green duffel bag, passed the open living room door. He looked in and said, "Okay. Bye." *Good timing*, Dyer thought.

"James," Wolfe said, beckoning him in. "Dyer, this is my son. James, meet Mr. Martin."

The boy dropped his bag and took a reluctant step through the doorway.

Dyer pushed himself out of the couch, crossed the room, and shook James's hand. "Hello," said Dyer.

"Hi," said James in a quiet voice, glancing at Wolfe. Dyer saw the likeness in the deep set of their eyes, their thin, white lips.

"James will be in your 250 class," Wolfe said to Dyer.

The boy took a long breath as if the prospect depressed him. He dropped Dyer's hand, returned to his duffel.

"See you in class," said Dyer, trying to sound cheerful.

"Bye, Dad," said James, pausing at his father's side.

Wolfe patted him on the back but said nothing. James looked reluctant to leave — but eventually he did, dragging his feet as he moved into the hall. Wolfe frowned at him over his shoulder. The front door opened and slowly shut. Wolfe panned his attention back to Dyer. "I'm sort of throwing him to the wolves."

"Oh?"

"I've sent him to live in the dorms. Staying here keeps him isolated. Sets him apart." He looked briefly out the window. On the far side of the street, James crossed the quad toward Elson Road, weaving under the weight of his bag. "Boarding school wasn't a happy time for me, either," he said. "I spent four fairly miserable years at Hawkins Prep. In Connecticut?" Dyer shook his head. "The social hierarchy was a little severe."

"Teenagers can be cruel," said Dyer.

"The elite can be. The popular kids." Wolfe studied Dyer. "Were you popular?"

"Not really," Dyer said quickly, finding his seat, trying to shake off a familiar gloom. Twenty-five years old, and it still depressed him to catch the resemblance between fathers and sons. "You had to be an asshole to be really popular," he said. Oops. But Wolfe didn't seem bothered by the word. "I had decent grades, but North Richmond High was no Britton School. Ran cross-country. Yearbook staff."

Wolfe scratched his cheek with a fingernail — a low, rough sound. "You know Britton's motto?"

Dyer's mind raced. "Not by heart, I'm afraid."

" 'Youth from Every Quarter.' Sounds nice — except when you consider that for the last two hundred years we've been a game preserve for New England Wasps. 'Youth from Every Quarter' means no power class, no hegemony of thought. No *elite*. The word itself should be meaningless."

Wolfe paused. Dyer sensed a cue. "That's what is exciting about teaching —"

"But our elite is alive and well," said Wolfe, interrupting. "Last year we had Henry Fieldspar in the upper form. You recognize the name?"

"Son of Angus?" Angus Fieldspar was a Republican senator from Tennessee.

"Major donor to the school. Or ex-donor, I should say. Henry thought his name meant he could get away with anything, but then he was caught drinking and what they call 'cruising' in the same night. We give you two strikes here. Those were his."

"What's cruising?"

"Leaving the dorm after sign-in."

"Got it."

"Discipline is a question for the collective. You'd call that a radical cliché, perhaps." Wolfe thought for a moment, then held his hand flat above his stomach. "Think of the school as a balanced seesaw. Privilege one class of student over another . . ." He tilted his hand up and down, then let it drop to the arm of the chair. A puff of dust rose like smoke.

Outside, in heavy, syncopated tones, a carillon began to ring. Dyer felt a headache coming on, a bunched feeling in his forehead. He tried to assure himself that he'd made no major missteps, that they were still building a rapport. "Do we have many senators' sons?" Dyer asked, smiling.

"I'm getting rid of them one by one." Wolfe deadpanned a stare, then smiled and leveraged himself up from the chair. "Good to have you, Dyer. I told Roberta to give you a light schedule this fall," he said. "While we break you in. Come winter term, we'll load you up with more."

"Great," said Dyer, standing. The meeting was over.

Wolfe followed Dyer to the front door and set a hand on his shoulder. His grip wasn't warm and soft as Alice's father's had been; it was more like a leather strap. "I do a sequence of choson do forms in the morning here in my backyard."

"Is that a . . . ?" Dyer couldn't think of the word.

"It's a Korean exercise technique. Six in the morning on Wednesdays. Optional of course."

Six in the morning. "Sounds terrific," Dyer said.

Outside, the carillon bells in the bell tower rang some tumbledown melody Dyer didn't recognize. The heavy notes hummed the air.

Wolfe shook his hand, holding his gaze a second too long, a

stare that felt like a warning. "They're not bluffing," he said. "The North Koreans. Take my word."

Bad news, thought James, standing inside the door to Weiss Hall, staring at a printed sheet of room assignments on the bulletin board. He traced a line with his fingernail under his name to the room number on the left. He tried to swallow. Twelve, the only single in the dorm, up on the third floor: Henry Fieldspar's old room.

Through an open door down the hall came the sound of a computer game. Upstairs he heard heavy footsteps and a door slamming shut. A thin cloud of dust drifted down from the ceiling. Weiss Hall had last been renovated in the forties — big rooms, high ceilings, wood floors, but also moldy carpeting in the hallway, warped floorboards, no phone lines in the rooms. A rank, nose-tickling scent of old sweat hung in the air. There were newer, cleaner boys' dorms at Britton, but the rowdiest, most popular guys all wanted to live in Weiss.

And of all the rooms, the single on the third floor was the biggest and the most sought-after. It was usually assigned by a summer lottery; this year it had been given to him.

Chris Nolan drummed down the stairs. He saw James at the bulletin board and clapped a hand over his face. "Say it ain't so."

"Hi, Mr. Nolan," said James. Chris Nolan taught photography; James had taken his portraiture elective in the spring term last year. For his final portfolio, he'd submitted ten angles on a dead pigeon in the grass behind Ramm Hall. Grade: 4.0.

"Our VIP," said Chris. "Welcome to Weiss."

"Why am I in twelve?"

Chris worked his teeth with his tongue, as if trying to dislodge a piece of food. "Nepotism?"

"Mr. Nolan."

"Plum assignment, James. Just take it."

"Did my dad cut a deal with Residence?" How unlikely was *that?* James thought. Privileges were not his dad's thing.

"I just post the list," said Chris. He had a sonorous, lilting voice. James remembered it from class. "Think of all the privacy," Chris said, raising his eyebrows.

James blushed. "This is not the way I wanted to enter the boarding community."

"Listen to you. 'The boarding community.'" A series of rapid gun blasts came from the room down the hall. Chris half turned and called out: "See that little knob on the speaker? Turn it left."

No answer, but the volume went down.

James lifted his bag off the floor and passed Chris, keeping his eyes low. "Does everyone know?"

"Only a couple of guys have moved in so far. But," he pointed, "your name is on the list."

James sighed and grasped the banister. It swayed right with a creak.

"You'll be fine," said Chris.

The third floor of Weiss consisted of four double rooms, a group bathroom, and one single. The hall was empty and quiet when James reached the landing at the top of the stairs. The brass number plates on his door were missing—in their place lay darker paint studded by nails. James crouched down and sniffed the circular tan stain at the base of the door. Mildew, then an acrid chemical scent, then, running underneath, the sweet rot of meat.

James knew the story from eavesdropping on lunchtime gossip last year. That spring—before they all got busted for drinking and before Henry got kicked out—the third-floor Weiss guys had engaged in two weeks of Property. It began small, as Property always did: Henry Fieldspar threw a stack of Cary Street's CDs out the window, smashing them on the brick walk. Cary then dropped a framed photo of the Fieldspar family in the toilet. Property had to escalate, so Henry slid a chicken leg behind Cary's radiator. A week later, with pudgy maggots climbing his wall, Cary recruited Sam Rafton and, from the chemistry lab, stole a specimen jar with a calf's brain floating in a quart of formaldehyde. At 2:00 A.M. they upended the thing outside Henry's door and knocked.

James stared at the stain on the carpet. By tomorrow night, he thought, the seniors would be up here. Sam, Cary, Buddy Juliver, Brian Jones, the others. Each one of them must have put their names into the Weiss room lottery for room 12. And the headmaster's kid had had it handed to him.

All last year, crossing campus, eating lunch in Commons, studying in the library reading room, James had felt independent and anonymous. Hardly anyone paid any attention to him; no one even seemed to know or care that he was the headmaster's son. In class, he made a few friends, Jeffrey Cohen from Chemistry, Volker Stein, the German exchange student, in U.S. History. He hadn't been lonely.

He'd told his dad all of this, but Wolfe had made it clear that his decision was final. "You can't go on isolating yourself from your peers," he'd said. He'd made James pack or box up everything in his room, relenting only on the framed picture of his mom that James had wanted to leave. "You need to commit," Wolfe had said. "I don't want you to think you can just come back if things get difficult."

James figured he was being taught a lesson. Like when he was eight and his dad swore off gift-giving. "The spirit of Capitalism," he'd said of the Christmas tree James and his mother had decorated. Or the time Wolfe had sat James down, at age fourteen, for a documentary on the My Lai massacre. "See what your government will do," he'd said warmly in James's ear as a gray heap of Vietnamese bodies filled the screen. The lesson could be about equality, the unity of the collective—like the sheep farm in Vermont his parents had lived on briefly their first year out of Harvard. They made cheese and walnut bread that they sold at the local farmers' markets. "Our year in utopia," his father called it.

But Weiss was the opposite of a commune. The seniors took whatever they wanted out of the rooms of the lower-form guys on the ground floor—CDs, DVDs, any food they could find. Lowers had to clean rooms and answer the communal pay phone on the third floor, even though they lived two flights down (the head-of-dorm apartment filled the second floor). It would ring, and one of the seniors would shout "Lower!" till someone started climbing the stairs. More than six rings, and a lower would get tackled on his way to the shower, have his head dunked in a toilet. Any new kid, no matter what year, got hazed. James slumped against the hallway wall feeling a tense, held-breath quality in the silence around him. He'd wanted a small room in an uncool boys' dorm, a safe place to hide out till spring. This special treatment was a disaster.

He let himself into his new room.

Sunlight poured in from the big window on the east wall. A single bed was tucked into the corner. The closet door stood ajar. An extension cord snaked across the wood floor. Bright rectangles of white marked the locations of old posters.

A girl sat against the far wall.

Her name was Jane Hirsch. James recognized her from Calculus and Chemistry. She sat cross-legged, her hands cupping her ankles, a Polaroid camera resting in her lap like a pet. Her eyes were closed. Photos lay scattered around her knees.

James pushed his bag inside the doorway with his foot, and Jane's eyes snapped open. She blinked at him for a few indecisive seconds, then lifted the camera. The flash went off; the camera whirred out film.

"Hi," she said.

James nervously eyed the photos. Henry Fieldspar smiling. Henry frowning. The side of Henry's head. James remembered —also from Commons gossip—that Jane and Henry had been a couple in the spring. That they'd logged multiple afternoons in this very room, on that bed in the corner.

James and Jane stared at each other.

"Came in the window," Jane said, and pointed.

James crossed to the sill and leaned out. A fire escape, a vertical ladder bolted to the brick, lay six inches to the left of the opening, the rungs corroded orange with rust.

He turned around. He still hadn't said anything. What could he say? "How was your summer?"

"Fine," she said. "I did four weeks of Mandarin at Yale. You?"

"Waited tables at Scudo's in North Britton."

"Cool," she said.

He shook his head. Jane stacked the photos in a pile and turned them facedown. She didn't seem to be leaving. "You taking 250?" he asked.

"Yeah," she said.

"I saw the guy teaching it," James said.

"What'd he look like?"

"Young, I guess."

He tried not to stare at her heavy black eyebrows, at the white skin of her neck. She wore frayed jeans, flip-flops, and a Britton soccer T-shirt. She played center forward, cocaptain of the team, James knew. He remembered crusty scabs on her knees in Calc. He remembered once seeing her cross campus after a game — her wet black hair pulled into a ponytail, her soccer shorts rolled on her hips, her shins flushed, mottled from the guards.

"So you're taking Henry's room," she said.

"I don't want it. It's been assigned to me."

"Better you than one of those assholes," she said, nodding in the direction of the empty hall.

"I'm not sure the assholes will feel the same way."

"They won't do anything."

James just stared at her.

Jane stood and slid the photos in the back pocket of her jeans. The camera dangled from her wrist. "Do you mind not telling anyone I was here?"

"Why are you?"

She made a quiet, relieved sound, as if pleased James had finally asked. "I didn't think anyone would be moving in yet." Silence. "I miss Henry. I know it's stupid or girly or whatever."

"Have you heard from him?" James finally asked.

"I saw him this summer when he came up to Yale. He's gone to this boys' school outside of Lexington. They have to wear uniforms."

"Funny," said James, keeping his voice dull and neutral.

"He's trying to get back in here to save his chances at Georgetown. Or, like, Choate. Exeter might even take him. His grandfather went there or something."

"I didn't know him that well," James said, his gaze leveled off her left shoulder.

"I know," she said, and pushed a few strands of hair behind her ear.

"I guess I'll see you in class."

"Class isn't until next *week*. Come over to Bachelor tonight. Bunch of seniors who're here already are getting together. Sign-in is lax since school hasn't technically begun."

Was that a joke? She must know he didn't go to parties. "I have to unpack," he said.

Jane grinned at the single duffel on the floor. "Want some help?"

James nudged the door. It swung on a whiny hinge.

"Well," she said. "You know where Bachelor is."

She turned to go, and James's eyes fell on the photos stuffed into the seat pocket of her jeans. He also noticed the silver anklet that hung between her frayed cuff and callused heel. A gift from Henry? She hadn't worn it last year. He would have seen it. She passed down the stairs, out of sight.

James closed the door and sat down on the corner of the bed. Through the open window, he could see straight across the road that separated East and West Quad, could see the shingled corner of Bachelor beyond the roof of Commons and the leafy tops of birch trees.

He kept swallowing, trying to calm down.

He imagined Henry waiting for Jane with his window open, some night in April before he got kicked out. He imagined Jane sprinting from her dorm, from hedge to hedge, skirting the sides of buildings, following the shadows on the ground. He imagined Henry listening for Jane on the ladder outside. There were campus patrols, and cruising was a probationary offense. Still, Henry had had the privacy of a single, they'd had this narrow bed to themselves, and they'd been falling in love.

James lay flat on his back. Glow-in-the-dark sticker stars spelled FUCK BRITTON on the ceiling.

Home could be anywhere, James told himself. The less you cared about where you lived, the better off you were. *I'll be fine.* What could they do to him? How bad could it be? He thought of the photo, the one Jane had taken of him when he came in. He took a deep breath, and a delicate floral scent reached him. Perfume — and running underneath like a fetid stream, that damp, meaty rot.

He thought of the calf, wondered if it had ever been born, if it had ever had any thoughts, even dumb bovine thoughts, before losing its brain to science.

Dyer retraced his steps toward his new home: Bailey House, a three-story, ski chalet–style boys' dorm beyond Reservoir Road. Maybe Wolfe hadn't known about Dyer's tutorial at Oxford. Maybe he'd just been sounding him out. The new History teacher — check out his politics. Still, what had he said? *You'd call that a radical cliché.*

Why would a guy with enough ego to hang a portrait of himself on his own wall give up a big-shot professor's post at Harvard? An institutional role, Dean O'Brien said. But Dyer figured there had to be something else. Prestigious or not, Britton was just a prep school. Maybe it was money; maybe Britton was paying him a load.

He slowed his pace; he'd been charging along. *Relax.* He stared at the school's prim, mowed lawns, told himself how much more restful this was than L.A.'s smog halo and bug-crawl traffic. It was the reason he'd gone for the M.Phil. at Oxford in the first place — to sweeten his résumé, to get a teaching job just like this one. Alice had had the idea of moving to Hollywood. "I hate this," Alice had said during their second winter at Oxford, wiping the condensation off the window in her room at Christ Church. "Hate what?" Dyer had said, sitting on the floor by the radiator, admiring naked, unbashful Alice. "Let's move somewhere warm," Alice had said, turning to him. "Let's get real jobs."

Up ahead on the path, another teacher was headed his way, a guy about Dyer's age with a narrow head and short, carefully mussed dark hair.

"Hello, hello," he said, reaching Dyer. He held out his hand. "Chris Nolan."

Dyer took it. "Dyer Martin," he said. Chris's hand felt soft and smooth, like baby skin.

"You're the new History hire?" asked Chris. He took a step back and looked at him with approval. "You don't look like a History guy."

"I don't? Why not?"

"You're not bookish," he said. "History teachers usually are. Where're you headed?"

"Bailey House," said Dyer, pleased.

"Hey. I was head of Bailey last year. I'll take you." He pivoted around, and Dyer thought he was going to offer his arm. They walked in silence for a few steps.

"I just met the headmaster for the first time," said Dyer.

"Comrade Wolfe? He's an oddity, huh?"

"I didn't know what to expect."

"We're all still getting to know Ed."

"What do you mean?"

"Just that it's only his second year. He was some kind of hot-shit History professor at Harvard before. Did European intellectual history." Chris frowned, thinking. "But then I think he wrote a book on China — or something. Anyway, rumor is he bedded one of his students."

"Jesus. Really?"

"But I'm not sure I believe it. Wouldn't exactly qualify him for prep school work." Chris glanced at Dyer. "Still."

"Has he done anything like that here?"

"Listen to me," Chris said, laughing, glancing over his shoulder to see if anyone had been nearby. "Loose lips. No, no. Not that I know of. And I'll shut up." But Chris looked as if he wanted to say more, so Dyer waited.

Chris tipped his head from side to side as though he were trying to decide whether to talk. "A college friend of mine is in grad school at Harvard," he whispered. "He told me Ed left under a cloud. Undergraduate complaints, he said. An affair or two is his best guess."

"Wow," Dyer said. "Is he married?" he asked.

"Caroline Fuller," Chris said. "As in Fuller-Reardon Aerospace. As in military weapons-maker heiress. As in meal ticket. So take that sixties radical stuff with a grain of salt."

They headed up a grassy hill, behind the library.

Commons rose up on their left, marking the center of campus. Commons was Britton's biggest building, and, as Chris told him, pointing, the oldest. Above the banks of double doors, a marble carving of the school seal—a bigger version of the one in Wolfe's ceiling—sat embedded in the brick. A book crossed by a scepter and the date of incorporation, 1790. "This is where the lower form hangs out," he said, nodding at the wide stone steps, worn shiny from feet. "Like vagrants." Seniors, he explained, spent most of their free time in a lounge in the basement of Commons; upperformers took the foyer of the library. Freshmen hid out in special freshmen dorms.

Dyer and Chris rounded the corner of Commons and headed down a pine needle–strewn path. Dyer recognized Reservoir Road. Up ahead was Range House, a girls' dorm; unlike the other oblong, barracks-style dormitories on campus, it looked like an ordinary house with a front door, two large ground-floor windows, white wood shingles, a gray slate roof.

Lying flat along the peak of the roof and leaning over the edge, a young woman reached for black cable lines connected to the side of the house.

"Greta?" said Chris.

She lifted her head. "Hi, Chris," she said.

"What are you doing?" he yelled.

"Trying to fix the cable." Her face was red from leaning over the edge.

"There are people who do that sort of thing," said Chris.

"I called weeks ago."

Chris and Dyer crossed the street and moved under her. She held the cable line with one hand. In the other she held a rubber-handled tool, like an oversized wire stripper.

"Is that safe?" asked Chris.

"I installed cable one summer on Long Island," she said. She was having trouble positioning herself to reach the connection with both hands. An old lightning rod at the end of the roof's peak was in her way. Dyer could see droplets of perspiration on her forehead as she hooked her neck and shoulders around the rod.

"How'd you get up there?"

"Tree," she said. Dyer took a step back and looked toward the rear of the house. A big maple stood in the backyard.

"This is our new History guy," said Chris, and then, to Dyer, "Greta Salverton. She teaches Chemistry."

She smiled down at him. Her cheeks were plump; one was smeared with dirt. "Hi," she said. She maneuvered around the lightning rod, working her body down the shingled slope to gain a better angle.

A sudden scraping sound—slate coming loose. Greta slipped sideways. She scrabbled her feet and shot both hands up as her body started to slide. She snatched the lightning rod just as her lower half dropped off the side of the roof. The tool fell; Chris and Dyer jumped back as it smacked the ground at their feet.

"Shit," she said, dangling, kicking at the side of the house. Dyer could see Greta's white fingers curled around the metal. The rod began to bend. "Shit," she said again, her voice lifting with panic.

Chris ran for the front door.

Wildly, Dyer looked around him. For what? Leaves?

Her flip-flop fell, narrowly missing Dyer's face. He took another step back and spotted the tree at the rear of the house.

A window slid open, and Chris's head appeared. Winded, he reached for her legs. "Can you swing this way?" he asked, grasping at the air near her ankles.

"This thing's gonna go," she said, looking up at the rod.

"Dyer?" Chris asked. "Can you catch her?"

Was he serious? The ground beneath him was hard-packed dirt and gravel.

Greta kicked at the side of the house again. She let out a little frightened breath.

"Hang on," said Dyer, dropping his blazer and running toward the backyard.

The maple was squat and old, and, despite the slippery soles of his loafers, Dyer had an easy climb through its gnarled, thick branches. He'd climbed trees in the alley behind his mother's house as a boy and, pulling himself higher, he remembered that if you kept your attention on what you were doing, you'd never notice how quickly the ground dropped away.

The roof was edged with a tin gutter. He gripped the sticky bark of a branch, at least twenty feet up. His breath was hard and heavy.

Dyer leaned toward the roof and tested the gutter with a hand. He pulled himself to a higher branch and rested a foot on its lip. Seemed sturdy, but as he shifted his weight, the stays broke with a rusty snap. Dyer lunged and slapped down on the slate. His breath caught; he slipped and grabbed the edge of the broken gutter with one hand.

Bracing with the hand, Dyer could just pull his knees up to the roof's edge and shimmy his body higher. An awkward grappling, but after a moment Dyer lay flat halfway up the slope, the hot slate warming him through his shirt. His heart thumping, he looked up the rest of the way. A bare patch of tar ran along the edge where Greta had slipped. He could also see the base of the lightning rod, a metal plate screwed into a block of wood. Greta's knuckles were bunched around it.

"Hang on," he said again, and he worked his way up on his

hands and knees. He wiped his face on his sleeve. The sun beat down all around him.

On all fours, Dyer made his way up the slippery slate to the ridge of the roof. He swung one leg over the sandpapery nylon strip running along the top. Anchoring himself with his thighs, he reached for Greta's free hand. "Can you take this?" Greta waved it at him wildly.

With a splintery, shearing snap, the rod pulled out of its block of wood.

Dyer lunged, falling forward onto his stomach. For a second, he had Greta by the wrist, her skin bunching in his grip.

Then his hold slipped.

Dyer watched her go down, her arms wide and flapping. When she hit the ground, that dirt and gravel, she let out a sound like a laugh. She landed feet first, put her hands down, then rolled and crumpled into a ball.

Chris, back outside, was crouching over her. "Greta?" he said.

She didn't say anything. Slowly, by degrees, she uncurled herself, holding her wrist, eyes squeezed shut.

"Greta? Are you okay? Can you hear me?" Chris asked.

Dyer tried to speak but found he couldn't. He was still feeling her wrist in his hand, feeling the skin bunch, then slide away.

They could hear her rough, jagged breath. She rolled onto her back and stared up at Dyer. Though there were tears in her eyes, she was trying to smile. She croaked something.

"Should I call an ambulance?" asked Chris.

She waved one hand in the air, shook her head.

"I'm okay," she finally managed. "Wind . . . knocked out." Her eyes went to slits.

Dyer gradually let his body relax, let the tendons in his neck go slack. He sat up and looked down at his filthy shirt. He considered the bent, broken gutter, the branches of the maple tree, the girl laid out on the ground, fighting to breathe.

Fresh start. He almost laughed.

. . .

"Fracture," said Greta, coming through the examination-room double doors into the infirmary's lobby. Smith Infirmary was a tall, steepled stone building with grids of leaded windows, ivy-wrapped columns, and poorly joined pale blue linoleum floors. It reminded Dyer of Oxford's Radcliffe Infirmary, also stone and tall, the patient wards long and wide with rows of curtained beds. He and Alice had spent an afternoon there the previous winter during a pregnancy scare. The test from Boots said no, but Alice had been eight days late and worried.

Dyer tried to make the memory disappear, the pints of Carlsberg they'd drunk at the Lamb and Flag to celebrate — no baby! — their vows to be more careful. A Durex every time. The way they'd staggered back to Christ Church and done it just inside her door, unprotected, again.

"It's just a little one," said Greta, and Dyer set down the magazine he hadn't been reading. Her left arm hung in a sling, splinted, with ice packs wrapped around the wrist. She'd regained some color in her cheeks.

"Does it hurt?" asked Chris.

Greta rattled a bottle of pills in her good hand.

"Oooh, what'd you get?" Chris whispered.

"Vicodin," she said.

"I'm really sorry," said Dyer, his gaze fixed on the bulky wrapping around her arm.

"You tried."

"How many refills did they give you?" asked Chris.

Greta raised a finger to her lips. A thickset nurse poked her head through the door, her hair done up in a net. She gestured at Greta with a clipboard.

"Orthopedist'll be in tomorrow. Come back at ten for your cast. Meantime, keep the ice on. Sign here."

Greta gave her a salute as Chris and Dyer rose from their metal chairs. She signed with her good hand, and the nurse disappeared back through the double doors.

"How long did she say you'd have the cast?" Dyer asked.

Greta looked at him, her smile weakening a little. She swept her blond hair out of her face, showing off her high, wide forehead. Her level stare held Dyer's for seconds. He wasn't responsible, he thought. She'd have fallen anyway; she might have pulled him off the roof; he couldn't have held her forever.

"Six weeks," she said.

Four rings, and Dyer nearly hung up; then came a groggy hello.

"Hi," he said.

"Not awake yet," Alice said.

"I can call back," he said.

"No," she said, and yawned, her voice squeaking at the end. He thought of her bed, the white duvet jammed down around her feet, her hair curled on the pillow. He couldn't help it. "No," she said again. There was a lag. "I should be getting up anyway."

Dyer looked at his things, his clothes, his laptop computer, and the few books piled on the wood floor of his narrow, railroad apartment in Bailey House. After coming through the door and standing motionless for a few seconds, he'd picked up the phone and dialed without thinking. Now, what to say? "I climbed onto a roof this morning," he said. It was the only thing that came to him.

"Why?"

"There was this other teacher up there. She'd slipped. I thought I could help her."

"My hero."

"She fell anyway."

"Oops," said Alice. She yawned again. "Was she okay?" The question was polite. He was sorry he'd brought it up.

"Broken wrist," he said and hurried onto something else. "How's the writing going?"

"Not bad." She would be out of bed now, padding into the kitchen. Catching her reflection in the living room mirror. Opening the cabinet, unfolding the package of ground coffee.

"I'm doing the finale," she said. "Jessica and Bruce's climactic, love-in-the-face-of-death moment. I'm still missing a big line of dialogue, though. A closer. A zinger. 'Here's looking at you, kid.' 'You had me at hello.' One of those."

"Remind me where we are?"

"Embassy communications are down, and Jessica and Bruce have no idea that U.S. troops are on the city outskirts. They've opened their last tin of caviar. Radiation levels are critical."

"Does Bruce still think Jessica is Iranian?"

"She *is* Iranian, Dyer. But, no. She's admitted she's CIA."

"And he still loves her?"

"More than ever. I'm thinking of getting him to quote some Rumi. To show his sensitivities. But I'm guessing that'll go over people's heads."

Dyer felt calmer than he had in weeks. He lay flat on the floor and tried to think about Shiites and errant U.S. missile strikes and dirty bombs and dead embassy personnel, and two people falling in love over a tin of caviar.

"I don't know," he said finally.

"It's a tough one," she agreed.

"The headmaster here had a page from Hoover's COINTEL-PRO files framed in the hallway of his house with his name on it. Says he was SDS."

"Cool. Is he a hippie?"

"Reformed. Or semireformed. He asked me if I would agree that capitalist nations tend toward war."

"Huh. So things are okay? You're meeting headmasters and saving girls from roofs."

"I didn't save her. She fell."

Nothing for a while. Dyer wondered if she was looking out her window at the complex's shady courtyard. If the palm was tapping the pane.

"Alice," Dyer began. He cleared his throat. "If I'd stayed, it would have been bad for both of us. I would have driven you crazy." He knew how insistent and formal he sounded, as if trying to reason with her. "I wouldn't have been very much fun to live with."

"*Fun* to live with? I wasn't worried about that."

"Do you know how much money I cost your dad? Even if he gets out of the contract, there are the lawyers' fees."

"You have to learn to do something else with guilt," she said. "Process it in a different way. Make it run around the block. Take it out for a drive on the highway."

"Six weeks ago you said I did this thing on purpose."

"Are you saying I was right?"

Dyer told her he didn't understand how he was not supposed to feel guilty about a half million dollars, and she let out a ragged sigh.

"I don't want to talk about the money," said Alice. "I don't know what to say. Why did you call?"

After unpacking his clothes, after putting them in the dresser and hanging them in his closet, after lying down on the bed, neatly made with a set of white sheets and a blue wool blanket, and reading fifty pages of *Huckleberry Finn* in an hour, James set the book down and stared at the bare dresser against the wall. Why had he left the picture of his mom? He supplied his own answer: to see if his dad would pack it away or leave it.

But that was a pointless experiment. They were getting divorced. He guessed they were just waiting for him to go to college to tell him. He said the word to himself, *divorce,* testing it out, gauging its effect. An image needled him: Ms. Salverton leaving by the back kitchen door too early on a Sunday morning in the spring. There was the evidence, if he needed it. And maybe the real reason his father had kicked him out of the house.

I should commit, James thought, pushing the memory away. Last year, he'd asked Jeff Cohen if he missed home. Jeff was from Montclair, New Jersey; he was a lower, fifteen years old, a new boarder living in Cowley Hall. "No," Jeff said, blotting his runny nose with a wadded tissue. "This is home. Once I decided that, I was fine."

James could be adaptable. He'd had to be. Eighteen months ago, after his dad accepted the Britton headmaster appointment, he and James had had dinner at their home in Cambridge, a dinner of liver and onions. James's mom had been working on campus with her MBA group.

"Bachelor food," Wolfe had said. James took his eyes off the acrid-smelling slab on his plate. "Get used to it, kiddo."

James waited as his dad took two hungry bites, chewed, swallowed, wiped his mouth with the back of his hand. "What do you mean?" James asked, and then listened as carefully as he could to the news that only the two of them would be going to Britton in the fall.

"What about Mom?"

"She's committed to her career," said his father, and then opened his hands, gestured at the empty kitchen. "See for yourself."

And he went on eating as if that was all the information James needed.

Are you separating? James's tight throat kept the question down. His parents used to kiss full on the mouth unloading the dishwasher; they used to spend whole Sunday afternoons behind the closed door of their bedroom. He never thought he'd miss such gooey stuff. But ever since his mom had enrolled in Harvard's MBA program, there'd been a newer, colder air in the house, a chilly atmosphere of stalemate. Caroline spent more and more time across the river at the Business School; his dad spent less and less time in the History Department, his teaching load down to one graduate seminar a year. They were drawing apart, and James knew his dad resented her newfound interest in her family's company. But they didn't fight. They didn't raise their voices, or let bitterness into their speech.

"Not that commitment is a bad thing. It's a good thing," his father said through bites of liver. His voice rose, his gaze leveled on James. "It's a principle to live by." The eye contact, the volume, the force of his father's voice, meant that was a line James should turn over in his head till he understood it. He'd been getting a lot of lessons then, declamatory, angry-sounding mini-homilies about idealism, dissent, sacrifice. Just the week before, his father had told him: "To be a part of something larger than ourselves relieves us of pettiness." James had been afraid to ask exactly what he meant, but he held his father's gaze until he looked away. Their lives were changing — that much he understood. James felt confused, but he also thought that these speeches were messages, direct communications of the sort that hadn't passed between them in years. His father's attention stirred him up and made him think of the ways they used to spend time together, Saturday mornings, just the two of them, walking to his office in Harvard's History Department, talking about his third-grade teacher, Ms. Nossiter, or drilling multiplication tables. His father did grading or typed out a lecture, and James would build teetering barricades of books, or later, when he was a little older, he'd read. His father's semester-long research trips to China disrupted the routine, and when he came back, he needed his office to himself to work on his book. James had grown out of the excursions, but nothing similar took their place.

How long had it been since they'd spent a Saturday morning together? Two years. More.

But now their lives were changing.

"By which I mean commitment to an idea," Wolfe finished, clattering his fork on his plate. "Since ideas are more reliable than people."

James took his plate to the sink and wrapped his liver in aluminum foil, reminding himself that *he* was being taken along to Britton. They were going together. His father was staying committed to *him*. He wasn't being left behind. That was what he was telling him.

But James was also going, apparently, because free tuition and a Britton diploma were too good to pass up. "It's an incredible opportunity for you," his mother explained later that night, kneeling beside his bed. He was being admitted into the upper form with only a rudimentary application. She combed his hair with her fingers. She seemed steady, her voice matter-of-fact: "I need to be here; your dad needs to be there. We can be adaptable, can't we?"

So *were* they separating? Maybe the family was just taking on a new shape. Maybe it *was* just a question of being adaptable. James wondered right through his move to Britton. The family spent a nearly conversationless August weekend in Vermont on Lake Champlain, rotating through solitary activities: someone read, someone worked on a lighthouse puzzle, someone took a walk to the town store. Trade and repeat. Back in Cambridge, movers followed color-coded stickers marking James's and his father's things. James returned to find the house half-emptied, rugs missing on the floor, bookshelves with their teeth knocked out.

The day he and his dad left Cambridge for Britton, James kissed his mother good-bye. She smiled as if it were nothing — just James going off to boarding school. He'd be back to visit in two weekends. Or that was what he told himself, waving at her through the car window.

James and his dad didn't speak on the drive. Arriving at the headmaster's residence on Smithson Way, with its pillars, its peaked glass windows, its brilliant white paint, they separated into the house, exploring the rooms in silence. James found the armchair and sofa, the kitchen table and chairs, the reading lamps configured around the ground floor. Upstairs, James discovered his books stacked flat on a shelf above a desk. Setting his fat duffel on the floor of his new bedroom, examining the lint where floor and wall met, the bare mattress, James finally felt the force of what had happened. He felt the miles between this place and Cambridge open up inside him, like a gash down his middle. He sat at the desk, in a hard-backed wood chair. Who had left whom? He wouldn't think about it. He would think about what had happened as little as he could. He rummaged through a small box, labeled JAMES, under the desk, through a set of great-works comic books, his fifth-grade spelling bee trophy, and a few CDs, and drew out a wood-framed five-by-seven of his mother. His dad had taken the photo on a family whale-watching trip a couple of years back. That day had been warm in Provincetown — and freezing on the ocean. James had spent the whole trip sipping hot chocolate in the cabin, while his mother stood against the rail in short sleeves, tossed and restless water behind her, smiling a chilly smile as her hair blew sideways. James dusted the photo off with his sleeve and set it up.

Running through all these memories in his dorm room at Weiss, James pushed himself off the bed, crossed to the dresser, and opened the top drawer. He found his house key underneath balled socks and stuffed it in his pocket.

Outside, James crossed the quad behind Weiss, avoiding the corner MassTrans bus stop on Elson. Over the summer his mother had been down and back to Fuller-Reardon corporate headquarters in Knoxville a half-dozen times. A few weekend visits with him in Cambridge had been all she could manage. This fall she'd be in Knoxville nearly full-time. The last communication he'd gotten from her had been a week ago. He could recite the whole e-mail: *Knoxville Hyatt is Yuck! Very busy but thinking of you and your senior year. I'll want to hear everything when I get back. One week, two at most. Love Mom.*

He wanted to tell someone how important his mother was (business development adviser to Fuller-Reardon's unmanned aerial-weaponry division) and how much he missed her. But who? His dad said she had "sacrificed her principles for profit." Who else? There wasn't anyone.

James let himself in the front door to the house on Smithson Way. "Dad?" he called out. No answer. James jogged up the steps and to his bedroom. Inside, four bare walls and airborne dust in a shaft of sunlight. His dad hadn't touched anything. James took the framed photo of his mother from the top of the dresser. Standing in the middle of the room, he did an internal check. Nothing. Good riddance.

Roberta O'Brien, dean of faculty, lived on Reservoir Road in a brick house beyond the graveyard. From where Dyer stood inside the first row of headstones, he could just make out her lit windows like lanterns hanging in the trees. The dean was hosting a cocktail party to welcome the faculty back from summer holiday. Dyer had spent the last half-hour pulling wrinkled shirts and pants out of his suitcase, laying them on his unmade bed. He finally chose a striped cotton shirt and khakis — more casual than what he'd worn that morning. Though it was too warm for long sleeves, he'd buttoned them at his wrists.

He blamed his mother for his nervous fixation on clothes. Even in those early days after his father left, she'd told him that clothes could articulate all kinds of things he was unable to say: I'm serious, I'm incapable of seriousness. I'm worthy of trust, I am unworthy of trust. How to tell this roomful of teachers, *colleagues,* that he was informed on the cultural, political, and economic currents of the twentieth century?

Stalling, leaning against an old headstone, staring through the trees, Dyer realized how badly he wanted this part to be over with, this introducing himself to others, this making of impressions. Having been in it for most of his life, school was something he understood, understood better than, say, real estate. And yet he couldn't shake the feeling that he was just passing through, like a tourist, as if any moment he would return to his car and head out to the interstate.

He told himself he knew his history. After World War II was especially fresh. Dyer had done the bulk of his Oxford tutorials on that period. But World War I? The Russian Revolution? The Spanish civil war? Unlike 110, his other class, a textbook-supported, carefully mapped survey of European history (Holy Roman Empire to the present) for sophomores (*lowers,* Dyer had to remind himself), 250 had no formula, just a directive: over two semesters cover the major intellectual and political developments in twentieth-century Europe. The course wasn't meant to be exhaustive. Like many of the senior-level classes at Britton, 250 was modeled after a college seminar — little lecturing, engagement with questions of historiography, "alternative" histories, discussion throughout. Britton's History Department office had shelves of primary source material — declassified government files, news articles, stock photography — plus a heavy cuboid text for his own use, *Modern Europe: An Overview,* edited by McArthur, Streatham, and Brewster. It surveyed the major episodes in microscopic print. Dean O'Brien had shipped him a copy in L.A. She'd also included a few old class plans — for the most part bare outlines: "Unit 1: WWI; Unit 2: Communism (emph. Trotsky); Unit 3: Berlin (blockade, currency discussion); Unit 4: Spanish Republic (Abr. Lincoln Brigade)."

During his run that afternoon around the school boundary wall, Dyer had imagined the first day, his class a jury box of appraising faces. He'd picked up his pace and on each controlled exhale reminded himself of his plan: nationalism and militarism in central Europe . . . Sarajevo assassination . . . trench warfare in Verdun, Somme . . . readings from Siegfried Sassoon, Wilfred Owen, and *All Quiet on the Western Front* . . . two weeks to Versailles . . . backtrack to Lenin.

What if he forgot facts? What if no one spoke up? He'd cut his run short and crossed the baseball diamond for Bailey House, trying to catch his breath. He'd seen the slate roof of Range and felt, for the hundredth time that day, Greta's skin slip through his.

Roberta O'Brien's front door was slightly ajar, and Dyer wiped his feet repeatedly on the mat before going in. He took in a carpeted hallway, a claw-foot bench covered in a pile of coats, and the open double doors down on the left. Standing in front of them were Ed Wolfe and Dean O'Brien herself. She wore a black skirt and a black sweater and held a glass of wine. A chandelier lit them like actors. Dyer caught the second half of Wolfe's sentence: "which is why it's a case of deterrence."

Rumor is he bedded one of his students. Dyer could see it; Wolfe was tall and broad-shouldered, trim through the middle for a man his age. His loosened tie and unbuttoned collar showed a triangle of throat, and suggested a touch of vanity, like maybe he judged that the overall effect — corduroy blazer, peppery stubble, and uncombed hair — delivered a rugged, just-in-from-the-woods look.

"Come on, Ed," Roberta was saying. "You can't seriously be happy about a nuclear North Korea."

"Why not?" said Wolfe. "I have to be happy about U.S. nukes on Guam."

Apart from their voices, the house seemed strangely quiet. Dyer took a step inside, and a board beneath his foot creaked. "Am I early?" he asked, as they turned their heads.

"Dyer," said Roberta, exhaling relief, moving to him, hand extended. She was a thin woman with a nest of gray-black hair. A familiar face from his interview; Dyer smiled. "Not at all. Good timing, in fact," she said. "Ed and I were stuck on the news."

"We've heard you've been climbing trees," said Wolfe. "Chris and Greta were rhapsodic on the subject."

"I didn't do much good."

"First-day heroics," said Wolfe.

Had that been sarcasm? "Hardly," said Dyer.

"Let me take you in," said Roberta.

"I'll get him a drink," said Wolfe.

"Would you like one?" asked Roberta.

"Sure," said Dyer, trying to sound casual. He did, desperately. One would be okay. His stomach, still healing from the summer's ulcer, could tolerate that much.

Dyer followed Roberta through the double doors. The living room was spacious, but barely half-full, with groups of three and four teachers standing around talking quietly, holding napkin-wrapped glasses or beer bottles to their chests. Dyer recognized Chris and Greta near the card table in the corner of the room. This was the bar, covered in a white cloth and topped with a few bottles, an ice bucket, and mismatched glasses.

Floor-to-ceiling bookcases lined two walls of the room. There was an unlit fireplace along the third, to Dyer's left, and a cluster of faculty sat around it in slatted wood chairs, their legs crossed. Above the bare mantel hung a row of what looked to Dyer like African tribal masks—elongated, sinewy faces carved out of ebony. One seemed to be screaming at him, the gaping oval mouth lipless and toothless. A fringe of twine sprouted from its head.

"They're my husband's," said Roberta, at his side. "Arnold Lambert. He's the dean of students."

Dyer remembered Wolfe mentioning Lambert. "Are they African?" asked Dyer.

She nodded. "Arnold spent a year in Mali, doing research for his doctorate. They're originally for Bambara trial ceremonials, for the judge to wear when he hands out sentences to tribal miscreants."

"The one in the middle's pretty fierce," said Dyer.

"When Arnold holds disciplinaries in here, he seats students in that direction to spook them. Have you met Arnold?" she asked, nodding for him to follow her deeper into the room.

A man intercepted Dyer with an arm. His hair was silver and gauzy, and he wore reading glasses low on his nose. "Mr. Martin," he said, and Dyer liked the formality of hearing his last name. The man's grip, when Dyer took it, was firm. "Thomas Blanton. Fellow historian. Welcome." Each word seemed struck against a bass drum.

"Mr. Blanton," said Dyer. "Pleased to meet you."

"Nice to have another Oxford man on the team."

"Oh," said Dyer. "I guess I don't really consider myself—"

"Did you row?"

"A little, yes," he said, and experienced a single memory, like a slide projected on a screen: a frozen March morning, the shock of cold water lashing at him, a finger crushed beneath the oar as the guy in the two-seat crabbed.

"Bow or stroke side?"

It took Dyer a second to remember. "Bow."

"Good man," Blanton said. "I rowed head of the river at torpids and eights in sixty-six. Did a Marshall at Oriel. Nice to have a rower's discipline in the 250. Tough course, or it should be."

"Yes, I've heard."

Blanton's gaze jutted left toward Wolfe, who crossed the room with a drink. Blanton leaned forward an inch and moved his grip up Dyer's arm. "Have any questions on the material, need advice, whatever, come talk to me."

"Thank you," Dyer said, meaning it. Blanton released him.

Wolfe handed Dyer the glass: "Do you drink gin? We have a lot of gin."

"It's fine," Dyer said. "Thanks." Wolfe, he noticed, wasn't drinking anything.

"Has Tom warned you about me?" asked Wolfe.

"Dyer's an oarsman," Blanton told Wolfe before Dyer could answer. He peered at Wolfe over his glasses. "Could use him on the river."

"IM program needs a head," said Wolfe.

Blanton made a guttering sound in his throat.

Dyer swallowed a mouthful of what tasted like straight gin. He stifled a cough.

Roberta O'Brien beckoned Dyer from across the room. "Excuse us, Tom," said Wolfe, detaching Dyer from Blanton, walking him over. "The man's kind of a relic," he said on the way.

Wolfe led Dyer toward a semicircle of teachers small-talking in the glow of a lamp. Wolfe introduced a man with a beaked nose and small, nervous eyes — Milton Greenley, English. Beside him was Jennifer Mercer, Math, who pressed his hand between both of hers. Next to her was Isadora Felton, the carillonneur Dyer had heard that morning. Through the lenses of her heavy black-framed glasses, her eyes looked overlarge and bulbous, like marbles. She clutched her hands together at her waist. Her nails were painted pink.

"We certainly enjoyed your efforts today, Isadora," Wolfe said.

She looked bashfully at her feet, and her hair fell into her face.

"Copland's terrific," said Dyer.

"Don't you think?" Isadora said in a high, trilling voice, lifting her head. "I'm *wild* about him."

Dyer caught sight of Chris and Greta, giving him sympathetic looks over their drinks. He sent them a helpless smile. "Sam," Wolfe called out. "Meet Dyer."

A muscular man in his forties walked over, his hair in a neat crewcut, a chunky digital watch on his wrist. He wore a short-sleeved golf shirt, jeans, and basketball shoes.

"Sam Morris," he said to Dyer. "Athletic director."

"Dyer Martin."

Sam's handshake was piston-quick. "Ed tells me you'll be running intramurals. They're a cakewalk," he said, crunching an ice cube in his mouth. "As long as you ensure a modicum of physical activity, I'm happy."

Dyer bobbed his head.

Isadora and Wolfe were talking about the acoustics in the Peabody Hall theater.

"Jogging before scrimmages, even some sprints, calisthenics. I'll leave it up to you," Sam said.

"I'm not clear on how the whole program is put together," said Dyer.

Sam swung a hand through the air. "I got a packet for you." A firm, blank stare. Dyer realized he'd finished his drink.

Chris appeared at his side. "Sam!" he said in a hearty voice. "We set to thump Loomis?"

"You betcha," Sam said, frowning and jiggling his glass, his eyes searching the room, the high ceiling, the brass electric wall sconces with their tulip bulbs. He clapped Dyer hard on the shoulder. "Excuse me, fellas," he said, moving past.

Chris watched him for a moment. "Sam's not a fan of mine," he said. "Threatened, I think."

"By what?"

Chris laughed. Dyer hadn't meant to be funny, but he smiled anyway. As he refilled his glass from one of the bottles on the bar — they did have a lot of gin — he considered the delicate state of his stomach lining. Out the window, big trunks were scattered around, as if they'd lost their way in the dark. He set the glass down.

"Pretty small group," said Dyer.

"The married faculty, especially the ones with kids, rarely come to these things," said Chris. At waist height, he extended a closed fist. "Want this?" he said, barely moving his lips.

"What is it?" asked Dyer.

"Vicodin," said Chris. "We all took one." He nodded at Greta, her arm in a sling, and two others, a diminutive black woman with close-cropped hair and a tomato-faced guy holding a beer.

"Not sure I should," said Dyer, though he realized he wanted it. Early after they arrived in L.A., he and Alice had taken painkillers recreationally: Vicodin, Dilaudid, and some Percocet he'd gotten from a college friend who lived in Santa Monica. Overwhelmed by the new city, the new job, Dyer had taken to the drugs' warm, woolly calm. He and Alice had sat on their apartment balcony, listening to the traffic on Santa Monica, sipping beer from the can.

"Let me know if you change your mind," said Chris.

Coming over, Greta blinked lazily. "Fabulous party, huh?"

"Doing the rounds is a little tough," Dyer said, turning and scanning the room. It was filling up, thanks to new faculty coming in from the hall. Dyer was relieved to find no one staring at him. Blanton was talking to Roberta. Sam whispered something in Isadora Felton's ear. She giggled behind her hand. Then Dyer found Wolfe. His eyes seemed to be fixed on Greta.

Did she notice? Greta looked up at Dyer and gently touched her earlobe, as if he'd been in the middle of a story and she was waiting for the end. "Ready for your first class?" she asked him.

"I hope," said Dyer. "I've been kind of cramming the material."

"Don't be nervous," she said. "These kids are ruthless. They'll know if you're nervous."

He waited for some advice, not wanting to ask.

"Learn the stare," she said.

Chris, biting his nail, said, "Done right, even the heiresses go submissive in a matter of seconds."

"Try it," said Greta. She squared herself in front of Dyer, rolled her eyes, and mock-chewed gum. There was a surly look on her face. He got the point — she was playing a role. Still, he felt a flush of heat in his cheeks and tried to laugh it off.

"No. Show lots of scorn," Greta said. "My daddy buys Nigerian oil fields. My kid brother gets a three-figure allowance. Smile, and you lose me forever." She cocked a hip and sent a bored look over his shoulder.

Dyer set his mouth. He did stare at Greta. He stared at a shallow wrinkle in the skin on the bridge of her nose. He stared at a pimple forming on her chin.

"Not bad," said Chris. "Now add a little pity."

Greta went on snapping at her imaginary piece of gum, her eyes rolled up and left. Dyer imagined Greta's fingers tearing on the rough metal of the lightning rod. He remembered the sound she'd made, that single breathy laugh, when she hit the ground. Slowly, incrementally, Greta's eyes met his.

"Good," she said.

"I'm really supposed to do this?"

"In cases of disrespect," she said.

Wolfe crossed the room toward them. "Or you can just hit them with a ruler," he said.

Greta's posture went through a subtle change; her neck bent a degree or two, and she pulled her wrist in its sling closer to her stomach. She took a long sip from her glass.

"Drink blunting the pain?" Wolfe asked Greta.

She didn't answer.

Dyer glanced at Chris, who returned his gaze and then nodded him toward the two younger teachers standing nearby. Behind him, Wolfe and Greta stood in silence.

Dyer met Will Hemmer, Physics, and Angela Grant, Theater. Searching for conversation, Dyer's resolve broke. He nudged and nodded at Chris in what he hoped was a significant way. Chris fished in his pocket, pulled out a white pill, and dropped it into Dyer's palm. Pretending to cough, Dyer threw it into his mouth and crossed to the bar for his abandoned gin.

A half-hour later, Dyer felt much better, vaguer, as calm as he'd expected. He chatted easily with Angela about her planned fall production of *Lysistrata*. He found out that Will Hemmer grew up in Maine, coached ice hockey — and that at the end of their first year all new teachers had their contracts "reviewed." "Sort of a formality," Will told him. "But it gives them a chance to dump you if you really screw up." This was news to Dyer—but it didn't alarm him as much as it probably should have. His senses were relaying confused signals to his brain. Lamps left comet tails as he moved through the room. The African masks seemed to bob and shift on the wall above the mantel. In the bathroom, the water from the tap felt polar.

He still hadn't introduced himself to Dean Lambert, but he wanted some air. He came out of the bathroom and headed for the door. Outside, tipping his head back to count the scattered stars, he heard the door open and shut behind him. Someone had followed him out. Her shoes scraped on the steps. He felt the rough texture of her sling brush his arm.

James stood in a fan of streetlight. Bachelor Hall was in that direction, ahead of him. He tried to imagine showing up, producing a casual, relaxed smile for the surprised faces, hunting for Jane's.

She was nice to ask him. It was enough to be asked.

People don't change so easily, James thought, turning around. Move into a new room and suddenly be a new person. He thought of the dead pigeon from last spring, the one he'd photographed from ten different angles for Mr. Nolan's portraiture class. He thought of the dirty, razor edge of its wing, its bloated body, its absolute plantedness, snug in the high grass behind Ramm Hall.

He moved ahead in the dark, the woods of the reservoir rising around him. He'd just go for a walk; because it was still preterm, sign-in was on the honor system. He could go around Ramm Hall and see if the pigeon had lasted the summer—but, even as he set off, regret began to drag at him, slowing his pace. A few more yards, and James stopped, let out a deep sigh. He looked around.

Beside James, in the shadows, two figures stood under a tree. They were pressed together—kissing, it looked like. Who was it? James squinted into the darkness.

That was the teacher he'd met in the morning. Mr. Martin. And wasn't that Ms. Salverton? He recognized her blond hair, her wide forehead.

Relief blew through him. James almost laughed. Instead he pressed his lips together. The new guy moved his hands around Ms. Salverton's waist.

Dyer woke to the outside sounds of trunks clicking open, engines idling at the curb, parents' voices ("David, *help* your father"), luggage thumping up the stairs. It was a Sunday, the morning after Dean O'Brien's party, Moving-In Day.

Dyer rolled into his pillow and thought of the textured cotton of Greta's sling, the static charges it sent along his arm. He remembered tipping Greta against a big oak near the gates to the reservoir, bumping her bad arm by accident, making her wince. He remembered shifting the strap crossing her back out of the way of her bra clasp. He remembered a dizzy plunging out of control, and then, when his lips touched hers, calm relief, like falling into a net. Under her shirt, Greta's skin was cool; the way she gripped him and smiled into his teeth made it seem as if they were old friends, like she'd known him for years.

The phone rang. Still sandbagged by the Vicodin, he struggled out of bed to get it, pushing his cinderblock feet across the floor, staying out of view of the windows.

"Hungry?"

"Hello?"

"It's Chris. Commons is open till nine."

"Oh, hi."

"Let's go."

"Don't I need to introduce myself to parents?" Dyer asked, rubbing his face.

"Not on an empty stomach. And not hungover. Ten minutes, I'll meet you behind Bailey."

"Hang on," Dyer said, taking the cordless phone to his door, opening it an inch, and peeking out. Suitcases, trunks, and plastic milk crates jammed with books, desk lamps, and poster tubes crowded the hallway. A silver-haired man with glasses was coming up the stairs with a cellophane-wrapped carton of Cup Noodles. Dyer shut the door. "How do I get out of here?" he whispered into the phone.

The answer was the back stairs, to the left out of his door — make a break for it when the hall was clear. Dyer got dressed, waited ten minutes, then did as he was told, dashing for the fire door and rumbling down the stairs and out to the small, triangular lawn behind Bailey House. Chris Nolan beckoned him from a grove of evergreens. They cut through the cool woods, circling around to the left, toward the brick hulk of Commons, its tall windows glinting with sun.

Around them, the campus was teeming. The bollards were down for the day, so airport shuttle vans, station wagons, and SUVs jammed the crisscrossing paths. "It's like a Mercedes car show," said Chris. There *were* a lot of Mercedes, Dyer noticed, and fathers in blue blazers and Britton caps, and thin mothers with painted nails. "There are scholarship kids too," Chris said. "Or so they tell me. Good luck finding one."

Dyer warily eyed the packs of returning students. The wealth didn't bother him — he'd expected to be surrounded by rich kids (as he had been at Oxford; three of the guys he'd rowed with had had titles in their families). What made him nervous was the sheer, raucous number of teenagers, all of whom knew this place much better than he did. The girls traded shrill greetings; guys slung luggage out of their parents' cars. Chris led him through a gauntlet gathered outside the Commons steps; Dyer noted how coolly he handled it, the faces like scenery, Chris giving a general wave.

"Commons is strictly segregated," said Chris once they were inside, guiding Dyer toward a quiet dining room to the right of the entranceway. "Jocks and postgraduates eat upstairs." Chris pointed over Dyer's shoulder, behind them. "Popular kids in that wing; theater clique, Goths, and homos one floor above them. And faculty's in here, with the social outcasts."

The kitchen staffers were putting breakfast away, but Chris pleaded for a plate of toast and bacon, two grapefruit halves, and a silver pack of Pop-Tarts. They filled mugs with coffee and took high-backed slatted seats near a window. Dyer was admiring the dark-stained wood, the heavy, polished table surfaces, the cathedral light falling through the high windows—when Chris told him that Ed Wolfe and Greta Salverton had had an affair the previous spring. Greta had broken it off abruptly just days before commencement.

"Say that again?"

"Greta should have told you before she let you drag her outside."

"I didn't drag her."

"Okay."

Dyer was still trying to put the information together. "She and Wolfe were a couple?"

"I think she was bored. It was sort of a fling."

"Why didn't you tell me this before?"

"She doesn't want anyone to know. He's married. Or separated. I'm not sure."

Dyer pushed the food away and glanced around him. They had the dining room to themselves. "Nothing happened," he whispered. "We made out a little. I was drunk."

Chris folded a piece of bacon into his mouth. "Wolfe can't really do anything since it was supposed to be this big secret," he said, chewing. "But people knew."

"She likes older men?"

"Not exclusively. Apparently."

"Why'd she break it off?"

"Came to her senses? You'd have to ask her. But better maybe if you don't think about it. Greta should have told you, but she probably wanted to send Wolfe a message."

"What message?"

"I'm moving on?"

Dyer's stomach cramped; up came a piny burp of gin. *Your first day,* he thought, rubbing his closed eyes, his thrumming temples.

• • •

On the way back to Bailey, wondering whether to say anything to Wolfe when he saw him next, Dyer spotted Greta outside Range House, leaning against the railing on the front stoop, her arm in its sling, black, plastic-framed sunglasses on, chatting with a girl holding a field hockey stick.

Stiffly, he walked over, thinking that they might laugh the whole thing off. He worked up a hopeful smile.

"There's no comparison. It's three windows compared to two. And a way bigger closet," said the girl with the hockey stick, raking Dyer with an up-and-down stare.

"Hi," said Greta.

"Hi," said Dyer.

"Seniority says I have first crack at the third floor. And Katie's not a quote, manic-depressive. She just wants a single."

"Later, Jen," Greta said.

"But will you talk to someone in housing?" The girl was still staring at Dyer, picking at some loose tape on the stick's grip. A small red dot on her left nostril marked a closed-up piercing.

Greta didn't answer, pushing her sunglasses into her hair, squinting. Her eyes were puffy and tired.

The girl exhaled noisily. "Fine. Later." And jumped off the porch, the stick bouncing on her shoulder.

Greta waited, as though she expected Dyer to start, then let out a flat laugh when he didn't, her look sliding away from his.

"Whoops," said Dyer.

"Whoops," said Greta.

He wanted to sit next to her, close enough on the porch railing to touch his arm to hers, but a column of girls exited Range, and he backed off to let them move through.

Greta tipped her head at the girls as they passed — and hooked one of them by the arm. "Sabrina," she said, then reached down and tapped something hard and circular in the tight seat pocket of the girl's jeans.

"Fuck," whispered Sabrina, trading wide-eyed looks with the other girls. A couple of them mouthed it back: *fuck.*

"Throw it out, or stash it where I'll never find it," Greta said, and then pointed back inside Range.

Sabrina and her friends hurried back inside, leaving a vapor trail of perfume, masking, Dyer thought, cigarette smoke.

"Dipping is a Range tradition," said Greta. "Smoke detectors mean you can't have a cigarette, so it's the next best thing. Seniors like Sabrina sort of haze the younger ones into it." She shook her head. "Pretty girls spitting into Dixie cups. I tell them, gum cancer. They're like, not if we quit before we're twenty."

"Smelled like they were smoking too."

"Take some advice? Ignore it unless it's blatant. Unless it's insulting. Where are you, Bailey? That's sort of a geek house. Lucky guy."

Sabrina and her friends were barreling out again, and this time Dyer stepped around them, backing up to Greta on the porch railing, leaving plenty of space. They took quick, appraising looks at him as they went by.

"Sorry, Greta," Sabrina murmured.

"First day you get a pass," Greta called after her.

Then they were gone, and Dyer waited through what felt like a full minute of silence. "So," he finally said, fumbling for a joke. He lifted his gaze from her sling to her face. "Should we blame the Vicodin?"

Greta's eyebrows moved; her lips tightened almost imperceptibly. Dyer saw that it had been the wrong thing to say. She shrugged. "Britton's a lonely place," she said.

"I can imagine," Dyer said.

"I doubt it," she said, and flipped the sunglasses back down over her eyes. "You've been here how long? A day?"

Through his window James watched Sam Rafton — tall and lean, his khaki shorts frayed at the hem, a cord of threaded seashells tight against his throat — oversee two skinny Weiss lower-formers playing sherpa with his luggage. Sam's roommate Cary Street arrived in a Logan airport van, dragged out his own set of bags and suitcases. Rafton flashed him the peace sign. "*Bonjour,* faggot," he said. "How went Paris?"

"Good, good," said Cary, and they slapped palms.

More third-floor seniors arrived throughout the morning. James heard them outside his room — Buddy Juliver, Josh Fishbein, Brian Jones (nicknamed "Brain," James knew, for his habit of "hanging brain," or dangling his balls through his open fly). James put a desk chair under the knob, wondering if it would hold.

Just before Commons closed for lunch, he shot out of his room, slipping along the hallway and down the stairs like a reporter under crossfire, his head ducked, his shoulder against the wall. He wasn't stopped. Same thing coming home. Throwing his door open, he scanned the space for what he assumed he'd find: a message in blood, a neat pile of shit on the floor.

The room was untouched. And nothing happened that day. Nothing happened that week. For the rest of the month, Sam, Cary, Josh, Buddy, and Brain paid no attention to him at all. If James met them blocking the hall, they wouldn't move; James would thread his way through, eyes on the floor. It felt like a free pass, but James knew there was no such thing. In sixth grade, at his old school in Cambridge, in front of dozens of other middle-schoolers, Brad Hingiss threw him into the lockers without warning. That was how it worked. They came at you suddenly. And since last spring, since their disciplinaries and Henry Fieldspar's expulsion, these seniors had bonded into a close-knit team. James stayed alert. At night, he listened through his wall to them all gathered in Sam and Cary's handsomely furnished room (Cary's dad owned a furniture company in New Jersey and had arranged for movers to install a calf-leather sofa and rosewood coffee table in Sam and Cary's common area). They belched and hacked phlegm. They wrestled until Chris Nolan banged on his ceiling with a broomstick. James heard a lot — Dylan Wald's tits were asymmetrical, Hans Jorgen had a hard-on in the gym shower after practice, Chris Nolan was definitely a fag — but not one mention of the headmaster's kid in 12.

The weeks passed. James stopped listening at the wall, began tearing through his homework. By the end of September, he found himself checking for the sound of his own footsteps on the stairs, the groans of the wood beneath his feet. He began seeking reassurance in bathroom mirrors and reflective window glass. Affection colored the memory from sixth grade: Hingiss grasping his shirt, the slap of the lockers, the attention from the other kids in the hallway.

It started to feel lonely, this waiting for whatever was coming. Maybe they weren't going to haze him; maybe they barely noticed him at all.

So, at the end of the month, when he heard the call through his door — "Skin up!" — and the drumbeat of footsteps, he considered joining in. Nighttime skin runs were a Weiss senior-year tradition, and James normally would never have imagined going along. But what if he surprised them? This month of isolation had created a roaring in his ears. Unsteady on his feet, he peeked into the hall and saw them heading down the stairs, stripping off clothes.

He didn't allow himself to reconsider. He threw off his T-shirt and ran after.

Running hard, James caught up to the blue-white bodies on the grass of the quad, a dozen yards from the dorm. The target was the bell tower. One loop. As he ran, James caught sight of Sam Rafton's hairy arms and Brain Jones's bouncing gut. He felt the night air sheeting around his body like water, the cold grass numbing the soles of his feet.

The pace was fast, but James reached the bell tower with the rest of the group. He noticed a few surprised stares; Rafton even smiled at him, his white teeth reflecting the bell tower's sodium light. On the leg home, Brain edged in close, then dropped behind James, his elbows pumping, his breath tearing in and out of his mouth. James — losing ground to the others, pounding away on the lawn, his lungs hot — felt the nick at his trailing foot. He went airborne, crashed facedown, skidding across the grass.

Brain blew past him, laughing. James spat grass, touched his lip, checked for blood, came up on his knees. His torso was streaked with lines of red, as if someone had taken a cheese grater to his chest.

Up ahead the other guys had reached Weiss's propped exit doors. They were waving at Brain, his ass jiggling as he covered the last few yards. He made it inside; the doors slammed tight.

James hobbled the distance and wrenched the handle. Locked. He heard the guys laughing on the other side of the door.

His head snapped around, looking for campus patrol. He crouched against the side of the building. His chest still hurt, there was a click in his jaw. He fought to catch his breath.

Hunched over in the narrow shadow cast by the building, James circled to the front, to the base of the escape ladder that led to his room. The moonlit campus was laid out before him; he could see two parked campus patrol cars beside Ramm Hall. A big girls' dorm, Gillman Hall, stood across the quad, its windows lit. The rungs made no impression on his numb feet as he climbed, his gaze rooted to the ivied brick, his ass, he was sure, like a rising balloon. His window was open an inch, and throwing it up, he launched his body through.

A wild look around him — the room was empty. He scrambled to his feet, yanked some underwear on, and through his open door saw Sam Rafton coming at him, down the hall, dressed now in lacrosse shorts and an Atlanta Braves cap. James lunged across the room and threw the door shut. His back to it, James caught a view of himself in the mirror above the dresser, his scraped chest heaving, his eyes like saucers.

The knob turned. James dug his heels into the floor.

"Hey, kid," Rafton said, his voice just on the other side of the wood, muffled but close. "Wolfe," Rafton said, his voice low and even, as if he hadn't just sprinted halfway across campus. "Open sesame."

James pulled the desk chair over with his foot, jammed it against the door, and sat down.

A shuddering blow sent James flying. The door slammed against the wall. Buddy Juliver and Cary Street landed heavily on his floor. Buddy had Cary's head locked in the crook of his elbow. Cary's skin was bright purple; his eyes were squeezed shut. Buddy was tickling Cary's crotch with one end of a stereo remote control. Cary's hands batted the remote away and slapped for purchase on Buddy's sweaty, naked frame. "Get his arm," said Buddy in a breathy growl.

James stayed sprawled beside his bed.

Rafton came inside and stood on Cary's arm.

Buddy started whacking Cary's testicles with the remote control. "Get his fucking *legs!*"

James edged toward Cary's scrabbling feet. "The *fuck* off me," Cary shouted, kicking violently. In a lunge, James threw his weight on top of Cary's ankles.

"Liftoff!" Buddy announced, pointing with the remote at Cary's erection. He met James's gaze with his own, sent him a wide, wolfish smile. "He can't control them."

Cary ripped one foot free and kicked James in the face.

2

October

DYER STOOD WITH his back to the class. The clock read 8:31
A.M. He rolled the cylinder of chalk in his fingers and gazed
into the green expanse of board. He could picture the scene
behind him — the dim basement light, the two rows of glassy-eyed
paralytics.

So far, the morning, the first really cold morning of the fall,
had felt confrontational. Putting his winter coat on in his apartment at Bailey, Dyer had breathed in stale, closet air. The radiators sounded their angry clangs on his way out the front door. Following the path through the lawns, spiky with mean-looking frost,
he'd buried his nose in the coat's musty collar.

Dyer chalked the day's date on the board, then wrote, in all
capitals, "LEAGUE OF NATIONS, 1919."

Dyer turned around. He surveyed the blank faces.

Though he prepped late into the night, rereading chapters
from his college texts, taking notes from sources in the History
office, watching documentary tapes from the library, Dyer still
never felt ready to bridge the hour-long session twice a week. Even
when class went well, when students made comments on the reading and Dyer got through all his notes, he left depleted and dry-
mouthed, longing for bed.

Chris Nolan had provided some comfort: "I nearly threw up

every morning my first month, and that was for *Photo.* So relax, give yourself a while to get comfortable. In the meantime, don't try to be nice or cool or funny. If you crack a joke, deadpan it. Don't smile until Thanksgiving."

Smiling wasn't a problem. Dyer had lectured through his first week of classes with his face turned toward the board, his expression in rictus, his trembling arm carefully chalking up his outline. He knew lecturing was a mistake, and in his peripheral vision he'd seen the slack, bored faces, the arms crossed against chests. For the third class, he'd drunk three cups of coffee and turned his outline facedown on the desk in front of him. Once they'd filed in, Dyer asked the class to push their desks against the classroom wall. Using a football-style diagram of x's and o's on the board, he'd positioned them into a tableau of the Sarajevo assassination, June 1914. He'd walked them through the imperial limousine route; the first, unsuccessful bombing attack by the Black Hand terrorists; the confusion of the driver, the way he'd taken a wrong turn en route to the hospital, and, forced to reverse direction, had backed into the assassin's sightline. Two shots, killing both Hapsburgs. The class had seemed pleased by the new approach. Dylan Wald, otherwise stone-silent, had even shown some enthusiasm for her role as the duchess, clutching her stomach after the "shot," falling slack into the arms of Greg Smile, the archduke.

For the rest of September, Dyer had tried similar experiments. A debate on objective realism, comparing contemporary newspaper stories with the work of Remarque and Sassoon. A mock military-planning session for the Battle of the Somme. He'd also assigned a short paper, two to three pages on a single cause of World War I.

So his confidence was growing. But now, this October morning in the damp, subterranean seminar room he'd come to hate, underneath the towering, quadruple-story Morrow Hall, a building with dozens of better rooms with big windows and good views, Dyer stared at the class — at Caroline Jermann, Randy Holiday, James Wolfe, Sam Rafton, and the others, fifteen altogether — and found himself with no creative ideas on how to proceed.

"Let's start," he said, "with word association. I want crude emotional reaction. One-word answer: *good* or *bad*. Ready? *Collective security.*"

To kill time, he wrote the words on the board.

When he turned back around, Jane Hirsch glanced up from the surface of her desk. "Jane," he asked. "Gut reaction."

"Ambivalent, I guess."

"Can't be ambivalent," said Dyer.

"Good."

"Jane says good. Chip?"

Chip Lee, his pen laid neatly beside his notebook, said, "Good."

"Two goods. Sam?"

"Don't even know what it means," said Sam Rafton.

Sam's legs shot out in front of him like planks of wood, and he drummed his fingers on the desk. The soles of his hiking boots had dripped dirty puddles on the floor. He wore a Britton lacrosse windbreaker and a baseball cap. Stringy bangs curtained his face.

"Did you do the reading?"

Sam shrugged.

Dyer ignored him. "Show of hands," he said. "I say collective security, and your instincts tell you that's a good idea."

Most of class made their hands visible, lifting them an inch, a half-inch off their desks.

"Who thinks 'bad'?" Dyer's gaze found James, seated in his customary spot against the back wall of the classroom, his head tilted over his notebook. He rarely spoke up, and yet his paper, a summary of the roots of Serbian-Austrian hostility, convinced Dyer that he followed the material.

James worked his hand into the air.

"Anyone side with James?" Dyer asked.

Randy Holiday, a trunk-limbed football player wedged in the small, old-fashioned desk chair, spoke up: "Yeah."

Randy's paper had compared ultranationalist early-twentieth-century Europe to the hard-core patriotism of the present-day United States. A little off-topic, and yet Dyer had given him a 3.5

for a creative take on the assignment, and to counter his surprise that a football player could write such a thing. Dyer had even put check marks next to his conclusion: "Accepting dissenting points of view gives a government extra plays in its foreign policy playbook."

"Anyone else?" Dyer asked.

Samantha Twiss raised her hand. Dyer nodded at her.

"I don't support the United Nations," she said.

"Why not?" asked Dyer.

"They seem anti-U.S." She pulled on a silver chain at her neck. "I read an article in the paper about it."

She meant the statement the secretary-general had made two days before, warning America against preemptive action against North Korea. Since the start of term, Dyer had done two news quizzes to ensure that they read a paper regularly.

"It isn't," said Dyer, getting a frown from Samantha. "Not categorically. But good that you're up on the news." He went on, "In 1919, was the U.S. for or against the idea of internationalism?" Silence. He had to answer his own question: "Both. Congress blocked joining the League of Nations despite the fact that it had been conceived by their own president." He paused. "Can anyone tell me why Wilson wanted a League of Nations?"

"To stop another war from happening," said Jane Hirsch.

"Good," Dyer said. "Wilson opposed competing treaties between nations, the same kinds of treaties that had drawn countries like Russia and France and Italy into the war to begin with. He wanted an open society of free nations, everybody protecting everybody else." He spread his hands and glanced at Sam Rafton. "Collective security."

Dyer turned to Randy and James. "Why isn't this a good idea?"

Randy shrugged and looked over at James. James said, "Because you can't trust nations to act outside their own self-interest."

Dyer let that sit for a few seconds. Then he marked his notes and told the class to move their desks. He asked most everyone to form a cluster by the door; then spread James, Randy, and Samantha out in isolated spots against the wall.

Dyer pointed to the larger group. "Here we've got a multinational body. And three nonmember states of various military and economic strengths." He paused. "Now, let's say one of the nonmember states, the biggest," Dyer pointed at Randy, "decides he wants . . ." Dyer crossed over to where James was sitting and picked his backpack up off the floor. "James's backpack." Dyer carried the backpack to Randy and set it down beside him.

"What can the smaller nation do?" Dyer asked. "Given that he's isolated from the international community."

"Nothing," said Chip.

Dyer returned James's backpack to his desk. "But what if James were a member of the international body?"

Anticipating Dyer's next move, James slowly rose out of his desk. Dyer slid the desk over to a space between Allison Wucsinski and Greg Smile. He nodded for James to sit.

"Doesn't this change the equation?" Dyer asked as James took his new position. "With the combined resources of the multinational body acting as a kind of deterrent—"

Randy pushed himself to his feet and crossed the room in three big steps. He scooped James's backpack off the floor and returned with it to his desk.

"Okay," said Dyer. He turned to the larger group. "Okay," he said again. Randy unzipped the top of the backpack. "Now, given the premise of . . . um . . . collective security," Dyer started, avoiding James's face. Randy was rummaging around inside his bag. "What's the international body obligated to do?"

Sam Rafton let out a sarcastic laugh.

"Wonder why we don't have door locks?"

James recognized the Atlanta drawl—the lazy stretch of *won-duh*—but he didn't look up from his History reading. "School constitution," he murmured.

Sam Rafton snapped his fingers. " 'There shall be mutual trust among students.' Fucking optimistic, if you ask me. I shove my bed against the door when I need my privacy, but what a pain, moving the furniture around."

"Can I help you?" James glanced over his shoulder. Rafton was leaning against the open door, digging between his teeth with a fingernail.

"Come to my room for a sec," Rafton said.

James shook his head.

"I need to show you something."

"No."

"Dude, 'there shall be mutual trust.' Come on."

James heard the command in Rafton's voice and turned in his chair. His jaw still hurt from where Cary had kicked him. The glare from the desk lamp blinded him a little so he switched it off.

"Move it, Wolfe."

James stood up out of his chair. Going along might be the smart play; take the chase, and some of the fun, out of it. He followed Rafton down the hallway and into his room, into a fug of sandalwood incense and cologne. Gypsy tapestries patterned with mandalas, starbursts, and concentric rings of paisley hung on three walls. The black leather sofa and the coffee table held notebooks, a math text, and DVDs glinting through strewn laundry like mica. In an adjacent room, James saw two twin beds, the bare mattresses visible beneath twisted sheets. Rafton unhooked a plastic tube from a nail on the wall above the stereo, a short length of what looked like surgical tubing with a funnel epoxied to its end. "I got this shoved down my throat fall of my lower year," he said, holding it out like a dead snake. "A fifth of Smirnoff, straight down. I threw up a lung that night. Soaked my bed with piss. This is what we're not doing to you."

"Thanks," James murmured. The mouth end of the tube, swaying gently in front of him, was fibrous with teeth marks.

"Too risky," Rafton said, rehanging the tube. "We're all still on probation. And you're the headmaster's kid. Which is why, I'm assuming, you got the best room in the dorm. Congratulations."

But James would never tell his dad what they did to him. He searched Rafton's expression, his smooth, tanned forehead, his sky blue eyes, wondering about his own dad. Rafton probably told him everything: grades, girlfriends, likely even the kid who had gotten the single down the hall. "Every one of us got funneled once upon a time," Rafton said, stepping around James, kicking the door to the hall all the way shut.

James heard footsteps moving in the direction of his room.

"You don't want to go through it?" Rafton asked, putting his face close to James's. "You know, voluntarily?"

"Not really," James said. *Get out of here,* he told himself.

But before he could move, Rafton took James by the throat, spinning him around, hooking the crook of his elbow under his chin. Tipped backward, James staggered on his heels. Cary Street came in from the hall. "Get his legs," Rafton said. James struggled, kicking his feet, swinging his arms, but Rafton's arm went tighter, cutting off his airflow. Small black gnats looped in James's vision. Cary squeezed his ankles together. They carried him, sacklike and writhing, to a closet—James saw sports equipment, a pile of dirty laundry—and tossed him in. James hit the floor, cracking his head against the wall. He had his airway back, but nothing was coming in or out. He coughed up hot bile; he spat and heaved in a lungful of the close, sweatsock air.

James struggled to his knees in the cramped space. The line of light below the door shadowed with movement. James heard the heavy dragging sound of furniture moving. He pounded on the door with his fists.

"Give it ten minutes," said Cary. Then, with a giggle: "Give it fifteen."

James threw his shoulder into the door. It met something hard, a dresser, or the end of the sofa. He settled back with a groan. They were doing something to his room and he couldn't stop them. He shifted soft mounds of clothes, hard-toed cleats, and bulky lacrosse shoulder pads out of the way. He caught colors blossoming out of the near total dark and rubbed the lump forming on the back of his head. Nothing he could do now but wait—and try not to think about what was happening. Try to think of something else. Think of Jane Hirsch, doodling on her notepad, lifting her gray-blue eyes, smiling at him. Imagine what Sam Rafton's dad must look like, jowly and gray-haired. Imagine his proud, lifted chin. Imagine locking his own arm around Sam's throat and squeezing.

Dyer and Headmaster Wolfe faced each other in the backyard of the house on Smithson Way. Both held Fighting Crane first position—legs spread, knees bent, arms stretched out at their sides. Dyer had been a choson do regular for over a month, but this morning, his body felt stiffer than usual—a combination of the cold and the tension at being the headmaster's only company. When Dyer realized they'd be alone, he'd wanted to turn and run.

Wolfe rocked his weight right and circled his left leg into a crouched, aggressive stance, his right arm rotating to Fighting Crane second position. Dyer watched Wolfe's fluid movements, his long arms sweeping gracefully through the air, his expression unfocused and serene.

He should have known this was going to happen—attendance had been dwindling as the mornings got colder. Also, the more often Wolfe pointed out choson do's North Korean roots, the more participants he lost from week to week. "This is still a basic part of North Korean military training," Wolfe said at one of the gatherings in late September, leading the group through Joint Manipulation, a grab-and-twist combination designed to dislocate the opponent's elbow. Later, in the faculty lounge, Thomas Blanton had mentioned that he'd heard about the most recent session: "Should come in handy," he'd said, lifting a tea bag out of his Styrofoam cup and tossing it into the garbage can. He'd started to leave the lounge, then turned and beckoned Dyer to him. "Been to his office yet?" Blanton murmured. "The complete writings of Kim Il Sung on his shelves, as a showpiece. See for yourself."

So what? You'd find *Mein Kampf* in the History office. Wolfe's interest in North Korea had roots in his research on U.S.-Chinese relations, or so said his bio on the Britton website, which also included the title of the China book Chris had mentioned, *East Rising: China's Political Economy and the Discourse of Material Production,* published six years earlier. Dyer wondered what he'd been writing, if anything, in the meantime. The bio also said he'd served in the Peace Corps in "southern Korea." It said nothing about a contrarian or radical past. But that had to be part of his enthusiasm too; as long as Kim Jong Il kept turning up in the headlines, threatening America, Wolfe would be tempted to cheer him on. In any case, Wolfe's North Korean fixation didn't bother Dyer. (And maybe, he thought, it didn't bother anyone else either. The other teachers were probably looking for an excuse to sleep in.) Attending choson do had no more bearing on North Korean–U.S. relations than on the cultivation of Dyer's physical or spiritual health.

Dyer mimicked Wolfe's slow, sweeping movements, tried to hold postures with the solidity and breathlessness that seemed to come so easily to the headmaster. Dyer focused on his balance, on chasing away anxiety and worry. At the same time, he stole glances at Wolfe, at his still, mannequin face, to see if he was being forgiven for leaving the party with Greta.

The silence in the backyard was broken only by a chorus of birds from the surrounding trees.

"Sweeping Hip Throw," Wolfe murmured, and lifted his left leg, flattening one hand and pushing it toward the ground. He wore rough-cotton gray pants and the same old Harvard sweatshirt Dyer had seen him in the first day. Dyer hopped a bit trying to stand on one foot. He steadied himself, then tried again.

Wolfe glanced at him. "Throw the hip *down,* Dyer. Let your body unlock."

Dyer tried to loosen his hips. He tried to drop his center of gravity, allow his limbs to glide into position.

"Release," Wolfe said, and sighed. "You're not getting it."

As was customary at the end of the half-hour, Wolfe and Dyer bowed at the waist, then stood upright, facing each other.

"Coffee?" asked Wolfe.

"Oh," said Dyer, rubbing his cold hands together, thinking: *Don't.* Thinking: *Say no thanks and leave.* "Okay," he said.

Wolfe's kitchen was basic—a porcelain sink, a small fridge, a wooden knife block on the countertop. Wolfe turned the knob on the stove, struck a kitchen match, and lit the burner, then ran a kettle under the tap and put it on the flame. "I heard 250 went a little haywire on Tuesday," he said, setting a jar of Folgers on the table.

Dyer watched Wolfe from inside the door. "I wouldn't say haywire. I was trying to get them to discuss collective security."

"Sort of a bankrupt concept," Wolfe said, rinsing two coffee mugs at the sink.

"Well, Randy Holiday may have been trying to make that point."

Wolfe chuckled. "They like to challenge at this age. And they like to be challenged. Get them away from their parents, and their minds open right up. It's gratifying for a teacher."

Dyer thought of the blank, bored faces in his classroom and didn't say anything.

"You need to anticipate better, Dyer. You shouldn't just assume they'll agree to the accepted order of things." Wolfe dried the mugs with a paper towel and set one at the end of the table, the end nearest Dyer, tapping it against the Formica. Stiffly, Dyer moved to a chair and sat.

"High school kids consent to radical ideas," Wolfe went on, sitting opposite Dyer. "Much more so than they will in college. Take it from someone who knows. The undergrads I taught at Harvard were little CEOs in training."

Wolfe twisted open the Folgers jar and poured some crystals into his mug.

Dyer wondered if he should bring up Greta. But how? And what would he say? Sorry? At the moment he didn't feel sorry.

"How's James doing?" Wolfe asked. "Keeping up, I'd assume."

"James is a good student," Dyer said. "Smart."

"Gets it from his mother." Wolfe sounded nonchalant, but Dyer noticed his firm grip on the glass Folgers jar. He had a wild thought that he was going to throw it at him. "Here," Wolfe said, handing the coffee over. Dyer spilled some crystals on the table shaking them into his mug.

The kettle blew out a low whistle, and Wolfe let it go shrill before standing to lift it off the burner.

"Caroline and I have been separated for over a year," Wolfe said, pouring.

Dyer felt Wolfe's eyes on him. His own found a sticky patch on the floor beneath the sink, found the battered metal rim of the table.

"Do you know what she does for work?" Wolfe asked.

"No," lied Dyer.

Wolfe explained that she'd taken an advisory position at the company her great-uncle had founded early in the century, Fuller-Reardon, number two military-weapons manufacturer in the country. "She's directing production of the Goshawk, their next-generation drone aircraft. It's lighter and flies farther than the UAVs the military has been using for the last decade. And it carries a nuclear payload." Wolfe's voice was still even and calm, but the sides of his neck had gone red. He shook his head. "You should have seen her shouting 'no nukes' at Reagan in eighty-four. Made the papers. 'Fuller Heiress Arrested at White House.'"

"What changed?"

Wolfe looked at him sharply. "*She* did."

Dyer searched the tabletop for something else to say.

"Caroline spends most of her time in Knoxville," Wolfe said, turning to the window, staring along the gentle grassy rise to Smith Infirmary. He let out a hard laugh and wiped his beard with the back of his hand. "So James doesn't get to see her nearly as much as he'd like."

"That must be difficult for him," Dyer said.

Wolfe seemed to consider this, frowning into his mug. His anger had peaked; the tension was out of his face now, his jaw, his brow. "Are your parents together, Dyer?"

Dyer shook his head. "My dad left us. He runs a dive service in the Caribbean. On Saint John."

Wolfe eased the kettle back on the stove with a quiet tap. Dyer stared at his shoulders, broad and rounded beneath his gray sweat-shirt.

Twenty-five years ago, Julian Martin left the house on Stuart Street with a slim suitcase of clothes to catch the Metroliner to New York. He had an interview at an insurance firm the next morning. Julian didn't return on Tuesday. Child support began arriving through a lawyer the next month. Dyer's earliest memories, brightly colored and poorly focused, were of his mother tearing open envelopes and pulling out checks.

Dyer thought of the FBI list in Wolfe's foyer, the portrait in the living room, its dead-center position on the wall. He conjured Julian in a sagging beach lounger, his skin sunbaked and cancerous, overcharging for tours and equipment. His wife was named Olivia; their three-year-old, Anton. No surprise Julian ended up on St. John, his mother once told Dyer. He had taken her there for their honeymoon and had been reluctant to get back on the plane. She still received a monthly check through Julian's Richmond lawyer, though Dyer never asked how much, nor did he want the news that occasionally accompanied the money.

"Leave anyone in L.A.? A girlfriend?" Wolfe took in Dyer's expression and nodded as if he knew the answer was yes. But Dyer didn't say anything. He was startled by the connection Wolfe seemed to have drawn. "Come on, Dyer," Wolfe said. "Make this a healthy exchange."

Dyer blew into his full, steaming cup. The overhead bulb threw a bright, trembling oval on the surface of the coffee. He forced thoughts of his father out of his head, replacing them with a memory of a Sunday, two years prior; he and Alice had known each other for a week. On an afternoon walk in Port Meadow, Dyer, acting on impulse, pulled her down into the high grass. They lay on the cool earth, spiky heather walling them in, a veil of sticky midday Oxford heat hanging over them both, and her mouth on his.

"I did," said Dyer. "Alice."

"What's Alice do?" asked Wolfe.

"She's written a screenplay," said Dyer.

Wolfe nodded as if this didn't surprise him.

"She was a Rhodes at Oxford," said Dyer. "Did a second BA in PPE: politics, philosophy, econ. Writing a screenplay was a new idea."

"So you followed her to L.A."

Dyer nodded.

"And why'd you leave?" Wolfe was leaning slightly toward him. Dyer didn't answer right away.

In the Port Meadow grass, ants had bitten him where his T-shirt had ridden up, bites like needle jabs along his ribs. He pushed Alice off of him, springing to his feet, beating his sides. "Shit, shit, shit," he yelled. Alice swiped more red dots off his calf and thighs. A swarm of them covered the ground. Back in her room at Christ Church, Alice eased a steroid cream into the rash of bumps. The pain disappeared, and they found each other again on her narrow bed, but the indoor heat was different, close and uncomfortable. There were library books stacked on the floor, a few strewn on the bed itself, and her laptop blinked an insistent pin light from the desk. The mood was wrong, and Dyer's hands were slick with sweat. Alice stopped them. "Too stuffy," she said, fanning her face. Though it was late in the day, and the meadow was far, Dyer still wanted to return to the spot he'd found. He'd endure the tiny pincers. He'd keep the two of them planted, the air moving and the sunlight pouring down, his mind empty of everything except the press of her body against his.

Wolfe was still waiting for an answer. Dyer sipped his watery coffee.

"She's in Tehran now," he said, exhaling the words, relieved to have them out, searching the headmaster's face for a reaction.

The week before, Alice had called: EDGE Films had bought her screenplay and was fast-tracking it into production. EDGE, a subsidiary of one of the major studios, had read and loved it — timely, sharp, romantic, the producers had said.

This was a Friday night; the boys of Bailey House were filing into Dyer's apartment for face-to-face sign-in. It was Dyer and Alice's second conversation since the start of September, and she'd been on her cell, shouting over the highway noise. "They want me to commit to being in Tehran for a month, to do revisions, to get the setting right. They got me a visa and they're putting me up in a hotel with a laptop."

Dyer waved the milling boys — *twelve, thirteen,* he counted — away from his bedroom door, the only room he kept private. Four weeks running, face-to-face in Bailey was as he'd hoped it would be: uneventful. Dyer had sniffed nothing but bad breath and ramen noodles.

"Dyer?" Alice asked.

"Do they do that for screenwriters? Fly them to Tehran for a month?"

He could almost hear her shrug. "They're doing it for me."

"Is it safe?"

"The Hilton Grand is."

The boys settled into Dyer's couch, a few studied his stack of CDs. Near the window, Oliver Frame, in oversized polar fleece pants, bent over and farted.

"Awww!"

"What was that?" Alice asked.

Tim, Josh, Benjy, and the others folded into hysterics. And Dyer laughed too because he couldn't help it. Everyone crowded away from Oliver, who grinned by the window.

"Nothing," he said, thinking of the distance, of all the miles of wires and transmitters that that sound, Oliver's almost plaintive squeak, had traveled.

"I'll call you before I leave," she said.

But she hadn't.

Dyer finished his cooling coffee in a gulp. He should go before he said more than he meant to; he should head back across campus to Bailey. He still had a stack of quizzes from — *Christ* — last Thursday to finish grading before class.

But curiosity got the better of him as he scraped his chair back from the table and stood: "If you don't mind me asking — why did you leave Harvard anyway? Not to take anything from Britton, but it just seems like a tenured position there is kind of the be-all and end-all."

Wolfe shook his head a little. Dyer searched for some sign that he was keeping secrets — but his expression was placid, impassive. If he was hiding something, he was good at it.

"From an outside perspective," Dyer added.

"I was the Timothy Dean Gillian Professor of History," Wolfe said haughtily, lifting his chin, then giving Dyer a hint of a smile. He waved his hand. "But Harvard's a bullpen for Wall Street. The investment banks would come to recruit, and the classrooms just emptied out." He pushed his chair back from the table and turned away from Dyer, clunking his coffee mug in the sink. "My last few rounds of undergrads were spineless. I'd lecture that a massive devaluation of the dollar would do our country good and lose twenty bodies the next day. I'd question the utility of nonviolent protest. I'd salute the prospect of a militarized China. You'd hear them gasp." Wolfe thought for a moment. "Kids lose something when they get to college. Maybe that's always been true."

There was more to the story — Dyer could tell from the abrupt way Wolfe cleared his throat and flipped on the water at the sink. He thought of what Chris had told him, the rumors of an affair. Dyer was still curious, but if he pushed and got Wolfe to make a confession, he'd be expected to make his own in return. And then they'd be talking about Greta. Dyer suddenly wanted to end the conversation. He took a step away from the table, moving for the door.

"And there were personal reasons," Wolfe said, glancing back over his shoulder. "Put it this way: I needed something else, something new. Some other commitment."

James stood behind the hockey rink, near a field shed and a line of parked mowers. He was five minutes late, but he'd meant to be later. He'd told himself to dawdle, which was hard. James was habitually prompt.

"Hey, squid."

James let a moment pass, then turned. Randy Holiday cast a humped, mountainous shadow in his XXL Britton sweatshirt. James noticed the happy, boyish blush on his cheeks, and dread crawled all over him. Randy was a postgraduate, which meant he'd put off college for one year to come to Britton, play football, and better his academic record. PGs were usually good for sports, but otherwise deadweight—dumb, wealthy athletes looking to attract Ivy League coaches. James had never even spoken to one before.

"Squid's a term of endearment," said Randy, reaching for James's shoulder.

James backed away, digging in his backpack. "Look, I've been thinking that it really would be better for everyone if you wrote this paper yourself. I did a very clear outline."

Randy's nostrils dilated. "What's that smell?"

"Does Springfield have a good community college?" James asked, taking a step backward.

"Seriously, squid. You reek."

"The point is, if you're caught cheating . . ." James knew his voice sounded miserable, pleading. And he did smell. All day, he'd been trying to ignore the ammoniac tang drifting up from his clothes.

Randy leaned in and took a whiff. "You smell like *piss*."

The piss had gotten into his pillow, which meant it was in his hair. It soaked into his mattress, which meant it got on his sheets, which meant it was on his skin. He'd dug down to the deepest layer of his clothes to find something to wear, throwing everything else in the laundry hamper, but laundry service wasn't till Friday. He wouldn't have clean clothes to wear for five days.

"You got—what do they call it? With the whiz in the humidifier?"

"Lacquered."

Randy threw his head back. "Fuck me. Was everything covered in it?"

"That's sort of the point," said James. Rafton let him out of the closet after twenty minutes — plenty of time to let the humidifier do its work. *You should have gone for the funnel,* Rafton had said.

"You gotta do something back," said Randy.

"No thanks," said James.

"Don't be a puss."

"Look," James said, surprised to feel a blush coming on. *Look at me,* he almost said. "About this paper."

Randy let a moment pass, then asked, "You read what? Like a book a week?"

James blinked. "I guess," he said.

Randy shook his head slowly, impressed. "I need some books to read. Fiction, nonfiction, whatever. Only the grade-A stuff."

"I have to be in class in five minutes," said James. A lie. He had nothing to do until IM soccer at 3:30.

"You should change," said Randy.

"My other clothes are worse."

"Here," said Randy. He lifted his gym bag strap over his head and dropped it to the ground. He unzipped the top and pulled out a Britton football T-shirt, as big as a tarp. "Take it. I've got a stack in my locker."

"I'm going to give you this outline," said James. He waved two stapled pages he'd taken out of his backpack. "And you can show me a draft or something."

"Deadline's when? Two weeks?"

"November first."

"You do it," Randy said, throwing the T-shirt at James. "You did such a nice job with the last one."

James held the shirt up to his chest; the hem reached his knees.

"Tuck it in," said Randy. He grinned, then swung an arm around, caught James's backpack, and ripped it off his shoulder, tearing the strap and spinning James on his feet. Randy rummaged around inside and pulled out a paperback copy of Fitzgerald's *Tender Is the Night.* "Can I have this?" he asked.

"No," James said, rubbing his shoulder. "I have to read it for class."

"I'll give it back," Randy said. He lifted his gym bag and started to back away. "Promise." He held the book up to his face, sniffed, and wrinkled his nose.

Inspecting his torn backpack strap, Randy's T-shirt billowing around his torso, his own stuffed in his pack, James cut in front of the bell tower and down the terraced grass of the central lawn. The girls' soccer field lay beyond a high row of dorms, below the peaked towers of the infirmary.

He couldn't help it. He was thinking seriously about Randy's paper. The assignment: an example of socialism after WWI. What if he did something on the Communist International? Contrast it with the League of Nations. He'd need another sports metaphor. Rival soccer teams?

As he circled Bachelor Hall, James gained a full view of the field. A line of girls in shiny blue Britton jerseys and black shorts ran wind sprints between rows of cones. There was Jane, leading, her ponytail bouncing around her neck. She braked hard, crouched to touch the ground, and tore off in the other direction.

James found the shade of a tree and sank down to a humped root. Jane streaked past her coach, who nodded, bent to a stopwatch, whistle in her mouth. Jane folded over and held her knees, breathing in deep swallows. She slapped the hand of a teammate.

The air was dry and cold, pushing around him. Would they scrimmage? It was useful when they scrimmaged.

Jane grabbed a green plastic water bottle from an open bag on the grass. She squeezed a stream into her mouth and noticed James. He'd taken a seat closer to the field this time, close enough to be recognized. She took another drink, staring at him — then dropped the bottle into the bag and headed his way.

"You're here again," she said.

"Just watching," he said quickly. He was sitting downwind. With the new shirt on, he couldn't smell himself.

She closed on him, narrowing the space between them into a line of grass. "What? Soccer?"

"We started scrimmaging in intramurals," said James, the words tumbling out of his mouth. "There're fewer people this year, so I have to play."

"What position?"

"Last time I was toward the back."

"Defense," she said, and nodded. James nodded back, as if they'd just agreed on something. "Funny about class the other day," she said.

The waistband of her shorts was rolled fat around her hips. James could feel her eyes on him, could feel her gentle look; his nose itched, but he wouldn't rub it.

"I mean, Randy's a nightmare," she said.

"You know him?" James asked.

"Oh God, not really. Do you?"

"Not really."

She lifted the hem of her jersey to wipe sweat out of her eyes. A slug of shiny skin reached from her hip toward her navel.

"What happened there?" James asked without thinking.

Jane dropped the jersey back over the scar. "They took some bone out."

"Where'd they put it?" James asked.

She pointed to her shoulder. "They used it to seal up my collarbone. Broke that two seasons ago," she said. The breeze blew, and Jane shivered. Two of the other girls on the field called out Jane's name in a singsong, and she shook her head, blinking slowly. She took one last look at James before turning, a quick roll of her eyes.

One of the girls passed her the ball as she reached the field. The coach blew a shrill blast of whistle, and the girls ranged out into position for a drill.

Walking through the open iron gates toward Forest Road, Dyer took a reflexive breath and held it. Dyer hated crossing Britton's old boundary wall and stepping onto Forest, a road that ran along the northern border of the school grounds, connecting to I-93 two miles west. For six weeks, Dyer had been telling himself that the

Britton School was home, or at least a version of it, busy but protected, circumscribed, hermetic. Crossing the wall, he thought of his father. He wondered what he must have felt as his cab pulled away from Stuart Street that Monday in May.

Dyer stood on the asphalt verge, checking the empty road for traffic. He thought of the classes he had to prepare for the week; it still took him hours of mostly wasted research to feel ready to face his students. He was overpreparing, he knew, but he couldn't stop himself. He'd get better, more confident, but it would take time. *Time,* he thought. He would spend months, maybe years here. At that, an instinct, a lurch in his gut, told him to turn left toward the faculty parking lot and get in his dirt-colored Honda. He shut his eyes and concentrated on the familiar drape of his shoulder bag, an ink-stained canvas satchel he'd had since college. Its weight reminded him of his responsibilities: his IM clipboard with the roster and game rules, equipment shed key, and the whistle Sam Morris had given him mock-ceremoniously that first week in September, looping it over his head like a medal.

There was no reason to leave, Dyer told himself, making for the line of oak and birch on the other side of Forest. There was nowhere to go, no other job waiting for him, and Alice was across the globe. He missed her. Just saying her name that morning in Wolfe's kitchen had sent their past thudding back—but he knew another instinct, another lurch in his gut, had told him to leave her in the first place. Since Oxford, his instincts confused and worried him. He'd signed that LOI. He'd left the party with Greta. He'd gone by her place and said that dumb thing about Vicodin. Earlier that day they'd crossed paths near Commons and performed their now-usual pantomime. She shook her head dizzily and gritted her teeth as if to say, *Busy!* Dyer bobbed his head with sympathy and let out a big sigh: *Me too!*

How stupid. A little foresight, a little impulse control, and Greta could have been a friend for drinks at the small, wood-walled bar in the campus inn, a go-to for decompression, for laughs at their students' expense. He could have heard firsthand, rather than through Chris Nolan, about the skinny girls in Range House who skipped the salad bar for bowls of brown rice with marinara sauce from the hot food line. They were convinced that Dr. Rombauer, the infirmary's "concerned" nutritionist, had ordered the dining service to spray the lettuce and raw vegetables with lard. Dyer could have gotten more advice from Greta than how not to smile in class — strategies for keeping up with the prep, the grading of papers, the writing of midterm exams, the work that meant he was up past midnight almost every night, listening to Benjy Duggan drilling the opening licks of Led Zeppelin's "The Ocean" on an unplugged Fender next door.

Dyer had no one to share this stuff with. He still had a couple of friends from college, but the one he'd kept up with best, Dave, the L.A. guy who'd given him Percocet, hadn't answered his cell phone the last two times Dyer had tried it. There'd been a drinking buddy at Oxford, Andy Gimble, but Andy was now a busy barrister in London, expensive to call, and five time zones ahead. Dyer felt alone, more so than ever in his life. Even his friendship with Chris Nolan had gone off track. On the walk back from the campus inn the previous week, after two beers each, the midnight Britton campus broad, empty, and lunar blue, Chris had invited Dyer up to his apartment in Weiss for a third. Both had early classes to teach, conversation had ebbed, the night was over. Chris, generally so easygoing, had rushed the question, his eyes on the ground: "You want another beer?" Dyer watched Chris toe a loose stone on the path. Suddenly awkward, he forced a big yawn, said he was half-asleep already. Next time.

Britton's a lonely place. Dyer could feel it. Packs of boys on the lawns shouting over one another or sticking lacrosse balls back and forth, lowers huddled on the Commons steps, and Dyer had to hurry to keep up with his routine — choson do to class to the History office to Commons to class to IMs to Commons to Bailey to bed.

He'd find Greta or Chris at dinner that night, Dyer decided. Crack a joke, smooth things over. If he was going to plant himself here at Britton, not fly off in his car on a weak, unsuppressed urge, he'd need friends.

The path to the outer sports fields threaded a dense stand of trees, the black asphalt cracked and erupting with moss. Following it into the cool woods, Dyer remembered how at an early age, with his mother working six days a week at a public interest law firm, he'd played solo baseball against the garage door in the yard after school. Divorce papers were signed, Dyer got older, he could drive and go to parties, but even still he kept up his routine, heading out to the aluminum door in the backyard with Wiffle ball and bat. Drive the ball into the top panel, single. The bottom panel, double; the doorframe, triple. Ricochet off the doorknob, home run. Jogging now (he was late, he realized), Dyer remembered how calming nine solitary innings could feel.

He thought of Alice leaning forward in a hard plastic garden chair, her gaze leveled on his mother's, not falling to the tremor in her hands, or her stiff frown, or the tendons standing out in her neck. This was two summers ago. They sat in the backyard of the house on Stuart Street, only a few feet from the garage door, in the corner where the sun pooled onto the patio tile. Alice, meeting his mother for the first time, had talked about her own parents, about her real estate developer father and her mother, an ex–television actress. Bethany had been rapt, even a little dazzled by this pretty Californian girl with the sun falling on her. Dyer could tell by the way the tremor in her hands stilled, by the loose way she held a handkerchief near the corner of her mouth.

There was sunlight ahead, an opening in the trees, the soccer field from this distance soft and green, the sky above a washed wedge of blue. Dyer passed out of the dark woods, out of the cool column of forest air, and onto the field's mowed sideline. His mother had really fallen for Alice that day, so much so that Dyer had wondered if he'd introduced them too early, before he knew whether the relationship would last. And look what had happened. Dyer had come through Richmond in September, and his mother had demanded to know if he'd left her. "Not sure," he'd said truthfully. "Can we not talk about it?" So she'd asked questions about his job instead: "Do they know you went to public school?" "How much are they paying you?" "Isn't that less than you were making in L.A.?"

Dyer shook himself, a full-body shake, trying to dislodge the thoughts now crowding his head.

Focus.

Players lounged on the sideline, an average-sized group. Sixteen, Dyer counted — more absences than last time, but enough for a game.

"Scrimmage," he said, unshouldering his bag. They let out a weak cheer.

IMs lacked discipline. Sam Morris had asked Dyer to change that, and for the first month, Dyer tried. He hadn't played soccer since sixth grade, so he read up on the fundamentals. He'd forced the players through offensive drills — passing, long crosses, shots on goal — but the ability level was too varied, and Dyer found he couldn't conjure the harsh tone needed to keep practice together. Short, asthmatic Jerome Katt kept dropping out to catch his breath. Louise Hampton said she had shin splints, and wouldn't run. And James Wolfe seemed reluctant to do anything but watch from the sideline. Meanwhile, the other guys — those who played spring lacrosse or rowed spring crew, guys like Sam Rafton, Greg Smile, and Anthony Laborde — liked to cannon the ball, scattering the others off the field.

Scrimmages, Dyer eventually decided, were the easiest way through the three-per-week, hour-long periods. Sweep the field for beer cans (away from the main road, where cops and campus security could patrol, Britton's outer sports fields had become a party destination for seniors from nearby East Britton High), mix the teams up — fifteen-minute halves. He'd run his first scrimmage two days before with some success.

"How's the field look?" asked Dyer.

"Clean," said Anthony, without looking up, fingering mud out of his cleats.

"Nobody's checked," said Jerome, his hair shiny and tangled, his cheeks feverish with acne.

Dyer shot Anthony a look and bent to pull the set of keys out of his bag. When he rose, Anthony had pushed himself to his feet. He nudged Greg, and they wandered out onto the field, looking left and right. Dyer felt a pleasant flush of authority. Sometimes it was easy, he thought. Sometimes they just did what you wanted.

"Somebody help me get the stuff," Dyer said to no one in particular.

Jerome and James stood and followed Dyer downfield toward the old equipment shed.

James, Dyer noticed, wore an enormous Britton football T-shirt, a new one, the fold lines still puckering the front, gym shorts, and old-fashioned tennis sneakers. Dyer admired the cracked white leather and clay-stained canvas, the metal eyelets. Cool-looking, but no good for soccer.

Dyer unlocked the thick padlock. He swung the wooden door open and entered the shed's thick air of mildew, gasoline, and cut grass. The mower was parked near the door, next to a couple of gas cans. A plastic first-aid kit hung on one wall, and humped mesh sacks lay like bodies on the cement floor. Two small, netted goal frames filled the corner. Dyer directed Jerome to one and lifted the other to his shoulder. James hefted the sack of balls.

"Do I have to participate today?" asked James.

"Everybody does," said Dyer.

"Last year I could just substitute," said James. "More people wanted to play."

Dyer eyed James, who'd set the mesh sack down to regrip the canvas strap. He wondered if the kid was angry about class, about being singled out.

"Me and Ben Wittleman found a dead cat in here last year," said Jerome. "Its head was ripped off." In the darkness of the shed, Jerome's acne looked better, flatter, like a shade of blush. "Ritual killing. There's this cult from East Britton High who come in at night." Jerome smiled, his teeth lumpy with braces. "See?" He pointed to a mound of candle wax in the corner, next to sacks of lime.

Prep school paranoia, thought Dyer. It wasn't the first time he'd encountered it. Even the teachers here had gone to prep school: Chris at Loomis Chafee; Will Hemmer, the Physics teacher, was a Britton alum. Over dinner, Arnold Lambert (Exeter, then Amherst) mentioned concerns about Britton students getting harassed in town. He'd said there were a lot of disadvantaged kids who "naturally" resented the presence of a wealthy school on a hill. *Naturally*. Dyer had bristled at the word. He wasn't, or hadn't been, a prep school kid, but he didn't resent Britton. And the town looked empty and safe — four blocks of Italian restaurants, a coffee shop, an ice cream parlor, a Walgreens, the town hall, and Jingles, an outdoors store with canoes and fishing gear in the windows.

"How do they get through the padlock?" asked James sensibly.

"Loose board in the back," said Jerome, pointing. And there it was: a plank in the wall hanging askew, letting in light.

"We're all cat killers, you know," Dyer said, leering, meaning, *we public school kids.*

Jerome's face was blank. "You are?"

"Two-lap warm-up," said Dyer to the players, who sat or lay flat on the grass, faces turned to catch the slanting rays of sun.

Samantha Twiss sighed. "Can't we just play?"

"Jogging loosens muscles and cuts down on injury," said Dyer, reciting the manual on his clipboard from memory. "Let's go."

Slowly the group rose and started off down the field, only a few of them jogging. Sam Rafton stood on one foot, holding his ankle behind him, stretching his quad. He lifted his hard, angled chin. "Mr. Martin," he said, his voice low, his r's gentle and southern. Dyer knew Sam's dad was a millionaire developer in Atlanta. Chris had told him Byrd Rafton half funded Britton's athletic program. "I didn't mean to seem disrespectful the other day. In class," Sam said.

Dyer glanced sharply at him, then nodded and bent to fish in his bag for his whistle; when he rose, Sam was still standing there, motionless, like a heron. His 250 paper had been a regurgitation of the reading, full of grammatical errors and spelling mistakes — and yet Dyer couldn't entirely dismiss him as a dumb rich kid here for his family's donating potential. There was a quickness about him, in his jabbing penmanship, in the way he'd whip a notebook page over to a clean side, in his sly, superior smile. He offered a version of that now.

"You're falling behind," said Dyer, looping the whistle around his neck.

The players straggled back in, and Dyer chose captains quickly, absently, pointing at two who caught his eye — Louise Hampton and Jimmy Bertrand.

Shit. Mistake. Jimmy was a real athlete, tight with Sam, Greg, and the other guys. Louise was here because she had to be. She'd walked her second lap cross-eyed, examining her bangs.

Before he could redesignate, they began rotating picks. Louise took all five girls for her team, then Jerome, then, finally, James. "Like your shoes," she said, nodding at him. Jimmy's team was all-male.

"Mismatch," said Ryan Fried.

"If you say so," said Harriet Rosenfeld, yanking tube socks over her regulation shin guards. Like some of the boys, she wore real cleats; Dyer remembered that the girl could play.

"Spot you ten goals," said Sam, backpedaling onto the field.

"Fuck you," said Harriet.

"Hey," said Dyer. "Language." Could he call Sam back, call the teams unfair? He opened his mouth to speak, then reconsidered. Politically, he wasn't sure.

"Take goal," Harriet, taking over captain's duties from Louise, instructed James. She pointed at Jerome. "Sweeper." Jerome produced an inhaler from his backpack on the grass and took a short, gasping tug.

Jimmy's team took the field; Harriet directed the five girls into positions on their side. James and Jerome walked slowly toward the goal. Jerome wandered around the penalty box. James stood dead center on the goal line, his feet pressed together, his hands flat against his legs as if prepping a dive.

The eight guys huddled, hands on knees. They clapped simultaneously, a neat sound like a gunshot, and dispersed, five to the shaded sideline near their goal where they sat down, propping their hands behind them, crossing their feet. It seemed that only three — Ryan Fried, Jimmy Bertrand, and Sam Rafton — would play. They approached the midline.

"Guys," Dyer shouted. "We need full participation."

Nobody moved until Sam nodded at his teammates, and they slowly picked themselves up off the grass and stood on field.

"This good?" shouted skinny Tim Weir, the brim of his Britton cap rounded and low.

As an answer, Dyer slung the game ball, the firmest in the mesh bag, to Samantha Twiss. She trapped it neatly with the bottom of her foot. The move suggested a reserve of coordination Dyer hadn't yet seen. He wanted this to be true.

Dyer started the timer function on his watch and blew the whistle. Swinging her leg like a pendulum, Samantha passed the ball left toward Harriet. Ryan Fried charged from the circle boundary, raced between them at full sprint, and intercepted the pass. He dribbled the ball downfield, passing two of the motionless midfielders, Dinah Bulgarov and Cassie Dane. Jerome leaped out of his way, and Ryan hammered the ball by James. The shot billowed the net. Ryan looped back upfield, arms aloft, hands forming fists, shouting, "One-nil! One-nil!"

James watched Ryan do his prancing, high-kneed dance upfield. He'd studied the way he'd run with the ball, a loping rhythm, touching it gently with the instep of his foot, never letting it get too far in front. He'd thought of Jane, of the way he'd seen her head a ball off a pass, her back arched, his fists near her shoulders. On the kick, Ryan's body had curved over the ball, his head down, his foot at the end of the stroke pointed like a dancer's. James admired the combination, its grace and speed.

Dyer shouted, "Let's see some movement out there!" Dyer

stared at the blinking numbers on his watch and tasted the tinny whistle, killing time.

Harriet had her arm around Samantha's shoulders, whispering to her. She rolled the ball under her foot. In midfield, Dinah rubbed her arms vigorously. As usual the brisk, late-afternoon air had begun to settle and swirl inside the clearing of trees.

At Dyer's whistle, Samantha passed the ball firmly to Harriet, who touched it forward, then passed again to Samantha on her cross. The girls were running hard, and for a moment, Ryan, Sam, and Jimmy just watched. The other boys had reseated themselves beyond the sidelines. There was no one in goal.

Sam trailed Samantha, picking up speed, catching up, but she got a shot off — and turned with a grimace. The angle was wide of the goal and the ball bounced and rolled clear. Harriet shrugged and backpedaled.

One of the boys on the sideline hurled the ball to Ryan, who deftly touched it forward and charged downfield.

James, standing in goal, was slightly crouched. His knees were bent and he was facing Ryan's approach. Dyer noticed all of this and nearly inhaled his whistle when James met Ryan's shot — hard, straight, and waist-high — with two cupped hands. There was a hot slap. The ball dropped at James's feet. James picked it up and held it in front of him, as if he expected it to speak.

Harriet waved her hands wildly, and James threw the ball toward her. She was past Jimmy, free and clear to the boys' goal. Silently, Dyer cheered her on. No one stopped her as she raced downfield. She made an easy, side-of-foot pass straight through. Score.

James pressed his burning hands between his knees and felt tears bead in his eyes. There was cheering around him, surprised, semi-ironic cheering from the girls in midfield, even some applause from Ryan Fried as he jogged away. From the corner of the penalty box, Jerome's eyes were wide, his expression stunned. James's hands felt scalded, pulsing with blood. Zero elation; he just wondered if he'd be able to grip anything — a book, a pen, a key — ever again.

Dyer still couldn't call half, but he'd let the clock run for another minute, let Harriet enjoy her goal and James his block. Except it didn't look as if James were enjoying anything. His eyes creased in pain as he shook, opened, and closed his hands.

"James, you okay?" shouted Dyer. He moved down the sideline.

Sam dropped the ball at the midline, passed it to Jimmy, who passed it back.

"Take it again," Dyer called out, waving the whistle. "Wait for this."

But Sam ignored him, dribbling all the way to the outer edge of James's penalty box. James's eyes cut nervously to Dyer. Sam trapped the ball and backed off three long steps, his eyes angling down and up, measuring.

"Sam!" Dyer shouted angrily.

Sam leaned over, tensed, and broke for the ball, sweeping a foot through it. His shot followed an unerring line into James's face.

"Broke my nose twice already. All you got to worry about is the doctor not setting it back straight. Hurt yet?" A light tapping on his arm. "Hey, squid, can you hear?"

James knew he was in Smith Infirmary. He remembered coming with Mr. Martin. He remembered a woman with a fat neck and a firm grip helping him onto the bed, propping pillows behind him. He knew that was Randy's voice. And yet — what did he care? He felt happy and loose, as though he were floating on the surface of something — a warm updraft, a fountain of air.

"No," said James. "Nothing hurts." And nothing did. He sensed the bandage wrapped around his head, the faint chill of ice on his nose.

"Trust me. It'll hurt."

"I've got this idea for your paper," said James. "But I don't think I can ... um ..." Letting the sentence go, James felt his attention ease, his vision go wonderfully soft.

"Sure you can."

"You know that girl Jane Hirsch?"

"Ah, man. You are flying."

Exactly right! James closed his eyes and saw a campus of tooth-pick people, Popsicle-stick buildings, and wads of green cotton trees.

"Squid?"

"Huh?"

"Still feel like a puss?"

Dyer hurried across the brick library courtyard, picking his way through a cross-stream of students headed for dinner. He dodged a boy with an overloaded backpack, a pretty girl in a purple wind-breaker with a headband covering her ears, a boy shoving the hem of his shirt into the front of his jeans. He offered each a brittle smile, turning sideways, forcing his way.

"Dyer." The word was punched, impatient, and coming from the rear. The girl with the headband gave Dyer a startled look. The students' chatter fell into a hush. They knew Headmaster Wolfe's voice better than he did.

Dyer turned around. Wolfe emerged from beneath the library overhang. He wore jeans and an open-collared shirt, the sleeves rolled to his elbows.

"What happened?" Wolfe asked.

He already knew? Information was racing ahead, invisible, like sound waves. "Broken nose," he said.

"Is anyone with him?"

"The nurse gave him some codeine."

"Is anyone *with* him?"

"Randy Holiday," Dyer said, low and quiet. He braced himself for Wolfe's reaction.

"Randy's there?" Wolfe asked. He sank into the heels of his shoes, exhaling a small cloud of breath between them. The man was relieved, Dyer realized. Dyer rushed on: "He told me he'd take James back to Weiss. I realized I'd forgotten to lock up."

As Dyer and James had passed within view of the football prac-tice fields en route to the infirmary, Randy, still in his pads, had come jogging over. Dyer had tried to ward him off, but Randy had produced a clean towel from his waistband. It was what they needed; blood had saturated the first-aid kit cotton wadding James held to his face. Dyer caught another glimpse of James's nose on the transfer — swollen, wet with blood, like a lopsided plum. Dyer nodded thanks at Randy, who held the towel in place and walked with them all the way to the infirmary. He'd stayed while the nurses cleaned and packed James's face with ice. The same nurse who'd tended to Greta's wrist told Dyer that James would have to see the plastic surgeon for a reset. Randy had been full of questions — how'd it happen? is anyone in trouble? — but Dyer had been too addled to answer, racing off when he remembered he'd left the equipment out, unlocked, at the field.

"Were you going to come find me?" asked Wolfe.

Dyer fought off a wince. "Of course."

Wolfe headed in the direction of the infirmary. Two steps, and he turned again. "I want to see you in my office tomorrow morning. After your class." They were standing a few yards apart, and his voice easily carried the space. Two students, crossing the library courtyard, slowed their pace to listen. "You know where that is?"

Dyer nodded.

Then Wolfe was gone. The courtyard was empty, empty except for a raw sort of quiet. The sky held a feeble, gray dusk. Across the grass quad, the students bottlenecked the Commons doors. Dyer's spine felt like cable, like a braid of wires. He rubbed his face with his hands.

Now he'd continue on through the gates onto Forest Road, head down that narrow gloomy path in the gathering dark. Collect the sack of balls, the goals, shove them into the field shed, lock the lock — by himself. He'd then race back, catch a quick dinner, stop by Weiss to make sure Randy had brought James home, or that Wolfe had collected him. Return to Bailey. Prep the class he hadn't prepped for tomorrow. Check the boys in. Then, finally, fold himself into bed and try to forget that any of this had happened. Try not to run over the afternoon, over the past two days. And tomorrow wouldn't be better: another full schedule, a meeting with Wolfe.

He should have gone to Wolfe's house first thing. It was only a few hundred yards from the infirmary. A leaden guilt poured in.

"Hey, Mr. Martin. You okay?"

It was Oliver Frame, from Bailey House, headed toward the library with a stack of books leaning against his chest, steadied under his chin. The boy was overloaded, straining with the weight, and yet there he stood, turned toward him, his face a moon of concern.

"Sure, sure," said Dyer, smiling. "Just thinking for a second. You need some help?"

"Nope," said Oliver brightly. "Made it this far."

Oliver crossed the bars of light thrown from the building's windows, his shoes untied, the laces whipping the brick. At the double doors, he paused, then jutted his hip out, trying to hook the door handle with one finger. He extended a second finger, his body curved like a comma.

Success! But the heavy door wouldn't budge.

Oliver strained against it, his brow an arrowhead of effort. Watching this, Dyer felt a dim film fall from his sight. Proportion returned. He moved forward, resizing the events of the last few hours. A broken nose? In a soccer game? No big deal! James would be fine. What could Wolfe blame him for?

Simplest to call it an accident. *Why not?*

Oliver let out a little grunt of effort. The stack of books buckled; Oliver tried to steady them with his shoulder. Dyer lunged to help, but the books, a dozen library hardbacks, a couple as big as dictionaries, slipped out of Oliver's arms, flapping open like birds, plunging birds, splaying out, thudding the brick.

Wolfe's office felt sterile and provisional — an unused room, maintained for show. The meeting was brief. Wolfe greeted Dyer with a curt, oddly formal "hello" and invited him to sit in the only other piece of furniture in the room—a chair with the Britton insignia painted onto its wooden back. Besides the chair, the desk, and a narrow table running along the rear wall, the room was bare, the surfaces shiny and dusted. A phone and a computer occupied the desktop. Along one shelf lay a dozen small, maroon volumes with Korean characters printed on the spine: the Kim Il Sung books. The set did seem like a showpiece after all, a conversation starter. And Dyer would have said something about them, made some casual comment to break the silence in the room, but stress held him still and silent, his knees together, his hands in his lap.

The optimism he'd felt outside the library with Oliver Frame hadn't lasted. James was Wolfe's *son,* and he'd been hurt on Dyer's watch. Dyer figured he had, at the very least, a reprimand in store: a lecture about control in the classroom, about discipline on the field.

So when Wolfe began to speak, Dyer's nerves made the words echo in his ears. But he wasn't talking about James at all. "I want you to recruit the top students in your 250 class," Wolfe said. He handed Dyer a neat, paper-clipped file of forms. "Six or seven. Get them ready for a conference in March in New York. Be a first for Britton. All the information's there." He'd pointed to the file.

Dyer handled the clipped pages gingerly, like a gift, nodding with real enthusiasm.

It was only after he'd been dismissed and was padding down the marble hall outside of Wolfe's office, weightless with relief, that he really looked at what he'd been given, at the laurel leaf insignia on the letterhead, at the bold capitals: INTERNATIONAL MODEL UNITED NATIONS INSTITUTE. There was a glossy, trifold brochure, with photos of the UN General Assembly, the glass tower of New York's Crawford Hotel, serious-faced teenagers huddled over a table in a conference room. There was a letter of introduction addressed to Edward Wolfe, headmaster, Britton School, thanking him for his interest in IMUNI. There was a blank application form.

Dyer turned around, wondering if he should go back in and ask some real questions. You want me to do what? Start a model UN club? Dyer stood in front of Wolfe's shut office door and tried to think. *Was* this some kind of reprimand? The whole meeting had lasted less than five minutes. Nothing about James, but Wolfe's air had not been friendly. Dyer raised his hand to knock, and then held off. He'd take the forms back to Bailey, take a good look, and think things through.

But he didn't take a good look. The forms sat under a stack of student papers for the rest of October. Dyer taught the Communist revolution and the Russian civil war in 250, the fifth-century Hun invasion in his lower-form World History class. He knew nothing about the fifth century, but one of the other History teachers had finally shown him the meticulous, prepared notes in the History 110 file in the department office. Now class was like reading aloud.

Each time Dyer saw Wolfe on campus and both Wednesday mornings before the headmaster called choson do off for the winter, Dyer thumped the side of his leg with a clenched fist. *Model UN,* he thought. Wolfe never mentioned it, and Dyer wondered if he'd forgotten. Wondered and half hoped — until one morning when the folded page of headmaster letterhead appeared in his box (Wolfe didn't send e-mails), reading simply: "IMUNI??"

Dyer ran his hands along the hard cracked leather of the arm-chair and breathed in slowly through his nose. He liked Blanton's office — the mahogany desk, as broad as a dinner table, the metal globe tilted on its stand, the teak steamer trunk with the rusted latch against the wall. The room occupied a windowed corner on the fourth floor of Morrow Hall, but Blanton had hung heavy drapes to protect his collection of colonial-era maps from the sunlight. The gloom contributed to the room's closeness, to the smell Dyer couldn't get enough of, a condensed male odor, slightly sweet, like toffee.

"Ed's being provocative," said Blanton. "He was hired to be progressive, but he's got that confused."

"What do you mean?"

"He wants our brightest kids making the case for diplomacy. Britton stands behind the UN," Blanton said, bouncing the heel of his hand off the IMUNI forms Dyer had brought to show him. "That's the message."

Blanton flew a souvenir-sized American flag in the desiccated soil of the palm behind his desk; he reminded Dyer of his Oxford tutor Phelps, whose growling confidence in the market economy had captivated Dyer as much as the glossy sheen of his wingtips and the equilateral wedge of his tie. Phelps had barked his name good-naturedly when he entered his office; at the end of tutorial, he'd routinely offer Dyer a cigar. This was the swagger and throaty bravado of a man enjoying another man's company — intoxicating to Dyer, who'd grown up with only his mother to look out for him. The rapport wasn't as palpable with Blanton, but Dyer thought he could feel it building in the musky air of the man's office.

"Scotch?" Blanton offered, spinning his chair to a recessed shelf with smudged glasses and a bottle.

"Better not," said Dyer. "IM soccer at three-thirty."

Blanton cleared his throat, picked up and reset the Dewar's bottle on the shelf. "You have to understand where Ed is coming from with this. The highlights from his CV."

"I know he was sort of a radical."

Blanton nodded. "New Left — but not Age-of-Aquarius New Left. He was in that anarchist clique of the SDS, the bring-the-war-home, days-of-rage gang. He used to have a photo of himself in his office, hands in cuffs, grinning, blood dripping down his face. Charming."

"I didn't see it," Dyer said.

"They made him take it down last year — after, I believe, an angry letter from a parent. So he stripped the headmaster's office bare in protest."

"They who?"

"The trustees."

"Actual blood dripping down his face?"

Blanton nodded and peered at him over his glasses. "Your headmaster may not have actually blown up buildings in the seventies, but he certainly cheered on those who did."

"But the trustees would have known all that when they hired him."

Blanton waved his hand. "It seems chic. Maverick, disgruntled Harvard History prof with a dark past, his outrage channeled into education. And Britton's bastion-of-privilege thing doesn't play as well as it used to. These days, everyone wants a 'progressive' institution — or everyone talks about it. I don't know what they mean exactly, and I don't think our trustees know either. They certainly didn't anticipate what they were in for with Ed. You should know. Isn't he training you to dislocate shoulders in the mornings? To break kneecaps?" Blanton chuckled and rubbed his chin with one finger. "He'd love for us to haul off and hit the North Koreans," he said.

Dyer shrugged noncommittally. He'd taken a look at the day's newspapers in the faculty lounge and knew that a U.S. Pentagon official had leaked scenarios for a missile strike on suspected uranium storage and reprocessing facilities in North Korea. Critics said America couldn't be sure where all these facilities were, and Seoul was only forty miles from the border, an easy target if the North Koreans wanted to hit back.

"Start a war with the North Koreans, and Ed can throw up barricades around here," said Blanton, his volume rising. "That's what he's waiting for: the next Vietnam, the next excuse for revolution. Get these kids doing protest marches. Bullhorns outside Morrow Hall." Blanton was working himself up, his voice loud enough to be heard out in the hall. "And you noticed what he wore to Commons last night?"

Dyer had: a gray wool Mao-style jacket, buttoned up to his neck. From two tables away, he'd overheard Wolfe's explanation to Arnold Lambert, who wore a jacket and tie, typical dress for the older faculty at dinner. A Chinese factory worker uniform, Wolfe said. Souvenir from a recent research trip to Asia. Warmest thing in his closet.

"Someone needs to tell him that capitalism has won. In a rout. Someone — maybe his wife." Blanton laughed.

Dyer gathered his hands in his lap and fingered his ragged nails. Was it dangerous to be talking about the headmaster this way? Like it or not, Wolfe was his boss. That wasn't going to change. "I'm just a little overwhelmed by the idea of running the thing by myself," he said, shifting the conversation back to the forms on Blanton's desk.

"Not much sympathy for you there, I'm afraid," said Blanton, his voice dropping in a sigh. "Two courses? Ed gave you a light load, much lighter than I would have. He's probably been planning this club for some time."

Deep wrinkles and bags under Blanton's eyes buried his expression. A film of dust covered the lenses of his reading glasses, and when he pushed them up to take another look at the forms, Dyer couldn't see his eyes at all.

"You know he pals around with terrorists?"

"He what?"

Blanton met Dyer's gaze. "Tried to get a Weather Underground alum to speak here last year. I shot that nutcase idea down."

"Oh," said Dyer. "I thought you meant—"

"Real terrorists?" Blanton rubbed his eyes underneath his glasses. "I live near Ed, and so I get to see the folks he invites inside his house in the evening for drinks. Some pretty strange characters."

"Like who?"

"Scruffy buddies from Harvard. An Asian gentleman in a very expensive car."

Blanton's volume had gone back up. Dyer glanced nervously over his shoulder to check that the door was closed.

"For drinks?"

"Or meetings," said Blanton, raising his eyebrows. "They stay till well past midnight. I don't know what he's up to, and I guarantee the trustees don't either." Blanton started to speak, then stopped himself. The silence lasted; Blanton's frown grew nearly unbearable.

Dyer waited. "What do you think?" he asked.

"What do *you* think?" The senior teacher raised his hands to the back of his head and threaded his fingers through his silver hair. "Take down the government, one prep school kid at a time?" The dirty glasses slid down his nose, and his smile returned. He nodded at the IMUNI forms in front of him. "Why don't you ask Ed if he's serious?"

The idea cramped Dyer's stomach. "I know he's serious. He wanted to know whether the application was in."

"He asked you?"

"This morning," said Dyer.

"At ro sham bo?"

"He called that off for the winter. A note in my box."

"Huh," said Blanton, pushing the forms across the desk. Dyer was being dismissed. "Last year he kept that nonsense up until mid-December."

3

November

THE MASSTRANS BUS leaned into the corkscrew highway on-ramp, and fresh sweat dampened the skin of James's neck. Who'd told him that sitting over the back wheel cut down on nausea? He thought the principle through — point of axis minimized centrifugal force around the turns. Bullshit, thought James. He felt as though he were on a Tilt-A-Whirl.

He'd taken this trip at least a dozen times in the past and had never been sick. And yet, from the moment he'd swung his feet off his bed to the floor of his room and thought of the bus ride to Boston, the ride he'd been anticipating all term, he'd felt his stomach lurch and twist.

The day before he'd found an envelope slipped under his door in Weiss with two folded twenties and a Post-it with "For your bus tickets" scrawled in a nearly illegible hand. The terse note didn't surprise him. His dad had never been big on Thanksgiving.

He'd gotten to the corner bus stop a half-hour early and had been first in line and first onboard. What good had that done? He had the wheel beneath his feet, and ten miles from campus he felt ready to spew the Pop-Tarts he'd eaten at Commons. James stared at the pocked plastic on the seatback and rested his hands on his stomach. It seemed to be levitating into his chest. The nerves around his nose twanged like guitar strings. He set his head against the padded rest.

Mom's been remiss! Finally back in Beantown. Come the minute you can, and we'll get the turducken. CAN'T WAIT.

James had printed the e-mail, and he carried it in his parka pocket, the page folded as small as it would go. He jammed a hand in and flipped the thing over as if it were a poker chip. Last year when she was finishing her MBA, the e-mails came every day. *Dear James,* they began. *Love Mom,* they ended. Since the summer, since she'd taken the position at Fuller-Reardon, they'd started reading like memos. He drew out his clammy hand. His forehead breathed sweat.

They'd needed her in Knoxville this whole time. Fuller-Reardon lost a defense contract last year to a rival company, so in addition to managing the unmanned-weaponry division his mom was advising on restructuring. Layoffs in commercial aviation, heavy R&D in antiballistic warning systems — programs that gave the congressional lobbyists something to shout about. *You don't care about this stuff,* she'd written. But he did care! He asked her to decode the initials: UAV, ABWS, JDAM.

Along Highway 91, skeletal trees blurred into gray. Brain Jones and some guy James didn't know had the seats behind him.

"Fuck it. Guy's dimes were all shake," said Brain.

"You've got better options?"

"Shittle says he's got a cousin in the city with stuff that'll blow your mind."

Raymond Tranian had been expelled the previous week. Tranian had been the campus dealer until Mr. Hemmer, head of Blake Hall, found him weighing bags of pot at his desk on a scale lifted from the chemistry lab. Tranian, blasting Jay-Z, had forgotten to barricade his door. Hemmer came in wanting quiet. Now Tranian was home in Philadelphia, and Sean Shettle (nicknamed Shittle), a scholarship kid from Queens, who'd bragged all term about his weed connections, had a chance to take over.

The things James knew, living in Weiss. Since the lacquering and the broken nose, the third-floor seniors had warmed to him a little, talking freely in his presence, in the bathroom, at Chris Nolan's sign-in, lounging in the hallway, spitting sunflower-seed shells down the stairwell. They respected the fact that James hadn't gotten anyone in trouble. They laughed at James's black eyes, at the packing and nostril tubing in and around his swollen nose; Buddy Juliver shadowboxed him in the hallway and called him Raging Bull, which stuck with everyone except Rafton. Randy Holiday had cornered Rafton after class and threatened to break his teeth — the rest of the Weiss seniors knew about this and thought it was hilarious. "Bull's got a boyfriend," said Cary one night at sign-in. "Hey, Bull," he shouted over. "You blow Holiday for that or what?"

James refocused on the window. The atmosphere was easier in Weiss, but he knew better than to consider any of those guys his friends. A mileage sign swept past: twenty-nine to Boston. James started a slow count, backward from twenty-nine. Peppery bile hit the back of his throat.

He pushed himself into the aisle. Brain took one look at him, bulged his cheeks, and mock-retched into his lap. James shut out the sound. The pitching aisle, the gray door at the back, the eye-level RESTROOM plate — these commanded his total concentration. James pressed his lips to his teeth and moved for it, steadying his way, seat top to seat top.

He remembered being seven or eight, riding in the family car along the sharp curves of the Maine coastal highway. He'd been trying to finish a comic book version of *Moby Dick* in the back seat. Shifting his attention from the scenery to the panels of lockjawed Ahab and the thrashing, toothy whale turned his stomach upside down. He remembered puking on the pages, remembered his dad veering the car into a scenic lookout. His mom had found Wet-Naps in the glove compartment while his dad leaned against the coin-operated telescope, a look of distaste on his face, arms folded tightly against his chest.

James's vision tunneled to the twist latch on the bathroom door. He fumbled the metal half moon, got the door open, and shuttered himself inside. He bent over and groaned out a lungful of puke into the bowl. Dizzy, he knelt down on the damp, wadded paper covering the floor and felt the wet reach through his pants to his knees. His teeth hummed; his stomach lurched upward as if trying to climb out of his body. James inhaled and puked again.

He spat twice and took another cautious breath. The air pushed through him, and he felt his stomach settle a little. He felt better. His teeth stopped humming; he could stand. He flushed the toilet. No paper towels in the dispenser, but, thank God, plenty of toilet paper. He bunched a handful and wiped his mouth.

In the mirror his face was corpse gray and puffy around the bridge of his nose. Only a faint shading of purple remained under his eyes from the twin shiners he'd had all month. He rubbed his cheeks, coaxing out some color. His hair—*ughh*—his hair was pathetic, looping off the top of his head and around his ears. He hadn't had a cut since the summer, and whenever it grew past an inch, these loose curls developed. His khakis now had fresh dark oval stains on the knees. He dabbed at them with more toilet paper, leaving white smudges.

The bus swerved. James fell into the wall, clubbing his head on the coat hook.

"Need a Dramamine?" said a voice in the aisle to James's left.

James shut his eyes, but not before he caught Jane's grin. She sat opposite the bathroom door. She must have gotten on after him. How had he missed that?

Bracing himself in the aisle, still rubbing the side of his head, James could feel the damp circles of his pants touching his knees. Jane took a tube of pills out of her backpack, zipped the pocket, and moved the pack to the floor. "I won't get on one of these without them," she said.

James dropped into the seat. He tried to thank her, but couldn't loosen his vocal cords to speak.

She shook a small pill out of the tube, then snapped a bottle of water from the elastic seat netting and handed both over.

"Hope you don't have to, like, drive after this. Pill makes me a little looped," she said.

"No," he managed. He felt the cold water all the way down his throat. "Thanks, Jane."

"No problem, *James*," she said, and laughed.

"What?"

"You're so formal."

Should he get up and head back to his seat? Brain was looking down the aisle, tonguing the inside of his cheek. But Jane was looking at him too, waiting for him to say something, apparently unbothered by the stains on his knees or the nervous smell that rose up out of his shirt.

"Are you going to see your parents?" James asked.

She didn't answer, and James winced. He remembered a story about her mother, killed in a hit-and-run right before she arrived for her first year at Britton. Her father lived somewhere in the Midwest. He *knew* that.

"Aunt Carey," said Jane.

"I'm sorry," he said.

"For what?" she asked. "Keep it," she said, not taking the bottle back. "I go every year. She does a turkey, stuffing, mashed potatoes, the whole nine."

Jane was dressed up. She wore a gray wool skirt patterned with little pink herringbone V's and a black turtleneck sweater. There was something different about her hair. It fell at an angle across her face, cutting the corner of her eye, and held a glossy patina of reflected window light. In 250, the only class they shared this term, she usually wore a baseball cap. Likewise at dinner, or after soccer practice when he'd catch a glimpse of her heading back to her room at Bachelor Hall. He could picture the wet rope of her ponytail, the damp half circle at the neck of her Britton sweatshirt.

She'd said something he'd missed. "Sorry. What?" he asked.

"Who're you going to see?"

"My mom," he said.

Jane nodded.

"I haven't seen her since the summer. All term she's been in Knoxville working. Refinancing the UAV research division. Unmanned Aerial Vehicles. They're these drone aircraft."

"Your mom's in the military?'"

"Fuller-Reardon Aerospace."

"Is that . . . ?" Jane shook her head. "What's that?'"

The sentence rolled out of his mouth like a carpet: "They're the number two military-weapons manufacturer in the country."

"Oh," said Jane. She played with the seat tray latch, swiveling it left and right. "Is that a little weird?'"

"Weird how?" asked James.

"Isn't your dad all gung-ho liberal? What was the thing he said in chapel at the opening of school?" she said.

"I'm surprised you paid attention." The September assembly was a first chance for postsummer reunions. Dean Lambert had had to quiet the crowd twice. James, sitting in the back, caught only snatches of his dad's speech. *Let's create a school hostile to orthodoxy and friendly to dissent.* A line James had heard before.

Jane shrugged. "I heard he was some kind of hippie in the sixties."

"He was," said James, thinking as he often did of the framed black-and-white photograph of his parents, the one that had stood at their bedside all those years before the move. A photo from a march on Washington. Both Harvard undergrads, bused down for the event, they sat sprawled out on the Mall, squinting up into the camera, smiling. His mom wore a dress like an apron, with flat, checked straps over her shoulders and a bandanna in her hair. His dad's bangs hung in his eyes, and he'd turned the sheepskin collar of his vest up around his neck. You could see the elbow-cocked shadow of the photographer on the grass beside them. James pictured their startlingly youthful expressions, his mom's collarbone knobbing through her skin, his dad's skinny face, his dimpled chin. Though classmates, they'd met only that morning on the bus, both single and pissed off about the war.

"They're separated," said James.

"Since when?'"

"Year and a half. Mom's new job was a problem, but it wasn't just that," he said.

"What else?"

James's focus cut from Jane's face to the rushing trees beside the freeway. He thought of his father taking that girl by the arm on the Harvard library steps, whispering something into her ear. He thought of Ms. Salverton crossing the backyard. "I don't really know," he said. He wedged his hands under his legs and gnawed his bottom lip. "But this one time Dad told me —"

Chirping rose from Jane's backpack. "Hang on," she said, leaning over to unzip the pocket and draw out the phone, the little LCD screen glowing orange. James wasn't trying to look — but he did look. He saw the name on the screen as she brought it to her ear, flicking her hair out of the way.

Henry.

Her voice was soft, musical, drawn out, falling at the end into breath: "Hey." She gave James an apologetic glance and angled toward the window.

James pulled himself out of the seat.

"She give you a mint?" Brain asked as he came up the aisle.

That one time his dad had told him, *No one begrudges your mother a career — it's her choice of field. We're two different people, and we married young. We married before I figured that out. I never should have done it.* He'd delivered the little speech abruptly and unprompted on a Sunday night at the house on Smithson Way, the previous year. James had just returned from a weekend in Cambridge.

Another mile marker passed: twelve to go.

I never should have done it.

If he had Jane to himself, alone in this bus, she could help him figure that one out. Figure out where it left him.

The Dramamine worked. Not like whatever they'd given him in the infirmary; that had been a moonshot. This just settled his stomach, muffled the talk around him, made him sleepy. But he didn't sleep. Out the window the dead highway forest became the outskirts of Boston — a shopping mall in Medford, the rows of glossy SUVs at a Ford and Jeep dealership. The fused clapboard townhouses of Somerville, houses with narrow lawns. The highway bridged the gray strip of the Charles. The towers of downtown rose up around the bus, which jerkily navigated traffic. Through narrow streets, James caught slips of harbor.

He was thinking only of his mom. The fall was the longest stretch of time they'd been apart. No chance he could have slipped off to Knoxville — nor had she asked him to. James could feel every inch of seat against his shoulders, the rest pushing against the back of his head. Time moved slowly at Britton, with week after week of the same class routine, each day a pattern he could execute blindfolded. Five classes, IMs (though he'd sat out play since the broken nose), meals, work in the library, home for sign-in. Two and a half months felt like a year. Now that he was back in Boston, the bus sliding into the cavernous bay of the South Station terminal, he wondered if so much time could leave her looking the same — waving at him from the driver's seat of her Jeep, crawling through the clogged turnaround of the station's entryway. That day in August, he'd said he could take the T, but she'd wanted to drive him, despite the traffic. *A big year for both of us,* she'd said, dropping him off.

The bus parked in its slip, and James made his way down the aisle. He glanced behind him but couldn't see Jane in the line of heads. He walked through the passenger lounge, with its rows of bolted-down bucket seats, and out the bank of doors. A straight shot on the Red Line, but she'd wanted to pick him up. Beneath the overhang, James peered through the pluming taxi exhaust for the Jeep. The lane was all cabs, their trunks unlatched and bobbing. Fresh morning air from the harbor fingered inside his ears, swept across the back of his neck.

Then Jane was beside him, a red weekend bag hanging from her shoulder. "Your eyelids are totally half-mast," she said.

"Thanks for the pill," he said.

She nodded and lingered, zipping up the shiny black down vest she'd put on over her sweater.

"Is your aunt picking you up?" asked James.

She shook her head. "It's just a couple of blocks," Jane said.

James's gaze scanned the crowded street; this was downtown, all high-rises and hotels. A couple of blocks to what? Jane lifted her bag and tipped her head sideways at him. "So long," she said.

"Could I give you a call?" he asked as she stepped off the curb. He fought to swallow; he'd surprised himself. "Over the weekend?"

She returned his casual shrug. She gripped her fingers together and wagged them in the air. "Do you have something . . . ?"

James crouched over his backpack. Stuffed in with a change of clothes was his calculus notebook and a pencil. He dragged them out.

She scribbled her number on the inside cover, her hair falling over her face, blocking her expression. She tapped the page. "AP calc, huh?" she said.

"It's hard," said James. The class was small — eight people around a wooden table. Mr. Holstein's formulas were like cuneiform on the wipe board.

"Should've taken it," she said, handing back his pencil. "For my apps." She shrugged again. "Okay," she said, and spread her fingers.

He waved the notebook.

James heard his name and spotted his mother through the open passenger window of her car. She paddled the air as he lifted the backpack to his shoulder and hurried through the line of cabs. He'd missed the car, a green, low-slung sedan, idling in a lane reserved for city buses. James threw his pack into the back seat and tumbled into the front. They couldn't kiss or hug. A bus was coming in behind them, blasting its horn. Caroline jerked the car into the next lane and had to brake hard. James's head lobbed forward. Cabs were merging into traffic from the right. James pulled his seatbelt across his waist.

Now, stopped, there was a chance to hug. James's cheek

brushed the soft hairs on her neck. His mother held his face and kissed him. She grinned. "Who was that girl you were talking to?" James blushed at the cheerful emphasis, the hard *g* of *girl.*

"Jane," he said. "Jane Hirsch." His mother wore all new clothes: a trim brown sweater and dark pants made of some soft, textured material. Her hair, held back with a black clip, was shorter than it had been in August, and messier too, as if she'd just toweled it dry.

She hit the horn, then laughed at the bleating sound. "We're not going anywhere," she said. She turned to him sharply, as though he'd just spoken. "I can't believe how wonderful it is to see you," she said. "I can't believe it." He heard Tennessee in the flat *a* of *can't.* She'd grown up there, outside Chattanooga, but James hadn't heard her accent in years. She used to read him *Pogo* comics at bedtime, or, later, Mark Twain, making him laugh with her drawn-out drawl.

"Me too," he said. Did her forehead look especially smooth? Was there a plumpness around her eyes? The Dramamine was still in him, he knew, futzing with his vision. Yet he was grateful for it, for its waxy calm, the way it let him sit totally still in this slippery leather seat. The new car, the new hair, the new clothes — there'd been changes, he thought. Things he'd missed out on.

"Feels like just yesterday I dropped you off," she said.

The cars were jammed askew, their blinkers ticking. James shifted his attention to the dashboard, the orange dial lights and elegant square buttons. "It felt like a year," he said.

"Your dad all right?" she asked.

"I barely see him," he said.

"I guess he's busy," she said, and let out a dead laugh. "Everybody's busy."

Caroline kept tight to the minivan in front. She held the wheel with both hands and threw him glances.

"Your nose looks the same," she said.

He flipped down the sun visor; the mirror lit. "There's still some color under my eyes," he said. "And I'm puffy." He touched the bridge of his nose.

"Look handsome to me," she said, and hammered the horn. James snapped the visor closed.

"Be prepared," Caroline said, unlocking the front door to their brick townhouse on an oak-shaded street in Cambridge. "I had cleaners come through."

The living room looked like an exhibit, the throw pillows on the couch plumped and symmetrical, months-old magazines fanned out on the coffee table, the wastebasket by the leather chair empty. The air smelled of floor polish, of sweet lemons and cream. Though his mom cared about appearances, about nice things, more so than his dad, neither was tidy. His dad's newspapers used to gather all over the house in dusty, browning stacks. Likewise his mom's coffee mugs and reading glasses, stranded on tabletops, on seat cushions.

Gently, James set his backpack down. After the move to Britton, his mom had refurnished, throwing out some of the holdovers from her early years of marriage, the sagging director's chairs and Indian sunburst rug that hung on the wall. James was still getting used to the glass end tables, the stain-free navy sofa. Caroline dropped her keys in the ceramic bowl by the door and switched on a new lamp with a silver base. A familiar gravity tugged James through the living room, past the stairs, and down the short hall to the kitchen. His entire life, James had done his homework in here, at the broad cherrywood counter that ran through the middle of the room. Had done homework and eaten his meals, picking at the knotholes and soft, oily surface of the wood. When they'd installed the counter the year James was born, his mother had argued that the wood wouldn't stay clean. Formica's bourgeois, had countered his dad. And less expensive, she'd said. They'd replayed the argument for James at Sunday dinners, the three of them lined up at the counter, watching *60 Minutes*. Over the years, the counter had darkened to a rich, oil-soaked brown. One morning when he was twelve, fixing himself breakfast before school, James had sliced through a bagel down to his finger. The bloodstain still shadowed the grain.

There it was: chest-high, jutting into the center of the room. Hesitantly, James stepped onto the glossy kitchen floor.

He took one of the stools at the counter, hooking his feet behind its legs. Every dish in the room was put away, the spatulas and ladles bunched in an earthenware jug by the stove. Even the cabinet doors had been scrubbed — gone were the oily finger smudges around the knobs. The sink was dry, the drain shiny. He spun in the stool, rechecking the polished floor for dust. A thought hit him.

"Was I a bad homemaker, or what?" Caroline asked, following him in. "Look at that stovetop."

No sign out front, thought James. But maybe they don't advertise good properties. Or maybe they already had a buyer.

Caroline opened the refrigerator, stared into the empty racks. "The larder's bare," she said. "We should go around the block to Corso's."

"Are you selling the house?"

Her back was to him. She let out a breath, a low, quiet laugh, and gently shook her head, impressed. She wasn't saying no.

"I just thought because the place is so made up," said James. "It's not that big a deal."

"No one's seen it yet," she said. She clapped her hands together. "I bought a pad in Knoxville."

James covered the bloodstain with his thumb. It *wasn't* a big deal, he thought. Over the last year he'd been visiting his home of sixteen years with a suitcase, a toothbrush, a disposable razor. The lesson? Home could be anywhere. The less you cared about where you lived the better off you were. "So Knoxville's permanent?"

"It's what makes sense." Her eyelids fluttered, as if against a hard light. "I should have told you we were selling. I suppose I thought it could all wait until you were through exams."

"All?"

She shut the refrigerator and approached the counter. She pushed up the sleeves of her sweater and sat next to him. She winced. "Your room's a guest room. I boxed up the few things."

James shrugged; old school folders, a yearbook or two. Nothing he wanted. He could tell there was more.

She placed her hand flat on the counter. She wore a new, braided gold bracelet around her wrist. James noticed the bare finger on her left hand. He followed two cracks in the wood to where they met in an X.

"Is there anything else?" asked James. "I'll be fine with it all."

"You don't have to be fine with it all," said Caroline. She tapped one finger on the wood. "Okay, ready?"

James nodded.

"There's someone new in my life, I guess you'd say. I actually don't know how you'd say it." She paused. "He's at the company. I didn't know how to bring him up. I wasn't sure I should bring him up."

James nodded again.

"Your dad already knows."

"He does?" asked James.

Caroline nodded. Faintly she cleared her throat. "He and I spoke about a week ago. Business stuff."

James struggled to get this out: "Business stuff?"

Caroline was silent. She clicked her teeth together — new mannerism, thought James — and sucked her bottom lip.

"I thought you'd wait for me to go to college to divorce."

"There's no timetable," she said.

He thought again of Ms. Salverton hurrying through the yard of the house on Smithson Way, the screen door slapping shut behind her, crossing beneath his window, head down against the low morning light. Last spring. James up early, going over his Chemistry notes for the midterm. Her hair had been tangled, the tail of her oxford shirt stuffed at an angle into her jeans. She passed through the back gate and stepped into the alleyway that ran out to Elson.

Downstairs, in the kitchen, he'd found his dad at the counter, reading the paper standing up, a coffee mug steaming into his face. James hadn't said a word, moving around him, gathering bowl, milk, cereal, spoon. His dad, evidently startled, had set the mug on the counter with a thunk.

James had been silent then, just as he was silent now, just as he'd kept quiet after getting lacquered, and after the soccer game last month, though he knew Rafton had been aiming for him, had seen him measure the angle before taking the shot.

But what if he spoke up? The idea was appealing, though he didn't know what he'd say. Still, he wanted to do something irrational, something impulsive. James thought of the applications sitting on his desk at Weiss, the thick envelopes of essays and transcripts ready for the admissions offices of the good northeastern schools, the ones his college adviser, Mr. Greenley, told him he "had no choice but to apply to." He thought of the mail slot in the basement of Peabody, and pictured an incinerator on the other end, or teeth slicing the envelopes to ribbons. Growing up in Cambridge, he'd seen the undergraduates on the library steps, hanging outside the Coop, crisscrossing the Yard. They lived in dorms, wore jeans, sweatshirts, ski jackets, baseball caps — same as Britton kids. Another dorm, more work, tests to study for, papers to write — four years that would spool out like a blank tape running to the end. He'd written good essays, he'd send the applications in. He wasn't crazy. But what if they were misdelivered, mislaid, what if, despite his grades and scores, no one wanted him?

What if he didn't go?

The longer James sat silently listening to his mother scratch the wood with her fingernail, the edgier and more unpredictable he felt. What if he did something reckless? Would all future certainties — graduation, college, career — disappear? What would take their place?

"Hungry?" asked Caroline. "I am. Been starving myself for tomorrow."

His single bed was gone. Also gone: his shallow, wooden desk, his bookshelf and dresser. The floor space in his old room consisted now of a lane of wood ringing a new, queen-sized bed.

James sank farther into the mattress than he expected. His bed at Weiss felt like a Styrofoam pallet by comparison. James didn't mind — he'd always had hard beds, he was a hard-bed person. Wrong, he thought, spreading out like a starfish. He'd just never tried anything else. A familiar rumble came from under the floor — steam heat making its way to the radiators. James had listened to this sound falling asleep his entire life. He could sleep now — his stomach full of Jimmy Corso's horseradish roast beef and cheddar.

He ran his thumb along the rubber buttons of the cordless phone. He dialed the number on the notebook at his side. He held his breath through the short bursts of sound.

"James?" Jane answered.

"Hi," he said, twisting a pillowcase with his free hand.

"What's up?"

He propped himself against the bed board, tried to loosen his grip on the phone. He couldn't hear any voices behind Jane's. He wondered if she were alone. "Mom and I just picked up the turducken."

"I've heard of that."

"Chicken stuffed in duck stuffed in turkey," said James.

"Like a food chain," said Jane.

"The smallest one they have is nine pounds. Which is way too much, obviously, for two people. How big is your turkey?"

"God," she said. "I don't know. Turkey-sized." She waited. "Everything going okay?"

He squeezed the pillow in his fist. "So-so," he said, and tossed the pillow away. "Would you want to come over here Friday? For leftovers?"

Jane let out a long breath, a sad sound, James thought, almost a sigh. She hummed a bit at the end, as if to cover up.

"What time is it?" she asked.

"Just past four."

"How about tonight instead? You want to drop by?"

"Aunt Carey's?" he asked, trying to keep the excitement out of his voice.

"No. I'm at the Mark."

"The what?"

. . .

"Take the car," said Caroline. "Are you insured?" She shook her head. "Who cares? Don't hit anyone."

She was back at the kitchen counter. Four thick, leatherette notebooks embossed with the Fuller-Reardon logo lay at her elbow. A stack of yellow pads sat to the side. She held a glass of wine and wore her reading glasses low on her nose. A muted CNN ran on the small white television tucked against the wall. This scene could have been two years old, conjured from her MBA days. Back then, outside of mealtime she'd commandeer the counter for a desk.

The CNN footage was a slow pan of the outside perimeter of a heavily guarded compound, identified by a caption as the U.S. embassy in Seoul. Zooming past two tanks flanking the gatehouse, the shot ran along coils of concertina wire and steel fencing. Concrete barriers lined the curb.

"She told me she was at her aunt's," said James.

Caroline's smile was broad; she liked the subject of Jane. "And the Mark's such a fancy hotel. What a mystery," she said. "Don't worry about me. Look at all the work I have. The car key's a little square thing in my purse."

"I'm not going right now," said James, though he almost would, as excited and helpless as he felt, his head dizzy, his body like a twig in a stream, lightweight, borne along by the current.

"Well, go early," she said. "Parking might be tricky."

James leaned against the counter and stared at the TV.

"Down in Knoxville, this seems like the Second Coming," said Caroline, tilting her wineglass at the screen. "Pentagon's promised a contract for the next-gen Goshawk, so we're cracking the whip at the engineers."

A reporter stood outside the embassy gates, dressed in a flak jacket and an open-collared shirt. He spoke into a microphone and gestured behind him with one hand. The shot then switched to a crowded protest march, angry young Koreans waving banners lettered in red: U.S. OUT, ONE KOREA, AMERICA GO HOME.

· · ·

Jane slumped low in one of the plush, purple chairs by the hotel's revolving doors, her hands bunched in her puffy vest. James missed her at first, radaring around the wide, marble-floored space. The lobby was cold, and light from no visible source flooded it like water, setting aglow the reception desk and the blank, bored faces of the employees behind it. A cluster of Japanese businessmen stood silently by the chrome elevator bank.

James finally spotted her, her boot-clad feet up on a black plastic cube. She lifted her hand.

"You drove?" she said.

"Yeah," he said. He hadn't driven since the summer, when his dad had lent him the station wagon for the trip to Scudo's. So he'd kept under fifty on the Mass Pike, stayed in the right lane, molding the wheel against his palms.

"Cool," she said, standing. "Check it out. This place is wild."

Past the elevators the hotel ran back through a set of interlocking lounges, each room dimly lit, windowless, and carpeted in purple. The chairs and loveseats were upholstered in purple as well. On the walls hung six-foot abstract paintings of bright red rectangles jammed together like buildings. Black cubes supported oversized art books, small vases of yellow flowers, and stone chessboards.

"You can get drinks in any one of them," said Jane. "There're these roaming waiters." She frowned. "Who card."

Two waiters stood beside a beaded entryway through which James saw polished wood backed with glowing bottles of liquor. The waiters wore loose, purple pajamas embroidered with a capital, cursive M. One, with a patch of hair beneath his lower lip, stared hard at James, his smile flattening, his lips forming a pucker. James cut his attention to the slick nylon of Jane's vest, the little pink chevrons on her skirt. He knew he was out of his depth. He'd never been in a place like this, never been in a bar, never had a drink in his life. And yet he wasn't as nervous as he might have been. He still had that light-bodied feeling, that twig-in-stream feeling; he was still in the current, racing along.

James trailed Jane a step or two as they passed deeper into the hotel, passed through circles of light cast by the metal-shaded wall sconces. The rooms continued the farther back they went. An older man with unnaturally gold-tinted hair peered at him over his glass of wine. A young couple played a game of checkers, their legs spread around the cube supporting the board. Jane strode through the lounges as though she'd been here before.

"There's pretty much no one in the back," said Jane.

Sure enough, they reached a small, empty room, more sparsely decorated than the rest. Purple velvet benches lined one wall, and a loose circle of chairs with no tables filled the corner. A red EXIT sign glowed above a curtained security door.

They sat in two chairs near an arching palm, which seemed to be growing out of a rock. James fingered the leaves — plastic.

"So," he said, forcing a smile.

"So," she said.

James gestured around him and gave her a questioning look.

"I'm staying here," she whispered, though there wasn't anyone else around to hear her.

"I figured."

With both hands she pulled out of her vest pockets two airplane-sized bottles of Bacardi and a can of Coke. She displayed them as evidence.

James nodded.

She cracked open the Coke and noisily gulped off the top third. Then, one-handed, she unscrewed a bottle of rum and poured it in, stifling a burp. She shook the can back and forth and took a more experimental sip. She unscrewed the other bottle and added it until rum rounded up from the can's mouth. Jane handed it over.

James tried not to hesitate. He took the can, slurped off the top — and held his face still so he wouldn't grimace.

"You said so-so," she said. "You said things were going so-so."

He took another swallow, and with his mouth and throat stinging said, "My parents are divorcing. I found out today."

She tipped her head at him and pressed her lips together in a kind of helpless grin. "Practically everyone I know has divorced parents," Jane said.

"And they're selling the house and Mom's moving to Knoxville. And she's got some kind of boyfriend."

"Well, good for her," said Jane. She dropped James's gaze, grinding her foot on the carpet as if mashing out a cigarette. "Are you mad about it?"

James understood how unimportant, how low-gauge, his news must sound — his mom was alive, back at home, yawning over her notes, swirling her last inch of wine. The rum made his throat quiver. "Do you miss your mom? Can I ask you that?"

"You could, but don't," Jane said, slumping into her chair, matching her posture in the lobby, gazing around the room proprietarily. "Not until I've had some more of that." She reached for the can.

Someone cleared his throat. A waiter had come in, the one with the tuft of hair below his lip. "We're fine," Jane said over her shoulder. The waiter touched the tuft, rubbing it with his finger, staring at the mini-bottles on the floor beside Jane's chair. "Thank you!" she said, waving. "Room five-fifty-one," she said, thrusting a key card in his direction. "Jane Hirsch. Look it up." He pursed his lips at her and turned to go.

Jane took a long pull on the Coke and burped behind her hand. "So," she said. "I bet you've figured out there's no Aunt Carey. No turkey-sized turkey."

James shrugged.

"Remember Henry?" She tucked a stray bit of hair behind her ear.

"He called you on the bus."

"Yes he did," she said, gunning him with her finger. "With some bad news. We're supposed to have this great long weekend. He booked the room and was supposed to be in it when I arrived. But guess what?"

Rhetorical, but James found himself answering anyway. "He's not here."

"Not till tomorrow at the earliest, he said," Jane said. "The Fieldspars are in D.C. for the holiday, and apparently his dad's watching him like a hawk. He can't get to the airport or something," she said. "So it's just me and the minibar." She lifted the Coke and smiled again, but this one was all teeth, a grimace. "And now you."

James thought of her at soccer practice, running sprints. He thought of the skinned knee she'd had last year. He'd spent slow moments in Chemistry watching it heal—first white gauze, then crusty scab, finally, pink wrinkled skin. Tonight, her skirt ended above the knee, exposing the shadowy patch beside the knee-cap.

"What I should have done," Jane went on, "is to go see Dad. But holidays depress the hell out of him. He actually asked me if Britton had some kind of on-campus thing for orphans. Ha-ha. Dad's got this weird sense of humor. Last year we went to this Chinese place for Thanksgiving dinner, and he made a drum set with the water glasses and chopsticks. I think he was trying to tell me something."

"Like what?" asked James.

"'Dad's crazy. Don't come home expecting Dad not to be crazy.' Have some more of this." She handed back the Coke. "It's not my first of the evening."

James took another, braver swig.

A familiar, chirping sound—from her vest pocket. She arced her back in the chair, opening an inch of white skin between sweater and skirt, and drew the phone out. She checked the screen. "And there's Henry now," she said. She overhanded the phone into James's lap. "Answer."

"No way," said James, wiping spilled Coke and rum from his jacket.

"Come on," she said.

"You're kidding," said James, and threw the phone, still ringing and blinking its angry red light, back to her. Jane caught it one-handed and flicked it back.

James managed to catch it this time. "I'm not going to answer this," he said.

"It'd be funny," she said.

Would it? Jane's gray-blue eyes were bulging. A strand of hair stuck to the corner of her mouth. She nodded vigorously. She really wanted him to play along. James flipped the phone open. Fuck it, he thought unfamiliarly.

"Hello?"

After a moment, a low, southern voice, one James faintly recognized, said: "The fuck is this?"

"James Wolfe," said James.

Big smile from Jane. Angry, staticky breath in James's ear. Henry said, "Put Jane on."

James tried to give Jane the phone. She crossed her arms against her chest. She shook her head.

"She's not . . . available," said James.

Jane rocked her head back with another big smile.

James waited through a long silence on the line. Can alcohol grab you this quickly? James's head began to swim lazily. He rubbed his eyes.

"Your dad's the headmaster," Henry said. "You're the kid living in my old room."

"Right," said James, realizing neither was a question.

"Dude. You want to hear something?"

"Sure," James said.

"Your dad had me kicked out."

"You were busted for something, weren't you?" James asked. "Drinking and cruising."

"So my dad would stop donating to the school."

Oh.

Henry made his voice gentle. He sounded like a doctor delivering bad news. "I wasn't in the room when they found the beers."

Senator Fieldspar. Republican. "But you were cruising," he said.

Jane lost her smile.

"Which is why I wasn't there, genius," said Henry. "Dean Lambert was fine with giving me probation, but your dad said I should get nailed for both. No special treatment. Ask Jane. She knows what I'm talking about."

Jane's hand was out, grasping for the phone. James rocked back in the purple seat. "She does?"

"Oh, dude," said Henry, making his voice gentle again. "You think she digs you for your personality? Because you're so smart?"

James pulled the phone off his ear, glancing at the little orange screen, the letters: HENRY. He handed it to Jane.

"What did you just tell him?" Jane asked into the phone. She twisted away as she had on the bus. "Don't be such a dick."

Henry's quiet voice lingered in his head.

"Tomorrow?" Jane asked. "Tomorrow day or tomorrow night? Okay, okay. I will. Whatever." And she snapped the phone shut.

"Wasn't there beer on his breath or something?" asked James, trying to remember the gossip he'd heard.

"But they couldn't prove he'd actually been drinking. Since he wasn't there. It was circumstantial or whatever. The guys in his room got put on pro; he got thrown out. He thinks your dad had it in for him."

"I don't know anything about it," said James, holding up a hand. "If that's what you're thinking."

She pushed her hair out of her eyes, detaching several strands from her lip. She opened her mouth and closed it. She moved her foot to the arm of his chair, propping it beside his left knee. She tapped him with it, and said, "All it is is I told him you were living in his room and we were hanging out and he wondered if you could put in a good word."

Her foot rested lightly against his knee. It was the first time any girl had touched James like that — deliberate contact — and the air went right out of him. His lungs sat empty for a full half minute. *We were hanging out.* He saw Jane in 250. He'd see her in the library, bent over a thick, messy three-ring binder, running her pen along her knuckles. They never shared a table. Nor would they sit together at Commons. Jane sat with the other soccer girls and some of the Weiss guys in the building's most elite room. No, they didn't *hang out*. Not the way Sam Rafton or Cary Street or Buddy Juliver hung out with girls. Those guys kept a strip of butcher paper, the "Scoresheet," tacked to the wall in Cary's room. On it was a tally of names with columns for dates, "Extent of contact," 0–10 rating, and a "Confirmed by" signature. They'd added a row for James, then wrote "N/A" in each column.

James pressed his knee against Jane's foot.

"He thinks Georgetown will take him if he gets a letter of circumstances from your dad," she said. "Apparently it's a really common thing. To go with his application."

"And you want me to —"

"Talk to your dad about it?"

"I don't really talk to my dad," said James. His lips were humming and damp from the drink. "Not since he moved me out of the house. He must have felt guilty, giving me Henry's room."

"Guilty about Henry."

"No," he said, and glared. But how could she know? "Dad wanted the house all to himself. He didn't want me around to see what he was doing."

"What do you mean?" she asked.

But he didn't want to get into it. He shook his head and looked down at the floor.

Jane tapped his knee with her foot again, then let it settle against him. For a moment James stared at the sole of her boot bunching the fabric of the chair. He stared at the place where her calf disappeared into the boot, at the pale chafing line where the leather bit into her skin.

Reversing the Honda into a tight spot on Stuart Street, Dyer spotted an envelope taped to the storm door of his mother's narrow, clapboard house. He threw the car into park and got out without turning off the engine. The letters of his name were printed in capitals, in red ink. He took the front steps by threes, bounding up as he had thousands of times, and tore the envelope open.

"Dyer, it's Mary Joyce. I don't believe you have a cell phone, so I couldn't call." Dyer's eyes raced down the page. "Your mother tripped in the yard and fell. I'm afraid she knocked herself unconscious, though she woke right up when I found her. She doesn't remember falling, and I've taken her to St. Elizabeth's, 368 Lakeside Rd., 4th Floor, Dr. Alexander's office. Come when you can. Mary."

Dyer steadied himself with one hand on the glass of the storm door. *Unconscious,* he read again, sounding the word out in his head.

He ran back to the car.

Dyer had never heard of St. Elizabeth's, but Lakeside wasn't far away, and he sped there through familiar streets, repeating the address aloud. In his head he saw the flagstones in the backyard. He saw their sharp, uneven edges and pictured the way one could rock under your feet. He pictured his mother tripping and falling, smacking her head. He pictured the spill of her hair, her slow and shallow breath, her sprawled body.

Gunning the gas through a yellow light on Brook Road, Dyer remembered the shuffle-and-drag rhythm of his mother's footsteps in August, the sibilant sound of her moccasin slippers sliding against the dusty wood floor of the hallway. At the time, he'd shelved the sound at the back of his brain. He wouldn't let himself get worried or alarmed.

During the autumn of Dyer's first year at Oxford, a neurologist diagnosed Bethany's left-hand tremor as early-stage Parkinson's. She didn't tell Dyer the news until he came home that Christmas. The first evening of his visit, she sat him down in a corner of the living room, away from the TV and the stacked magazines on the coffee table. Dyer sank into the couch, under a window that looked out onto the street. The window fit poorly in its frame, and Dyer felt a familiar draft on the back of his neck. Bethany took the upholstered armchair a few inches away. The twin ceiling bulbs inside a frosted glass globe threw a hard, wintry light onto the whorls of lint clinging to the chair's legs.

Bethany rested her hands in her lap, the left cradled in the right. It shook from the wrist, the fingers trembling against her stomach. Dyer had noticed the tremor the previous summer, attributing it to caffeine or nerves; seeing it again, he felt a flushed premonition (canceling the cold draft on his neck) of bad news.

She explained the diagnosis. "I still drive to work," she said. "I still use the computer and phone. What can't I do? I can't thread a needle, but I never could." She delivered this speech in the fake-casual, anger-suppressed tone she used for news of Julian Martin's latest whereabouts.

"Why didn't you tell me before?" he asked.

"I wanted to see you," she said. "To do it in person." She crossed her legs and flexed her right foot so that the moccasin dangled from her toes.

"What does the doctor say to do?"

"Treatment's Sinemet. But I'm putting it off," she said. This didn't surprise him. All his life, Bethany had never liked taking any kind of medication, preferring to treat the occasional headache or cold with liters of water and an extra hour of sleep. "After a while the pills don't even work," she said, then listed the side effects: "sudden, uncontrolled muscle spasms, bad sleep, depression, hallucinations." Dyer flinched at the last word.

"If this slows me down in a few years, so what? I'm fifty. I'm sure I'll be ready to slow down," she said. Dyer tried to speak, but his throat was too tight. Her posture in the armchair was how he'd always remembered it — still impressively flat-backed, her neck arched, her chin up, her shoulders spread, her brown and unblinking eyes on his. Dyer took all this in, then dropped his gaze and took a long, unsteady breath. She leaned forward and touched his arm with her left hand, the fingers wobbling on his skin.

That night Dyer woke up, hearing pops and shifts around him, quiet, old-house sounds he must have listened to his whole life but had never noticed or never heard so distinctly before. He lay there for an hour, trying to catalogue each one.

Dyer spent a month of the following summer at home (a stay that began with Alice's visit), and he came again the next Christmas for a week and a half. During this time Bethany's tremor spread to her right hand, and her face and neck tensed — tendons standing out in her neck, a curved line molding around her cheeks, her lips pressing into a flatter line than before. She still did work at the law firm, representing nonprofits around the city, though she'd cut her week to three days. Bethany never mentioned quitting, nor did she ever mention Sinemet or the neurologist she'd seen. She didn't attempt to hide her tremor, and as the days of Dyer's visits home passed, he could almost get used to it. He'd stiffen when she tried to fit her house key into the lock, or when a piece of broccoli shook off her fork, and yet they proceeded as before. Dyer helped with the cooking and dishwashing as he had since high school; he took out the trash; he shoveled snow in the winter and weeded the garden in the summer. When he was back at Oxford, Bethany's voice on the phone (they spoke once a week, on Sundays when the rates were low) sounded unchanged, an accentless, nearly Californian voice, unusual for someone who'd grown up in Virginia. Dyer could imagine nothing was different, and he could ignore his lurking guilt over not asking questions about the shaking or stiffness. "How's work?" he'd ask. "The same," she'd say, then ask, "Are you going to bring Alice home again?"

Dyer was doing fifty in a thirty-five when he spotted the Lakeside Road sign. He stood on the car's brake to make the turn. The Honda shuddered, and the tire bounced over the curb, jolting Dyer in his seat.

Alice used to tell him how brave he and his mother were not to mull and feel sorry for themselves. To this, Dyer would generally nod, never pointing out the obvious: not talking wasn't the same as being brave. He thought of L.A. He thought of the kitchen sink crowded with Alice's coffee mugs and his cereal bowls. He thought of the curdled, tofu smell of the natural foods store they went to on Sunday mornings for the organic coffee Alice liked. He'd been unhappy, he reminded himself, certain that he'd made the wrong decision in moving to L.A., unhappy that he relied on his girlfriend's family for a job, sure that he and Alice were moving too fast. But he'd never said anything to Alice. Not a word about how he felt.

Up ahead on Lakeside, Dyer saw a sign that read ST. ELIZABETH'S CONTINUING CARE. He navigated the car down a short asphalt drive that led to a three-story brick-and-smoked-glass building surrounded by landscaped gardens of densely planted tulip trees and gardenia bushes.

Dyer made for an open spot near the arcaded entrance. He missed a carved-wood STOP sign and had to swerve to avoid an oncoming Lincoln. The Honda hopped onto a parking lot median and scratchily wedged into a shrub. Framed in Dyer's rearview, the man inside the Lincoln — white hair, brimmed hat, jacket, and tie — slapped his dashboard angrily. Dyer held his head with both hands, his fingers laced in his greasy hair, staring into his lap for a moment before gingerly gearing the car into reverse.

Through the sliding glass doors of St. Elizabeth's, Dyer found himself in what looked like the sitting room of an English country inn: wing-backed chairs with cabbage rose pillows, pale yellow curtains generously folded above the paned windows. A wrought-iron umbrella stand, full of tidily closed umbrellas, stood by the doorway. Against one wall was a wooden horseshoe desk, but there was no one behind it, and once he spotted the elevator bank down a narrow yellow corridor he decided not to wait.

Up on the fourth floor, the pale yellow hallway drew Dyer down, down, down, as if into a narrowing throat. Jogging past parked wheelchairs and numbered, hotel-style doors with brass knockers, Dyer realized what "Continuing Care" meant. An old folks' home. Why bring her here? The carpeted floor with its linked chains of flowers matched the yellow wall, and the uniformity of color threw Dyer's balance. He took wide, stabilizing steps.

The hallway came to a T. Still no sign for Dr. Alexander, but down the hall to Dyer's right lay another lounge decorated like the front lobby. Going in, he spotted antique horse prints, two overstuffed sofas, and a bureau with brass latches and a lace runner. A glass panel was set into the wall, glowing with fluorescent white light. Through it, a woman tapped loose medical files into tidy stacks.

Dyer caught the wood ledge below the glass with both hands. The woman peered at him over the rimless lenses of her reading specs. Her blond hair was pinned into a neat, spherical bun, and she wore a string of thick, plastic pearls. At her side sat a can of ginger ale with a lipstick-tipped straw. She slid the panel noiselessly open.

"Bethany Martin?" Dyer asked. "She's been admitted here?"

"Is she a resident?"

The woman's tone was sweet, but Dyer was startled by the question. "She's my mother," Dyer said. "Is this Dr. Alexander's office?"

"Is your mother a resident?"

"No. Does it matter?" Dyer asked. She blinked at him, then pushed her glasses higher up her nose, bubbling her eyeballs in the lenses. She licked her thumb and began picking through the stack on her desk. "Bethany Martin?" she asked.

"She fell down and hit her head," he explained. "She must have just come in."

"My shift began a minute or two ago," said the woman, still thumbing through the files.

Dyer shrugged his coat off and bunched it in his fist.

The woman placed all the files except one back onto the desk. "Give me a second, dear," she said without looking at him, and rose from her desk chair. She left the office — a cube lined with shelves of color-coded files — by a side door.

"She only sounds friendly."

Dyer turned and saw a hunched man with neatly combed white hair, in shiny gray pants, brown loafers, and a green cardigan sweater. Dyer forced a smile and a nod. The man supported himself with a black metal cane. His sweater hung down to his knees. Dyer wiped a bead of sweat off his forehead with his sleeve, wondering how old he was. Eighty? Ninety?

"You made it." There was Mary Joyce standing in a doorway beside the office window. She was tall with hard cheekbones and a narrow-hipped, narrow-shouldered frame.

"Mary," said Dyer, feeling more hopeful, taking a step toward her as if she were offering him a hug.

"I didn't want to take your mother to the ER," she said. "And I'm on the St. Elizabeth's board. Dr. Alexander took care of my mother when she lived here." Mary touched his arm and nodded her head in the direction she'd come from, a gray, windowless door. "She's fine," she said. "A little banged-up. Don't worry."

Through the door, another hallway stretched away, but here were hospital-style rooms with coiled blood pressure gauges, heart monitors, IV trees, and the chrome railings of canted beds. Dyer relaxed a little at the sight of all the equipment. Nurses in white uniforms crisscrossed the hallway. The air held the knifing scent of disinfectant.

Mary covered the floor in long, confident strides. Dyer knew she'd been a Wall Street financial adviser who'd moved back to Richmond for a quieter life. As teenagers, she and Bethany had been classmates at St. Agnes School. Her brown, highlighted hair was finely brushed and bobbed, the ends turned in neatly under her jaw. Dyer trailed her, behind by a step, hurrying along.

Mary pointed at a door up on their left, evidently Bethany's room. She stopped and leaned against the corner of the wall, against a shell of thick, protective plastic. Out in the waiting area, Mary had looked young; in the new, harsher fluorescent light, Dyer saw the lines around her eyes and the loose skin in the hollow of her neck. Filaments of gray ran through her hair.

"She has a concussion, but not a serious one," Mary said, dropping her voice to a whisper. "Nothing's broken. She got one hand in front of her that sort of half stopped her fall, but also scraped up her palm and fingers. And then there's the bump above her eye. Tell her she looks tough. That's what I've been doing."

"She was knocked unconscious?"

"Which means they have to monitor her here overnight at least. After that I'm taking her away."

"Away?"

Mary tipped her head, nodded, and gave him a sympathetic smile. "She wants to go on a cruise. She started talking about it once I got her inside the house. The Caribbean."

"The *where?*" Too loud. Dyer caught a glance from one of the nurses, wheeling a cart stacked with sheets.

Mary startled him by taking his hand. She squeezed it hard, and Dyer felt the bones beneath her skin. "Tell her she looks terrific in her johnny," said Mary.

His mother wore a crisp, scoop-necked hospital gown. A gauze pad covered a golf ball–sized lump above her left eye. Her thick, dark brown hair spread behind her on the pillow. She was asleep, her mouth parted slightly, her hands completely still.

Bandages wrapped her left palm. An IV drip ran under a piece of tape on her wrist. She was missing a fingernail on her left middle finger, and the skin showed tracings of dried blood.

Dyer sat heavily in one of the vinyl-padded plastic chairs next to the bed. In his head—he couldn't stop himself—he saw her tripping on a flagstone and slamming onto the ground.

Above the bed hung a painting of a shoreline. The gray water was laced with bone white ripples. There were black smudges for birds and boats, and a black pier jutted into the water as if it were a piece of charred wood. The autumn trees behind the beach were dark blooms of orange and red.

Dyer wanted to rip the gloomy thing off the wall and shove it under the bed. He took a deep breath. He focused on his mother's still face.

Bethany's eyelids fluttered open. She closed her mouth, looked around, and blinked hard twice. Her hands began to wobble.

Dyer was on his feet. "Hi, Mom."

"Dyer," she said, her voice raspy with sleep.

"How do you feel?" he asked.

"Help me up," she said, holding out her hands. "Put a pillow behind me," she said.

He did and caught an acrid, nervous smell rising from the tight tendons of her neck. She swam in the loose hospital gown.

"You've got a nice lump," said Dyer.

She raised her hand to her face, but she didn't touch the bandage.

"Do you remember what happened?" asked Dyer.

She shook her head no. "Where's Mary?" she asked. It was the quietest and weakest he'd ever heard her speak. His mother had a strong, declamatory voice, and she'd raised Dyer to speak the same way, slowly and clearly. *People have to hear you,* she used to say. *Speak up and get their attention.*

"She's just outside," said Dyer. "She's in the hall."

Her bandaged hand came up from the tan blanket and sank down. It came up again and played in the air, looping and stirring. "I don't remember anything," she said.

"Does your head hurt?" asked Dyer.

She shook it no. "They gave me something," she said. "I suppose they had to." She looked out the window on the wall to her left, past Dyer's shoulder.

Through the pane and down below them, Dyer saw lines of parked Lincolns and Cadillacs and the tall floodlights, like watchful aliens, arcing over the lot. One of them blinked on. A glare-cutting film of plastic covered the glass, and through it the floods threw a dim and feeble light.

Dyer moved closer to the bed, touching the soft blanket at the side of the mattress with his fingertips. His mother's dark mass of hair and her olive skin — he hadn't inherited either — made a stark contrast against the white sheets. He placed his whole hand on the blanket, in the region of her hip.

"I don't do well in the cold," she said, her voice so quiet that Dyer thought she was speaking to herself.

"Warm in here, though," said Dyer dumbly. A question about

the cruise would come out wrong. Accusatory. *Will the boat stop at St. John?*

She nodded and looked directly at him, pinching her brow. She seemed to be drawing him into focus. "How is the job?" she asked.

He answered immediately, firmly: "Terrific. I'm really getting my feet under me. It's a really good school."

"That's two reallys," she whispered.

Dyer smiled. *You are or you aren't,* she used to tell him. *It is or it isn't.*

"You're not sorry you left Alice?" she asked, her voice gaining volume, though still thick with breath.

"No," he said, but every muscle in his stomach tightened, urging him to tell her about the regret he'd felt in the car, the regret he realized had been building all along. "She's in Iran. A movie studio sent her there to revise her screenplay."

Bethany's left hand shook the IV tube.

"Careful, Mom," Dyer said, gently stilling her hand with his own. The skin was warm, her knuckles knobby and hard.

"Is that dangerous?"

"I don't think so," said Dyer. "I guess the studio is looking after her." Dyer hadn't heard from Alice since October, since that night she'd called from her car.

"When is she coming back?" Bethany asked.

Dyer didn't know, so he didn't answer. "You really don't remember anything about your fall?"

She shook her head, then closed her eyes. "I remember the mail coming, and I remember going out to the yard to get some air. I needed air. I remember Mary touching me, waking me up."

"Is walking more difficult?"

Bethany's trembling left hand took another violent shake. The plastic bladder of fluid swung gently on its hook above the bed. Her eyes snapped open. She'd remembered something. "Have you been home yet?" she asked.

"Not inside."

"A package came from Julian." She used to say "your father"

until the year Dyer turned sixteen and asked her if she'd refer to him by name.

"A package?"

"Addressed to you."

Dyer took a step back from the bed. "Did you open it?" he asked. He'd never received anything from his father before. Not a letter, e-mail, phone call, not one thing.

"No," Bethany said. "I went out back."

"And fell."

"I was agitated," Bethany said, her voice quiet again. "I wasn't watching my step." Her eyes squeezed shut. Dyer could see she was in pain. "Can you get Mary?"

He nodded, but stalled for a moment, staring down into his mother's stung, wincing face. He could feel the coastline hanging there, edging the top of his vision, a dark smudge on the wall above the bed.

A small cardboard box, hand-addressed to Dyer, waited on the table by the front door on Stuart Street. Mary, who had come to the house to get a few things for Bethany, stood silently behind Dyer as he sunk a dinner knife into the seam and sawed through the packing tape. Inside the box, embedded in Styrofoam peanuts, sat a green leather case. Folded square and taped to its top was a letter, handwritten on a plain sheet of copy paper. The handwriting: long-tailed and looped, like doctor's script, leaning across the page.

> Dyer,
>
> Wasn't going to write a note. Just thought I'd send the watch, but then I wondered if you'd accept it. Diving client gave it to me. 77 vintage, Soviet issue. Maybe some day we'll have a whiskey and share adventures, huh? Some day! God, what a thought!! You know I've tried to help you and your mom. Here's my address. Write me. An old dog with his paw out wants a shake.
>
> Dad

Dyer dropped the letter onto the front hall table.

"Are you okay?" asked Mary.

Dyer nodded, breathing through his nose.

"It's from your dad?" asked Mary.

"Can you leave me alone for a minute?" asked Dyer.

Without a word, Mary slipped around him and headed toward the kitchen. Dyer noticed how forthrightly she moved down the hallway.

He reached for the note, to take it and reread it, then stopped himself. *Don't,* he thought. Take the box, the green case, the letter, the whole thing, out the kitchen door, back to the trash cans in the alley, and dump it.

Dyer moved his hand past the note, to the green case in the box. He lifted it out, hearing Mary move around the kitchen, hearing the water running in the sink.

He brushed off the clinging peanuts and opened the hinged lid.

Inside was the face of a heavy steel watch, the crystal covered by a protective steel lattice. The watch's face was at least two inches across; when Dyer placed it in the palm of his hand, the steel felt slightly warm. Red Cyrillic characters and a tiny submarine in profile decorated the center of the black dial, and a thick, ridged knob jutted from the side, the end of which was attached by a linked chain to the body of the watch. Beneath it lay a folded certificate, the card stock typed with Cyrillic and stamped with a triangle in which was handwritten "1977." Beneath this sat a flat, wide leather band, a black tongue at the bottom of the box.

The second hand was stuck motionless above the nine. The minute and hour hands, with green, faintly luminescent inlay, tapered sharply to points. On either end of the face, the steel curved smoothly downward to the band joints. Dyer pinched the knob between his thumb and finger, but didn't turn it. He replaced the watch in the case and replaced the case in the box.

In the kitchen he said, "I didn't mean to be rude."

Mary pushed a button on the dishwasher, and when the water started rushing through the machine she turned around. She waved her hand and shook her head. "What was in the box?" she asked.

"A watch," he said. He opened the cabinet above the sink and pulled out one of the blue plastic cups he always used. He ran the tap and filled it. " 'Absentee Father Gives Son Watch,' " he said, his hand blocking out the headline. He drank the cup of water in one go.

An awkward moment passed, Mary smiling a gentle smile, Dyer tapping the cup with his fingernail. Dyer moved to the counter and picked up a slippery bottle of olive oil and set it back down. He wished Mary would get his mother's things and go. Apart from a few dinners with his mother in this house, they'd never spent any time together, and Dyer didn't know what to say to her. He was grateful his mother had a close friend, someone to look after her, but right now he wished Mary would leave him alone so he could figure out what to do.

Dizziness struck Dyer. He steadied himself against the counter. He realized he hadn't eaten since lunch.

Mary touched his arm. "Why don't you sit down," she said. Dyer nodded, thankful for the suggestion. They moved together into the living room and Dyer settled in the couch under the windows.

"Back in a moment."

Dyer stared through the house, through the windows into the ashy dark of the backyard. He thought of his mother, asleep at St. Elizabeth's. He should have told her more forcefully, more convincingly, that Britton was working out. That's why he'd come after all, to reassure her (to reassure himself) that leaving L.A. had been a good thing.

Mary came back into the room, holding a fork and a plate with a large wedge of pumpkin pie. "This was for tomorrow," she said. "But what the hell."

"Oh God," Dyer said, his eyes wide, taking the plate. "Perfect. Thanks."

Mary sat beside him. Dyer ate a forkful. Crushing the sweet, cinnamony pie against the roof of his mouth, he sank deeper into the couch and sighed.

"She's going to be fine," said Mary.

Dyer chewed slowly, nodding. It was good to hear. "She wanted to go on a cruise?" he asked, between bites. "That's what she said?"

"She said she didn't do well in the cold."

"She told me that too."

"Then she grabbed my hand and said take me on a cruise. I said where, and she said, the Caribbean."

"That's where he lives," said Dyer, his mouth full.

"She doesn't want to see him."

Dyer nodded because Mary sounded so sure.

"She wants to go because it's beautiful, and warm, and an escape from her routine. Everyone wants to go there. She wants to go to be with me."

Mary hit the last word hard. Dyer pulled his gaze off the backyard windows and looked at her. What did she mean? They were close. Mary knew how to take care of her. What else?

"Daiquiris by the pool," Mary said, returning Dyer's open stare, her knees crossed and her hands fitted neatly in her lap. "Sounds great, right?"

It did sound great. Pushing what remained of the pie around on the plate, he wished, faintly, that he could go too. He saw himself poolside, slathered in sunscreen, airport thriller wedged in his hand, flat on a lounger beside his mother and Mary. *Paradise,* he might say, saluting them with his coconut drink, green, humpy islands passing off the boat's rail. St. Croix, St. Martin, St. Whatever. Who cares? You can't tell them apart anyway, not from the deck of a ship, not with propellers plowing you forward, comfortingly so, toward the horizon.

Dyer took the last two bites and set the empty plate down on the floor. He shivered with an anticipation he had to remind himself was foolish. *He* wasn't going on a cruise. He looked over at the green case sitting cockeyed in the cardboard box. "I don't know what I'm supposed to do about this," he said, nodding at the hall table. "Throw it out?"

"Let me see."

So Dyer stood and crossed the room, floorboards sighing under his feet, to the table by the front door. Peanuts littered the wood, half covering a stack of bills. Without looking at the letter that lay open on the table, he withdrew the green case from the open box and took it back to the couch. He sat, placing it on the cushion between them.

Mary weighed the case in her hand. "Heavy," she said.

"The watch is huge."

She opened the top of the case, and her eyes went wide. "No kidding," she said. She lifted the face of the watch out and held it to her ear. "Should we wind it?"

Dyer shrugged. He was feeling better, thankful that Mary had taken care of him. "You do it," he said.

She pinched the fat knob on the side of the watch and turned it in her fingers. It unscrewed like a cap and hung from its tiny chain, revealing a smaller knob, also ridged. She gave Dyer a questioning look, and he nodded. "Go ahead," he said. She turned it two full turns.

The second hand stirred. A quiet ticking sound emerged from the body of the watch as it stuttered around the face.

"You can't throw this out," she said. "It could be worth something."

"I could sell it online, I guess," said Dyer.

"Or just keep it. Who cares where it came from? Here," she said, handing it to him.

The steel underside still felt warm on his skin. The lattice, he noticed, was hinged; a small latch held it to the side of the watch. With his fingernail Dyer lifted the latch, and the lattice swung open like the cover of a book. Staring through the crystal into the black face of the watch, with its wickedly pointed hands and large red numbers, Dyer felt a trace of excitement, an illicit thrill snaking through him. He liked the watch, and he wanted to keep it. What he didn't want was to read that letter ever again. *An old dog with his paw out wants a shake.*

Dyer stood, crossed to the table, and balled the handwritten page in his fist. He dropped it into the trash can and kicked the can to mix up the discarded litter.

"So," said Dyer, turning to Mary. "We'll meet at St. Elizabeth's in the morning. Bring her home?"

"And get Chinese," said Mary. "Or sushi. Last thing anyone needs to do is cook a turkey."

"True."

"You don't object," Mary said, rising from the sofa. "To the cruise idea?"

"No," said Dyer. "God no. I was just worried—I just didn't want her to see him. That's all."

"We won't," said Mary. "She doesn't want to see him." But this time the sentence felt a little forced, as though she were convincing herself as well as Dyer. Mary didn't hold Dyer's stare. She pushed her hair out of her face and moved toward the stairs. There was something she wasn't telling him. "I'll just get those few things."

"You know where everything is?"

Mary nodded as she passed him.

A little surprised that she did, Dyer trailed her up the stairs, leaning on the banister as he climbed.

Dyer thought of his mother alone, climbing these stairs herself, with difficulty now, with shuffling, trembling steps, gripping the wood railing for support. Affection for Mary flowered in his chest, for this woman who would put his mother on a boat in the middle of the sea. He reached his mother's bedroom door and stood there, watching her move swiftly, knowingly, around the room. She slid open the top drawer of the dresser and pulled out a pair of white underpants, folded them neatly, and dropped them into a canvas tote bag on the floor. She took a pair of pants from the closet, a gray knit sweater from a hook on the door. From beneath the bed, the moccasin slippers.

· · ·

In his own bed that night, Dyer singled out a new sound amid the popping and shifting in the walls around him, a low, even ticking, rising up through the floorboards, a sound so quiet he could hear it only when he held his breath and closed his eyes, a metronomic rhythm in the darkness that marched him into sleep.

4

December

AS PROMISED," said Dyer, tossing a piece of chalk onto the grooved ledge beneath the board, clapping dust from his hands. "I'm giving you five essay questions; two will be on the exam." He flipped a paper clip off a stack of printed pages on his desk and began distributing them around the room.

Greg Smile had his hand up. "How much does the final count?" Since his midterm (a grade of 1.5; he'd left fifteen IDs blank), Greg had been doing late-term damage control.

"Forty percent," said Dyer.

Randy Holiday leaned across his desk and clapped James's arm.

James sat in a *Thinker* hunch, staring through Dyer, through the board at his back. James used to dress neatly and sit upright in his chair, his eyes on the floor, murmuring correct answers when no one else would. Though his hair had been growing all term, in the last couple of weeks it had become a pasta bowl of curls, dangling around his eyes and ears. This morning James's shirttail hung out of his pants, and two soggy, untied laces wormed onto the classroom floor. Six more minutes to go, and he'd already stowed his notebook in his bag. This was a new, distracted James, thought Dyer. Something was fermenting in the kid's head, and Dyer wanted to hold him up after class and ask him what. Why?

Probably, Dyer thought, because he still felt guilty for telling Arnold Lambert that Rafton's shot had been accidental, thus averting the annoyance and time waste of a disciplinary action. For telling the dean, "If Sam can hit a kid's nose from twenty yards out, why's he not playing varsity?"

James had a neat stack of 4.0s in Dyer's grade book and would surely ace next week's final. James's preoccupations were no business of Dyer's. Who knows? Maybe James had gotten a girlfriend. Occasionally, for no obvious reason, a sleepy smile would surface on his face.

Sam Rafton inserted his middle finger through the spiral ring of his notebook and hoisted it off his desk like a flag, spilling loose pages into his lap. Body turned, legs crossed, Louise Hampton watched him, capping her fingernail with a pink wad of chewing gum. Sam rotated the notebook in her direction, his middle finger wagging in her face.

"Sam," said Dyer, sliding his hands in the pockets of his pants. Sam liked attention, he knew, and admonishing him in front of everyone would be a reward. Better just to throw a review question his way. A hard one. "What would a determinist say is the foundation of capitalism?" Dyer asked.

"Pass," said Sam, dropping the notebook with a flutter of pages back onto his desk.

"That could be an ID question on the exam," said Dyer.

Sam leafed through his thick, water-swollen notebook, pages covered in messy scrawl, others blank.

"Human acquisitiveness," Dyer finally said. "What's that mean?"

Sam shrugged.

"Somebody else," said Dyer.

"People want stuff," said Chip.

Sam's blue eyes were just visible beneath the curved brim of his hat. The cotton sheath was frayed to the cardboard on the brim's right edge. According to Chris Nolan, Sam's father phoned Sam every Sunday night to talk company strategy, a service for which the older Rafton paid his son a consulting fee out of payroll. "Entitled little shit's a shoo-in at Duke," Chris had told him. "Byrd Rafton golfs with the university president. Try not to think about it." Dyer tried not to — and failed. He didn't care about Duke. The part that rattled him? The detail that struck a personal nerve? Rafton's family business was real estate development.

"Here's a gimme," said Dyer, holding Sam's stare. Dyer would take no pleasure in seeing him fail next week's exam; a failing grade at the end of term entailed paperwork to Dean Lambert, a letter home with evidence and justification. "Who said, 'We repudiate all morality taken apart from human society and classes . . . We say that our morality is entirely subordinated to the interests of the class struggle of the proletariat'?"

"Marx?" asked Sam. Dyer had had them read post-glasnost commentaries on Lenin's terror campaigns and concentration camps. For balance, he'd put those side by side with pro-Soviet material: *Daily Worker* eulogies coming out of the United States, and excerpts from John Reed's *Ten Days That Shook the World.*

"Lenin," Dyer said to Sam. "Who's 'we'?"

Sam stifled a burp with the back of his hand. "No idea."

"The Bolsheviks. What's he mean?"

"We kill who we want to kill," Sam said.

"Whom," Dyer said to Sam. "But yes, basically."

Dyer glanced at James to see if he'd paid attention. A month ago, in mid-November, returning James's (excellent) paper on Italian Futurism, Dyer had said, "You and your dad must discuss the material." James froze, his hand extended for the paper, his body half swiveled out of his desk. "It's all my own work," he said, dropping his hand, giving the paper an alarmed stare. "Oh, I'm sure," said Dyer. "I wasn't suggesting that. I just thought, surely, since he was a History professor . . . and you know, your dad. It would be only natural. I know he takes an interest in this class." Dyer blushed at his own stumbling sentences. James stared at him as if he were crazy. "We don't ever talk," James said. "Ever?" Dyer asked, his head at a skeptical tilt, his smile forced and stiff. James took the paper out of Dyer's hand, slid it into his bag, and zipped his jacket all the way to his neck. The rest of the class had piled into the hallway, and James clearly wanted out too. Dyer tried to meet the boy's nervous, dodging eyes. James looked as though he were keeping something to himself. Dyer didn't ask what it was, his gaze settling instead on the curve of purple that delicately shaded the skin below his left eye. He let James go without a word.

But if James wasn't telling Wolfe what went on in his class, who was?

Randy Holiday's hand went up. Dyer nodded at him. "Are you grading on a curve?" Randy asked.

Here was a kid Dyer liked. Occasionally, Randy still forgot to bring a pen to class, and just last week during a mini-lecture on Mussolini, Dyer caught him dozing, his thick head folded down on his thick neck. And yet with only the exam to go, Randy had managed a 3.0 average, had written two decent papers, and had turned in an okay midterm. All during football season. For this, he had Dyer's respect. Also, for the way Randy could still Sam in his seat from across the room with an open-mouthed zombie stare.

"I'd give everyone a four-point-oh if they earned it," Dyer said checking the big black face of his diver's watch. "One last question before time's up." Dyer perched on the edge of the desk; he'd put this off, worried he'd get no takers, worried he'd have to cajole, or bribe. Well, fine. He would cajole; he'd throw a little salesmanship their way.

Dyer forced a wide smile, spread his arms. "Who wants a free trip to New York?" he asked.

"So, squid," said Randy, banging the gray bar, flinging open Morrow's rear fire door. "What're we doing about the exam?"

They couldn't walk abreast along the narrowly shoveled path, so Randy fell into step just off James's shoulder. The weak December sun threw no heat at all, only a white, slanting light that rebounded off the day-old snow. As they turned the corner of Morrow, the lawn to their left began to fill with coat-bundled students, heads down, hats pulled low, hurrying between classes.

New York was on James's mind. New York, and the Crawford

Hotel especially, which Mr. Martin had said was in "midtown" and "four-star." He wondered what the hotel looked like, and if it bore any resemblance to the Mark. "Three nights you get the run of the place," Mr. Martin had said. And then Jane had put her hand up.

As soon as Mr. Martin had copied down the names — a handful including Jane's, his, Chip's, Greg's (not Sam's, not Randy's, James noticed with relief) — Jane had raced out of class, disappearing down the basement hall and up the stairway that led to French. James had been all packed up and ready to intercept her, but she'd been too quick, launching out of her desk and through the door. She'd exited class the same way on Tuesday. And on Monday.

"Squiiid," Randy said, rapping the back of James's head.

James ducked away. "We're not doing anything about the exam," he said through his teeth, rubbing the top of his head. Thinking about Jane tightened some mechanism inside him, a wheel ratcheting to the right of his heart. He wanted to turn around and shove Randy, knock him down if he could.

Which would be suicide. Or just look foolish. The guy was twice his size. He knew that. And Randy wasn't the problem anyway. Randy had threatened Rafton in October, warning him that he'd break his teeth if he fucked up James's room again. James was grateful, though he took it as quid pro quo for two 250 papers. Now he wanted to be left alone to figure out what to do about Jane. She'd slipped out of the Booker Reading Room in the library the night before, just as she'd slipped out of class today. A breeze swept up; bare oak branches collided above their heads, showering down snow.

"Forty percent of my grade," whispered Randy. "We're doing something about it."

James wanted to clap his hands over his ears before Randy could say anything else. He spotted Volker Stein on the steps to Ramm Hall, hooking shaded lenses over his wire-framed glasses. "Hey, Volker," he said, hopping over the ridge of the shoveled path, sinking his shoe through the snow's icy crust.

"Hello, James," said Volker, wiping his nose with the back of his sleeve. He wore a black pea coat, wool suit pants, and on his back a neon pink and green German backpack.

"How are things?" asked James, bounding up the Ramm steps, loose snow falling off his pant legs and into his tennis shoes. James realized that he and Volker hadn't spoken for weeks, maybe months. Last year they ate lunch together every day, right after U.S. History with Mr. Blanton. This year their schedules put them in Commons on different class rotations, and James had adjusted to eating alone. He preferred it, in fact; James could just take a seat in the anonymous, statusless dining room where the faculty ate, do some reading, stare into space, or he could take a small corner table on the other side, close enough to Jane and the other soccer players to overhear their conversation.

Volker nodded. "Good, thank you," he said, his voice high-pitched and precise. Neatly parted, his bangs lay like paint, motionless in the breeze.

Randy called James's name, but James didn't turn around to look.

"He's your bodyguard?" said Volker.

"Where did you hear that?" said James.

"Not sure," said Volker, after a moment of careful thought. "Maybe it's just a thing I overheard."

"He's just ... a friend, sort of," stammered James. Through the semi-opaque gray of his sunglasses, Volker gave him a puzzled stare.

"More like an acquaintance," said James.

Behind him, from the path, James heard Randy say his name again, drawing out the *a*: "Jaaaaames. Come talk to me." James turned and saw Randy take a step into the snow toward them.

Volker tucked his thumbs into the pink straps of his backpack and threw James a concerned glance. "You should come by the dorm. We should get caught up."

"Or you could come to Weiss," said James, nodding vigorously. It seemed possible — Volker would make the place seem less volatile — but Volker frowned.

"Hey," Randy said to Volker, extending one thick hand. "Randy Holiday."

Volker shifted his weight. "Volker," he said, and delicately placed his hand in Randy's.

"Cool." Randy gave Volker's arm a violent shake. "Any friend of James's . . ."

The Ramm doors burst open, and a stream of students flowed toward them down the stairs.

Volker slid his hand out of Randy's and slipped around him, joining the traffic headed down the steps. James wanted to call out, tell Volker he'd see him later, soon, but he wouldn't draw attention to himself, not with Randy standing right there grinning at him. He watched Volker go, admiring his upright posture, watched him cut left on the path, his pink and green bag bobbing as he made his way toward Morrow. "Leave me alone," he said as sternly as he could.

"The usual spot, squid," Randy said, backing down the steps. "Three."

After class, Dyer checked his mail in Peabody Hall—nothing. Inside the men's room off the faculty lounge, one of the student-safe places for a teacher to piss, Dyer took the middle urinal.

The door swung open. "Mr. Martin," Wolfe said with gusto, striding in, his shoes squeaking across the tile floor.

Startled, choked off and dribbling down below, Dyer nodded. Had Wolfe followed him in? Dyer hadn't seen the headmaster in the hallway outside the bathroom. Wolfe's office was upstairs—and there was a bathroom up there too. "Headmaster Wolfe," he said.

"Ed," Wolfe said.

"Ed," Dyer agreed.

Wolfe bellied in to Dyer's left, so close their shoulders nearly brushed. "Been meaning to ask—where are we in 250?"

"I've been bouncing around a little, but basically interwar," said Dyer. He'd gone totally dry. "Twenties, thirties."

"Don't simplify Stalin," Wolfe said, using one hand to unzip and pull himself out. In his navy blue corduroy jacket and woven tie, Wolfe smelled musty, like an old book. "Make sure they understand the scope of the Soviet experiment. The vision thing, you know? Comparing Soviet industrial gains with the U.S. Depression would be my approach." Wolfe's hearty stream gushed against the porcelain. "Not that you want my approach."

"I think I've been balanced," Dyer said.

"I know you've been talking to Tom Blanton," Wolfe said. He rocked back from the urinal and blew a breath out at the ceiling, his chin up, evidently thinking. "Tom's ideological. Reactionary. Don't get lured in."

Dyer had seen it before he could stop himself. Glimpsed the thing just over the lip of the metal barrier: Wolfe's penis, stubby and wide like a soda can wedged in his fly. Dyer shut his eyes; it butted across the backs of his lids. Dyer flipped them open, staring hard at the crosshatched tile in front of his face.

"Blanton is a senior teacher in the department," Dyer said. *Shit.* Wolfe was smiling at him. Had he seen? Dyer hadn't looked on purpose. He returned a brittle smile. "It's natural for me to —"

Wolfe's free hand went up. "I'm saying he has an agenda, but you're smart enough to see that for yourself." He paused. "I'm sure, by the way, he reminds you of your old pal Phelps."

Dyer didn't know what to say to that. Blanton did remind him of Phelps, but so what? Dyer hadn't even seen Blanton for weeks. "There's no bias in my class," Dyer said. "Sit in if you want. See for yourself."

Wolfe patted Dyer's shoulder. "Maybe I will." Wolfe's hand slid off Dyer's shoulder. "You all right?" he asked.

A vise was squeezing him down below. "Fine," said Dyer.

"Everything okay at home?" Wolfe asked.

Dyer thought of Thanksgiving Day, the morning his mother had come back from St. Elizabeth's with Mary. The painkillers put her off food, and she spent the whole afternoon in bed. Did Wolfe really care? There was a baiting light in his eyes; they caught a glinting ricochet from the overhead bank of fluorescents. *Let's make this a healthy exchange,* he'd said over coffee in his kitchen. But his questions felt interrogative, overly insistent; Wolfe's interest in him wasn't heartfelt. He wanted something from Dyer. Wanted his trust. What had Blanton said? *I don't know what he's up to, and I guarantee the trustees don't either.* Dyer put himself away, his bladder still full. Nearly simultaneously, Wolfe shook, tucked, and rezipped.

They took side-by-side sinks. Dyer told himself to calm down; he was wringing his hands under the faucet. He should offer something, if only to be polite, to maintain the relationship. "Thanksgiving went well. Good to see my mom," he said as brightly as he could.

Wolfe nodded but didn't seem to hear him. Running water over his hands, he said, "I'm meeting one of the trustees later today, and I'd like you to come along."

"Okay," Dyer said.

"Tipton Pal," Wolfe said. "Bit of an asshole, but I have to cozy up to him from time to time. Tipton's the endowment's chief investment officer, which means he liaises between the board and me on budget issues. He's a fund manager in Boston."

" 'Tipton Pal'?" Dyer asked.

" 'Tip' to his friends," Wolfe said. "Whoever they are." Wolfe shook his hands over the basin and banged the paper towel lever twice. "I'm asking for money for Model UN," he said, tearing a length of paper and drying his hands. "The school's fee is not inconsiderable, and I'm making the case that the students shouldn't have to pay for travel or hotel rooms. I'd like to introduce you as faculty adviser for the club. Can you make it? Late lunch. Norwood Room at Commons."

"I can do that," said Dyer.

Wolfe frowned. "Forget about Tom," he said, gently scolding, as if Dyer himself had brought up the subject. "I'm sure you're doing a fine job in the classroom."

Just before third period, upstairs in room 12, on the floor inside his door, James found her folded note:

James

Sorry we haven't talked. Forget the letter.
Don't say anything about it to your dad.

Jane

James backed into the hallway and stood where she'd stood, testing the air like a psychic, feeling it for here-and-gone vibrations. The calf brain stink had finally faded. The air smelled like air, like sweat, like wet wood. Brain Jones came out of the bathroom, chewing on a straw, and said, "Ho, fuck! Bull, if you'd been here five minutes earlier . . ."

"Did you see her?" James asked.

"Her who? I mean me rubbing one out. In full view, in the hall. Ten points in the Mastur-Derby. Your loss."

Dyer lingered at the top of the Commons stairway. With the center of his palm, he polished the newel post, an oblong globe, tightly leaved, like an artichoke. Above him on the landing hung life-sized portraits of Warner and Constance Britton, the school's founders. Warner's silvered hair swept back off his head in curls, and he stood with one foot on a stool, one hand grasping the phallic hilt of his saber. A dart of wrinkles fit neatly between his buckshot eyes, and his lips pressed into a line of admonishment. Over time, Dyer had developed a strong preference for Constance. For the pearl gray half circle of her neck, for her wide, tapering feet, which poked like arrowheads beneath the ruffled hem of her silk dress, for the stack of books on the wooden table beside her chair. The fingers of her left hand hovered above the top volume. She had a flat, brown shell of hair, no chin (the contour faded into her neck), and an unfortunate asymmetry to her eyes. Warner left the school for a seat on the Massachusetts legislature; she stayed and taught Classics and History. Her mouth gave her an unhappy, put-upon look, but given how rare women teachers were in 1790, she must have been determined, Dyer thought. She must have really wanted to do the work.

He took a breath and puffed out his chest to match her upright, serious posture, filling himself with a little of her determined air. He wanted to do the work as well. He was getting used to being in the classroom; he was more confident in front of his students, some mornings holding the group's attention for the entire period, or nearly. They listened to him; they did the reading, had even seemed reasonably prepared this morning for next week's exam. Dyer could picture himself doing it all again the next year, and possibly the year after that (the furthest into his future he could imagine)—provided that the year-end review Will Hemmer had told him about went well. Staring at the portrait, he took a deep breath, then exhaled noisily, fluttering his lips, feeling silly. Silly for channeling Constance, silly for his unsettled stomach. Don't worry so much, he thought, reminding himself that he'd gotten the Model UN application in. He'd collected the names he needed for the club from the 250 class—even if it had meant adding a promise of extra credit on their final grade for the trip to New York. So what? He'd pitched them the idea, and they'd responded.

But like it or not, the prospect of seeing Wolfe dumped hot acid into his stomach. He watched the needle sweep the face of the diver's watch. He glanced back at Constance, pulling himself up onto the landing. He remembered the way Wolfe arced his back at the urinal, gazed at the ceiling, rocking away. Had he been showing off? Because of the thing with Greta? *That* seemed so long ago now, Dyer thought. She acted like a total stranger to him now. If Wolfe was still bothered, he shouldn't be.

Dyer dropped his hand off the newel, trying to put the scene out of his mind. He shook his wrist, dislodging the watch. Its band joint kept snagging the hair on his arm. He knew he could leave it in the dresser drawer back in his room, the place he stashed it at night to muffle the ticking, but each morning, when he was getting dressed he remembered Mary's advice—to keep it, to strip the thing of father associations, to make it his. Who cared where it came from? The boys in Bailey had pronounced the watch "highly cool" and demanded to know where he got it. "My mother," Dyer had said. In fact, Dyer had hid it from his mother the entire weekend in Richmond, and after their one conversation about it at St. Elizabeth's, neither had brought up the box that had come in the mail. "Wish my mom gave me cool shit like that," said Tim Olsen, who smelled distinctly of cigarette smoke. *Ignore it unless it's blatant,* Dyer remembered. *Unless it's insulting.* He was taking Greta's advice.

The door to the Norwood Room, a small dining room for alumni meals and faculty conferences, stood slightly ajar, and through the crack at the jamb Dyer could see a polished strip of wooden tabletop. He could also hear two voices.

"You do actually read the investment reports?"

"Eleven percent off."

There was a deep sigh. "The board's not panicking, Ed. The board accepts ups and downs."

"As they should."

"But they're not going to get excited about unorthodox fundraising. I'm all for whatever academic programs you want within budget constraints. But don't tell me play-acting North Korea is going to help with contributions. We've taken a hit this year losing the Fieldspar money. Nobody's blaming you for that. But we'd all like to close the gap."

"I've launched Campaign Britton—"

"Modest returns so far, Ed. That'll need shepherding."

"Which I have every intention—"

"And you're coming to me with other priorities."

When Wolfe finally responded, his voice was weary, almost pleading. "I'm talking about a program that will give Britton's top students national publicity. I need a budget allocation to get it off the ground."

Dyer had never heard Wolfe sound so scrambling and defensive. He'd been interrupted — *twice.* Dyer wanted to stay where he was and listen, out of sight, but he was expected, and so he forced himself to rap lightly on the door.

Wolfe cleared his throat, a shallow, ragged sound. "Come in, Dyer," he said flatly, as if he knew Dyer had been there all along.

Dyer pushed the door open. Wolfe sat at the end of the long, oval table, a cup of coffee just off his left hand. His hair lay closer to his head than usual, combed and neat; he'd also clipped his beard to a tidy half inch. And yet, Wolfe had a bedraggled look. A loose thread dangled from the top button of his jacket. His head hung slightly forward, and the skin of his neck was flushed. His jaw jutted outward, angrily, the set of a man under attack.

Tipton Pal swung his head and shoulders in Dyer's direction. He had alert, widely spaced eyes, pink cheeks, and an inflamed pimple just below his jaw. The guy was not much older than Dyer. *This* was Britton's investment manager? Tipton wore a double-breasted pinstriped suit, with a blue Britton tie, knotted in a fat Windsor. When he saw Dyer, Tipton struck the table with both hands and rose out of his seat. "Here's the new guy," he said heartily. He was short but wide-shouldered, with stiff, blond hair — hair that looked squeezed out of a tube. He swung himself around the corner of the table and came at Dyer with the squat, low-gravity swagger of a wrestler. "Tip Pal," he said, proffering his business card in one hand and smacking the other into Dyer's. A diamond-shaped white napkin hung from his waistline, one corner tucked into his belt.

A vise grip: no surprise. "Dyer Martin," said Dyer, taking the card and trying politely to keep his eyes off the napkin.

Tipton smiled up into Dyer's face, lips crooked as he explored a back molar with his tongue. He threw off a scent like oiled leather. Two plates sat on the table in front of his chair. The smaller one held overlapping rinds of melon and a corkscrew chain of orange peel, the other a sticky smear of ketchup, scattered fries, a pickle, and fork and knife, neatly aligned. Wolfe had nothing in front of him but the coffee cup and a white, legal-sized envelope, the upper corner printed with the IMUNI laurel-leaf crest. Above their heads hung a tarnished brass chandelier with candle-flame bulbs.

"You think this is a good idea? Play-acting terrorists?" Tipton asked. On release, Tipton's palm adhered stickily to Dyer's. Tipton frowned at Dyer, as if that was his fault, and snatched the napkin out of his belt, wiping his fingers like a mechanic.

Wolfe pulled a page out of the envelope beside him and flapped it over the tabletop. "We've been assigned," he said.

"North Korea?" Dyer asked him, sliding Tipton's card into his pocket.

Wolfe nodded.

"You're learning this for the first time?" Tipton asked, turning to look at each man — also like a wrestler, thought Dyer, one of those bolt-shaped guys he saw around the school — a full body turn, head, neck, and shoulders fused, arms bowed out from his body.

"The letter just came in the mail," said Wolfe.

"Did you request that?" Dyer asked.

"Sure," Wolfe said, lifting the mug to his lips and taking a sip. He set it noiselessly back on the table. Coffee beaded his upper lip. "What an opportunity," he said.

Dyer had to suppress a smile. Blanton was right. Model UN was a political statement, a chance to speak up for the other side. Three months after North Korea's nuclear announcement, there had still been no test, nothing to prove that Kim Jong Il's claims of a nuclear arsenal were real. And yet Defense Department talk of a preemptive missile strike still dominated the headlines. Just that morning, Vinnie Dick, Dyer's guilty-pleasure radio DJ, called North Korea a freak state of Stalinist midgets who should be blasted into oblivion.

Dyer turned his attention to Tipton, who had been studying him. That leather smell was cologne, Dyer realized. It rose up off the guy in waves.

"You're not convinced it's a good idea," said Tipton. "I can see it in your face."

Dyer took a step out of Tipton's airspace and gave the headmaster a generous, reassuring nod. "No, it's great. A great opportunity," he said. *Why not?* Play along, see what happens. "We could be bombing these guys by spring. It would be good for the students to find out why," said Dyer. Then to Tipton: "They're really excited about the program."

"So maybe they can pay their own way," said Tipton.

Wolfe shook his head. "I explained that," he said. "Britton picks up the tab. We send the parents donation letters after the conference."

Tipton clapped his hands together. "That's right. They're so pleased to see their kids in the paper. Whammo. Money rolls in."

Wolfe scraped his chair back from the table. "So don't allocate the funds," he said, gathering the letter and the envelope, intent, it seemed, on leaving. "I'll drain the discretionary account instead."

"You're wasting time on this," Tipton said. "It's not something to depend on."

Wolfe asked Dyer: "Which kids are onboard?" He was standing out of his chair now, gripping the scrolled back.

"I've got seven," said Dyer.

"Who exactly?" Wolfe asked.

Dyer listed the names.

"Add Sam Rafton," said Wolfe.

"I don't think he's interested," said Dyer.

"Draft him," said Wolfe. "He'll do it."

"I'm not sure he will," said Dyer.

Tipton laughed. He was sitting on the table now, staring out into the hallway. "Tough talk, Ed. But I'm following you here. The Raftons practically own Atlanta."

What did Dyer know about North Korea? Wolfe hadn't asked him. Maybe, thought Dyer, making his way to Bailey House, he assumed Dyer had the basic history, and a more enlightened attitude than, say, Tipton, who ended their meeting with a parting shot: "'Historic Boarding School Puts Friendly Face on Terrorism.'" This jab pulled one last embattled sigh out of Wolfe. "North Koreans aren't terrorists," he said wearily, as if stating the obvious.

Were they not? Hadn't they bombed a plane? Hadn't they abducted Japanese citizens? Dyer recalled some mention of that from one of his Oxford tutorials: "Theaters of the Cold War" with Bradley Tease at Worcester. They'd covered Egypt, the Congo, Korea, and Vietnam. Back in his apartment were Dyer's notes. Korea divided up by the United States in 1948? The 38th Parallel drawn just after Hiroshima by . . . ? He searched for the name, turning his head against the cold breeze bending around the corner of Commons.

Dean Rusk. Not bad. But he was clearly in for some research. He kicked an icy chunk of snow out of his way, and wondered — with a jolt of surprise that he hadn't wondered before — what went on at a Model UN conference anyway. Was it like a debate? Did you compete? If so, the group of seven (eight if Rafton came onboard) couldn't fake it. They would actually have to get North Korean history down, also its diplomatic attitudes, foreign policy goals, stuff Dyer didn't know. Stuff he'd have to find out, because if the March thing in New York was some kind of competition and Britton got trounced, Wolfe wouldn't be pleased, and then his year-end review could go badly. There was his future here to worry about. Reflexively, even though his ulcer had long since healed, Dyer rubbed his stomach, anticipating the stress to come. Wolfe would want a positive spin on North Korea, ideals of Socialism, a small Communist country resisting the West. But how about abductions and bombings? Good stories, Dyer reminded himself, got their attention. Just the other day, he'd read an editorial in the paper about the unnaturally hot tempers of the North Koreans, their pugnacity, their historic tendency toward violence.

Historic tendency toward violence. Not a bad place to start.

Dyer lifted a hand to wave to Isadora Felton, who strode down Elson, wrapped in a gray overcoat and fluffy, flamingo pink scarf. To Dyer many of the faculty members were still anonymous, graying middle-agers, but Isadora stood out. She always wore a flash of bright color like that scarf, and once the winter set in and temperatures dropped into the forties she'd begun loudly complaining that the bell tower carillon room wasn't heated. Just last week in the faculty lounge, she'd wondered aloud to Dyer and a couple of other teachers reviewing class notes and sipping coffee, "Why with all the money in this school's endowment can't they provide a little warmth for the arts?"

How much money was there? *Eleven percent off,* Wolfe had said. The market was down this year, but not 11 percent. When Tipton had mentioned losing the Fieldspar money, Dyer had made the connection — Henry Fieldspar, the kid who got kicked out last year. So there was fundraising pressure on Wolfe, Dyer thought. Pressure to do well with Campaign Britton. Pressure from Tipton, a young guy, obnoxious and swaggering in his pinstripes, but backed by a (Dyer suspected) fearsome stock portfolio. Dyer read about the market in the paper but had no money to invest; apart from two decent paychecks from Virgenes, Dyer had never made any real money in his life. Tuition had always been paid through Julian's Richmond lawyer, a fact that radiated a uranium-like shame from the base of his brain. Now he was free of that, but barely; Britton paid him next to nothing. Perhaps, thought Dyer, the poor endowment performance explained why Wolfe had hired a guy with no teaching experience, a guy with no salary history. A guy who would think a thousand or so direct-deposited into his bank account every two weeks, room and board provided, was pretty darn okay.

Gloomy now, Dyer tried, and failed, to keep his gaze off of Range House, just down the angled path and across Elson on his left. The blanket of snow laid earlier in the week had slid down the roof, exposing the upper third and the newer, bullet gray shingles on the rear side where Greta had slipped in September. The lightning rod hadn't been replaced, and splinters from the wood mount made a rough fringe on the end of the peaked frame.

Closed curtains filled Greta's second-floor window. She was likely to be in class, in her Ramm Hall lab. Dyer had seen Greta there only once, back in September, when he found himself peering through the wire-latticed window in her classroom door, gripped by the memory of her thin lips on his, the juniper taste of her mouth. He'd watched her move behind a wide aluminum lab table, fill a beaker from a plastic-wrapped tub of solution, set it down, and spark a Bunsen burner to blue, flapping life. Safety goggles covered half her face, and she operated awkwardly, one-

handed, her other arm in a sling, held tightly against her stomach. Behind her, a dry-erase board displayed geometric chemical
compounds and neat lists of formulas. He'd lingered as long as
he dared, not wanting to get caught staring, fascinated at the same
time by how tightly she held the class's attention, her lips moving
even as she adjusted the Bunsen flame and set the beaker into a
steel frame above it. Her students' gazes cut up and down. They
jabbed notes as fast as they could.

Dyer headed up Bailey's brick steps and through the front
door, desperate for something to take him out of his own head,
Tim Olsen blaring Metallica too loud or Oliver Frame reassuring
his mother that he was all set for his exams. Anything but this: the
hallway lit by a single ceiling globe, the shut doors, the cherry red
fire extinguisher bolted to the cheap, gray sheetrock, the building as silent and still as a mausoleum. He counted himself lucky
for getting a "geek" dorm, a place where the boys actually studied, where there was no drinking or smoking or cruising (or none
that he knew about), but at that moment he wanted distraction. He
wished some lazy, jackass kid was just getting up, shuffling down
the hall to the showers in his boxer shorts, scratching his waistline,
ready with a joke. Dyer could use one. He fumbled his apartment
keys out of his pocket and dropped them with a *thunk* against the
wood floor. Bending over to retrieve the key ring, blood pooled
inside his head and he had to shake and blink away a shimmering, silver-white fog. Vision returned, but silence didn't; a low-fre-
quency murmur filled his airspace:

*You can't avoid checking Greta's window at Range. And you'll
check your answering machine and laptop for an I'm-back message
from Alice. You'll make a pot of coffee and feel sorry for yourself measuring the grounds into the filter, doing it just the way Alice taught
you, leveling each spoonful with the side of your finger. You'll think
of your mother and Mary, of their holiday cruise, one week away,
scheduled through the New Year.*

Dyer worked his jaw, popping his ears. He fit the key in his
lock, reminding himself that he'd told his mother that he probably

wouldn't make the drive down to Richmond anyway and that he'd also turned down Chris's invitation to spend Christmas at his family's house in Rhode Island (the invitation, he'd sensed, was half-hearted and motivated by pity). To his mother, he'd said that he needed the holiday vacation to prepare for the next term's classes. Her swelling was down, she and Mary were ready to go, and by all means they should. "Don't worry about me," he'd said. "Have fun."

Inside, the answering machine on the floor beside his desk blinked a frantic red light. Bending over to reach the small white box, Dyer's satchel swung around his body and smacked into his leg.

Alice's voice rose out of the machine. "Dyer," she said. "I'm back in L.A. They're sending me to Dubai for production, but I'm home for now. It's like six in the morning here, but I'm up. Jet lag. Give a call."

Dyer sat on the lip of his desk chair, staring out his single living room window down the snowy grass slope to the baseball diamond, the longest view he had, the one his eyes inevitably settled on, relaxing into the distance. This was it, he thought, the solution to the yawning gap of vacation. She'd come see him, maybe, or he'd go to her.

"Hi," she said, after two rings.

"When did you get back?" Dyer asked.

"A week ago, but my sleep is still fucked up."

"I'm so glad you called."

"Well sure," she said lightly. "I mean, I haven't spoken to anyone but studio people for what? Two and a half months?"

Dyer heard the deflection. He clenched his toes inside his shoes and wished he'd waited a couple of hours before calling. "How was Tehran?" he asked.

"Crazy. There were anti-U.S. protests every day for a month. The studio sent Haddie to shoot some footage of the marches. He's going faux-documentary with my script, which I guess is pretty cool. I mean, he's keeping the romance, but everything's hand-held, and no sets or anything."

Haddie? She must know that he wouldn't have a clue.

"You said something on the message about going to where? Dubai?" he asked.

"We can't take a crew to Iran, so major shooting is supposed to happen there in the spring, and Haddie wants me with him. The rewrites never end. All that stuff about Jessica and Bruce? Kaput."

Dyer remembered that she always talked about her work this way, the words falling out of her mouth in wads, in sticky clusters. "But you said they're keeping the romance."

"Yep. But now it's this Iranian student leader who's involved in the reform movement. She falls in love with her CIA contact. Haddie wants nonactors, but that seems risky to me."

"I don't know who Haddie is," said Dyer. And that was the right thing to say, even though he'd already guessed — her new boyfriend, or just someone she was sleeping with. The idea wasn't as painful as it might have been, reminding him as it did of certain incontestable facts: Dyer had left; he hadn't had to; there had been schools in L.A.; she'd wanted him to stay. A weight settled through him, as if his desk chair were an elevator finally arriving at its floor. He heard breath in the earpiece, and he wondered if her nerves were firing, wondered if she had the phone cord in a tourniquet around her arm, wondered if she was lifting her coffee mug to her lips and cursing it for being empty.

"Haddie's the director. And I'm chattering," she said.

"You're working yourself up to something," Dyer said.

And he let the silence run, because he knew an awkward silence was as intimate as this phone conversation would get. He'd been replaced by a movie director named Haddie. Dyer wouldn't make her admit it.

The usual spot meant the equipment cul-de-sac behind the hockey rink, a narrow strip of gravel out of view of the practice fields. Three on the dot, and James was clapping his gloved hands together and pacing to keep warm. Through the corrugated aluminum siding of the rink, James could hear the hockey team tearing around, their blades slicing up the ice. He kept looking for Randy beyond the corner of the rink, down the path behind the baseball dugout. He was angry that he had to endure this cold, this nothing-to-do, because he couldn't help but be on time and Randy was always late. He'd already spent five minutes brainstorming strategies to end writing his papers, *cheating,* but only one came to him, one sure solution, a last resort. Go to the dean. Admit everything.

Strategy was his mom's department. Maybe, James thought, if she weren't back in Knoxville, busy again, supervising prototype tests, she'd be right here, by his side, and Randy wouldn't have a chance. She'd come up with some leverage James could use against him, and then they could move on to more important matters: Jane's evasiveness, her mind-change, her phantom swoop through Weiss just hours before.

James stopped pacing and stood, knees locked, feet spread. Finally. There was Randy, behind the baseball dugout, headed his way. James spat sour, tacky spit onto the frozen gravel.

Randy hitched his jeans, loped up the hill, and glanced each way before ducking around the corner of the hockey rink. He asked James something, but the knifing, steel-on-ice sounds coming through the wall of the rink were too loud. James kept his expression set and waited for Randy to ask it again.

"Something wrong, squid?"

"I'm not helping you with the final," James said, moving his left foot forward to break the stiffness that had already set in through his legs and arms. He thought of those exercises his father had started doing the year before, the Korean thing, the stances and postures he could maintain for minutes. James wished he knew a few.

Randy stopped a few paces from James. "Wanna learn how to fuck a guy up?" he asked.

"I'm not helping you with the final."

"You get him on his back," said Randy, jamming his hands in the pockets of his letter jacket, "and drive the heel of your hand into the chin. Chances are he bites through his tongue."

"I'll tell my dad you threatened me. I'll tell Dean Lambert. That I had no choice."

"You're wondering how you get him on his back," said Randy, nodding reasonably. "A guy your size taking on, say, a guy my size." Randy shrugged his shoulders in exaggerated circles. He pulled his hands out of his jacket pockets, stretched his fingers out, then clenched them into fists, popping his knuckles. Randy nodded at James's knees. "Go low, below the center of gravity. Tie 'em up and tip 'em over."

James retreated a step along the gravel path, and Randy moved with him, filling his chest with one long breath, swelling it into a slab. He was blocking James's exit now, and James glanced to his rear. Two riding mowers and a midsized tractor with a covered cab formed a parked line where the gravel ran into the trees. "I don't know why you're telling me this," James said, his eyes on the narrow-set trunks of birch trees, thinking he could get around Randy by running through them.

Randy rotated two fused fingers in the air. "Stab a guy in the neck with these, cut off his airflow. Doesn't matter how small you are."

"You're on your own for the exam," James said. "That's all I came here to tell you."

"Try it," said Randy. "Not the neck thing. Knock me down." He smacked his knees. "Hit me right here. Use your shoulder."

"Are you kidding?"

"Say I'm that fag Street, or Rafton. Say I'm not expecting it."

James blew out through his teeth. "Hey," he said. "Did you hear me? I'm not helping you with this exam."

Randy hacked phlegm out of his chest. He curled his tongue, tipped his head back, and shot a green mass into the air. It arced, wobbled, and flopped behind him.

"You did fine on the midterm," said James, taking another step backward.

"I copied off yours. Watched right over your shoulder."

"You did not."

Randy closed the space between them and shoved James in the chest. James struck the blade-hood of a mower with his heel.

"You need to toughen up," Randy said.

James regained his balance, and when he met Randy's amused gaze, some safety switch inside him flipped off. Feet tingling and fingers splayed out, he threw himself forward, half-bent, crossing the space between them in a flash, driving his shoulder through layers of sweatshirt and nylon windbreaker into Randy's soft gut. On impact, Randy said, "Oomph," and expelled a cloud of vapor. James rebounded off Randy onto the ground; a vibration of pain ran up his spine, tailbone to neck.

Randy crouched down, touching the ground for support. "Pretty good, squid," he croaked at the gravel. "Unexpected."

James scrambled to his feet, and threw himself forward again, landing his shoulder on the twin boulders of the football player's knees. He felt the collision in his collarbone, felt a pain in his shoulder and neck, but kept lurching forward onto his stomach as Randy toppled. His sneaker caught James in the chin as they both went down. James's teeth clicked shut on his tongue. His mouth went hot. He tasted salt.

On his back, Randy's face creased in pain. "Fuck," he said.

James's skin felt feverish; he wanted to sneeze or throw up. Crackling static filled his ears. He spat blood.

"Fuck," Randy said again. "Didn't see that coming."

James was on all fours now. He spat more blood, coloring a nearby patch of snow pink.

Randy shook his head and struggled to his feet. He took a few tentative steps, moving in a circle.

"Is it okay?"

Gingerly, Randy did some slow knee bends; he shook one foot, then the other. "I should come over there and pound you," he said.

"You said go for the knees," James said.

Randy jogged in place, his windbreaker shifting on his body.

"You said the knees," James said again. The noise in his head, the roaring static, slowly cleared. His head was like a radio finding its station.

From far off, Elson Road most likely, came the sound of a police siren. James listened to it drone away. He moved his head back and forth on his neck, wincing.

Randy quit jogging; he rubbed his kneecaps through his jeans.

"What do you do if a girl's avoiding you?" James suddenly asked.

No answer from Randy; nor did he register surprise. Just that semicircular rubbing and a few more cautious knee bends.

"Who's the girl?" Randy finally asked.

"Doesn't matter," James said, flipping over onto his butt, no longer sure why he'd asked. He was wet all over, whether from sweat or snow soaking through his clothes he couldn't tell. There was a low throbbing pain in his neck, and his mouth still stung. He took a handful of snow and stuffed it in his mouth, onto his tongue.

"You get laid?"

"Come on," James garbled through the mass of melting snow. Never. Jane hadn't invited him up to her room at the Mark that night, and James had no idea what he'd have done if she had.

"Are we talking about Jane Hirsch?" asked Randy.

James let melted snow and blood dribble off his numb bottom lip. He leveled a gaze at Randy. "You know Jane?" he asked.

"I know she's got a picture of you on her dresser. I've seen it."

James bent his head and spat out the cold slushy mouthful. A pink rope hung from his numb bottom lip.

Chris Nolan's living room was enormous, an echoing, high-ceilinged rectangle. Two windows gave a view across the terraced lawn to Elson Road and South Quad; tacked-up color photographs, their edges pulling off the plaster, haphazardly decorated the walls. Above a lamp, one eight-by-ten glossy depicted gridlock in a city intersection; next to the door hung a cluster of schoolchildren squatting over dirt. On the wall between the windows: a dripping, mossy bathroom sink. For furniture, Chris had only a wood-framed loveseat with gray cushions, two slatted classroom chairs, a small desk topped with camera equipment and stacks of contact sheets, and the leather recliner in which Dyer lay nearly flat. The windows let in the copper light of Weiss's floods.

Dyer rolled the sausage pillow on the recliner into the crook of his neck and took a long pull off his beer. It was Dyer's third; he'd drunk too quickly, outpacing Chris, twice helping himself from the minifridge in the kitchen. Dyer hadn't brought anything over with him and knew he was being rude. But tonight was his first real drinking since September, and he'd wanted the beers badly. He'd also wanted company, wanted to talk, and had just told Chris everything about Alice, a story that began two years ago and ended with their phone conversation that afternoon. It was midnight; thirty minutes give or take, he'd been talking.

"That must have been boring," Dyer said.

"Nope," said Chris. But he did look bored, gazing abstractly into the ceiling, fingering the hair that ducktailed off the back of his neck.

"I won't ask for your advice," said Dyer.

"Two options, I'd say. Leave the thing for now. Or redeye it to L.A."

"I've thought of that," Dyer said. He pictured charging the plane ticket, taking a cab from LAX to Sweetzer Street. Knocking on her door. "Though I guess it's pretty high-risk. What if Haddie's in residence?"

"Or in flagrante. My real advice is don't take my advice. You want boring?"

"Yeah," said Dyer.

Chris flicked something off the cushion of the loveseat. "My astonishing romances."

Had Chris made a pass at him, all those weeks ago? Dyer couldn't be sure. He was being friendly tonight, but not overly so. Minimal eye contact, no sympathetic smiles, and he'd tightened his bottom lip, dimpling the skin above his chin. Dyer felt a tug of loneliness and guessed he'd misread what had happened that night in October. He should have come up for a nightcap, as casually as he had tonight. Then they'd be better friends; then Dyer would've taken Chris up on his invitation home to Rhode Island.

Now Dyer wanted a re-invitation but didn't know how to get it. He felt a gloom coming on, and to distract himself he flapped his hand entreatingly. "Come on, let's have them," he said. "Let's have one."

Slowly, soberly, Chris shook his head and pushed himself out of the loveseat. "I used to see a guy in Boston," he said, plucking up a blue-and-white-checked sweater from the back of a wooden chair and crossing to the nearest window. "Rick. That was last year, when I had my car. Before the crankshaft, the thing that runs through the engine block? I guess it's fairly important. Before that snapped." Chris pulled the sweater on, the wool crackling as his head came through the neck. "I sold the thing for scrap," he added, shrugging the sweater straight on his shoulders and finger-raking static out of his hair. "Now, I refuse to ride the bus with students, and he, obviously, can't come here."

"Why not?"

"Don't ask, don't tell. Britton's like the army." He jerked the upper window panel down, opening two inches at the top of the frame. A frigid draft swept in and sank to the floor of the apartment. Chris slid open the top drawer of his desk and took out a pack of cigarettes and a black plastic lighter.

"Want one?" Chris asked. Dyer shook his head. "Really?" Chris asked, putting a cigarette between his lips. "I figured you for a closet smoker." Chris flicked the lighter, and sent his first lungful of smoke up through the opening. "My mistake."

Dyer was oddly pleased that Chris would think that of him. "Do the guys here know you smoke?"

Chris perched on the edge of his desk and took another long, contented drag, nodding. "Kid called Brian, they call him Brain — he's above us and says he can smell it. Says I'm a hypocrite if I nail him for smoking his own."

"Would you?"

"I'm not big on discipline," said Chris. "I make a lot of noise when I go upstairs, and I go nice and slow. Give them time to stash their liquor, their bongs, Lysol their rooms, whatever. Catching anyone gets me more trouble than I need. The dorm head in here last year used to do raids after sign-in. You'd think he'd know better than to pound on doors, especially with a Fieldspar upstairs. But the guy was ROTC in college. Kind of hard-core all around. Left to do a Ph.D. in Math."

"I heard Britton lost a major contributor when Henry got kicked out."

"Hard to blame the Fieldspars," said Chris. "There were five guys drinking in Henry's room when ROTC barreled in, but Henry himself was halfway across campus, headed for his girlfriend's dorm. Campus police pick him up and say he smells like booze, and no doubt he does — but that's hardly catching him red-handed. Still, he gets cited for cruising and drinking: two strikes. The guys with beers in their hands get probation; Henry gets tossed."

"Seems a little harsh," said Dyer.

"Ask me, Ed was looking for a reason to throw Henry out before his father got his name on a new library wing." Chris flicked ash out the window. "So he pushed Lambert for expulsion." Chris shrugged and took another drag.

It was Dyer's turn to make conversation. "Blanton told me Wolfe buddies around with terrorists. Said he's up to something."

Chris laughed. "Tom *hates* Ed. Thinks he was passed over for the headmaster position himself."

"Really?"

"Tom's been here for fucking years. Which of course is the problem. The trustees wanted someone from outside. Snagging a chaired professor at Harvard was a coup. Even one who'd been banging his students."

"They couldn't have known about that."

Chris shrugged. "And maybe he wasn't."

"Blanton said the trustees wanted a progressive institution."

"That's part of it, I'm sure. And for all I know, Ed's popping anthrax into envelopes as we speak. Or building a bomb in his basement. My advice: Stay out of it. Keep your head down."

Dyer nodded, finished his beer, and let out a satisfied sigh. "You could borrow my car," he said. "To go to Boston."

Chris lifted his cigarette in salute. "Rick's a moot point by now. Thanks all the same." He took a thoughtful drag and turned back to the window. His eyes fixed on something outside. "Oh fuck," he said. He slid open the bottom window, and more cold air rushed inside. Dyer's eyes teared against the draft. "Fuck, fuck, fuck," Chris said, peering into the night.

James sprinted across the snow-encrusted lawn, beelining it for the gray strip of Reservoir and the elderberry hedges that rose up on the road's far side. Before him, thrown by the Weiss floodlights, lay the path of his elongated, alien shadow. He wished he could fold into it like a jackknife, tucking himself neatly into the darkness. The brilliant sodium light surrounded Weiss like a prison perimeter, and James was taking what he'd judged the shortest distance through it, the shortest distance to Reservoir Road and the hedges that made a thick, shadowed barrier on the far side of the pavement. Fifty yards across the lit grass, and then he'd collapse into the dark strip of asphalt and burrow under the hedge.

Chris crushed his cigarette on the outside of the building. "Fuck," he said again.

"Who is it?" Dyer asked, pulling himself out of the recliner.

"James Wolfe, but maybe I can't tell," said Chris. "Maybe the glare makes it too hard to see."

Dyer moved, a little unsteadily, to the window and peered out. The buzzing floodlight bolted above them threw a hazy veil over Dyer's view of the school grounds. The terraced lawn running to Elson descended into pewter gray, and the distant trees made a brown scrim.

"I think he headed left, toward Reservoir," said Chris. He sighed. "Better check his room."

"I wondered if he had a girlfriend," said Dyer.

"Unlikely," said Chris, sliding the window shut. "Let's hope he's all tucked in. Ed's fucking kid. This is not someone I want to catch."

• • •

Reservoir Road ran in a straight line behind the bell tower, the music building, and the gym, before breaking into the patch of woods that filled the southeast corner of Britton's grounds. Once in the trees, Reservoir horseshoed right, just inside the boundary wall, emerging again at South Quad near Bachelor Hall. Though roundabout and heavily patrolled by campus security cars, the Reservoir route offered tree cover from the moon and headlights. Despite being on probation, Cary Street cruised this way to see his girlfriend Lane Newinski in Bachelor after sign-in every Friday and Saturday night. "So easy," James had heard Cary say to some of the other third-floor guys. "Wear black, stay off the road, and watch for patrol."

James mapped the route in his head, lying on his belly at the base of the hedge, gulping the cold, earthy air. He squirmed sideways, the elderberry branches raking his back. Convinced he was out of sight, he brought his arms to his sides, laid his cheek down on a pillow of cold soil, and tried to catch his breath.

Your picture, squid, Randy had said out by the hockey rink. *On her dresser. This is good news.*

James hadn't been able to bring himself to ask why or when Randy had been in Jane's room; he'd just felt sick, as sick as he'd felt in the bus to Boston, though this time he didn't vomit. He'd stalked past Randy, off the gravel verge, stumbling down the slope to the baseball dugout, ignoring Randy's trailing questions: "So, we're good? For the final?" Walked all the way to Weiss and his room. He vetoed homework and dinner. He tried phoning his mom, but the number at her new house in Knoxville just rang, no answering machine, no voicemail. He replaced the pay phone receiver gently, with some relief, unsure of what advice he would have asked for. He thought of heading to the house on Smithson Way but then remembered what his dad had said, sternly, back in August: *I don't want you to think you can just come back if things get difficult.*

James read Jane's note over and over, running his index finger along the cramped, printed words: *Forget the letter. Don't say any-*

thing about it to your dad. But forgetting the letter broke his tie to Jane. He felt the irony down in his gut — without Henry, they might never speak again. He swallowed two Tylenol for his sore shoulder and his throbbing, tender tongue. He paced back and forth. Sometime after midnight, he tried to sleep, but found himself staring at the glowing FUCK BRITTON star pattern on his ceiling instead. What had Henry been complaining about? He'd had Jane in this very bed — or he'd sneak across campus in the night to hers. Following the shadows on the ground . . . Taking the Reservoir route . . .

James had put on his shoes, put on his black turtleneck and darkest blue jeans, pulled on a fleece ski cap. He slid open his window, monkeyed carefully onto the rusty rungs of the fire escape ladder, and climbed down the face of Weiss Hall. The cold made its way through the thin cotton turtleneck to the small of his back. He shivered, noticing the lit windows of Mr. Nolan's apartment. He hit the ground as quietly as he could.

If he could get Jane away from everyone else, he'd thought, get her in private, not after class or in the library, at night, this night, right now, when no one else would know, she might explain her note, explain where things stood with Henry and why Randy had been in her room.

James had his breath back, and he pushed himself through the hedge to the other side. Bent low, he moved in the shadow, the shoulder of his turtleneck snagging on the branches as he ran. He pulled his fleece hat down to his eyebrows. He kept his gaze on his feet, afraid to look around, sure he'd see the high beams of a campus patrol car cutting toward him. The music building passed by in his peripheral vision. The brick finger of bell tower.

When he reached the woods — after two hundred yards of hunched running — he edged off the road, into the rows of pine and spruce, and slowed to a walk. The footing was easy, a soft layer of pine needles and snow, but the darkness under the evergreen branches was total, and James moved carefully, straining to see. When twin headlight beams pierced the woods ahead of him, he dropped flat behind a tree, gripping an exposed root, tucking his face into his armpit, listening to the humming engine of the cruiser approach and pass.

The air turned rotten and thick with the scent of a dead animal. James breathed through his mouth and stepped carefully, wary of squishiness underfoot. Quiet hung between the columns of trees like thick lengths of velvet. His sweat cooled, and the cold lashed icy ropes around his chest. He wished he'd had a coat or a sweater dark enough to wear. His hands were numb inside his gloves. Inside his tennis shoes, an old pair, navy with gray trim, his toes had fused into grooved paddles of flesh.

James made his way to a row of buildings, peering at them through the streetlights. To his right lay Bachelor, another hulking brick dormitory, identical in its oblong, rectangular design to Weiss. He followed the tree line, bending to collect a pebble on the way, scanning the rows of windows, some lit, some dark.

Oh — shit.

He stood still and rocked his head back. *I am such an idiot.*

James walked the periphery of Bachelor twice, slowly, dejectedly, staring up at the dozens of windows, pressing the cold, dimpled pebble in his fist. If he'd gone to that party on the first day of term, he might know which was hers. In a second-floor window Louise Hampton stood in her bra, hair loose around her shoulders, leaning into a mirror above the dresser, swabbing her face with a cotton ball. In another he saw the top half of a Monet waterlily poster. In a third, the burning planet of a desk lamp.

Louise moved out of the window's frame, and James slowly trudged back toward the woods. He'd have to retrace his route all the way to Weiss. Cross the lit grass, climb the fire escape, try to get some sleep. The prospect exhausted him. He turned and gave Bachelor a final, defeated stare. He'd never really had a plan, he realized, just an impulse to get out and see her. He hadn't thought the thing through. He wasn't even sure she'd risk coming out to talk to him. Now he wondered if he should take the night's screwup as a sign and just do what she'd asked: forget the letter, forget about Randy being in her room, forget about Jane altogether.

A few hundred yards to his right, down Smithson Way, was his father's house. He hadn't seen the place in weeks. Instinctively, his gaze found his old bedroom window on the second floor. The curtains were open, and he could make out a length of the wall, the white paint through the glass pearly and luminescent. He imagined breaking in and spending the night up there, sleeping in his old bed, pretending it was last year, before he knew Jane, or Randy, back when he was an anonymous new kid. He'd just go to class, do his work, study for his exams, keep his head down, get through the year. The idea drew him so hard, his longing to roll back time, to uncomplicate his life, that he jerked forward on robot feet, moving in the house's direction.

That's when he noticed the spill of light coming from the kitchen window in the rear and the sleek, low-slung sedan parked in the driveway. James recognized the aerodynamic lines, the round headlights, the silver trim on the door — and the cold ran stiff rods through his legs. He stumbled, his knees not operating correctly. His face flushed.

What was *she* doing here? Why wasn't she in Knoxville?

His legs shook, and he thought he might have to sit, or lean against the side of the house to keep himself upright.

When he was ready, when he knew he had to see, and couldn't leave till he had, he inched closer to the kitchen window.

His father sat at the table in a clean white oxford shirt, rolled at the sleeves, pointing his meaty finger at a stranger, a tall Asian man with military straight posture and meticulously combed hair. The man wore a black suit and stared at James's father with interest. He jotted notes into a small notebook he held in his palm. On the table sat a squat bottle of cognac and two bell-shaped glasses. James backed up, confused. He spun around, peered through the dark, and realized that that wasn't his mom's car at all in the driveway. Up close he could see that it wasn't green.

Then a flashlight beam stabbed him in the chest.

"Wouldn't have figured you for cruising," said Chris. Dyer, standing beside him in the middle of Smithson Way, noticed the gentle way he moved the flashlight beam off James's skinny, shivering frame. James's teeth chattered, there was dirt smeared across his face, and his thin turtleneck showed a tear at the shoulder. Dyer took off his overcoat and offered it to him.

James shook his head, retreating along the driveway, cutting a nervous glance at a black Mercedes parked there.

"I came to see my dad," he said.

Chris switched off the flashlight. "In the middle of the night?"

"Who's in there with him?" Dyer asked, noticing the kitchen light was on.

James's chin sank to his chest, and he shrugged and blinked at the ground.

Dyer took a few steps down the driveway, gaining a better sightline through the kitchen window. An Asian man in a suit sat at the table, swirling liquor in a glass. Dyer could see only a portion of his arm, a small notebook in his hand.

Chris whispered Dyer's name. "We're headed back," he said.

That's when Wolfe appeared in the window, one hand on the frame. Dyer ducked back into shadow. Wolfe stared through the glass, rubbing his chin with one finger.

Feeling Wolfe's eyes on him, telling himself he couldn't see out into the dark, Dyer retreated quickly into the street, out of view, then turned and jogged to catch up with Chris and James. When he reached them, out of breath, he asked James again: "Do you know who that was?" James shook his head as they walked, wiped the dirt from his cheek, and glanced up at Dyer with eyes that seemed to search inward, tracking the braided convolutions of his own head.

Dyer decided against telling Blanton about the man he'd seen in Wolfe's kitchen. Chris's advice came back to him: *Keep your head down.* That could have been a parent, or a prospective hire, or just an old colleague. But if so, why meet in the middle of the night? "He's not up to anything," Chris said. "Or not anything we need to worry about."

Keep your head down.

The school emptied of students for Christmas break; Chris and most of the other faculty left as well. Dyer told himself he'd be fine, and he started research on North Korea for Model UN and wrote World War II class plans for the first weeks of spring term. He warmed soup on his kitchen hot plate and logged on to the Neptune Cruise Lines website, tracking his mother's ship (a turquoise trident icon on his computer screen) past Vieques and Virgin Gorda. For exercise he ran a few desultory miles on the treadmill at the school gym, and he slept sweatily through the sound of clanging radiators in his bedroom. On Christmas morning, a call from his mother woke him. She was anchored off Tortola, and though a lag in the connection threw the conversation's rhythm, her voice stayed bright and steady on the line. The food was no good, but the ocean was the bluest she'd ever seen, and she and Mary were getting fat on virgin daiquiris. "I'm so relaxed I'm not even shaking!" she blurted. Dyer nodded hard at this, as though she might need his reassurance to make it true. He told her about a faculty holiday dinner that night in Commons with turkey, token gifts, and hot, spiced cider. "Should be festive!" he said, nearly shouting into the phone. Really, there was no dinner; Britton on Christmas Day was a deserted, snowbound postcard. Dyer had no one to see, nothing special to do, no one but his mother to talk to. But at a dollar a minute, they didn't talk long. She told him she missed him; he said the same. They hung up.

Dyer passed a few hours reading, then took a long walk around the school grounds, avoiding the few glowing windows of faculty family apartments, worried that he'd be spotted, taken pity on, invited inside. For dinner he ate takeout Singapore noodles from Dragon Express, the only place he could find open downtown, then tried to read a true-crime bestseller, listening to carols on the radio, wishing for the first time since September that he had splurged on a cheap TV along the way. The MSG doubled his vision and made his hands shake. He put the book down. He switched off the radio. He turned to sit-ups and pushups, a hundred of each, rinsed himself of sweat in a lukewarm shower, and, finally, when sleep seemed impossible, slugged a glass of warm Scotch from a bottle he'd laid away for emergencies.

All in all, a tough Christmas—but the day hadn't killed him. Sure, the empty hours in the afternoon had drawn a hard contrast with his childhood, when he and his mother had spiraled colored lights on the banister in Richmond, when there really had been spiced cider, fragrant with nutmeg and gently steaming from a steel pot on the stove, when he'd wake to find a wool sock stuffed with GoBots and trick yo-yos and sachets of SweeTarts hanging off his bedroom doorknob. But Dyer was determined not to be sentimental, not to feel sorry for himself—and to keep the past where it belonged. The past was *past,* a length of time the tick-tick of the diver's watch on his wrist ratcheted out steadily behind him. He could even forget, for days at a time, the origin of that grid-faced thing. The evening when he and his father would get together over a whiskey and "share adventures" would never come, he was sure. He watched the trident icon at NeptuneLines. com swim steadily through the Caribbean Sea, skirting St. John by a hundred miles or more. His mother was happy, happy with her childhood friend Mary. Her friend of many, many years. After the divorce, his mother had never had any boyfriends, or none Dyer had met. He'd been grateful at first, and then, when he went to Oxford, he worried that she'd get lonely without him around. But at least there had been Mary, a buddy for movies, for dinner twice or so a week. He'd been glad to hear that his mother had a friend. But thinking back now, Dyer hadn't really known just how close they were or how much time they spent together. Did Mary sleep over? And what did it mean if she did? He tried to put the whole subject out of his head, but when he closed his eyes he saw them in bed together—not doing anything, thank *God*—lying there, propped up on bulky pillows, in high-necked nightgowns, sipping tea. *Don't think about it.* Or think about it this way: Mary Joyce was her companion, her protector, her ward against solitude.

On the afternoon of December 31, just as he was wondering how a solo New Year's Eve would feel, Chris knocked on his door.

"Rick's throwing a party in Boston," he said, unspooling a scarf from his neck. "Rick, my ex. Turns out he's not moot after all. Can you drive us in?"

"God, yes," said Dyer. He hadn't known Chris was back from Providence.

"Greta's going to be there too. Which won't be weird, right?"

Dyer shook his head. "I can't believe I have something to do."

"You've been on your own this whole time?" Chris asked, looking past Dyer to his cluttered apartment, to the stack of Korean books on his desk, to the clothes on his floor. "I assumed you had plans."

They drove out of Britton in Dyer's Honda, the back tires squealing on Elson. Jumpy with anticipation, Dyer had popped the clutch. Still, it got him a hurrah from Chris as they raced toward the freeway ramp.

Dyer felt good on the drive to Boston, good when he and Chris got to the party, good when Rick Stonehouse (peroxide hair, Buddha belly, mascara) pressed a white ecstasy tablet into his palm, good swallowing it down. Then, later, dancing in a crowd on the polished hardwood dining room floor, with an aerosol taste in his throat and his stomach humming, he became as joyful as he'd ever been in his life. At midnight, he kissed an advertising copywriter named Monique Trembly. He'd been telling her that in North Korea you could get sent to a gulag for stepping on a newspaper with a picture of the Dear Leader on it. "And they only let good-looking people live in the capital," he'd said. Across the living room Greta stirred a martini with her finger, then held it out for some broad-shouldered blond guy in a spread-collared dress shirt to suck.

Later, Dyer found Greta in the scorchingly lit kitchen and told her how sorry he was that they'd become estranged. "Whose fault is that?" she asked, and tucked her chin into her neck and mimicked his baritone: "'Should we blame the Vicodin?'" Under the kitchen's powerful halogens, her bangs and eyelashes threw thin shadows around her eyes, like wrinkles or stress lines.

"I'd just found out about you and Wolfe," he said — and immediately doubted the wisdom of bringing this up.

"Old news, even then. Chris must have told you that. Unlike your girlfriend. What's-her-name."

"We broke up," he said. Greta gave him a dead-straight, line-drive stare. Dyer felt a muscle in his neck spasm with excitement, and he wondered if this was another party they could leave together. It was arctic outside, but they both had cars with heaters. Dyer returned the stare, the chemical in his system proposing a bear hug.

Greta put out her hand with the healed wrist bone, and they exchanged a serious, Wall Street–banker handshake instead. "Estranged is too strong a word," she told him. "Let's say awkward."

WINTER TERM

5

January

D YER RETURNED TO BRITTON late on the first, serotonin-
depleted, sunk into an ocean-bottom gloom. Chris was staying at Rick's for another night, and Greta had disappeared
back to Long Island in her own car before the sun came up. Dyer
was alone, again, and faced with, he realized, a lot to do.

By the time Tim and Benjy and Oliver and the others poured
back into Bailey, two days later, Dyer had forgotten the party and
had lost a mental picture of Monique Trembly's face. He was
scrambling to prepare for a schedule that now included History
250 and 110, IMs (a rotating menu of gym sports: dodgeball, bad-
minton, indoor soccer), and Britton's first Model UN club. Dyer
had barely looked at the fifty-page IMUNI instructor manual that
had arrived via e-mail over the break. UN parliamentary procedure had its own lingo (plenary approval, caucus, point of personal privilege), and though he'd already, sort of, covered North
Korean history, it turned out that there was much more issue-spe-
cific research to be done. How did North Korea view the Situation
in Angola for instance, or the Impact of Transgenic Crops on De-
veloping Markets? His delegation had to have speeches planned
for March. Two thousand high school kids were going, and though
Wolfe hadn't been in touch, he knew the headmaster would expect
a decent showing from the Britton team. Dyer also knew his volun-

teers thought they were getting a free trip to New York, not a major bump in their workload, and he could see their faces when he explained what lay ahead: 6:30 P.M., his place, right after dinner. He'd bought ice cream and Nutter Butters to kick things off, to introduce a little false enthusiasm and the no doubt short-lived hope that all of this might be fun.

James tailed his father out of Commons, tracking him down the stone steps onto the path behind the library. His dad moved with hip-thrusting strides, his attention targeted on some point south of Elson Road. They hadn't spoken since James returned from Knoxville eight days before — hadn't spoken, now that James thought about it, for weeks. James wondered if his dad was angry at him for going to see his mom — the idea was subtly appealing, implying as it did a question of loyalty — or, more likely, if James was just slowly becoming invisible to him, undetectable, one more bobbing head and overfull backpack on the Britton grounds. That depressing thought settled through him, sinking from his head to his feet. But then, when James stepped on a twig lying on the path, snapping it in half, Wolfe's head came up like a marionette's, and he glanced over his shoulder and spotted his son.

James broke into a jog to catch up. "Dad," he said.

Wolfe landed one hand in the middle of James's back, then patted his shoulder: the half hug James had been receiving ever since he turned thirteen. "Welcome back," Wolfe said. His red flannel shirt, visible beneath the Mao jacket, matched the chapped skin of his cheeks. His eyes had sunk deep into his face, deeper than usual, and James wondered, with a sympathy emerging from some low burrow within him, if he'd been sleeping. He'd taken care of James when he'd had nightmares as a child, dreams of suffocation, of being slowly pushed into a bog, dreams that would sit James, age seven or eight, upright in his sheets, crying for help. Wolfe would come in and perch on his bed murmuring sleepily that he was there, it was just a dream. Then he'd push a chair into the corner, near the night-light, and read by its glow for as long as it took

James to go back to sleep. The room felt warmer with his father there, the air touched with sweat and cigarette smoke. James could still remember his easy slide back into sleep, the view through narrowing eyelids of his father's bent head in the corner, the feeling of being cared for, protected.

Was anyone protecting his dad now? His nose was blade-thin, and the stubble on his neck, below his beard line, was ash gray and rough, like iron bristles. He looked as if he'd lost weight. With a sideways tip of his head, Wolfe motioned them both toward Elson, his eyes resetting on some point in the distance.

"Happy New Year," said James, matching the pace and directing his eyes forward as if he too had business to take care of, as if this were just a chance meeting on the way to South Quad. Truth was, he had his new astronomy elective with Mr. Jeffries in fifteen minutes back in Ramm Hall.

"I saw your very fine term grades," said Wolfe.

"The exams were pretty easy," said James.

"All your applications go in on time?"

James felt a shock, as though he'd tripped on a half-buried wire, and he fell a step off his father's pace. Had it really been so long? He'd given up the fantasy of sabotaging his applications and sent them in on December 1; today was January 10. Surely something had passed between them in the interim — but what? The last exchange James could remember came just after Thanksgiving, when his father had asked James how his mother looked. How she'd *looked*, as if he'd known that the answer would be more glamorous, more expensively dressed, with a newer, more modern haircut.

"All of them," said James. "Totally out of my hands." Distance had opened between them, a tidal drift had been pulling them apart, since . . . well, James thought, since the days of the Saturday walks to his office at Harvard, since the days he'd sit by the nightlight while James fell back to sleep. He shouldn't be surprised that his dad hadn't asked before about the applications; James hadn't asked what he'd been doing drinking with a strange Asian man at the kitchen table in the middle of the night last month. He thought of the fat cognac glasses, the squat, brown bottle and the screw top lying on its side like a capsized boat. His dad had always had friends over, scruffy bearded friends from his past, or one or two colleagues at Harvard, the other China historian, the Latin America guy — they all came to talk politics and drink. This man (he'd looked Korean, James thought) had been taking notes, and his father's expression had been solemn, concentrated. Even Mr. Martin had wanted to know what had been going on. James still didn't know, but it was easier not to try to figure out what it meant, easier to let the weeks continue to carry them further from their roles as father and son through the relatively few weeks left until summer and college. He thought of Ms. Salverton crossing the yard at dawn. He thought back, four years (or so) ago, to Beebie Warner, the art student he'd seen his father grab roughly by the elbow in front of the Fogg Museum. Henry Fieldspar's words came to him: *Your dad had me kicked out.* Henry had sounded like a guy wanting someone to blame — but could James really be sure about anything regarding his dad? Ms. Salverton had spent nights in the house with him last spring (down the hall, in his father's *room*), and he'd had no idea until he saw her out on the back lawn.

He should confront him right now, striding purposefully past the wingbone-shaped, iron and steel-cable sculpture that abutted Elson, titled *Stress.* This was why he'd followed him out of Commons anyway: to stop this drift. To blurt something about Randy and the final exam; about Jane, who continued to ignore even James's hardest, most plumbing looks; above all, to talk about Knoxville and *Dennis,* even though he knew his dad was exactly the wrong person for this.

Wolfe plowed on, jogging down the brick steps to the sidewalk along Elson. A cluster of girls, bulked out by their backpacks and shoulder bags, fell silent and traded nervous grins as they passed.

"Hello, hello," Wolfe said heartily.

Berin Allan, a thin lower with gold hoop earrings and fur-tipped boots, pulled her earbuds out by the cord and said, "Hi, Headmaster Wolfe." She was one of the Bachelor girls; she lived with Jane. Her steady eye contact, sweet smile, and her boots, her boots especially, hit James like an adrenaline shot.

He waited for the girls to pass out of range, then said: "I need to ask you a favor."

"How's your mom?" Wolfe asked.

"Did you hear me?"

"And the new place?"

His father's instincts spooked James; he could anticipate, mind-read, and outmaneuver you somehow. The few times in junior high when James had scored less than an A on a Math or Spanish test, Wolfe would take one look at James's funereal slump at the cherry-wood counter and swell with pride. "I distrust perfection," Wolfe would say, as if he knew about the grade, even though he couldn't. "So you're mortal like the rest of us. Sit up. You'll get a back like mine." He'd straighten James's posture with a warm palm.

"James?"

"Big," James said. "The new place is huge."

James had been shocked by how big: a rich person's house, with runway-lengths of floor, sixteen rooms (he'd counted), and bathrooms you could park a car in. "Everyone has big houses in Knoxville," his mother warned him on the ride from the airport — which didn't seem like something she'd say. And clearly everyone didn't. Beside the freeway, near the riverfront downtown, James spotted shabby row houses. Then, tucked behind the strip malls on the wide four-lane they took to the suburbs, he'd seen bland, institutional, cinderblock condos hung with banners reading LEASING NOW! in red, white, and blue. Out of town, the road turned into a country highway studded with the sweeping entryways of gated developments.

His mother's was called Highbury Estates, and when they drove up to the guardhouse, stern-faced security men greeted her as "Mrs. Fuller." The black-painted, spike-tipped gate swung on silent hydraulic hinges, and James and his mother followed winding tarmac roads through neat grids of bare willow and cottonwood trees. Nickel gray mailboxes marked driveways that led off the main road. "Where do people walk?" James wanted to know as they took deserted S-curves through the development. "There are these nice trails that go through the trees," she'd explained.

That night, he met Dennis, the boyfriend, another project manager at Fuller-Reardon. Dennis was in his mid-forties and short, with a droopy left eyelid, a clean-shaven, brick-shaped jaw, and a belly that stretched his dress shirt into a dimpled sack. Dennis had grown up in Los Angeles, spoke fluent German, and restored antique BMW motorcycles as a hobby—information that came via Caroline in bright-voiced non sequiturs. James could tell she was smitten, but with what? Dennis was average-looking at best. He arrived with a pizza and a box of store-bought tree ornaments for the four-foot fir in the empty living room. He wore jeans, a yellow dress shirt, a dark blue blazer, and duck boots—each piece clean and new-looking. His jeans had creases down the legs, as if he'd worn them out of the store. Coming through the door, he transferred the pizza and the box of ornaments to his left arm and softly squeezed James's hand, offering a courtly "How do you do?" He hung the ornaments in silence—apparently content to listen to James and Caroline reminisce about Christmas trees past (the potted fern, the live spruce, the plastic one that smelled like chlorine). He'd smile whenever James looked at him, but otherwise kept his expression blank, scratching occasionally at his neck. He didn't stay the night. This, James guessed, was for his benefit. Dennis and Caroline spent a long interval in the front doorway touching waistlines, kissing earlobes, and whispering phrases James heard indistinctly as "good to take this slow . . . love you . . . see you tomorrow."

Christmas had never been a major event for James. When his father swore off presents, it fell to Caroline to buy a few things —books, wool socks, once a camera, once a Discman—to put under the tree for James. No surprise then: James slept in the next morning, oblivious to the holiday until he switched on the light in the bathroom and rubbed the focus back into his eyes. Downstairs, he found his mother pacing the kitchen, a giant mug of coffee in her hand. The table lay buried in Fuller-Reardon folders and printed reports on stiff, heavy-stock paper. Though she wore a change of clothes — Harvard sweatpants and a snap-buttoned cowboy shirt — James wondered if she'd slept. Her short hair was tangled, her eyelids swollen and red, her fingernails ragged. She gave him a grassy-breathed kiss and mussed the hair on his head. "Merry Christmas," she said, and cleared a space at the table. After cereal and half a grapefruit, she sat him on the only piece of furniture in the cavernous living room, a putty-colored leather sectional sofa framed in chrome.

Under the tree lay a full set of Fuller-Reardon gear — hat, T-shirt, button-up shirt, sweatpants, tie, fleece pullover. All in his size.

"Hey, thanks!" said James. He pulled each piece on, hanging the tie around his neck, turning the hat backward on his head, and giving his mother a goofy smile. Nothing worked. Perched unsteadily on the edge of the sofa, a distracted expression on her face, Caroline kept biting her lower lip. "I know I said don't bother," she said. "But I wanted you to have something."

"These are great, Mom," said James. "Really."

"NO GIFTS!" she'd e-mailed him. "Your coming is gift enough." But at the Boston airport bookstore, James had picked up a hardbound edition of *David Copperfield*. Still wearing the Fuller-Reardon gear, he dashed upstairs and brought the book down from his bedroom, unwrapped, and handed it over. The handsome, embossed lettering triggered tears (she used to read him *A Tale of Two Cities* at bedtime), and Caroline went to him for a long, sniffly clutch. "I'll read it," she said. "I'll find time."

But over the next week, between Christmas and New Year's, it was James who read the book beginning to end, 950 densely typeset pages. He also watched news footage on CNN of U.S. troop deployments to the Sea of Japan for war game exercises, and, at the warmest point of the afternoon, bundled up in his new gear and walked the Highbury Estates trails, peeking at lookalike brick-and-glass mansions through the leafless trees.

Caroline had to work. She'd had to work Christmas afternoon and every day afterward. Coming through the door at 6:30 or 7:00 P.M., she looked depleted, her face pale, her suit jacket wrinkled, her mouth crooked, as if she'd been sucking on something sour during the drive home.

"What's going on at work?" James asked the first time he saw her like that, hoping for a salvo of abbreviations, those coded descriptions of her job he used to love. "Nothing," she said, pinching the corners of her mouth. "I mean 'Classified.' Sorry, honey. I hate that I'm so busy."

"Classified?" James asked.

"Weird, I know," she said with a sigh, and headed into the kitchen. "Since we got the new Defense contract I can't talk about anything." This statement came out grimly, straight into her brimming wineglass. The recycling bin was full of green bottles of pinot grigio, and, watching them pile up, James tried to remember if she'd ever drunk so much. At night, she didn't totter or slur her speech, but her breath always smelled sharp, like cut grass and disinfectant.

Left alone day after day in the empty, pinging rooms of the house, James's mood darkened, then went black. The week dragged by, and he began wishing he were back at Weiss, a place less foreign than this. He missed his mother more than he ever had at Britton, but here the feeling was unpleasant and embittering. One day, bored senseless, he'd scuffed the gleaming oak floors with the heels of his shoes, found a tennis ball in the monkey grass by the Highbury tennis courts, and bounced it against the side of the house, leaving marks on the new white paint.

By New Year's Eve, James was desperate to leave. Dennis came for dinner and handed him a Van Gogh sunflower card with a $100 bookstore gift certificate inside. *From one reader to another,* the note said. At the dinner table, James brandished the certificate like a winning lotto ticket, and said, "Gosh. Great. Jackpot." Dennis studied his food, then looked up at James expectantly. The silence held until Caroline said, "*Thank* him."

But James didn't want to thank Dennis. He didn't want to act grateful for any part of this lonely, bewildering week. He'd expected a wonderful visit, days of exploring Knoxville, a VIP tour of Fuller-Reardon headquarters. Not seven days of solitude, not seeing his mother push breath over her top lip and shake her head, as if just as relieved as he was that his plane was leaving the next day.

James met Dennis's gaze with his own — and shivered at the patience and intelligence he saw there. The one heavy eyelid sent a look of scrutiny right through him as if it were an x-ray, straight through to the wall at his back. Did Dennis have a family of his own? James guessed that he had, that he'd run out on them to make room for Caroline. James aligned his fork and knife on his plate, pushed his chair away from the table and the gift certificate, and went upstairs without a word.

Wolfe noticed the embroidered Fuller-Reardon insignia on James's pullover when they reached the crosswalk at the corner of Elson and Reservoir. "Nice sweatshirt," he said.

"Mom gave it to me," said James.

"Did she tell you that her beloved Goshawks carry miniaturized nukes?"

"No," said James.

"And that they break North Korean airspace every day?"

"She didn't talk about what she was working on."

"Didn't or wouldn't? The CIA thinks North Korean uranium labs are buried under their mountain ranges, and the nuke-armed Goshawks can blow them apart. Just flying them around sets off a nice little arms race in the region." Wolfe flashed an angry look at his son. "Did she look guilty at all? Weight of her conscience on her back?"

"I need to ask you a favor," said James for a second time.

"Wait till we're home," said Wolfe gruffly, picking up his pace. They angled toward Smithson Way. James had heard his father's raised voice and seen his angry, lifted chin so many times. He pictured his father talking back to the evening news, or smacking the paper with the side of his hand over coffee at the cherrywood counter in Cambridge on mornings before school. James had learned to wait these episodes out. The papers got folded and put away; the brow unfurrowed; the outrage went; there was nothing James could do to speed any of it up. Walking the route to Smithson Way side by side with him now, the route James took every day last year, he felt a renewed affection for his father, a longing to close the gap between them. All around him, Britton took on the comforting, familiar look of home, and Knoxville seemed like a different planet.

James closed his eyes and caught the low sun in his face, the unseasonably warm January air resting gently against his cheeks; this week had seen record high temperatures in the fifties, prompting the Britton Earth Club to leaflet the school with global warming fact sheets. Snow hunched in oily black crusts along the curbs.

They made their way down Smithson through South Quad, past the numbered mailbox and up the steps to the front door of the house. Inside, they settled in the living room, sitting at right angles to each other, James on the couch, Wolfe in the sunken armchair, dust pinwheeling in a shaft of sunlight between them. The air in the room was warm and smelled lightly of cigarette smoke. If his father had some pressing business to do, he didn't let on. He glanced once up the wall at the portrait of himself, squinting at it as if it had fallen askew, rubbed his eyes, and waited silently for James to speak.

"Would you write a letter of circumstances for Henry Fieldspar?" James asked.

"A letter of what?"

"Circumstances. Explaining why he was kicked out, and what kind of record he had while he was here. And send it to Georgetown."

Wolfe stared at him, spending long, frowning seconds on the embroidered Fuller-Reardon logo on his breast. "I didn't think you and Henry were friends."

"We weren't," James said quickly. "Aren't. Some guys in Weiss have been in touch with him and apparently he thinks he needs one to get into Georgetown. They told me to ask you."

"Why doesn't Henry ask me himself?"

"I don't know. Pride?" James knew how unlikely and vague all of this sounded, and he half hoped his dad would challenge the story and force out the truth. That morning, he'd woken to the buzzing of his clock radio, thinking he could claim that he never got Jane's note and follow through on her original request, the one she'd made at the Mark. If Henry could use a letter, she'd be indebted to him; if not, she could explain. Either way they'd be talking again.

If his dad asked, he'd tell him everything. And maybe that would bring them closer.

"Was your mother wearing a ring?" Wolfe asked.

The conversation kept falling off track. James slumped into the couch. "The one you gave her."

"Really?"

"I didn't check."

Wolfe stared hard at his son, then let out a belly laugh. "God, you fooled me. I bet she's not. This guy's a Fuller-Reardon company man, right?"

"I don't want to talk about this." But he did — he wanted to say how much of a mystery his mother had become, how unhappy he'd been in Knoxville.

"Did he give you a Christmas present?"

"A gift certificate. I left it down there."

"Good boy," Wolfe said. "What do you want me to say about Henry? That he was a star student? His grades were good. Shame he got himself in trouble."

"So you'll write it?"

"I don't think he really needs one. Not with a senator for a dad.

Georgetown'll take him." He cleared his throat, and James heard the thick churning of phlegm, another hint, like the smell in the room, that he was smoking again. "How's Dyer doing?"

"Who?"

"Mr. Martin. Your Model UN instructor."

Dyer. Teachers' first names sounded so strange, like passwords to a club. "Model UN's only met once."

Wolfe nodded to indicate he knew this already. "Tell me how it went."

"Mr. Martin did a kind of pep talk thing," said James. "He gave us some facts and figures and then handed out research projects. He said how much fun it would be to be the country everyone was afraid of."

"How much *fun* it would be? That's what he said? Exactly?"

James nodded.

"Was Sam Rafton there?"

"Yeah," said James. "I guess he needs the extra credit."

"It's important work you'll be doing in that club, James. I want you to throw yourself into it."

Important work. James searched his father's face for some clue as to what he meant; his stare was blank and unreadable. James felt the tidal gulf reopen between them, roil with waves and chop. He dropped his gaze and nodded at the floor. He had never had to be encouraged to throw himself into anything. He took a long inhale of the close, ashtray air of the living room.

"North Korea is a deeply misunderstood country," said Wolfe.

"Mr. Martin told us some North Koreans hacked up a bunch of U.S. soldiers with axes in the DMZ," James said casually, as if predicting the weekend's weather. This is how distant I can be, he thought, absently glancing around the room, checking his watch. How out of touch with what you consider important. "He said they're naturally violent people."

Wolfe's face went stiff; he laced his fingers and bowed them. James tried to hold his father's stare; the effort emptied his lungs of breath. "That's a distortion," Wolfe said.

James's gaze rose off his father to the painting above the mantel. One day, when James was in eighth grade, it appeared in the living room of their house in Cambridge. James's mother pronounced it ugly and demanded Wolfe take the thing away, hang it in his office at the History Department if he had to hang it somewhere. Though James couldn't make it out from where he sat, he knew the signature in the lower left-hand corner read "Beebie Warner," the Harvard art department undergrad James had seen his dad grapple with outside the Fogg Museum. He'd cupped her elbow and leaned into her, his lips touching her ear as they formed words. She'd torn away, whipping her arm out of his father's grip. Though James could still see this scene in his head with all the color and clarity of a snapshot, he had never wondered if his dad had been having an affair with the girl. Why not? James must have known what he was seeing and yet he'd slipped into a neutral gear, a disengagement of the brain that allowed him to see, register, and not interpret. Revisiting the scene again these four and a half years later, seeing his father's lips brush windblown strands of Beebie Warner's hair, James's body warmed with deferred shock. His dad's first affair? And so easy to hide. An undergraduate art student painting his portrait. He must have sat in Beebie Warner's private studio for hours at a time.

Had his mother known? Had she found out? It bothered James that he didn't know.

The caulk-thick red paint pulsed at him wetly, like blood.

"No chance you'll do it?" James asked.

"Do what?"

"North Korea is the size of New York State. It's one of the last Communist regimes in the world. Kim Jong Il is the leader. The army has 1.1 million people in it. There was a famine there. They have an illegal nuclear weapons program and support terrorism. We hate them." Sam Rafton stuffed the folded sheet of notebook paper in his back pocket and reseated himself in his chair.

"That's your whole presentation?" Dyer asked.

"Sounds like the encyclopedia," said Louise Hampton.

"Online version," said Sam. "I kind of condensed things down."

Dyer shook his head. "You're going to have to do it again."

"No way," said Sam, his voice low and flat. "You said basic overview, and that's that."

"I asked you to present the character of North Korea from a historical, geographical, and socioeconomic perspective," said Dyer, trying to be patient.

"That's what I did," said Sam, still calm, still flat-voiced, seemingly aware that there was no way Dyer could coerce more effort out of him. Model UN wasn't a class; there was no grade. Though Dyer had promised him that by signing up he would bump last term's grade a full point or more, Sam hardly needed the favor. A 1.5 was a low pass, and a low pass was all the Admissions Department at Duke would need from a legacy applicant of the Rafton family. And of course, four years in Durham was really just a prologue to a career in Atlanta real estate. Rafton sat slouched in the wooden desk chair, his knees apart and his hands behind his head, his lacrosse cap low, his blue eyes visible beneath the brim. He stared past Dyer, out his window as if catching an outline of concrete mixers, cranes, and backhoes idling in the darkness. He stretched his elbows backward like wings, and shrugged.

"Mr. Martin?" said Greg Smile.

"Greg?"

"Any idea how long this is gonna go?"

"Forty-five minutes," said Dyer. "Just like always."

"Last week you let us out after fifteen," said Sam.

"Tonight we're going the full forty-five," Dyer said, feeling the moment slide through his hands like a wet rope. He looked around the circle of six (with two empty chairs) he'd formed in his living room, trying to linger meaningfully on each face. "Guys, we need to take this seriously. The goal here is to get to know North Korea, to kind of *be* North Koreans at this conference in March. You're going to have to give speeches, do debates, write resolutions. We have to prepare."

Chip Lee yawned, dropping his jaw so low that Dyer saw the retainer lining the rear of his lower teeth. Dean Lambert had made a point of telling Dyer that Chip Lee was allowed to yawn and otherwise exhibit signs of drowsiness. It wasn't disrespect; the kid had sleep apnea, diagnosed by Dr. Abrams at Smith Infirmary. He also had a 4.2 average, an early admission to Harvard, and a lock on the school's Warner Scholar prize.

"We could prepare," Sam said generally to the group. "Or we could just go to New York and party in the hotel."

"Hey, Sam, do me a favor," Dyer said, standing and crossing the room to his bookshelf. He withdrew the heavy, oversized world atlas he'd taken from the History Department office and, squatting, laid it flat on the floor at the center of the circle of chairs. He rotated it to face Sam Rafton, opened the book to a political map of the globe, and tapped the page. "Point to North Korea," he said.

Sam didn't even glance at the book on the floor.

"Jane?" Dyer asked. "Just nod if you know where it is."

Jane nodded, her eyes locked on the open book.

"Louise?"

"It's been, like, all over the news," she said, puckering her lips and winking at Sam. Flirty or derisive, Dyer couldn't tell. Chris Nolan had mentioned to Dyer that he'd heard Louise's shrieky laugh in the vicinity of Sam's room on the third floor of Weiss two Saturday nights in a row — after sign-in. "She's severely testing my capacity to look the other way," he'd said. Tonight Louise wore jeans that sat two inches below her navel, a tight red tank top, wool ski cap, and makeup. Her gaze stayed fixed on Sam, her eyelids low, and her bottom lip tucked behind her teeth. Dyer wondered if she was the reason Sam joined the club. If his willingness had nothing to do with the promised grade bump after all.

"Chip?" asked Dyer.

Chip nodded.

"James?" Dyer asked.

"Sure."

Sam Rafton squeezed the shoulder of his teammate, Greg Smile.

"Sorry, dude," he said. "I totally can too." Greg had managed a turnaround 3.5 on last term's 250 exam — and still seemed aglow with accomplishment.

"So what's your point?" Sam asked Dyer, clipping the last syllable off with his teeth.

Dyer wasn't sure what his point was. He resented the fact that Wolfe had ordered him to get Sam onboard, adding to Rafton's healthy balance of self-importance. "Why do you want me so badly?" Sam had wondered aloud to Dyer the previous week, after the first meeting of 250. Dyer hadn't known what to say. *He* didn't want him; Wolfe did. And the only reason was fundraising. Wolfe wanted to flatter Rafton's parents by handpicking their son for the little group. But Dyer couldn't tell Sam any of that, and so he'd mumbled something about how Sam would add a quality of leadership to the club. "Give it some thought," Dyer had said, struggling to keep a pleading tone out of his voice. But Sam confirmed what was already in the air: "As a favor to you," he'd said, clapping Dyer on the arm.

Sam's winged-out elbows, his reclining posture, the curve of his jaw: it all read privilege, and arrogance, and toward Dyer, a load of magnanimity. The combination sent Dyer back to his own high school, and the clique of baseball players, the football quarterback, Danny Ryan, and that inexplicably popular short kid Fred Place, who all slouched around as if waiting for the school to pay them a per diem just for showing up. He'd hated those guys, just as he didn't much care for Sam Rafton and had hauled out the atlas on a gamble that he could put Sam in his place. He enjoyed the payoff as long as it lasted, the book open on the floor, Sam not looking at it.

The door opened a few inches, and Liem Du stuck his narrow head through the opening, blinking rapidly at Dyer, as if trying to place him.

"You're late, Liem," said Dyer.

Liem pushed the door wider. In his free hand he held a square of carrot cake on a small dessert plate. "I forgot," said Liem.

"Can you find North Korea on this map?" asked Dyer, nodding at the book.

"Of course *he* can," said Sam.

Seconds of silence slipped by.

"I'm Vietnamese," Liem finally said through a mouthful of carrot cake. He set the plate on the empty chair and stood over the atlas. Delicately, like a dancer, he toed North Korea with his hightop sneaker. "That's North Korea." He moved his shoe southwest. "That's Vietnam."

Jane Hirsch turned to Sam, and said quietly, "You're a total idiot."

Liem settled into his chair and focused his attention on the rest of his dessert.

Dyer cleared his throat and plowed ahead. "You're in luck, Rafton. Most Americans can't find North Korea on a map either." Dyer paused. Sam scratched at something on his pants leg with his middle finger. "You *are* getting another research assignment, though. There's a lot to cover, and no one gets a free pass."

"Slut," said Sam.

Dyer blinked rapidly. Jane rolled her eyes. She lifted her fingers and flicked them sideways, a gesture that read: *Let it go.*

Oh. Dyer had thought Sam meant *he* was a slut. "Get out," he said, nodding toward the door in what he hoped was a resolute way. But did anyone care? Jane Hirsch kept her cool; she even looked pleased. Greg, Louise, Chip, Liem — they all maintained relaxed, unruffled postures in their chairs. Only James Wolfe seemed unsettled. He'd slid to the edge of his seat, both feet planted squarely on the floor, as if he were on the verge of leaping across the room. He stared at Sam's knees, a filament muscle below his left eye twitching.

"I'm serious, Sam," said Dyer. "Go back to Weiss."

Sam held himself still for another moment, his hands laced behind his head. He snorted breath through his nose and let out a low chuckle. Then, with a convulsive jerk, like a trap snapping shut, he clapped his knees and stood. Without a word, he crossed the room, swinging a messenger bag over his head, smoothing the strap on his chest.

"We'll talk later," said Dyer.

"Promise?" said Sam, passing James's chair.

Dyer listened to Sam head down the Bailey staircase. A bit of attitude as the kid left the room, but who cared? Dyer had thrown his first student out of class! He felt a hot draft of power and wiped a sheen of sweat from his brow. Chris had told him about this, this sirocco of authority, the tingle of it along the skin. Dyer had no idea what he was going to say to Sam later, but he didn't worry about it. Greg Smile's dark burr of a mustache; Louise's diving, parabolic neckline; the expensive fountain pen Chip Lee waggled in his fingers: all costumes and props. Dyer was the only real adult in the room, and they would do whatever he told them to do. Amazing that these kids had ever made him nervous.

"Sam's most salient point came late in his presentation," said Dyer after a satisfying interval of silence. " 'We hate them,' Sam said. Let's substitute 'scared of' for 'hate,' and let's switch the pronouns. We're a tiny, impoverished nation with no real allies in the world, and the U.S. is scared to death of us. Why?"

Dyer didn't wait for an answer, ticking the points off on his fingers. "The U.S. can't predict us. Can't understand us. We're Communist. We don't participate in the global markets — and we prefer it that way. We have nuclear weapons — no one knows how many. We've got a dictator for a leader who likes cognac, girls, and *Friday the 13th*. During a famine a few years back, he let a couple million of us starve while he built a movie studio. As a country, we don't have freedom of speech or freedom of the press. Our radios have dials fixed at one station — the government broadcast. CNN and the Internet are totally forbidden. Speak out against the Dear Leader, and you get sent to a gulag. It's like thirties Russia all over again."

"Cool," said Greg.

"But we don't have unrest. We're not racked by revolution. We're not yearning for international investment, and we don't want tourists. We don't like people telling us what to do, or showing us

how to live. We like our misfit status. Last week I told you how naturally aggressive and violent North Koreans can be. That talent for
belligerence is a national asset. Our volatility and unpredictability
keep us safe. Mess with us, and we'll launch an invasion across the
DMZ. Or we'll fire a missile at Japan. Or test a nuke."

"Or bomb the U.S. embassy in Seoul," said Louise, a new, sour
look on her face, her eyelashes clotted with mascara. She certainly
kept up with the news, Dyer thought. There'd been a small blast
at the U.S. embassy in Seoul two days prior. A backpack of ex-
plosives left near the gates; South Korean authorities suspected an
activist student group from Yonsei University who'd been organiz-
ing anti-U.S. demonstrations for months. There'd been no injuries, but the news was full of State Department officials predicting
more serious attacks to come. Dyer remembered Louise's exam at
the end of last term, the perfect handwriting, the thorough, point-
by-point essays, all her IDs nailed. Grade: 4.0. Louise was one of
Dyer's best students, and she hadn't liked seeing Sam leave. She
was frowning at Dyer.

"Maybe North Korea had something to do with that, maybe
they didn't," Dyer said, offering her a firm, plaster-cast smile. Louise was pretty: cream white cheeks, big brown eyes, freckles trailing
down her bare arms. But Dyer didn't feel a thing for her, not one
tingle of lust. That was a happy fact — Britton girls didn't arouse
him. They were too bony, their voices too high-pitched, their
frank, flirty stares (and Dyer had received a few of these) backlit by
insecurity and self-doubt. Ten years ago, he'd have thought girls
like Louise — rich, pretty, popular — were infallible, like the pope.
"North Korea has certainly used terrorism in the past. We've taken
hostages and blown up airliners. But there are plenty of young, politically motivated South Koreans who want to see the U.S. with-
draw its troops from their country. Was North Korea supporting
them? That's an open question."

James had his hand up, and Dyer nodded at him. "Did they really chop up a bunch of U.S. soldiers with axes in the DMZ?" he
asked, leaning back stiffly in his chair.

"In 1976. You can look it up," Dyer said. "The officers were mutilated so badly, the bodies couldn't be identified. Kissinger, secretary of state at the time, thought Kim Il Sung was deliberately trying to provoke a war. And maybe he was. Who knows? That's the point! We're a little bit nuts!"

Dyer was getting into it, the history he'd stored inside him during the holiday rising into his head like bubbles from a gassy swamp. The group watched him with unfocused, owlish stares. That was boredom; Dyer knew the look well. But he didn't care. Newfound authority still warmed him from the inside out, and for the next thirty-odd minutes, no one was going to talk except him.

So he went on about Korea's forty years of massacres, forced labor, and sexual slavery under Japanese colonial rule. He described the way the United States had arbitrarily divided the peninsula in two after World War II, without consulting anyone but their own State Department, essentially ensuring a civil war. He hammered a single message throughout — North Koreans exist on the losing end of history. We've got a grievance, we're angry, and retribution-minded.

"Did you know the U.S. dropped more napalm in the Korean War than in Vietnam?" Dyer asked. "People talk about Dresden and Berlin. They talk about Nagasaki and Hiroshima. No one mentions Korea. The Americans bombed the country so thoroughly they ran out of buildings to hit long before the war ended. So then they went after the dams, flooding North Korean farmlands. And they didn't have smart bombs. The Americans killed two million civilians in the air campaign. Two million."

"Can I go to the bathroom?" asked Liem.

"And no one won. Armistice means a tie. It means let's stop shooting at each other. So we're technically still at war. That's a big source of pride for the North Koreans."

Chip Lee's eyes were closed. His chest lifted and sunk in slow wavelike swells. Jane Hirsch had her hand up.

Dyer nodded at her.

"What's that thing you told me to research? Joos? Jook? I forgot to write it down."

"Juche," said Dyer. "It means self-reliance. National philosophy. Very important. Louise, you're on diplomatic goals. Greg,
you've got the story on nuclear weapons. And James?"

"Religion," he said.

"Right. No more encyclopedia summaries. Got it? Chip? You
awake? Somebody hit him."

James's door stood ajar two inches. Behind him, Cary Street and
Sam Rafton's door was closed. Down the hall, Josh Fishbein and
Buddy Juliver's door was closed as well. The third floor of Weiss
was unusually quiet and still, and James felt a flutter of panic, a
butterfly tickle that traveled along his scalp as he pushed his door
open the rest of the way with his foot.

They wouldn't lacquer him twice, he figured. A round of Property? It usually started with personal items, and so James's eyes
went straight for his mother's photo, the one of her on the Provincetown whale watching boat. There it was, cockeyed on his
dresser, unmoved. His computer — still there. His textbooks stood
evenly above his desk on the single shelf. His blue wool blanket
lay folded at the base of the made bed. His pillow, plumped and
white.

A dull, yeasty smell hit his nostrils, and James's foot crashed
through a small pile of empty beer bottles half-hidden under a T-
shirt on the floor. They clanked together and spun, spitting beer
into the floorboards.

James stared at the brand name he'd seen a million times as if
it were a message in a foreign script. Strips of the labels had been
peeled to the sticky glue. He gathered the bottles up, six in all,
clutching the necks with his fingers, wincing at the ringing sound
of glass on glass. Where to put them? Not the trash can, not for
contraband. Kicking the closet door open, James set the bottles
behind a line of shoes, arranging them neatly like bowling pins
against the back wall.

"Place stinks like a brewery."

James gripped the doorframe of the closet. He turned around
slowly.

"Careful, dude. Or you'll get on pro like the rest of us," Sam said, and then took two quick sniffs of the air in the room.

"Get caught drinking, and you'll be out," said James.

"Hoo boy. Knew it," Sam called over his shoulder. "Wolfe's spoiling for a fight." James heard the chuckle of someone down the hall. Sam moved deeper into the room, both hands jammed into the back of his sweatpants. He stood above the small puddle of beer on James's floor, and his cheeks bulged with a burp. He blew it at James through pursed lips. "Holiday been training you to do your own fighting?"

James hadn't had trouble from Rafton or any of the guys in Weiss since the broken nose earned him a nickname and a measure of respect around the dorm. The Mastur-Derby, with its complicated system of awarding points for semipublic stunts of self-abuse, had passed him by, as had two recent midnight skin runs. James went unmolested to shower in the mornings. He brushed his teeth without incident, eventually training himself to stare through the dried pus spattering the bathroom mirror. The invisibility he'd so hated in the fall felt like a blessing to him now.

"Saw you get pretty tense in there tonight," said Rafton, rotating one hand inside his sweatpants around his hip to his crotch, where he gave himself an emphatic scratch.

"What are you talking about?"

"When I called your girlfriend a slut. Looked like you wanted to take a swing at me."

The word *girlfriend* whipped James like a wet towel.

"Hey," Sam said, tipping his head in a friendly way, gesturing with two fingers for James to come toward him for a private chat. James didn't move. "I'd hook up with Jane Hirsch if I was you. For the social-climbing potential alone."

"That's not . . ." started James. He didn't trust Rafton, and yet he had to fight off an instinct to confide in him anyway. "She's not my girlfriend."

Sam burped again, and this time James got a whiff: beer, the same musty, damp-cardboard smell coming off his floor.

"Confidence, Wolfe. She wouldn't be too big a challenge," Sam said. "Considering."

"Considering what?"

"Girl's easy. I bet she's even got a thing for you."

"Sam—"

"And if Holiday can bang her."

James made his legs move, crossing the room, away from Rafton, to the nearest window. He slid the pane up and took a long, steady breath of fresh night air. He leaned against the sill, staring out. How many weeks since he and Jane last spoke? James had stopped counting.

"Your study buddy," said Rafton. "Nailing your girl."

With his thumbnail, James chipped white paint off the soft, rotting wood of the sill and waited to hear what Sam would say next.

But Sam just stood there, watching James.

It was 9:10, ten minutes past the weeknight sign-in, and Britton was quiet. The bare branches of the oak trees lining Peabody Hall formed a black tracery in the darkness. A plastic bag sailed across the lawn. Waist-high safety lights spread hazy circles on the paved walks crossing the quad. Directly below James, Chris Nolan jogged the last ten yards to Weiss's front door, taking the brick steps two at a time. Mr. Nolan saw him and waved. Weekday sign-in was on the honor system — a list for signatures tacked to Nolan's door. Nolan wasn't supposed to let Weiss go unsupervised, and he tapped his watch and raised a finger to his lips as he went inside.

James liked Mr. Nolan. He was grateful that he hadn't told the dean about his late-night run to South Quad, and yet he wished the school hadn't assigned someone so weak on discipline to Weiss. The Weiss guys, despite being on probation, smuggled in a supply of beer and vodka pretty much every week. Having a drink or two, or even a heavy session, on a Tuesday night was pretty common. Nolan never came upstairs, and the seniors — understandably, thought James — had come to believe they could do anything they wanted. Nolan was a pussy, they said. And a fag. Over the past couple of weekends, James had heard Louise Hampton's voice through the wall separating his room from Sam's. Just yesterday, the humid stink of bong water had hung in the hallway like a fog. He tried to imagine Mr. Nolan facing down Sam Rafton, and couldn't. Not as Mr. Martin had tonight at Model UN. *That* had impressed him. Mr. Martin looked as though he'd enjoyed it himself, leaning back imperiously in his chair and lecturing at them for a half-hour straight.

Sam still stood in the middle of the room, feet spread as if he owned it, one hand down the front of his sweats, the other scratching under the rear of his cap, tipping it up off his head.

"What are you doing in here anyway?" James asked.

Sam shrugged. "I wanted to make sure we were cool. Dorm mates, you know. Looking after each other. Me after you, you after me." He rubbed his mouth and chin as if trying to iron out a grin and set his hat down firmly on his head.

"This is what you did to Henry last year."

"Did what?"

"Drank in his room."

"Everybody drinks in everybody's room."

"But he wasn't here when you guys got caught," said James, crossing toward the closet.

Sam tracked James with his eyes. "He was with us; then he left. And what the fuck do you care?"

James could just hear the wood-creak of Mr. Nolan climbing the stairs to his apartment on the second floor.

"Who told the dean he'd been drinking?" James asked.

"You in law school now?"

"He would have denied it in his disciplinary."

"They smelled it on him."

"You told Lambert."

"You're high," Sam said with a laugh. Never turn anyone in for anything — that was the most basic, most elemental law of life at Britton, and Rafton wouldn't have broken it. Still, James liked the way he felt making the accusation. Now he wanted to grill Sam about Randy and Jane, but knew he wouldn't get straight answers.

Anger ran through him like a spike. Acting on instinct, he gripped the knob with a sweaty palm, pulled the closet door open, reached inside, and gathered the beer bottles into his hands.

"What are you doing?" Sam asked.

"Don't come in here again."

"Where you going?" asked Sam.

James took three quick steps for the door, shielding the bottles with his body. Sam moved with him. Before the gap closed, James broke for the hall. Reaching the doorframe, he felt Sam's hand on his arm, his nails digging into the muscle. James spun his body, whipping his arm, tearing free of Rafton's grip. Stumbling now, James dashed for the hallway and the top of the stairs. Sam lunged after him, missed, then tripped James's trailing foot. James fell hard to the carpeted hallway floor, breaking his fall with his right hand. With a dull, snapping sound, the beer bottles broke in his fingers.

The blood came out easily, generously; James watched the flaps of skin on his fingers turn red and wet with it. Cary Street emerged from his room, took one look at James splayed out on the carpet, and stumbled back through his door. Rafton kneeled in front of James's face, and whispered, "What the fuck are you doing, Wolfe?"

James pushed Sam away from him, printing bloody oblongs on his T-shirt. *Our volatility and unpredictability keeps us safe,* Mr. Martin had said. Wasn't that Randy's lesson as well? The unexpected tackle, the jab in the neck. Doesn't matter how small you are. Don't be a puss, don't let people interfere with your life. James rose to his knees, just as Mr. Nolan appeared past the lip of the stairwell, one floor beneath them. The teacher headed for his apartment door, his key in his right hand. James opened his mouth to speak.

Sam smacked him with the palm of his hand. James's head snapped sideways. His cheek tingled with blood.

"What's going on?" Chris Nolan's voice drifted up the stairwell.

Sam backed away from the stairs, out of Nolan's sightline. Cary gestured for him, and Sam rushed toward the room. He glared at James before closing the door.

"Mr. Nolan," James started, tonguing the inside of his numb cheek, trying to massage the feeling back. He struggled to his feet. Black blossoms opened in his vision, and he took two body-jarring steps down the stairs.

"Mr. Nolan," James began again through heavy breath, brandishing the jagged neck of the beer at the teacher, feeling the blood drip off of his hand. Chris's head rocked back at the sight. "Look what I found in my room," James said.

Dyer's clock radio woke him with the morning's news. At talks in Beijing, the North Korean diplomat had threatened the U.S. undersecretary with "merciless extinction" if aerial espionage continued, as well as the "reckless and aggressive" buildup of nuclear-armed UAVs in the East Sea. The undersecretary denied the presence of any such aircraft. The North Korean called him a "liar" and "a proponent of imperialist moral leprosy" and stormed out of the room, ending the meeting early, hours before the security detail had cleared traffic along the American convoy's route back to the airport. In heavy traffic, the lead, dummy limo was hit by a rocket-propelled grenade fired from the roof of the Millennium Casino, a nightclub in the heart of downtown. Five bystanders and the two marines driving the dummy limo were killed in the explosion.

Dyer rolled into his pillow and buried his face, muffling the news anchor's grave, relentless voice. That might do it, he thought. That might be the trigger. U.S. intelligence suspected North Korean terrorists, sponsored by a Japanese organized crime syndicate with connections to Pyongyang.

He pushed himself out of bed. On the way to the shower, the phone rang.

"Hi," his mother said.

"Hi," said Dyer.

"Everything all right?"

"I'm barely awake."

"Should I call back?"

Dyer rubbed his face, trying to wake up. "No. Just let me . . . Hang on." He went back into his bedroom, opened the blinds covering his easterly window, and let the sun smack him in the face. He blinked and sat heavily on the edge of his bed.

"Well, I've got some news," his mother said.

Dyer squinted through the smudged windowpanes. He didn't feel ready for whatever it was.

"It's some fairly big news. Surprising maybe." Her voice was as bright and steady as it had been in the Caribbean.

"Okay," Dyer said, sitting up straight, trying to gird himself. He leaned over to the radio and snapped it off.

"Mary and I got engaged over dinner last night," she said. "We're having a May wedding. Or 'commitment ceremony,' I suppose it's called." She gave him the date. "Can you come?" she asked. "You could bring someone."

Dyer's gaze wandered through the door into the other room to the disorganized piles of paper at his desk and the red light of the cordless phone's base.

"Are you there?" his mother asked.

"I'm just absorbing it," said Dyer. His first clear thought was of the way Mary had cut him that piece of pumpkin pie last November. He remembered the restorative hit of sugar in his mouth.

Did Julian know? *Julian:* the name usually made him angry, but just now, nothing came. Only this news, like a fire blanket, smothering old feelings. His mother with a lover.

Jesus.

"This must be a surprise, I suppose."

"Yeah."

He wondered, strangely, if she was still getting alimony checks from Julian's lawyer. If so, this would end it, surely: the flow of money. Which would be a relief.

A May wedding.

"It's a recent thing," Bethany said. "In case you were wondering. And it's sort of a . . . surprise to me too. If that helps."

"It's big news," Dyer said. But he could already feel himself ac-

commodating it, adjusting to this new state of things. His mother
and . . . stepmother. Which meant she wasn't alone. Which meant
she had a companion, partner, wife, whatever.

"I wondered if you'd already guessed."

"I hadn't." Though that wasn't strictly true.

Dyer closed his eyes and raked his unwashed, cowlicked hair.
He'd only ever seen one picture of his mother's wedding to Julian.
It surfaced out of a drawer during an afternoon of spring cleaning when he was in high school. A professionally taken eight-by-
ten — torn down the middle. Time had bleached the colors into
pastels: Bethany in white, and her three bridesmaids in mint green,
girlfriends from Smith, clutching pink bouquets, a lattice altar behind them strung with white flowers. Julian's half of the photo
was gone. Sticky with dust and sweat, clutching rags, he and his
mother had stood over the photo laid flat on the dining room table and stared at it for a long time. "I was so angry once," she said
then, touching the photo's white ragged edge.

"But everything's okay, Dyer," said Bethany on the phone.
"This is good news."

6

February

Mr. Ryan Griffo
Dean
Office of Undergraduate Admissions
Georgetown University

Dear Dean Griffo:

I'm writing on behalf of Henry Fieldspar, one of Britton's finest students, an academic, social, and athletic leader at our school. Late last spring, Henry was the victim of some bad judgment — and a little bad luck — resulting in his expulsion. I'd like to explain the circumstances of his case in the hopes that you will consider him for your incoming class.

A faculty member discovered students drinking beer in Henry's dormitory room one evening in May of last year. Henry was not in the building at the time of the discovery. Dean of Students Arnold Lambert determined that he was to be cited for two offenses — leaving the dormitory after sign-in and a violation of the school's drug and alcohol code. In his disciplinary, Henry denied having anything to do with the beer in his room, and though we have a tradition here at Britton of taking our students at their word, Dean Lambert determined that the circumstantial evidence against Henry was too significant to ignore.

Henry was expelled, and the other boys were placed on

disciplinary probation. I must stand by Dean Lambert's decision; his was a strict interpretation of Britton's two-strikes policy. And yet it is an unfortunate truth that had Henry been in his room drinking with the other boys — or had he only been caught outside of his dorm, a lesser offense — it would have been unnecessary to expel him.

I'd like to stress Henry's academic record and his commitment to our athletic program, lettering in crew, tennis, and squash. Personally, I've missed his humility and good humor this year, and I wish him the best. It is my sincere hope that you'll look kindly on his application to Georgetown. Please don't hesitate to contact me if you have any questions.

Warmly,
Edward Wolfe
Headmaster, Britton School

Holding the page delicately by its corner, Jane peered at James over the top edge. "How did you get the letterhead?" she asked.

"What do you mean?" asked James, blocking the glare from the low sun with his bandaged hand.

"You wrote this," she said.

James shrugged and moved himself into Jane's shadow. The setting sunlight made stray strands of her hair incandescent. She dropped the page to her side and buried her chin in the blue-and-white-striped Britton scarf loosely collaring her neck.

"Henry says it was your dad, not Dean Lambert, who pushed for expulsion."

"He told me."

"This line about it might have been unnecessary to expel him," said Jane, pinching the page more firmly and giving it a tiny shake. Her eyes were bloodshot, the tip of her nose cherry red. "No headmaster would admit —"

"Can Henry use it?" James asked. He sounded impatient, but he wasn't, just nervous. Waiting for her to answer, James let his gaze run down the grassy slope to the cracked and snow-bleached asphalt of Reservoir Road, to the place where the road led into the woods.

"I don't know. It's February already. But I'll ask him," she finally said.

So she and Henry *were* speaking. One question answered. More were stacked up in James's throat — at the very top, *Have you hooked up with Randy?* James pressed his teeth together. He didn't really want to hear the answer. Best to drop all the questions and talk about something else. Jane might already be looking for a quick escape, and an interrogation would definitely justify it.

He'd cornered her into speaking to him. Letter in hand, James had intercepted Jane on the path the way he'd seen her intercept Pomfret strikers in the fall — an angling vector, cutting her off before she made it onto the main quad. He'd had a wild image of slide-tackling her, his foot connecting with her shin, knocking her to the hard-packed dirt beside the path, her hair fanning out along the slushy snowmelt. He'd been having a lot of violent fantasies these days — stabbing Rafton with a ballpoint, dropping something heavy (his math textbook, a fire extinguisher, his desk chair) on Randy's head from two stories up.

Jane let her backpack slip off of her shoulder and set it on the path. Crouching, she unzipped it and pulled out a folder. "There's a reason, I'm guessing, why you didn't do what I asked." She flicked her bangs out of her face and looked up.

"You didn't ask. You left a *note*," said James, throwing the word down at her. Annoyance was a fly buzzing around inside his head, behind his eyes, in his ears. "Slipped under my door. And no explanation." The bandaged fingers on James's right hand ached, and he gingerly inserted them into the back pocket of his pants. This wasn't going the way he wanted it to. He hadn't intended to get angry, and he took two deep breaths to calm down.

Jane sighed, rubbing her eye with a knuckle. "How are your fingers?" she asked, rising.

The buzzing in James's head flagged, sputtered like a motor, and stopped. "Is it too late to use it?"

Jane shook her head. "Decisions don't go out until March. How are your fingers?"

"Itchy," said James.

"They don't hurt?"

"They do. Sometimes."

"You didn't tell Mr. Nolan who'd been drinking?"

"I didn't know."

"Sure you did. Sam."

James shook his head. "I didn't see him do it. Could have been Cary or Brain or anyone. Mr. Nolan wasn't going to, like, dust for prints," he said, trying not to think about the exasperated look the teacher had given him when he made it down the stairs with the broken neck of the beer bottle. The blood had been dribbling through James's fingers, spotting his shoes, catching the cuff of his pant leg. Mr. Nolan had slowly replaced his apartment key in his pocket, pushing breath through his teeth. "I'll get your coat," he said evenly, starting up the stairs. "Tell me where it is. And get some toilet paper or something."

On the walk to Smith Infirmary, James pressed the soggy, bloody toilet paper into his fingers as the ache started to flow up his arm. Sneaking glances at Mr. Nolan, James thought of how kind he'd been in photo class the year before, expressing real admiration for James's dead pigeon photos. "These are heavy," he'd said.

"The beers were just sitting there in my room," James offered. "I thought you should know."

"Yeah. Terrific," said Mr. Nolan, staring straight ahead.

The day after the visit to the infirmary, Dean Lambert summoned James to his house and sat him in the living room. Fidgeting in the wooden chair, trying to find a comfortable position, pain in his fingers emerging from beneath the butterfly bandages, the layers of gauze, and the Tylenol he'd taken that morning, James had organized his story in his head. Dean Lambert would want to know who was responsible for the alcohol, but James would say only that the beers had turned up in his room and he'd wanted to get them out and had tripped heading down the hall.

"I have no idea who brought the beers in," James told Lambert, who frowned at his answer. "I just wanted them out of my room."

Dean Lambert plucked his glasses off his face and held them up to a lamp beside his chair. "No idea?" he asked, squinting through the lenses.

"I heard someone else up in the hall," said Mr. Nolan, leaning against the doorjamb, just inside the room.

James shook his head, his attention caught by the scariest mask of the three above the mantel, the one with the howler mouth, the blind, whorled-wood eyes, the crown of straw hair. "Just me," he said. "I tripped on my way to the stairs."

Lambert replaced the glasses on his face and sat perfectly still. James fidgeted in the seat, rubbing his ticklish nose, sweat sticking his shirt to his back. It had never been his intention to get anyone in trouble. His rational motive had been to force Mr. Nolan to pay more attention to what went on up on the third floor, and to send Sam a warning.

His other motive was less clear. *Unpredictability keeps me safe,* he thought. All his life, James had been predictable—polite, studious, adaptable—and where had it gotten him? Isolated from his parents and manipulated by guys like Randy and Sam. There was freedom in invisibility, but if James couldn't be invisible, he could be volatile. Do the unexpected thing. The cuts on his fingers throbbed meaningfully as the meeting with Lambert ended, and each morning since, reminding him of the power this new way of thinking gave him. Want to talk to Jane? *Talk* to her, then. Want to cut Randy Holiday out of your life? *Cut him out.*

"You've changed," Jane said.

"What do you mean?"

"I just mean you've changed. You look different. You seem different."

"Is that good?" James asked, too eagerly, he knew.

Jane just laughed, as though she didn't know the answer.

"Should get to the library," said James. She turned in that direction and moved with him.

"I feel a little gross for ever having asked you for the letter," she said. "That's why I left the note, I guess. I wanted to forget about it."

November to February, and yet he hadn't forgotten a thing. He should tell her, but they were walking now and there was no pressure to speak. James kept his gaze down, stepping over a moldering pile of *Britton Gazettes*, the student newspaper, its banner headline: "Girls Hockey Pucks Up Exeter."

"Writing the letter was pretty easy, actually," James finally said. He'd pictured Henry Fieldspar's face — the coarse swatches of stubble on his cheeks, the heavy waves of his hair that swallowed his ears down to the lobe — and the sentences began to trickle out of him. Henry wasn't as good-looking or as athletic as Sam Rafton or Cary Street — but he was smart, and he had had a near perfect GPA. Henry opened his mouth to speak, and even Brain Jones shut up long enough to hear what he had to say.

"Are you in any trouble?" Jane asked.

James blew out his cheeks. "Doesn't seem like it. Not sure Lambert knows what to do. Nolan's making nightly sweeps of the third floor, and I'm really unpopular."

"Could be worse," Jane said. "You know Berin Allan? In Bachelor?"

James nodded.

"Scary thin, right? Total nut case about food. She's this sort of outcast in the dorm — and Louise fucking Hampton keeps zapping her hips with a laser pointer at sign-in."

James remembered Berin's fur-tipped boots, the time she'd cheerfully said hello to his father on their walk to the house.

"A few of us are waiting for her to collapse in the hall or something," said Jane. "It could be that bad is what I meant."

They spent a long moment together at the bottom step to the library. Jane's cheeks were pale white, nearly blue in spots, and there were yellow crescents under her eyes the color of cigarette filters. Concealer smothered a pimple at her hairline. She fidgeted, she kept swinging her gaze around, but her feet held her in place.

A pack of senior girls emerged from the library. James recognized Kelsey Grimm, Jane's roommate. For a moment they headed directly for James and Jane, then angled their path away, giving the two of them a wide berth. A smooth, instinctive redirection; it wasn't clear that they'd even seen James and Jane, though James knew they had. Kelsey let out a barking, overloud laugh at something one of the other girls said. Jane kept her attention on her booted feet, on the length of dead grass they'd just crossed from Morrow.

"I get so tired of this place," said Jane quietly.

Maybe she was the one who'd changed, James thought. Henry had made her one of the social princesses in the school, but James always wondered if she really liked the status. At Commons he'd never heard her monopolize the airspace the way Christie Fontaine or Louise Hampton would. Then there were the days James spotted her walking back from soccer practice or between classes. Popular girls moved in impregnable groups. Jane seemed to like walking solo.

James knew his was a convenient fantasy, but he'd nurtured it anyway: given the chance, Jane would lose the popularity Henry had given her.

And now, after all, he could have been right. Two months ago, those girls would have grouped a few yards away in the library courtyard until she left James's side and joined them to head to dinner. They would have said: *Slumming. Very senior year.* Now they were halfway to Commons, and no one was looking back. Jane was still staring toward Morrow, her eyes unfocused and damp. She sniffled again.

"How's your mom?" Jane said. "The new boyfriend."

"I don't like him," said James.

Jane nodded — the correct answer — and sniffled again. "Dad has this girlfriend now. Good that he's not alone, takes the pressure off me, but I'm still like, *bitch.*" Maybe she had a cold. That would help explain the Britton scarf.

"Did you see him over the vacation?" asked James. The longer they stood there, the more ticklish the moment became. It was dinnertime — but they couldn't go to Commons together.

"Yeah. She came to lunch on Christmas. Ashlee. Double-e."

He imagined reaching out and grasping the woolly end of the scarf, gently unlooping it over her head. What would he see? A chain of hickeys, like purple steppingstones running along her bare neck?

James heard Rafton's voice in his head: *Slut.* The word like a knife slicing through fabric. *Girl's easy.*

"You're nice to have done this," said Jane. "Writing the letter."

"Anything for Henry," James said.

Dyer was surprised by the way Model UN caught on. Greg Smile gave a good blow-by-blow of the North Korean nuclear program — when it started, why the North Koreans need it, how many nukes IAEA inspectors thought they had. Louise Hampton's presentation exceeded his expectations as well. "The average North Korean settles the smallest dispute with a fistfight," she told the group. "At the UN we're unpredictable and dangerous. We like to blackmail the other delegates into giving us what we want, to push around countries twice our size." No one in the room actually cared about North Korea, but they were doing the research, going to online UN document repositories to find the positions they'd need for the conference.

"Take the assassination attempt on the undersecretary of state," Dyer posed to them one Tuesday night. "If there's a resolution at the UN to disarm nations who sponsor terrorism, what would be the response?"

"Any resolution is an act of war," said Greg.

"The U.S. is the world's terrorist," said Jane.

Perhaps this new enthusiasm was due to college decisions and the fact that extracurriculars still counted for wait-list admissions, perhaps because the idea of making speeches in front of a couple thousand delegates in New York seemed sufficiently intimidating, perhaps (unlikeliest of all) because they actually wanted to support Dyer. Sam Rafton certainly didn't, but he showed up and stayed quiet. Dyer hadn't talked to him after kicking him out of the second club meeting. Sam may have felt ignored or slighted. The word from Chris Nolan was that since James Wolfe's stunt with the beer bottles, the third-floor Weiss guys were on best behavior. Whatever the cause: Rafton wasn't a problem, and the vibe at Model UN meetings had grown steadily healthier.

Then, one morning Dyer picked up a note in his faculty box:

TO: Louise Hampton, Jane Hirsch, James Wolfe,
 Sam Rafton, Liem Du, Chip Lee, Greg Smile,
 Randy Holiday
FROM: Headmaster Wolfe

Please be advised that I will take over the Model UN team meeting on February 15 to speak on the particular challenges the DPRK faces in the world today. I have included some background information to give you a preview of the issues for discussion.

Take over. February 15 was next week. Jane Hirsch was scheduled to present on North Korea's Juche Idea that night. The memo went on:

Also, there is substantial media interest in our representation of North Korea. I expect a number of reporters will be attending future team meetings. I'd like each one of you to remember that you are a reflection of The Britton School.

Attached to Wolfe's message was a "DPRK Fact Sheet and Resource List," which included a timeline that began in the third millennium B.C. with Old Choson Kingdom ("Period of peaceful, glorious rule") and ran to the present ("DPRK emerges from years of natural disasters, economic hardship, and imperialist aggression as stable, independent nuclear power").

Below the timeline lay a short list of "Diplomatic Goals":

1. End illegal U.S. aerial espionage.
2. End imperialist war buildup in the East Sea.
3. Eradicate U.S. troop presence on Korean peninsula.

4. Block hostile UN nuclear inspection to reassert the Juche
   Idea and sovereignty.
5. Achieve independent reunification with South Korea.

Under the heading "Resources," there were two web addresses:
one for something called the Choson Coordination and Development Group and one for the Korean Central News Agency of the
DPRK.

It must be a draft, Dyer thought. But when he checked the student mailboxes, there it was, a folded slip of white paper in each of
them.

Dyer headed back to Bailey and went online. The Choson Coordination and Development Group was a Korean community
organization in New York City that gave school and church presentations in heavily Korean-American enclaves of New York on
the achievements of Kim Il Sung and Kim Jong Il. The CCDG
website offered articles on "Peaceful Reunification," "The Juche
Idea," "U.S. Propaganda and the Capitalist War Machine," all
written by CCDG Director George Choe, a former New York
City councilman. "George Choe has dedicated himself to teaching young Korean-Americans about their heritage and ending
the misconceptions over the aims of the DPRK," his bio read.
The CCDG site looked slick and corporate, with photos of immaculate boulevards in Pyongyang and a Flash-animated video
of Korean schoolchildren playing under a shower of cherry blossoms.

The Korean Central News Agency of the DPRK had a simple,
text-based site with a list of press releases by date. These included:
"U.S. and S. Korea's Military's Evermore Undisguised Moves for
War," "Rally to Vow Anti-U.S. War Struggle Held in S. Korea,"
"Supreme Commander Kim Jong-Il Inspects Korean People's
Army Unit." Dyer clicked the "About" link, and read, "The Korean Central News Agency is the state-run agency of the Democratic People's Republic of Korea. It speaks for the Worker's Party
and the DPRK government."

. . .

The shearing sound of steel eating wood covered Dyer's footsteps, his clearing of the throat, his "Hello!" Wolfe bit the whirring chainsaw blade deeper into the body of the dead poplar branch. His forearms, bare below the rolled sleeves of his flannel shirt, tightened as the chain saw slid through. Sawdust spattered his boots. Randy Holiday stood nearby, leaning on an ax.

They were out of view of the road, tucked into the section of the headmaster's yard where Wolfe used to hold choson do, their breath steaming in the crisp Saturday-morning air. A length of branch dropped free of the saw, and Randy, who wore a Bruins jersey, loose jeans, and basketball sneakers, knocked it toward him with the flat end of the ax. Randy hefted the cut log to the stump near the sloped cellar doors, and, setting it on its end, he bent his knees and swung the blade in a neat orbit above his head, bringing it down hard, splitting the log in one stroke.

Wolfe sawed two more lengths; Randy split both. His nose and cheeks were strawberry red and he sniffed repeatedly, wiping his nose with his sleeve. The two didn't talk, smile, or trade looks as they worked. Randy was even taller than Wolfe, but the headmaster's shoulders were nearly as broad. They took similar stances, their feet spread, their backs bent to the work. Their wordlessness struck Dyer as intimate, familial. Like father and son, he thought. Wolfe's chin dropped approvingly as Randy split another log with one hard swing.

Dyer balanced his palms on the tips of the picket fence and waited for one of them to see him.

Finally, Randy turned and Dyer lifted his hand. Randy nudged the headmaster, who looked over his shoulder at Dyer, bowed a kink out of his back, and shouted over the buzz of the saw: "Branch came down last night in the wind."

Dyer unlatched the gate and let himself through. Wolfe switched off the saw, set it down, and shook the vibration out of his hands. A brittle, triangular silence settled into the yard.

"So you've been drafted into the club," Dyer said to Randy.

"He did it," said Randy, with a nod to Wolfe. His voice was tinny and nasal. He wiped his nose again.

"You need a replacement for Will Pilone," said Wolfe. "He has yet to show up, correct?"

Dyer nodded. If Randy weren't standing there, he might have pointed out that the club was doing fine with the group he had.

Sawdust clung messily to Wolfe's beard. Randy hitched his jeans. The way they stood, squared with each other, nearly shoulder to shoulder, gave Dyer a twitch of alarm. Two big guys with a chain saw and an ax.

But Randy was a *student*. There should be an obvious hierarchy here.

"Did I catch you at a bad time?" asked Dyer.

"A bad time for what?" asked Wolfe.

Avoiding Randy's face, Dyer said as casually as he could, "I wanted to talk about Model UN."

"I can come back later," said Randy.

"Later's busy. Just grab a Coke inside," said Wolfe, clapping his hands on his jeans. "I'll give you a shout when we're done."

Randy hacked up phlegm and funneled it out of his mouth and over his shoulder. He propped the ax against the side of the house and took the porch steps by twos. The door slapped shut behind him.

"He's a useful kid to have around," said Wolfe, nodding at the split logs littering the ground.

"Good student," said Dyer, spotting Randy through the kitchen window leaning into the open door of Wolfe's fridge. "Surprisingly so."

"I like his self-confidence. You know, there's never been a football PG in an advanced History class."

"His papers aren't bad," said Dyer.

"And he's been good to James," said Wolfe. "Looked after him a bit. Toughened him up — that's according to Randy. Anyway, I thought having a football player on the Model UN team would reduce Britton's perceived elitism at the conference."

"Are we really getting media attention?" asked Dyer.

"I've gotten the *New York Times* to bite," Wolfe said.

"On what?"

Wolfe shook his head and sighed. "You don't see how subversive this is?"

"I guess I don't."

"We'll be at war with North Korea by spring. And Britton will be speaking for the other side. The right-wing news guys, the talk radio guys, that asshole on cable — they hear Sam Rafton talking about North Korean freedom fighters, and they'll lose their minds."

"But they're teenagers. Half of them just want to party in the hotel."

"They're America's great white hope. The *Times* puts them in print, the ball will roll."

"I think that's unlikely," said Dyer.

"I think you're naïve," said Wolfe.

The simplicity of that, a short sentence like a jab to the head, rocked Dyer to his heels. He felt the hot blood rising into his neck and cleared his throat. "I was surprised by the memo yesterday."

"Surprised?" Wolfe smiled humorlessly and scratched his beard.

"I was surprised you went over my head to the students. I was surprised you added a member to the club without discussing it with me. I'm surprised you've never discussed any of this with me before."

"We're doing that now."

"There's a student presentation this coming week. On Juche. Are you intending to preempt that?"

Wolfe maintained that grim smile.

"Last week, Louise Hampton presented on North Korea's diplomatic goals — not the same ones you identified in the memo, by the way. We've covered the history pretty well, and I'd say the students in the club would disagree with your assessment of the current situation."

"They would?"

"Emerged from economic hardship? A stable nuclear power?

That's not what I've taught them, and it's a little confusing to have mixed messages show up in their mailbox."

Wolfe was still smiling, but his gaze had focused on Dyer so tightly that the trees behind the headmaster, the blue of the sky through bare branches, went soft-focus and dim. For a moment, Dyer heard nothing but his own heavy breathing.

"North Korea is a serious attempt to construct an independent, self-contained economy apart from the global capitalist system," said Wolfe.

"Okay, sure," said Dyer.

"Not a police state of crazed Stalinist terrorists."

"That's not—"

"A nuclear program is Kim Jong Il's only avenue for deterrence. The U.S. has had nukes aimed at Pyongyang for fifty years."

"I've included all that in our discussion. The kids know this stuff."

"There is going to be a lot of attention on them at the conference, and I want each one properly informed."

"You want the party line."

"I want their minds opened."

"What do you think I've been doing?"

Wolfe's voice lost its evenness. "Stories about Kim Jong Il throwing orgies. Fantasies about cannibalism. Shadowy terrorist plots. 'We're the bad guys.'"

Dyer blinked. He remembered what James had told him in the fall: *We never talk.* But they were talking.

"That's all in the news."

"The news is lurid bullshit. Scary stories sell papers. Show me a reporter who has actually spoken to a North Korean. They print what's spoon-fed to them by the State Department." Wolfe glanced through the kitchen window and then turned his back to Randy, who had propped his feet up on the table. "The whole point of this exercise is to embody another country's position," he said, closing in on Dyer by a step. "To accept it as your own. Is anyone making that effort in America today? Any politicians or policymakers? When North Korea offers an antidote to U.S. power? Yep, yes, don't say it: no freedom of press, no freedom of speech, political prisoners in work camps. Should be a liberal's nightmare. But North Koreans have the freedom to be North Koreans."

"What does that mean?"

"To be other than what Western capitalism says one should be. To be *other*. To *resist* U.S. hegemony. You've read, I assume, the U.S.'s current National Security Strategy? Preemptive unilateral strikes on so-called evil regimes. Are North Koreans evil? That's the question these kids should be asking. They should be projecting themselves. Questioning who the bad guys really are, who the fanatics are, who's scary as hell." Wolfe wiped the back of his hand across his mouth and regarded Randy's pile of split logs.

"I'm doing the best I can," said Dyer.

"You're being lazy. You're handing them paranoia and misinformation. You told them that Kim Jong Il brainwashes his citizens."

"But he *does*," Dyer said. Just the week before, he'd shown the group a video of a roomful of North Korean schoolchildren chanting a song about Kim Jong Il's talent with a handgun. Subtitles to the singsong Korean had run: *The Dear Leader shoots every Yankee / He shoots them in the chest. / Bang bang!*

"I know this area much, much better than you do," Wolfe said flatly. "The West views noncapitalists in the East as a population of zombies. It was the same way with China twenty years ago."

Dyer nodded; he knew very little about China twenty years ago. "I'm trying to get their attention," he said. "They're not naturally passionate about the place, and telling a good story gets them intrigued."

"It's cheap pedagogy. It's not what I hired you to do."

"What did you hire me to do?"

"Educate," said Wolfe. "Teaching isn't a talent show, Dyer. You *believe* in what you're doing. Do you? Do you have a political position at all?"

"I try not to in the classroom."

Wolfe thumped his chest with a thumb. "I came to Britton to educate these kids about systems different than their own. I don't make any apologies for that." A vein surfaced in his neck; both nostrils dilated. He flinched, almost imperceptibly. "But it quickly became clear to me that the Britton trustees don't want me educating. They want me administrating. *Fundraising.*" He spat the word. "So I brought you here to educate in my place."

Dyer had to close his eyes to break Wolfe's tunneling stare.

"And I know as well as anyone what Communism has done. However many million dead, but North Korea isn't pure Communism. It's socialist, but it's also dynastic. It's unique to itself. Do you know the writings of Confucius? 'What all men speak well of, look critically into; what all men condemn, examine first before you decide.' That's practically a North Korean motto."

But Wolfe hadn't come just to educate. He'd been sleeping with Harvard students, Dyer thought. *And he left his wife.* Dyer kept his jaw clenched shut. The old anger at his father was pushing up and out. The smell of cut wood made his head swim; he felt as if he might fall over. He let his eyes go wide on the ground, on the trampled pine needles, on the dried mud beneath. He needed to regain his balance, his bearing. He'd been foolish charging over here, facing this man old enough to be Julian Martin. (But he wasn't Julian, Dyer told himself. Emphatically not.) Wolfe was the headmaster and could do anything he wanted.

Dyer backed off a step. He moved his attention to the trees surrounding the yard, the sunlight cutting narrowly through new leaves.

"They're good students," Dyer said evenly. "And apart from Sam Rafton, I'd say they're doing the work. But you can't force your own interpretations on them."

"Our president hammers day after day about North Korean pygmy terrorists," Wolfe said. "Congress passes a North Korean Human Rights Act that cuts food aid to the country. U.S. warships loaded with miniaturized, nuke-tipped UAVs bully up to the North Korean coast." He gave his head an angry shake. "Saying anything remotely forgiving about North Korea is a major political act. I know an educator in New York that gets death threats for telling school kids that the U.S. shares the blame for starting the Korean War."

"You'd like me to get death threats?"

Wolfe laughed humorlessly. "George's organization is high-profile. We aren't yet."

George. The guy from the website, from the Choson Coordination and Development Group, Dyer thought. The full name came slowly: George Choe.

"The Britton School has a reputation," Wolfe said, "and it's not for sympathizing with enemy countries. The students will say something. And the press will be there to record it. That's the first step."

"The first?"

Wolfe ignored him: "I won't take over your club meeting on the fifteenth, but I'm keeping an eye on what you're doing."

"They *graduate* in June," said Dyer, but the headmaster had picked up the chain saw and yanked the cord. The teeth spun, and Randy poked his head out the kitchen door.

Wolfe shouted over the blade's wicked hiss: "Be nice to the *Times* reporter when she calls you. Her name is Henrietta Talbot. About your age, but alas, not your type."

By 4:00 that afternoon, the breeze had dropped, but the air had dimmed and turned blue with cold. At 5:00, snow fell. By dinnertime, Britton had an inch, and students ranged out in the main quad to start a snowball fight — their first in weeks — but the stuff was too fluffy to pack. Puffballs of powder sailed back and forth. To Dyer, who'd spent the rest of his day inside the History Department office writing exams, the contours looked beautiful and clean, scallops of white on the steps to Ramm Hall, a haze of flakes in the pour of floodlights.

Battling Wolfe was useless. This fact slowly cleared the gnat-cloud of annoyance and irritation hanging around Dyer's head. He caught some fluffy snow with his bare hands. Maybe he had been a little sensational, lingering over the rumors of cannibalism in the rural areas during the worst of the famine, telling the group that Kim Jong Il kept a harem of girls at various pleasure palaces in the countryside.

Cheap pedagogy. It was a relief, in a way, to have that out. To hear him say it.

Dyer reached Reservoir Road, following its long curve past the dormitories on the southern end of campus. The snow fell gently around him. His footfalls made squeaks on the powder. Bullet gray luminescence filled the evening sky.

But wasn't Wolfe's approach just as cheap? Dyer hadn't been at this job for very long, but demanding specific interpretations of foreign policy from a bunch of high school students seemed to have little to do with education. Likewise, demanding that a teacher be a mouthpiece for a single set of views.

And why pick *him* for the role? Dyer was no power-to-the-people radical — though reading about U.S. history on the Korean peninsula had reacquainted him with how self-interested his own country could be. How — frankly — imperialist. Still, at Oxford he'd written essays expressing smug superiority over a decades-old countercultural movement that Wolfe had been a big part of. Of course, *that* had been about mirroring Phelps, seeking his tutor's approval, setting himself up with an academic advocate. Maybe Wolfe understood this better than Dyer did. And maybe the trustees, and senior faculty like Blanton, would have balked at Wolfe installing some podium-pounding Marxist in the History Department. Maybe Dyer's résumé was the best Wolfe could do.

Dyer told himself that he wouldn't be manipulated. He'd go on just as he had been. If Wolfe wanted to fire him at that year-end review, he'd surely have to come up with a better excuse than Dyer's reluctance to let politics dominate the classroom.

A snowball interrupted his thoughts, a loose one, breaking apart over his shoulder, sluicing his neck with cold granules. Dyer turned around and saw Randy bent to the grass outside one of the dorms on Reservoir Road, trying to pack another.

"I could write you up for that," said Dyer.

"For what?" Randy asked, rising, the snow falling out of his hands. He lifted his chin in the direction of Range Hall. "You visiting someone?"

"No," Dyer said, and turned to go. He had been walking straight for Range, but that was just his usual route home.

Randy jogged after, slipping a little on the sidewalk, spreading his arms for balance. He fell into step just off Dyer's left shoulder, his streetlight shadow falling like a giant kite on the snow.

Dyer stopped and turned. Range Hall stood twenty yards on. He'd seen that Greta's window was lit, her curtains open, and Dyer had decided in an instant that he didn't want to walk by with Randy in tow. He wouldn't be able to resist looking up, or worrying that Greta would hear them through the glass. He wouldn't be as cool, as nonchalant as he'd want to be. Randy would notice.

"So. You and Ms. Salverton, huh? That's the rumor." Randy's nasal, head-cold voice slid through the evening quiet. His nose was still red, and he wore a clown smile, both rows of teeth visible. His nutmeg eyes took Dyer all the way back to L.A. and Jim Simon, Alice's father, Dyer's boss at Virgenes. Jim Simon, by his own admission, was no genius. "Always been a doer," Simon had told Dyer once, gesturing with his thumb at the foundation of a new downtown office building, the biggest deal of his career. His eyes were that same dull tan, his smile just as full-bore and toothy. "Make the deal. Don't fuck around thinking about it."

Randy didn't shift from foot to foot; his gaze didn't falter. He stood like a pylon, dropped from the sky, soldered into place.

"Was there something you wanted to talk about, Randy?"

Randy nodded at Dyer as though agreeing with something. "I wanted to see if I could get caught up for Model UN."

"Fine. Why don't you hang out after class on Monday morning?" Dyer said. "We can talk then."

Randy kept those milky rows of teeth on display, and his arms away from his sides as if ready to block Dyer's path if he moved. Dyer had no idea how to make Randy vanish.

Randy nodded in the direction of Bailey. "We can walk and talk, if that's cool."

So they did, and Dyer avoided looking up at Greta's window, letting the snowflakes melt on his cheeks and forehead. Britton was a small campus, but he and Greta had managed to studiously avoid each other for weeks. Memories of her body, the warm skin at the small of her back, tacky with dried sweat, the rough edge of her teeth, the way she'd bit his lower lip kissing him all those months ago, had been dropping like slides into his dreams, into his distracted, classroom thoughts. Just the other day, in 250, listening to Samantha read aloud her mock proposal for Marshall Plan support, Dyer found himself back under the tree that night in September, knocking Greta's hurt arm, cupping the back of her neck. February doldrums, or just a hormonal pulse. Dyer was desperate for sex.

Randy had guessed right; he had come this way to see if Greta was home, to see if he had the gumption to go inside and knock on her apartment door. But now Dyer could do nothing but pass by, head down at his feet, only half listening to Randy's voice.

Randy blew snot onto the snow. "Headmaster Wolfe put me in your club 'cause I asked him to," he said, wiping his nose with his hand.

Get this kid a tissue. "Is that right?"

"Yeah. My dad tells me that if I don't get into Princeton, I'll owe him this year's tuition. And I'm a fucking long shot."

"You should have asked me."

Randy held his hands high. "I was talking to Headmaster Wolfe, and it just came up."

"Well, we'll make room for you."

"Dad's hard-core about Princeton. There's this huge banner above his desk: PRINCETON."

"Uh-huh."

"It's like the only place in the world. So I can't relax until the letter comes."

Dyer searched for something to say. "A Model UN–football player is a pretty niche applicant, right?"

"I sure as shit hope so. You know how expensive this place is?"

Bailey was in sight, a half a block away, and Dyer picked up his pace.

"Ms. Salverton, huh?" Randy nudged Dyer's arm. "Nice work, partner."

Dyer's reply was immediate and angry: "Drop it, Randy."

"Okay, okay."

They walked in silence. "But tell her to go easy on my midterm grade. That thing fucking killed."

"Randy—"

"She's pretty smokin', Mr. Martin."

Jane came in wearing the scarf, wrapped tightly around her neck, her nose redder than before, her skin more pale. James wanted to ask her how she was feeling, if she'd gotten sicker, but she didn't look at him, not once, as if their talk the previous week had never happened. James palmed his knees, stared at his feet, and reminded himself that he made his own opportunities now.

Randy Holiday kicked James's chair and leaned into view. "Hey, squid."

James looked around him and picked up the new, burdened vibe of the group. It was there in Liem Du's averted face. In Louise Hampton's curled lip. They didn't like having Randy in the room. The football player took a quick tour through Mr. Martin's apartment, checking the view from both windows, the books on the shelves, testing a loose board on the floor with his foot. He was empty-handed—no backpack, notebook, or pen, and he put off what felt to James like a sweaty, locker-room heat. Greg Smile tracked Randy with a steady stare. Chip Lee scraped his chair away from a vacant seat. Did Randy see any of this? He didn't seem to, but then before sitting, as if needing acknowledgment, he passed by James again and pawed his shoulders.

Mr. Martin, leaning over his desk, flipping loose pages, didn't look at Randy. He didn't look at anyone for minutes until Chip Lee said, "Headmaster Wolfe coming tonight?"

"Nope," said Mr. Martin glancing up from his desk. "Change of plan."

And James breathed a sigh of relief. He'd dreaded the stares and scrutiny that would come with his father in the room. James wouldn't even have shown if not for Jane's presentation—he wanted to hear that—and for the pressure he was putting on himself to be strong, forthright, not to care what other people thought.

Jane tapped her fingers on the folder she held in her lap. She sat with her back straight, her head tilted slightly forward. The scarf bulked up to her chin, but a keyhole of skin showed below, in the notched neck of her shirt. James stared at it so long that he didn't notice her closed eyes, her forehead shining with sweat. She was really sick, he thought. Her lips were together; she seemed to be swallowing something. Spit.

Randy took the seat to the left of Chip Lee. He sat in his customary way—his knees apart, his thumbs hooked into the waist of his jeans, his elbows wide. Taking up as much space as possible.

Mr. Martin came over from his desk and handed out two pages, one with committee assignments and another with a handwritten flow chart. James saw his name beside "Disarmament and International Security," Jane's beside "Economic and Financial." The flow chart was crude, a series of boxes strung together with arrows: "roll call" → "set the agenda" → "policy speeches" → "caucusing" → "develop working papers" → "resolutions" → "vote."

"First time for you guys, first time for me," said Mr. Martin, his hands in the air, palms out: defensive. "I'm not pretending to know how this thing'll be run. But here's parliamentary procedure, straight from the instructor's manual." He brandished a page, then began to read: "'Caucusing is a temporary recess in the committee meeting where proposals are drawn up and consensus-building, negotiation, and compromise take place.'" Mr. Martin looked up. "You basically huddle in the hallway with other delegates and whack out a working paper."

"Which is?" asked Greg.

"Glad you asked," said Mr. Martin, and moved a finger down the page. "Working papers consist of major points of agreement between allied nations."

"But you said we don't have any allies," said Randy.

"I said China. Look out for China. And maybe some of the rogue states will want to talk. Syria. Or Sudan."

"When do we give speeches?" asked Louise. "And what's UN-CHR?"

"United Nations Commission on Human Rights. That's your committee. You all have committees. You go and give your speech at the beginning of the session. You, Louise, explain what North Korea thinks about human rights."

"Anti."

"Well, yes, sort of." Mr. Martin read on: "'At some point in the debate, a group of delegates will bring their resolution to the floor of your committee. It will require a two-thirds vote to pass.'"

Through all of this, James felt a pleasant, gathering anticipation, as when the lights dimmed in a theater before a movie. Jane opened the folder on her knees and pulled out a short stack of note cards. She pressed them together by the edges. In a moment Mr. Martin would be done, and he'd call on her to give her presentation. James shifted and settled into his chair. He'd listen to every word, as if she were talking only to him, a short speech about everything she was going through.

She kept sniffling, swallowing with a wince as if her throat hurt, and every so often touching the middle of her chest.

Finally the moment came. "Jane, you're presenting tonight, yes?" Mr. Martin asked. She nodded, and he clapped his hands together. "Good. Juche. Let's have it."

Jane stood slowly, scraping the chair back with her calf.

She kept her face tucked into her note cards. "Juche is an untranslatable word," she began, her voice weak and raspy. She cleared her throat and winced again. "Sorry," she said, looking up. "I sort of have a cold."

"You and everyone else," Mr. Martin said. "Need a rain check?"

She shook her head. "I'd rather get it over with." She took a deep breath and continued: "The closest we come in English is 'self-reliance' or 'independence.' But the North Koreans use it in a much more all-encompassing way. It originated under Kim Il Sung in the fifties as a form of nationalism. It turned into something like a religion for the North Korean people after the war. It's the most important idea in their life. Everything they do boils down to Juche. They want to be independent from every other country in the world. They want to be entirely self-sufficient. They believe that their leader is entirely right about everything, that he is the brain of the country and they are the limbs, the arms and the legs. Excuse me." She blew her nose into a tissue she pulled out of the pocket of her jeans. She wiped her nose and sniffled again.

"North Koreans say things like 'A person must have Juche fully implanted to be happy.' 'Juche must unite the mind and body.' 'We must live in the spirit of Juche.' The Tower of the Juche Idea in Pyongyang is as tall as the Washington Monument. The roof of the nuclear power facility in Yongbyon is painted with a Juche slogan.

"In Juche, the right mindset will lead to the right action. If you believe in your independence and self-reliance—your ability to take care of yourself—you will act in the proper way. No matter what."

Jane blotted a bead of sweat on her forehead, then lowered her hand to the center of her chest. She was staring hard at the index card in her other hand. "With Juche, you think with your whole body. This is why North Koreans are so impulsive. They locate the brain right here." She tapped her chest gently. "They don't divide rationality and emotions. Mind and body."

When Jane's gaze came up and flashed like a minnow, silvery and quick, from Randy's face to James's and settled there, James felt a snow-globe calm in his head that he hadn't felt in as long as he could remember. Slackening limbs, heavy with what? Jane pushed out her lips, as if she wanted to give him the words. She let her hand drop.

He caught Randy's open, inclusive gaze. His centimeter nod. James glanced back, and Jane met his stare with her own.

They were trying to tell him something.

"They don't think," she said to him, straight at him, using the plummeting, bell-like tones of apology. "They just do."

Through the grid-wire porthole in the door, Dyer watched Greta Salverton rack test tubes upside down on needle prongs, a stack of exams on her left, sneakers hooked around the legs of a stool. *They don't think. They just do.* A seventeen-year-old girl's reductive assessment of the North Korean national character had started to seem, in the hours since the students had cleared out of his apartment, like words to live by. Dyer's hand found the knob. Greta's head came up. Dyer walked halfway into the room and stood beside a table with a sink in it, close enough to Greta to use a gentle voice, to gauge how welcome he was, to watch her brown eyes watch him through her plastic safety goggles.

She started. "I'd shake your hand, but I've got hydrobromic acid on my gloves." Greta held the pink gloves up, rubber mitts with dry whorled ridges.

"I saw you in here."

"I've been running through this experiment for class tomorrow. Finally got it to work." She peeled the pink gloves, turning the contaminated things inside out, giving her puckered fingers air. She tipped her head to the window that let out onto the path. She pushed the goggles up into her hair, flaring her bangs. "I saw you outside, and thought, I bet he's coming in."

"I should be working too. I've got tons, but . . . I needed a walk."

"I bet he's coming in to talk to me."

"I saw you were working late."

"And I thought, I've got acid all over my hands."

"I could walk you back to Bailey," said Dyer.

"Pretty presumptuous, right? I mean, I don't see everyone at Britton, and think, He's going to touch me."

Dyer waited. The fluorescent sizzled above him. "There's been the one time," he said.

"And not since," said Greta. "Zero human contact. Which makes it weirder that I thought you were going to."

She'd forgotten the handshake at that New Year's party in Boston. Or maybe she was ignoring it. "We could get it over with then. Rebreak the ice," Dyer said, the words glossing out between his teeth.

"Terrific. Since I'd already been thinking that's what you came in here to do."

Dyer crossed the rest of the room, positioning himself on the opposite side of her black veneer table, its surface glossy with chemical-proof laminate. The test tubes stood on their needle racks, and the water-thickened student problem sets lay in a stack. Dyer reached his hands over the pile of inside-out gloves and sandwiched Greta's hand between his own.

He'd touched her before — he'd run his hands under her shirt and around her back, and he'd felt the thin struts of her rib cage — so this was easy, almost natural.

"I could walk you back to Bailey," he said quietly, knowing that she'd say no. Sensing it in the saccharine lab air and in the hard edge of the table cutting into his waist. But there *was* the possibility, thanks to Jane Hirsch and her echo of what Alice's father had told him last summer: *Don't fuck around thinking about it.* Thanks to his impulsive decision to leave his paper grading and head out for a post-sign-in walk around the Britton campus, passing by the chem lab at Ramm Hall just in case. Sex — not now, but at some point — made his palm warm. He kept his grip firm enough to hold her, not too firm to stop her from pulling away if she wanted to.

"I've got another hour here," she said, sliding her hand from between his and patting the stack of problem sets. "Two. But thanks."

SPRING TERM

7

March

WHEN DYER HEARD the kid belch, a deep stomachy sound to his right, he closed his eyes and thought hard about the student-made, chemical compound models on the windowsill of Greta Salverton's bedroom—hub-and-spoke radials of red and blue foam balls on toothpicks, their labels reading FREON, MELATONIN, CALCIUM CARBONATE.

"Wait, wait," Greta had whispered the night before, landing a hand on his back. He'd wanted to wait, wanted the moment to last indefinitely, its giddy relief stretching into the night, but blood had been rushing through him, and he'd lost feeling below the knees, a sure sign that he was almost there. So he pulled his stare off the freckles scattered between Greta's teacup breasts, the damp skin flashing in the hollow of her neck. Still moving, still gripping the stitched corner of mattress where the sheet had come loose, Dyer turned his head and found the models on her sill. Their satisfying asymmetries, their toylike clutter, their primary-color good cheer, gave Dyer a few minutes of delay.

Now, standing in line at the registration desk in the banquet hall of the Crawford Hotel in New York, needing distraction from the groans coming out of the teenager in the corner, Dyer saw the models again. They brought Greta into the margins of his head. He saw the compound models, not *her,* and could resist wondering whether she'd come down from Britton tonight.

Okay, she'd said. *Maybe.*

He'd gone walking the night before (a habit he was getting into), out into the granite cold. Greta's light was on, she'd been sitting at her desk, her head bent, her hair bobby-pinned out of her face, chewing on the corner of her thumb. He'd stood outside where she could see him until she came to the window, and pushed it up, and whispered, "You must be freezing." He moved quickly through Range House, past the closed doors of the girls' rooms, up to Greta's apartment on the second floor. Every step sent wattage through him, the same shooting electricity he'd felt on his first date with Alice.

After sex, after two and a half hours of sleep, Greta nudged him. "What?" he'd wondered lazily, dreamily, rolling toward her, and running his hand along her arm. "Use the fire door in the back," she whispered. "Sorry. Eight-thirty class. Do you mind?" Her words forming, dissolving, and his head not clear of sleep. Dyer folded the blanket back; the cold air settled onto him. He didn't mind. He *should* go out the back, he should leave now and be discreet about it. He had eight kids to get to New York in the morning.

Groping for his pants, he knocked over her water glass. She let out a loud breath, a sick, tugging, regretful sound that landed on Dyer like a punch. "Sorry," he whispered through the dark.

Then he whispered again: "Come to New York this weekend."

She propped herself upright, pinning the sheet in her armpit. Take it back, Dyer thought. Say, *Joke.* Say, *Kidding.* His eyes dropped to her soft cheeks, her bare, bell-shaped shoulders, then wandered around to other things. The collated handouts on her desk. The books on her shelves, arranged by size, a perfect declension of spines. The morning's outfit, folded slacks and turtleneck sweater, neat and ready on the desk chair. And yet, Dyer thought, she can be impulsive too. Following him outside at Dean O'Brien's party. Or tonight, bringing him up to her room.

And she slept with Wolfe. The sentence ambled out of the darkness like a scurvy drunk to rough him up.

"Okay," she said. "Maybe."

In the Crawford banquet hall, the kid in the corner groaned and retched. One or two times already, as the registration line inched along, Dyer had noticed the kid's pink scalp, visible through his downy crewcut, his knees tucked into his chest, his yo-yoing Adam's apple. Dyer wanted to get away, but he couldn't drop his place in line. He'd been waiting to register for twenty minutes, and there were only a handful of teachers ahead of him: a thick man with silver hair, wearing a navy corduroy suit, holding a rolled conference brochure in his fist like a nightstick, and three middle-aged women sharing sections of the newspaper.

Not mine. Dyer kept his gaze rooted on the wispy neck hairs of the teacher in front of him. None of the dozens of smartly dressed kids flea-hopping around the banquet hall were Dyer's. There were masses of them, teenagers in blazers wheeling their suitcases to and fro, girls in skirts and flats dumping backpacks on the floor, full-throated teachers yelling at them: "Stay together." "Sit right here." "Don't move." So much noise, so many people. Dyer felt an unpleasant rattling in his ears as if small bones had come loose. His eight were still down in the lobby, staying, God willing, right where he left them.

But who knew? By now, they could be scattered all over New York. Dyer was the only chaperone for the Britton team, a violation of the rules laid out in the IMUNI teacher handbook. He didn't actually care if Greg or Sam or whoever disappeared into the city for a few hours, but he did want company, wanted Greta's company, and the rules mattered because the rules said he should have someone with him.

That was supposed to be Wolfe, but so far, Wolfe was a no-show. Dyer had heard that Campaign Britton was pushing for $1.2 million by graduation and was nowhere close. Wolfe would be working the phones, throwing dinners in Boston, letter-writing, flattering VIP alumni. Two weeks ago, Dyer caught the headmaster hurrying along the hallway in Peabody and asked if anyone would be helping him look after the team. Wolfe cleared his throat and spoke two carefully enunciated sentences: "I'll be coming. I'll help."

"You know if your dad is planning to show up?" Dyer had asked James at 7:30 that morning. James had been the only student waiting beside the Britton van, a Ford Econoline with loose steering and the candied air of spilled soda. They got inside for warmth. James shrugged and bounced his back lightly against the front seat, flipping the visor down and blinking into the mirror. Dyer started the engine, and they waited for the vents to cough up heat. The light from the east stalked in. Dyer still had Greta on him, the old perfume musk of her sheets rising off his skin and leaking through his collar, a heady mix of dried flowers and sweat. As the first students arrived, trudging out of the dark like vampires, Dyer lifted the inside of his wrist and licked the skin, releasing the smell, and he thought, briefly (how unexpected the mind is, how counterintuitive) of Alice. *Alice.* That artifact name out of his past, like the street he grew up on, or the name of the long-dead family cat.

Dyer took another half step toward the registration desk, and the kid by the wall started to groan again.

"Not mine," Dyer said out loud.

"I wouldn't claim him if he was. Were," said the teacher ahead of him in line. Dyer made one last attempt to put himself back in Greta's room, her shoulder notched under his arm, a strand of her hair in his mouth. But then the kid in the corner let out a deep, stomachy heave, vomit splattered on the carpet, and Greta and her spiky compounds fled. "Jesus," said Dyer, under his breath.

The stink clouded over, humid and enveloping. The teacher in the blue suit directed an ugly stare to their right. "Bet he's sick on Ritalin," he said. "Someone's going around selling them. If they take too many at a time, they puke." Dyer looked. The boy was on his knees, his glasses down to the tip of his nose, shaking his head, reading the star pattern of orange vomit like a map. Dyer tightened his throat, plugged his own bitter, rising bile. He caught fragments out of the din in the room:

"Who blew? Ian? Did Ian blow?"

"Nice one, Ian."

"Aw, man. That is so nasty."

The lobby was a refugee camp — glum, hungry-looking teenagers everywhere lounging on their suitcases, neck-bobbing to headphones, thumbing their cell phones to death. The hotel staff — porters, concierge, greeters, door holders — used the maple reception desk as a barricade, not just against the kids, but against the angry line of teachers waiting to get their room keys, the kinking, zigzagging line twice as long as the one Dyer had just waited in.

The veteran teachers, Dyer noticed, wore foam earplugs against the sounds that bulleted around the room, ricocheting off the marble floor, the marble columns, and the mirrored ceiling, shaking those loose bones in Dyer's ear like dice. Teenagers squeaked their shoes across the shiny floor; teenagers smacked down playing cards; teenagers sprinted for closing elevator doors, shrieking at one another to hold them. The energy was convulsive, spastic; a boy spiraled a leather penny loafer like a football over Dyer's head.

"Some guy from Brookline High just tried to sell me drugs," said Liem Du, pulling his earphones down to his neck. He stood alone, surrounded by bags. "Three pills for thirty bucks."

"Where's everyone?" asked Dyer.

"Bathroom," said Liem. "I think. Did you hear me? Did you get our room keys?"

"How would I have the keys?" Dyer asked, nodding at the line to check in.

"Don't yell at me. You said don't move."

"And you're the only one who heard me. Get in that line. I have to find people."

Don't bother, Dyer told himself, scanning the crowd. The Crawford was enormous, the ground floor covering half a city block, encompassing three restaurants, a bar and cocktail lounge, a row of souvenir shops, and a hairdresser and newsstands by the elevators.

Every inch of space streamed with noisy, scrambling teenagers. Had this been their plan all along? Get to New York, wait till Dyer wasn't looking, and beat it? *Oh well.*

"You can't leave us for an hour without food." It was Randy's voice, coming from behind Dyer. "Cuts down on our diplomacy skills." Randy, Jane, and James stepped over luggage, picking their way around the card game on the floor. Randy had a plastic shopping bag in his hand; Jane blew a pink, veiny gum bubble.

"Everyone else is in the bathroom?" Dyer asked.

"Some dude booted upstairs," said Greg Smile, suddenly standing behind Dyer. *Where'd he come from?* "You were there. I can, like, smell it on you."

"How about Sam and Louise?" Dyer asked.

"Making out in the bar," Chip Lee said, materializing from the other direction.

Dyer pulled a stack of white stickers from the manila registration folder. "Your nametags," he said, holding them out. "Wear them at all times, they told me to tell you." Eventually, James took the tags out of his hand.

The Crawford was nothing like the Mark. That was James's first, disappointed thought when they arrived. The circular drive was too mirrored and grand. The carpets in the entryway were straight out of generic hotel supply, red polyester edged with rubber. Through the spinning doors, a flush of orange, rusty light colored the marbled lobby (which lacked the pristine white glow of the Mark), and the furniture looked faux-antique, claw-foot chairs and upright settees. Beyond the front room, there wasn't a dim, quiet spot anywhere, not one corner to sit down and talk. And they might talk, now that Jane wasn't ignoring him, now that he, she, and Randy had formed some kind of bloclike affiliation, some weird clique.

For weeks they'd been sitting together in Model UN and 250, Jane in the middle, James and Randy on each side. Jane routinely smiled at James, giving him that inclusive look she'd debuted during her presentation on Juche. And Randy no longer pummeled him like a football dummy whenever they crossed paths. Were they his friends? With no other candidates — Volker didn't even say hello anymore — the tempting answer was yes.

Jane and Randy had begun lingering by the classroom door so they could all walk out together. They'd even started joining him for lunch, in the lower left quadrant of Commons, at an outpost table near the teachers. Randy did most of the talking, mimicking something Sam Rafton had said in class, or reporting his bench-press max, which climbed by the week. James, dumbstruck, could barely eat; being so near Jane was some kind of dream, but Randy queered it. She smiled at his round, thick face. She looked impressed when he bit into his third meatball sub. Had they or hadn't they? The falling-anvil question hung frozen over James's head.

He pinned his hopes on the Crawford. In the weeks leading up to the conference, James recalled the syrupy taste of rum, the crease Jane's boots made in the soft part of her calf, the light pressure of her foot on his knee. He thought: Get to the hotel, lose Randy, sit her down, get the information out.

But from the moment Mr. Martin squeezed the van through midtown traffic into the Crawford's turnaround, James knew that the place was wrong and that Randy was going to be hard to lose. He sat behind James in the van, his face bobbing over James's shoulder; he jammed himself into the revolving doors, crushing James's heel. Jane stuck close as well, but with Randy around, James couldn't say anything to her. Mr. Martin went to register upstairs, and Randy wanted to go "case the place." They did this together, James and Jane and Randy, checking out the gift shops, the magazine racks, the breakfast buffet, the shoeshine and manicurist. They crossed through the cocktail lounge and saw Sam and Louise making out on one of the banquettes. Sam had one hand on Louise's stomach, his chapped fingers tucked into the waistline of her jeans. Randy nudged Jane in the soft part of her side, at the base of her ribs, and grinned with both rows of teeth. Jane visored her hand over her eyes. James took it all in, thinking, a nudge isn't proof of anything, knowing that it was.

Passing out of the cocktail bar, too shy to look at Jane straight, James blurted the question: "What's Louise doing with Sam, anyway?"

"Working on her self-esteem." Jane's gaze slid over to meet Randy's. "He tells her how beautiful she is. He *cries* for her. He wrote her name on his bicep."

Randy rolled his eyes and scratched his armpit.

James shuffled the nametags he'd taken from Mr. Martin and handed Randy his: RANDY HOLIDAY, BRITTON SCHOOL, DPRK. Randy peeled the back and stuck it to his forehead.

"Can you really smell the vomit on me?" Mr. Martin asked.

"No," said Greg, nodding yes, sticking his own nametag to the hem of his shirt.

Randy turned to Jane with the tag stuck to his forehead; "Oh," she said, staring blankly. "Funny."

James flipped through the rest of the nametags, found Jane's. He peeled off the back and, turning quickly, pancaked it on Jane's shirt, high up, around her collarbone. He didn't touch anything soft — her breast was at least an inch south — but he'd been close. His fingers tripped over a knot beneath the skin, the titanium screws in her collarbone.

Jane didn't flinch or pull back. She took the sticker uncomplainingly, almost stoically. Without looking at James, she flattened its curling edges and coughed lightly.

"You cop a feel?" Randy wanted to know, nudging James off his feet.

"Says here," Mr. Martin said, reading a schedule, "buses leave for opening ceremonies at three. So once we get room keys, we'll drop our stuff, and —"

"This line is so not moving," Liem called over.

James still had violent fantasies. He imagined Randy's head cracking on the marble floor, the slippery blood pooling out. He'd already knocked Randy over once; he could do it again. In the off-season, Randy had filled out even more, the broad bridge of his nose going soft, his pants stretching tight against his bulky legs. Hit him low, below his center of gravity, and he'd fall harder, heavier.

You've changed, Jane had said to him, and he wanted it to be true.

Mr. Martin continued through the schedule for the next two days, but James didn't listen. He didn't look at Jane. He searched the faces in the crowded lobby, checking their nametags for the countries they represented. Not one ally in the room. James's mind went to his speech, the one he'd prepared for the Disarmament and International Security Committee. He let the blustery sentences come:

The Democratic People's Republic of Korea will not sacrifice our sovereignty.

We will fight before giving up our weapon programs or assenting to international inspections.

Our military is the fiercest, most highly trained in the world.

Provoke us at your peril.

It took Dyer a moment to place the name stuck to the breast pocket of the boy's shirt. A boy with shaggy hair that swallowed his ears and fell like a bird's wing over half his face, wearing a tightly cut blue blazer with brass buttons and a pink dress shirt, tucked snug into jeans.

He leaned against the wall talking to two guys in khakis and suede oxford lace-ups, each with a tiny flag pin on his blazer lapel. The delegation from Lexington Prep, representing Burkina Faso.

"You're Henry Fieldspar," said Dyer. No one heard him. "Hey," he said louder. "Henry."

Henry's hand came out smoothly, the motion as greased and immediate as a politician's. Dyer wasn't wearing a nametag, so Henry couldn't know who he was.

Dyer took his hand. "I teach at Britton."

"No shit?" Henry's hand squeezed his a fraction harder. He flipped his hair out of his face, and it slid, strand by strand, back.

"I've heard about you," said Dyer.

"What have you heard?"

"You were kicked out."

Henry pushed himself upright against the wall, as if he were proud to hear it. "Where's your team?" he asked.

"Around. Upstairs in their rooms."

"Headmaster Wolfe here? I'd like to say hey."

"What committee are you in? I'll tell him where to find you."

"World Bank."

"Good," said Dyer. "Burkina Faso, huh?"

"Fourth poorest nation in the world," said Henry. "Per capita. That kid James here too?" But before Dyer could answer, Henry nudged one of the other guys: "*Hola*, Nairobi." Three girls walked by, toting Barneys bags. "Heck yes."

Dyer held up his hand in a half wave and walked away, resituating the strap of his weekend bag on his shoulder. Headmaster and expellee to meet — should be entertaining. *Cheap pedagogy.* The line still nagged at him, as did all Wolfe's noise about press interest. No reporters had been in touch.

That was just as well. The kids were reasonably ready to play-act North Korean delegates, but there was no guarantee that they'd parrot Wolfe's message. Dyer wasn't even sure *he* could. *North Korea is a serious alternative to the global capitalist . . . something.* Granted, this morning's headlines were the scariest of the year. Surveillance satellites had photographed an explosion in northern North Korea, and intelligence analysts were calling it a nuclear test. Overnight the Pentagon had ordered B-1 and B-52 bombers to Guam, and had given the go-ahead for additional naval exercises in the Sea of Japan. One twitch from the North Korean army, and Wolfe could be proven right about war by spring.

Dyer stuffed himself into a boy-crowded, fart-gassy elevator. Things had turned tense between him and the headmaster since their talk in his backyard, and the less they spoke the worse it got. Wolfe came into Commons, and Dyer set his fork down and tracked him like a target, imagined Wolfe dropping another memo into his lap: *Services terminated.* But the fear wasn't just about losing his job. The fear was irrational, atavistic, slinging up out of his childhood. Dyer had never been to a shrink, but he could anticipate the analysis. Need to win commendation from older men stemming from significant developmental absence.

Dyer breathed through his mouth and stared at the illuminated floor numbers. Let's consider this problem from a happier angle, he thought. *I'm sleeping with his ex- . . . his ex-whatever.* Dyer didn't know anything beyond what Chris Nolan had told him all those months ago: Wolfe and Greta had had an affair. Was she bored? Or had she actually fallen for him? He should ask her. He should find out, and, sure, the man could always fire him on a pretext, or saddle him with a killing load of work — Wolfe was his *boss,* and that wasn't going to change — but once Dyer knew the whole story, the gory Greta-Wolfe arc, maybe then he could finally get over at least this part of his anxiety. Pose the question casually, and Greta might spill the whole mess. Get it out. Dyer's confidence would stiffen like iron in his blood.

New York's elephantine façade lumbered grayly through the bus window. The sidewalks clogged with people; cabs braided into the strobing yellows and reds of taillights and the ghost steam from grates. James had been trying to resist thinking about the future, the pending blank of his life past May, but watching this scroll of foreign scenery he started ticking through the colleges he'd be hearing from soon. Columbia was one (a "lock" according to Mr. Greenley), but the truth was he didn't really care where he wound up. Home had already become a figment, a label applied to wherever he happened to be. Smithson Way, Weiss, Knoxville — college would be more of the same, life like a series of brief touchdowns, a flat stone skipping across water. What if he never spoke to his father again? The boring pain in his chest surprised him, but it didn't last. Their life together had already ended. He channeled himself onto that sidewalk, into the body of a determined pedestrian, into the man in the back seat of a cab talking on a cell phone, craning, staring hard through the windshield. The pain in James's chest wormed down to nothing. They reached Times Square. Beneath the LED screens, the lashing, cascading color, the scrolling headlines (ATOMIC ACTIVITY IN NORTH KOREA: PENTAGON MOBILIZES TROOPS), a bald man in robes sat cross-legged on a pink, embroidered blanket spread out on the sidewalk, his eyes shut.

"Dude, you want some of these?"

The question came from two rows up. A kid with wraparound sunglasses and braces was talking to Sam Rafton, holding a closed fist over the top of the seat.

Sam tapped the guy's knuckles, then flicked through the capsules in his palm. "Tylenol."

"Incorrect."

Sam flicked again. "How much?"

"Three for twenty."

"Whatever."

"Okay, four."

"These the ones making you sick?"

"Take 'em one at a time, and they won't."

Turning back to the window, James caught Jane's profile in the reflection; she sat one row behind, her head tipped into the glass, her eyes trailing the scenery as it slipped by.

She doesn't know about the papers.

The thought brought James upright. He remembered the way she made fun of Sam Rafton at lunch. "I bet he's the dumbest kid here," she said once. "You can see it in that retard smile." And Randy said: "Second dumbest." Trying to self-denigrate. Meaning to charm.

She doesn't know about the *papers*. Sunlight flashed on her reflected profile. *She doesn't know about the cheating.*

What had Randy said, all the way back in September? *I need some books to read,* he'd said. *Only the grade-A stuff.*

He probably waved that copy of *Tender Is the Night* in her face like a flag.

She couldn't possibly have been fooled this whole time. She couldn't possibly have thought he was some kind of closet reader, some hyperliterate jock. No way she'd be that gullible. Right?

The knot of traffic slipped, and the bus lumbered ahead. Sam handed over a folded twenty. They turned left on First Avenue and the UN rose up on the right, the thin windowed tower of the Secretariat, the row of member-nation flags, the breeze-bothered East River beyond. Excitement trickled through him, burbling and tumbling along his spine. James would come out clean; she'd see that he'd had to write the papers, that Randy hadn't given him a choice. He rubbed his fingers together on his right hand, running over the place he'd touched the screw. It'd be clear who had done the cheating, the deceiving, who was to blame. He'd tell her.

"Kill me," said Chip Lee midway through the Economic and Financial Committee head's speech, and Dyer didn't shush him. The opening plenary ceremony had run over an hour already and showed no signs of winding down. The speeches were endless, the committee heads and conference organizers — power-drunk college kids — followed one after another, each sticking to the same script:

"I remember when I was in your . . ."

"I'm honored to be addressing . . ."

". . . truly learn something about the world . . ."

Their voices waved out into the conical, cathedral space of the UN General Assembly, breaking over the heads of the fidgety teenagers at the member-nation desks.

"I stand today on the bedrock of peace, in the hallowed halls of international cooperation," intoned one reedy undergraduate — the conference's secretary-general. Call it what you want, thought Dyer, watching a cluster of teenagers at the Germany desk swat one another with programs.

The head of the Commission on Refugees, dressed in a boxy,

double-breasted suit, with pomade-slick hair, spoke in crowded South Boston–accented phrases, scattered with gulping pauses: "We move as exemplars through . . . an anxious moment in history. Diplomacy offers the last . . . best chance for survival in a world of . . . uncompromising power and military might."

No one seemed to be listening. Not the boys over at the Australia desk playing paper football. Not the girls thumb-wrestling at the Mexico desk. Not Dyer's own students. Greg Smile and Chip Lee were asleep, Chip's head folded down on his neck, Greg's tipping tenderly into Chip's shoulder.

South Boston ended his speech, and another began: "The United Nations shines a beacon of peace into a gloom of tyranny, oppression, and violence."

"That's us he's talking about," said Liem. "We're the gloom."

Dyer enjoyed the scenery as long as he could, the spoked sunburst on one wall, the monster blue amoeba on another. The General Assembly walls themselves, an oddly cheap-looking veneer of veined wood, converged upward, like the inside of a witch's hat. But soon he slumped in his seat just as Chip and Greg, the two students nearest him, had; he watched dozens of others seated around him at the green-topped desks work their thumbs across the buttons of their cell phones.

James bent forward, his arms crossed between his knees. He kept turning and looking down the row of seats, toward Jane Hirsch. Dyer thought of a girl in his tenth-grade biology class he'd briefly dated. Amy something. They'd parked in the lot of the Episcopal church near his mother's house and kissed with such vacuum force that Dyer's lips had been purple and swollen for days afterward. His mother asked him if someone had punched him in the mouth, and Dyer told her yes. Jeremy King, he said; they'd been wrestling. Nearly ten years later, Dyer could still remember the angled lace fringe of Amy's bra, the insolvable problem of the clasp, the way his hand had covered her breast like a tarp thrown over a piece of furniture.

James gave Jane a magnetized, stuck-fast stare. Poor guy, Dyer thought. James was a kid who deserved the full menu: grades, friends, a girl, bruised lips he couldn't account for. But Dyer took in the problem at a glance. Jane's own stare went from James, down the aisle, toward Randy.

Randy lolled in his seat, one big leg blocking the aisle.

Outside, Dyer's group gathered on the concrete terrace in front of the General Assembly building, waiting to be loaded back into the buses. Nearby, some girls sitting on the concrete barricades placidly smoked their cigarettes; down on the curb, the dreadlocked driver with the bandanna tied around his neck dozed against the door of the school bus. Dyer beckoned Greg and Chip closer and started a head count.

Three whip cracks perforated the broad calm of First Avenue.

The echoes turned three shots into six. Dyer's students froze. He turned around.

A short Asian man with a dirty satchel slung across his body stood in the middle of the Peace Garden, a wad of what looked like flyers in his fist. He flung them into the air. They floated and sailed around him, a few borne away on the breeze.

Dyer felt an unpleasant shock: in the other hand the man held a small, black handgun, aimed down at the grass.

The man reached inside his satchel and pitched more flyers toward the crowd on the terrace. He took a step toward them, only a hundred yards off. Dyer felt rooted to the spot, still putting together what he was seeing. The man lifted the gun. Someone yelped in the block of students and teachers emerging from the tented visitors' entrance. Someone let out a bottle-rocket scream.

Dyer dropped into a crouch as three more shots broke through the air above him. Those are *bullets.* That guy is *shooting into the crowd.* Dyer tried to spot each of his students, sure one was down and bleeding on the concrete. Jane was nearby, on her hands and knees, Sam and Greg were pressed against the security fence, trying to see what was going on. The rest had been around him a second ago, but now the crowd was swarming toward the sidewalk, bottlenecking at the security gate, bodies starting to get packed in.

Dyer tried to move toward the street, but a formation of black-suited security officers in sunglasses were pushing through the crowd near him, pushing past the fractured brass globe on its ivory pedestal, across the terrace toward the Peace Garden. The lead man stiff-armed a boy off his feet; another boy and a girl went down with him, crying out. Dyer was crushed against the blue barrier fence, the steel tube cutting into his waist. The officers vaulted it and scrambled down the embankment, their handguns unholstered — heavy, long-barreled Glocks, dull in the sunlight. They were aiming at the man. They were shouting at him to drop his weapon.

Dyer stopped trying to get away and watched. The man wore a navy zip jacket and loose blue pants flapping gently against his legs in the river's breeze. Fixing his face forward, he let his gun fall to the grass. The security men were still shouting, their voices overlapping, their arms ramrod straight. The man raised one hand, slowly, above his head.

"They're going to shoot him," someone said loudly, right in Dyer's ear.

With the other hand, the Asian man reached into his satchel for a third time.

James couldn't pick whole words out of the shrill voices around him. Something had happened, but his senses weren't working properly, not after that endless opening ceremony, all those pointless speeches. The whole time he'd done nothing except watch Jane watch Randy, grimacing, as if she wanted to put her gaze somewhere else but couldn't. The sight left his brain dull and blunt with discouragement. Jane actually *liked* Randy. The way she offered that stare, however reluctantly; the way she waited for Randy to pass it back: this James had watched for an hour and a half, doubting his plan to tell her about the cheating, thinking, *Too late.* Too late to tell Jane anything that'll change her mind.

Bodies herded him toward the street, away from the UN building. People started to push harder, some girls crowding in on his shoulder, warm breath on the back of his neck, one boy ribbing him hard with his elbow. A low, harmonized wail came at him from the side.

But he'd tell Jane anyway. He would tell her before he lost the nerve. Force her attention one last time. Give up his only secret and spend whatever cheap hope he'd been hoarding since November.

He tried to turn around. Someone kneed him from behind; a fist lodged in the middle of his back, pushing. "Go, go, go, keep moving." This came from a bearded, balding teacher, white spit in the corners of his mouth.

What's going on?

The crowd had moved him only a few yards from the group, but he couldn't see anyone. Then he spotted Chip Lee's buzzcut a few heads over to his left.

James shouted the question.

"Someone shot at us," said Chip calmly. "You didn't hear it?"

James did his best to look around. One girl was crying; one guy seemed to be saying "fuck" over and over through an excited smile. The bodies were pushing together. A girl's hair brushed James's face. She stepped on his heel, and he stumbled, nearly went down. *Someone shot at us.* Really? Was anyone hit? But he couldn't look, only blunder along toward the street, alert now, carefully keeping his feet under him, stuttering baby steps moving him forward.

And then he wasn't moving at all. There was a jam up ahead, and someone in a blue uniform, a cop maybe, struggled to get the sliding gate open, trying to move students clear from its track.

A sheet of paper flapped through the air above his head. Two pages lay underfoot. Tracing paper it looked like, onionskin, thin, nearly translucent. James couldn't bend to pick one up — he was squeezed upright — but by squirming his arm free, he could reach for the one floating in air. He missed, someone gave him a solid push, and he had to grab the shoulders of the guy in front of him to keep from falling. Eyes down, he could see that the pages, half-shredded by feet, carried printed text and a flag, one James easily recognized: the broad red stripe and the swallowed red star.

The cop got the gate open, and the mass lurched hard. Some bodies went down to James's left. The crowd cratered in on top of them. Frightened by the screaming he heard, James focused on staying upright. Up ahead he saw a familiar head buoyed in the sea of heads, a profile he recognized, that rough, stubbly chin, and shaggy hair, longer now than he remembered it, slashing across his face. Henry Fieldspar stood still as the herd of students broke around him. James was elbowed and shoved in his direction.

A security officer with a plastic wire coiling out of his ear shouted something at Dyer, gesturing him toward the crowd clogged up by the narrow exit gate. But people were already backing up to where Dyer stood, and now there was no reason to move.

The shooter lay on the grass, on his stomach, his arms twisted around to his back. A security officer had his knee between his shoulder blades, cuffing him. The man had dropped the gun, but that hadn't stopped the officer from tackling him from behind. The sound had been like luggage landing in a heap.

And the others were still aiming at him. One of the officers kicked his handgun across the lawn. Another spoke intently into his sleeve.

The human traffic was closing in, and Dyer moved along the security fence, flanking the Peace Garden. As best he could, Dyer kept to the edge of the crowd. Pages of thin paper had drifted against the fence, a few within in arm's reach. The breeze swept one up, and Dyer snatched it out of the air.

He held the flyer flat and stared down into the North Korean flag, reading words printed in all caps: SANCTIONS FROM THE UN BRING DEVASTATION TO THE PEOPLE OF KOREA. IMPERIAL-IST AGGRESSION WILL CAUSE 3 MILLION SERVANTS OF THE GREATEST GENERAL KIM JONG IL TO STRIKE WITH JUCHE UNITED IN THEIR HEARTS AND BODIES. NO ENEMY IS SAFE!!!

· · ·

The police descended on First Avenue in seconds, suddenly, dozens of them, shouting orders, hustling kids into buses, waving the drivers out along a cordoned route down 47th. More cops diverted traffic south of the UN, emptying the entire avenue.

James and Henry were herded into bus 3. A few kids still looked scared — some had their heads tucked between their knees — but most jostled for views out the windows, tumbling down the aisle as the bus launched away from the curb, getting up, scrambling, taking open-mouthed, ravenous breaths, fogging the glass.

Someone shouted: "Anybody get hit?"

"Kidding me? Blood everywhere."

"Wrong."

"Your ass. I fucking saw it. Some teacher just whipped a gun out and started shooting."

"A terrorist, stupid. North Korean."

"The letter's pretty convincing," said Henry, taking the seat next to James. "But let's hope Georgetown doesn't follow up with a call to your dad. They do, we're fucked."

An ambulance passed James's window, and he tried to follow its progress, but there was no view out the rear of the bus.

"Wrote the letter yourself I'm assuming. Forged the signature?"

James shook his head.

Henry shrugged. "Okay, good. Good answer."

Three guys pulled their shirts over their faces, Palestinian-style, and mock-shot one another in the aisle, collapsing across seats.

"Fuck *off*," Henry said to a guy leaning across his lap, trying to look out the window.

James rubbed his closed eyes, watched stardust screen across his lids.

"Your dad's a bloodthirsty fucker," Henry went on. "I guessed he wouldn't actually write me a letter. But I knew Jane could get you to ask for one anyway — pussy-struck as you were likely to be. Then I get this envelope and it's got two things in it. One," said Henry, holding up a finger. "Letter of circumstances. Two" — another finger — " 'Dear Henry, I'm fucking a football player. Let's stay friends. Kisses, Jane.' "

James looked at Henry for the first time since he'd sat down. "She wrote that?"

"I'm paraphrasing." Henry rapped the back of the seat in front of them. The kid turned around. "You're listening. Fucking stop."

They were back in midtown traffic. The girl across the aisle was holding her camera phone up to the window, snapping shots of Broadway marquees.

"So, I'm hoping to get a look at this kid Randy," said Henry. He landed a punch on James's upper arm; James didn't flinch, but he felt the blood gathering, starting to sting. "Think I can take him?"

"No," James said.

Coming through the lobby, foot-sore from the long, crosstown walk (the buses had pulled away without him), Dyer picked his way through a group of students with their bags, staring glumly at one another.

"We look like wusses," said one of the boys, sitting on his suitcase.

"Tell it to your parents," their teacher called over from the reception desk. She wore a purple sweatshirt embroidered with a Manhattan apple.

The rest of the ground floor was jammed with kids, their chatter deafening in the marbled space. Dyer didn't see anyone from Britton. In the mezzanine conference room, Dyer found the IMUNI director explaining to a crowd of teachers that the conference would proceed on schedule. "We've arranged for additional security at the hotel," he said, his tie hanging loose around his neck. "But we understand that some parents may be concerned and that schools may feel the need to change their plans. We can't, unfortunately, offer any refunds on registration fees, partial or otherwise."

Upstairs, he found Chip Lee in his room. "Where's everyone?"

Chip shrugged. "Around, I think. Committee starts in ten minutes."

"You've seen them all."

Chip blew out his cheeks, thinking. "Randy, Jane, Sam, and Louise were on my bus. I just saw Greg and Liem down by the committee rooms. That's everyone — except James. Haven't seen James. This thing is still on, right?"

"Seems like it," said Dyer.

"Was anyone hurt?"

Dyer nodded. "One kid looked like he might have been."

He left Chip and headed for his own room. Inside, he flipped on the TV. Nothing yet on CNN, and the networks ran competing therapy talk shows. He found the report on NY1. The reporter stood on the far side of First Avenue. "Hundreds of teenagers participating in a high school model United Nations conference were congregating on the steps outside when the shots were fired," he said, gesturing behind him. "According to authorities, the bullets passed over their heads, and there were minor injuries as the area was cleared. U.S. Secret Service assigned to the visiting Cypriot president subdued the gunman, and police have blocked off the avenue . . ."

Dyer had stayed on the UN terrace long enough to see the ambulances arrive, to see one girl cradling her arm, her face stricken with pain, another girl holding a padded bandage to her cut lip, and then to see the boy strapped to a backboard. Minor injuries, the TV said. But the boy, who'd been wearing a navy suit, torn, dirty shirt, and loose tie, had seemed in pretty rough shape, his eyes wide open, his lips tight and white, his fingertips skating against the side of his leg as he was loaded into the ambulance bay. Three hovering friends and a teacher were kept from riding along. "Mount Sinai," the EMT said, pointing south, shutting the bay doors. "Ten blocks."

The news report ended, and Dyer told himself to find the rest of the group, find James especially, since Chip hadn't seen him. He should be accounted for.

But when he opened the door, he met a tall, black-haired woman in a trim blazer and wool skirt, standing in the hallway, scanning room numbers, a reporter's notebook and a pen in her hand.

"Are you Dyer Martin?" she asked.

Dyer nodded.

She stuck out her hand. "Henrietta Talbot. From the *Times.*"

"Hi," Dyer said, shaking Henrietta's knobby hand.

"Do you have a minute?"

"Not really —"

"Just a minute. I promise."

Her voice was firm, and she was already moving past him, into the room. Dyer pushed the door open for her and followed her in. The room was still neat, the bedspread wrinkled from where he'd been sitting on it, the remote control on the floor. He'd left the TV on.

Dyer bent to retrieve the remote and noticed, for the first time, a small, battered gray leather bag sitting at the foot of the second bed, its leather thick and wrinkled, like elephant hide.

Henrietta looked up at him curiously, wagging her pen between thumb and finger. "Something wrong?"

They were *sharing a room*? "No," Dyer managed, switching off the TV and dropping the remote with a clatter on the table. The bag was just big enough for a change of clothes, a toothbrush, a shaving kit. So, Dyer thought, Wolfe was already here. He must have dropped it off sometime in the last hour, passing through while Dyer was making his way across the city.

"Can we sit?" asked Henrietta, still watching him curiously.

Dyer nodded at the desk chair. He settled heavily on the edge of his bed and tipped his forehead into one palm.

"So you were over there just now? At the shooting," said Henrietta.

Greta's freckled breasts came into his head, the grip of her legs around him, the flash of sweat at the base of her throat, like a tiny mirror catching the light. He'd have to call her, stop her from coming.

Henrietta crossed her legs, and propped the pad on one knee. She straightened; most of her height was in her long torso, her thin neck. "You're really all right?"

Dyer rubbed his face. "Who was he? The guy with the gun."

"Lee Mi-Rang. A postal worker from Queens."

Dyer saw the blue pants, the zipped jacket, the satchel spilling pages. He saw him grimace as the officer wrenched his arms behind him.

"The police have yet to make a statement beyond occupation and name. I called USPS and got his district."

"Do you know if anyone was badly hurt? I saw this one kid put in an ambulance."

"I heard minor injuries."

"That's what they said on TV. But they took this kid to Mount Sinai."

"I'll call," said Henrietta, making a note on her pad. She swiped a line with her pen and leveled her gaze on his. "How sympathetic would you say your students are to North Korea?"

Dyer blew air between tight lips. Was she trying to surprise him? "A few seem genuinely interested in the place. You study a country long enough, and you start to identify."

Talbot scribbled this down.

"Are you quoting me? What story are you doing?"

"Student reaction to the shooting. You say they identify?"

"Most just came here for the extra credit, the weekend in New York."

Talbot nodded.

"North Korea's got this rogue reputation; some of them like that. The self-reliance thing, the outlaw mentality, thumbing its nose at the U.S. Easy for a seventeen-year-old to understand."

"How would you describe their reaction to what happened today?"

"I haven't seen everyone yet, so I don't really know. But I'm sure there wasn't any cheering for the home team or anything."

Henrietta gave a brief smile. "Your headmaster has been writing and calling me for months, saying your club is taking some radical positions on North Korea."

Dyer nodded that he knew. "You'd have to decide for yourself just how radical we are."

She scribbled a note, thought for a moment, then looked up.

"Have you heard of the Choson Coordination and Development Group?"

"I have."

"Do you know a man named George Choe?"

"I've heard the name," said Dyer. "Wolfe has mentioned him."

"Has Choe met with your students at Britton?"

"No."

She watched him closely. "Did you know that Choe and the CCDG are under federal investigation for connections to a terrorist organization?"

Dyer stared. "Which one?"

"The Yonsei Unity Coalition, the Korean student group suspected of bombing the U.S. embassy in Seoul. Financial support. Funneling money through the CCDG's charity operation," she said.

Dyer nodded dumbly.

"The feds won't confirm they're looking into it. I only know thanks to some angry New Yorkers who blocked Choe from making presentations at their schools. Older Korean-Americans mostly, a few of them veterans from the war. They have friends making statements about Choe to the FBI. They tipped me to the investigation because they're looking for bad publicity. They want the CCDG shut down."

"What does this have to do with what happened today?" asked Dyer.

Henrietta shrugged. "Lee Mi-Rang's postal district in Queens is the same neighborhood as the CCDG offices."

Dyer stared at her, trying to focus. "I'm not following."

"Could just be coincidence." She swiped another line on her pad. "Choe never had contact with anyone in your group?"

Dyer thought of the man in Wolfe's kitchen. "You should be talking to Wolfe."

She triple-clicked her pen and sighed. "Do you know where he is?"

"No idea," said Dyer. "But he's been through here. I'd check the hotel if I were you."

"And your students?"

Stiffly, Dyer looked at his watch. "They're just about to go into committee."

James sat in the back of Ballroom B, clicking his fingernails on the DPRK placard on his lap. Drafts of air conditioning fell from vents in the ceiling, and the metal folding chair chilled his legs through his pants. Alexandra, the committee head (she'd introduced herself as a "government major from Carnegie Mellon"), sat behind a podium on a dais at the front of the room; a cream-colored scarf whirled around her shoulders, and heavy purple eye shadow colored her eyelids. She held her gavel between pinched fingers, as if mildly disgusted by it. She rapped the thing to silence the hundred-odd delegates in the room.

"So I'm feeling a bit jealous right now," she said, leaning into the microphone, producing a peal of feedback. "The four years that I was a delegate at this conference, I never got to be the target of an actual terrorist attack. Delivers a certain *frisson* of relevance to the whole exercise." Then, more quietly, an aside: "And I'm sure we're all especially eager to hear from our North Korean delegate."

James flipped his country placard over, hunched his shoulders, and stared at the buttons on his shirt. The looks came by the dozen, delegates swiveling in their seats, craning to see whom she meant.

"Not to put you on the spot," said Alexandra, speaking with soft, European vowels. "There in the back." A thrum of nervous laughter and whispering. Alexandra finger-rapped the gavel again.

"You're in the Committee on Disarmament and International Security," she said loudly. "Are you in the right place?" She rocked back in her chair and shook a column of clattering bracelets down her arm. "Do you have your country placards with you?" Another pause. "Good," she said. "Roll call." And with a musical breath, she began reading each country's name — "Afghanistan, Albania, Algeria" — barely listening for "here" or "present," checking each off a list with a flourish of the wrist.

Dad. James was stunned to see his father slip in through the double doors near the podium, stunned that he'd come down from Britton after all. He was *here.* In James's committee. Wolfe slid along the wall, peering down each row as Alexandra went through the B's. "Bangladesh," she said. "Barbados, Belarus, Belgium." James clenched the hard edges of the note cards in his pocket, then let his grip go loose; his toes unbunched. Wolfe continued along the wall, squinting down the rows.

James tugged the cards out, stared down at the neatly printed letters. When he'd prepared the speech, he'd thought of those angry, pointed lectures about commitment and idealism his father had delivered two years before, when he was deciding, for both of them, to start their new life at Britton. James had wanted his father to hear this, this little speech he was about to give to the room. Wanted to hear that he could be defiant too. Committed. But he'd also tried to be realistic. His father could not be counted on to show up to anything that mattered. James shouldn't even care what he thought.

"Croatia, Cuba, Cyprus."

The stares from the other delegates were long gone; James raised his head and drove his gaze into the far wall. But he did care. And now that he was here he might raise the stakes a little, incorporate what happened at the UN. Why not? He thought of what Randy had taught him: the unexpected tackle, the jab in the neck.

"Czech Republic."

He'd have seen me by now, thought James. Seen me here in the back. Surrounded by all these empty chairs. Another line came to him, this one from his father, from all those months ago, back in the moving-out days of September. *You can't go on isolating yourself from your peers.*

But you could.

"Democratic People's Republic of Korea," said Alexandra.

"Present," said James.

• • •

Dyer drifted in and out of ballrooms and conference rooms. This was what the other teachers were doing: checking up on their students, making sure they were awake. He kept going back through what Henrietta Talbot had told him about the CCDG, trying to make the connections clear in his head. The CCDG supported a terrorist organization. Mi-Rang was a postal worker in George Choe's neighborhood. A federal investigation was under way. *Stop,* he thought. The idea was ludicrous. They'd all been in the line of fire. James had been in the line of fire. People had been hurt.

Still—Wolfe had gotten his reporter. She'd come right over to the hotel to do a story. *Student reaction to the shooting.* After months of not returning Wolfe's calls.

Dyer kept expecting to run into Wolfe, kept wondering what he'd say to him. Wondering whether he'd have the guts to say anything at all.

According to IMUNI rules, teachers weren't allowed to get involved with the committee proceedings—weren't allowed to pass their students notes or whisper messages in their direction—and there were stern-faced undergrads standing in each room, watching for interference. The teachers scribbled on pads and sent meaningful glances into the rows of seats. Joining them, Dyer received weary, collegial nods. "It's all on them now," said one, scratching his mustache with a pencil. "Just hope they're not too rattled by what happened." This was in the room housing the Commission on Human Rights. Louise Hampton sat in the back row, reading *Vogue,* her DPRK placard on the floor, under her foot.

After roll call, James's committee's first job was to select a topic to debate: chemical and biological terrorism or nuclear proliferation. Alexandra accepted a motion to create a speakers' list and appointed a delegate to take names on a display pad. Jerkily, as if tugged up by invisible strings, James's placard went above his head, and she smiled, pointed at him with her gavel. "DPRK" went down fourth. Speeches were thirty seconds. The Canadian delegate argued for the first topic, speaking of the threat from rogue states with access to chemical agents. Japan said the topic should be nuclear, and especially accounting for fissile material in the former Soviet Union. Saudi Arabia also went with nuclear, suggesting the committee set a goal of creating a nuclear-free zone in the Middle East. These early-speaking delegates were model-UN veterans, their speeches smooth, succinct, well under the thirty-second limit. Going for the gavel trophies, James figured as he headed down the aisle, the ones displayed in the registration hall. He brought the freestanding microphone in the front of the room to mouth height and cleared his throat.

Standing against the back wall, his dad shrugged off his overcoat and gathered it in one hand. With the other, he took off his glasses and polished the lenses with his knit tie.

James ran his tongue along the inside of his lips, trying to gather spit. He glanced over his shoulder at Alexandra, then swallowed what he could and leaned into the microphone's gridded bulb.

"The Democratic People's Republic of Korea does not recognize today's action at the UN as a terrorist act," he said, and then listened to the slight reverb his voice made in the big room. He took a deep breath that came through the speakers like a rush of wind.

"The essential principle of nonproliferation is that countries without nuclear weapons cannot be threatened by those that have them," he said. "And yet the U.S. has deployed miniaturized nuclear weapons mounted on unmanned aerial reconnaissance drones in the East Sea. These weapons represent a travesty of international treaties and the UN charter and a provocation to war. The UN was designed to block such provocations, to protect countries such as ours, ones with few allies." James paused. "But the UN has become a tool of capitalist imperialism. Despite its principle of collective security, the UN is nothing more than a front for the United States, supporting its criminal, destabilizing international policy. In the absence of an effectual international organization, the DPRK reserves the right to respond with whatever means necessary."

The silence in the room was complete. James felt the attention coat him like a glaze.

Alexandra spoke into her own microphone: "I'd like to remind the delegate that the purpose of these speeches is to decide which topic—"

"The DPRK won't allow weapons inspections," interrupted James, "or bans on research of any kind—nuclear, chemical, or biological—to infringe on our sovereignty." He let a second slip by. "The Korean people have stood at the receiving end of Western aggression and betrayal for decades, and we are committed to meeting force with force." James was totally loose now, his fingertips tingling at his sides. He glanced at his father at the back of the room. "We are *committed.* We will defend our sovereignty. We have the most highly trained, highly motivated military in the world. Provoke us at your peril."

A whistle from the audience and a smattering of laughter. Alexandra tapped her gavel again.

James noted the surprised grin on his father's face, then moved down the aisle as calmly as he could. He took his seat, willing himself not to turn around and look again, to check on the approval there. Gradually, over the next few speeches, the desire to do so gentled, and his breathing slowed. Australia spoke, then Senegal. When Bulgaria reiterated Australia's point about strengthening the chemical weapons ban treaty, a roaming courier-delegate delivered James's first batch of handwritten notes. A scrap of paper from the Sudanese delegate. From the Iraqi group. From the Chinese. Three more: "Meet me during the first caucus, Kazakhstan." "Libya's ready to work with you." "Great speech. Let's build a bloc: xo Liberia."

Alexandra approved a motion to caucus, and the delegates rose to huddle. Warm hands grasped on James's shoulders. "There's someone I want you to meet," Wolfe said, gently squeezing.

"I'm supposed to caucus," said James.

"Make them wait," said Wolfe. "Was that memorized or off the cuff?"

"I added some stuff," said James. He glanced at his dad's face. The approval was still there, the wrinkled pride.

They left the ballroom together, entering the long mezzanine hallway that ran the length of the hotel. James and Wolfe walked in silence, past another ballroom door with a sign reading ECOFIN, past another reading WORLD BANK.

"I sat next to Henry Fieldspar on the bus. He called you a bloodthirsty fucker."

Wolfe's pace faltered; then he let out a big, bursting laugh. "Verbatim, I bet." James dropped his head, smiled. They kept moving, walking side by side, nearly in lockstep. Wolfe's arm brushed James's; James brushed him back. His father's eyes kept cutting over, lingering on his face.

"You were okay," Wolfe said. "In the crowd."

Neither, James noticed, had been a question. But he nodded anyway. "I got pushed around a little. I didn't even know what was going on at first."

Wolfe responded with his own quick nod.

Up ahead stood an Asian man in a dark gray suit. A needle of silver clipped a maroon tie to his shirt. A star pattern of pinprick moles lay just below his right eye. James was startled. This was the guy from the kitchen. Black Mercedes in the driveway.

"George Choe," Wolfe said. "Meet my son."

"Provocative speech, James," said Choe, shaking his hand, his accent full of pushed V's and T's, slippery R's. "Jolted the room, I thought."

"You heard it?"

"Stuck my head in," he said. "Scary afternoon, huh?"

"Not really," said James. "Honestly, I didn't even know what was going on."

"Others were though, yes?" said Choe. "Scared."

Both men waited for James to say something. They seemed to want him to nod, so he did. "There were some freaked-out kids, I guess."

"I hear parents have called a few dozen homes already," said Choe, trading glances with Wolfe, and pulling some documents out of a briefcase that sat on the floor between his feet. "I want you to read our mission statement. There will be reporters contacting you later tonight, and I wanted you to know what we're up to when they ask."

"What we're up to?" James repeated, confused, turning to look at his dad.

"That bit about your mom's nukes was powerful," said Wolfe. He swept his hand through James's hair, a gesture he must have picked up from some movie. He'd never done anything like it before. "You really nailed the argument."

The World Bank doors clicked open, and out came caucusing delegates, a few already scribbling in notebooks, boys loosening ties, girls pulling their hair into ponytails.

George Choe raised his voice over the hallway chatter. "When reporters ask you how it feels to represent an avowed enemy of the U.S. A state-sponsor of terrorism. When they ask if the message of today's action resonated in any special way—"

"Today's *action*?" James asked. His father glanced at Choe: a warning. Choe tapped the top page of the documents, above the type, where the letterhead read CHOSON COORDINATION AND DEVELOPMENT GROUP. His fingernail was immaculate, trimmed and glossy-smooth.

"You tell them that the U.S. wants a new Korean War, to finish what they couldn't fifty years ago. That the U.S. sees a stabilizing North Korea as an intolerable threat to military and economic interests in the Far East." Choe was talking more slowly, more quietly, now that delegates were milling near them in the hallway.

"Mr. Choe's organization is sponsoring a trip to Korea in May," Wolfe said to James. "For the club. For you. The eight of you. The CCDG wants us to be peace missionaries. Mock talks in Panmunjom, in the DMZ with a group of North Korean students. Right in the war zone." Wolfe's mouth stayed open, his tongue loitering along his bottom lip. "Isn't that amazing?"

James stared blankly at his father. He had no idea what to say.

"We'd like you to be the spokesperson for the trip," continued Choe quietly. "We'd like you to tell the international press that there's still an opportunity to bring global pressure to bear against the U.S. nuclear buildup in the East Sea. That you know there's no evidence North Korea had any involvement in the attack on the undersecretary, or the bombing in Seoul. Tell them that you represent a younger, more enlightened generation of the U.S. cultural elite, one free of Cold War paranoia. Free of Cold War logic. Angry at the renewed threat of nuclear warfare. Willing to accept North Korea as a nation without Western interference."

"Give the *Times* a few lines from your speech," said Wolfe.

George Choe's nostrils flared. "No," he said without looking at Wolfe. "Now that we have their attention, it's time to get our message out."

"What message?" James asked quickly, his voice more urgent than he wanted it to be. "Dad?"

But Wolfe's attention had turned. Henry Fieldspar stood in the hallway, his shirttail untucked, a rolled *ESPN* magazine sticking out of his back pocket. Their eyes met, Wolfe gave Henry a slow blink, then ignored him. "Keep it up in there," he said to James, nodding in the direction of Ballroom B. "I'm proud of you."

"Read the documents, James," said Choe, handing them over. "It'll be clear."

"*What'll be clear?*" James nearly shouted the question. The heavy, yellow light in the hallway hurt his eyes.

"Said it yourself," said Choe quietly. "A political provocation. Not a terrorist act."

James tried to get his father to look at him, but Henry had closed in. Henry swept his bangs out of his eyes, threw his shoulders back. Wolfe put a hand out, offering a shake, which Henry took in a firm grip.

"I know you threw me out because you couldn't stomach my dad's money coming into the school," said Henry. The statement drew looks. George Choe began gathering up his briefcase.

"Hello, Henry," said Wolfe, withdrawing his hand.

"But you're finding that Senator Fieldspar has connections with donors."

Wolfe directed an apologetic glance to Choe, but he was already turning, moving quickly for an elevator bank, not saying good-bye.

James backed away as well, holding Choe's documents in front of him, his stomach lurching, his throat pinched. His breath was short and shallow, his vision wobbly at the edges.

"It's been a long time," Wolfe said to Henry. "We should get caught up."

"Campaign Britton, right?" said Henry. "Not going well, I hear."

The notes from other delegations kept arriving; James let them pile up in his lap. This all seemed like a stupid game to him now, but playing along was his only option. What else could he do? Call the police?

James scribbled noncommittal responses to those demanding that he comply with existing chemical and biological weapon controls. In caucus, he stood near other rogue-state delegates across the room from the bigger, Western-nation bloc. The Syrian delegate, a pretty, tomboyish junior from Providence, started to outline a working paper on her yellow legal pad. Each country to police itself, she wrote in big, bubbly capitals. No UN supervision.

James told himself he had the wrong idea. "Political provocation" could mean a lot of things.

Back at his seat, James pulled the CCDG pages out of his pocket, reread the bulleted "Organization Goals."

1. Focus international attention on the plight of the North Korean people.
2. End United Nations support of illegal U.S. aerial espionage.
3. End imperialist war buildup in the East Sea.
4. Eradicate U.S. troop presence on the Korean peninsula.

James folded the paper carefully, scoring the folds with his fingernail, and tore each page into fourths, into eighths, into tiny, illegible pieces. *Focus international attention on the plight of the North Korean people.* He jammed the shreds in his pocket.

He remembered his father's reaction to his speech, the warmth of his hands on his shoulders, squeezing. But his dad had been thinking of other things, of the future, and the press. Pleased only that his plan was working so well.

James thought of all those years of armchair outrage: his dad smacking the newspaper, talking back to Jim Lehrer on TV. The time his mother had taken James to an antinuke rally at Harvard, and his dad had stood in front of the crowd, an apple red flush climbing up the sides of his neck, his fist bouncing off the podium. "He's still so committed," she'd said that day. "Still hears the drumbeat. The protest song playing a loop in his head." Then there'd been letters to senators, to the *Times,* even once a guest editorial in the *Globe* after a violent string of WTO protests in France. James had read them all. "Violence that isn't sponsored by the state is considered insane or criminal," his father had written. "But can a protest movement stay peaceful when nonviolent dissent ratifies state violence?" The letter of reprimand from the university's chancellor had been framed prominently in the front hall.

But he'd never *done* anything before.

I've got the wrong idea, James told himself again, then thought: Impossible to believe I'll be at this conference for two more nights. There were committees all day tomorrow, then a dance on Saturday night, then a plenary session on Sunday. James would go to it all, but he wouldn't give any more speeches. And he certainly wouldn't talk to any reporters.

Sunday afternoon, they'd go back to Britton, and life would return to normal. A trip to Korea, to the DMZ. What an insane idea.

The longing for Jane fell on him like a chill. Randy, Henry, Sam Rafton — fuck every one of them. That future he'd imagined in the bus, all the possibilities on the horizon, like a distant sparkling skyline, now looked like a fragile mockup, a thin, Disneyland diorama of the years to come. He was scared. He watched the wall clock, watched the seconds crawl along.

Committees broke up on a staggered schedule, between 7:00 and 8:00 P.M., to rotate kids through the dinner line — a steamy buffet in the lobby restaurant. James ate his vegetarian lasagna, Fritos, and cheesecake slice with the Syrian delegate, half listening to her advice. "No way to get authorship of a passable resolution as a rogue state," she told him. "But you can screw around with other peoples' working papers. Ultimatums, poison-pill amendments, debate them to death. Last year I scored a gavel as Iran, just being a nuisance." She ate only Fritos, three small bags, and sipped a Diet Dr Pepper.

No Jane. No Randy. No Henry. James took a few laps around the lobby bars, then headed upstairs to the block of Britton rooms. Coming out of the elevators, he spotted a reporter sitting cross-legged in the hallway, talking to Greg Smile.

"North Korea proves that the globalized market economy isn't just, like, the natural order of things," Greg was saying.

The reporter nodded, jotting on her pad.

"I mean, this tiny country goes to war with the most technologically advanced nations in the world, and *ties*. Pretty cool."

James kept his eyes down, picking his way by the pair, jamming his keycard into the door. He wouldn't talk to her. Even if the reporter asked a question, he'd ignore it.

He got inside and shut the door hard. Sam Rafton and Chip Lee, lying side by side on James's bed, looked up. The TV was on — news commentators waving fingers, the caption filling the bottom of the screen: CRISIS IN KOREA.

Chip pointed the remote at the screen. "They're talking scenarios for a surprise attack. But, you know, how's it a surprise if they're *talking* about it?"

"I heard you actually spoke in your committee," said Rafton. His pupils were dilated. His head swayed gently, a flower on its stem. He cracked his knuckles and laced his fingers behind his head to steady it.

"This isn't your room," said James. Randy, Sam, and Greg were staying next door. He was in here with Chip and Liem, who must be in the shower. He could hear the water running.

"Mine's occupied," said Rafton. "Wanna know by who?"

"I can't get him to leave," Chip said.

Rafton blew spit bubbles between closed lips. He hooked his fingers into quotation marks. " 'Not a terrorist act,' " he said. "You should say that to the reporter. Get yourself in the *New York Times.* Fucking showoff."

Chip twisted sideways, bending over the edge of the bed to gather the three stapled pages of *MUN Today,* the newsletter put out by the Model UN Press Corps. "You're the most interesting thing that happened all afternoon," said Chip, winging the newsletter at the foot of the bed.

The lead column's headline ran, "DPRK Delegate Calls Terrorist Shooting Political Action."

Rafton held his thumb in the air, looped it around. "Everyone's very proud."

James read: "James Wolfe, DPRK delegate from the Britton School, spoke in support of today's terrorist shooting at the United Nations."

"I gave a speech too," said Liem Du, coming out of the bathroom in his towel. "Kind of had to. South Korea was going on and on about the refugee crisis. I was like, '*What* refugee crisis?' "

"Is this all over the hotel?" asked James, holding up the newsletter, thinking of the reporter in the hall. He peeled his nametag off his shirt and crumpled it in his fist.

Chip nodded. "The *Times* wants to know how we feel about the guy with the gun. Like we should be on his side or something."

Liem Du paraded his reedy body in front of the TV.

"Nice abs, Ginger," Rafton said, watching it all go by: soft skin like suede, knobby, puckered knees. Whatever he'd taken — that Ritalin from the bus, maybe something else too — had drained away his tense cool. He kept breaking out this goofy smile, his eyes sliding around.

Liem flung himself on the other bed and hiked a pair of briefs over his hips. Rafton's eyes stayed on him. He tried patting Chip's cheek, but Chip batted his hand away. Then Rafton was standing, unsteadily. "Hey," he said, coming down along the side of the bed and laying a hand on James's arm. "Heard your boy Holiday got into Princeton. Congratulations." Rafton brought his face in close. His breath smelled like cheesecake. He laughed. "Holiday said if I ever fucked with you, he'd break my teeth. That's the guilt talking."

"Leave me alone."

"You think Randy Holiday's your friend." He drew air through his nostrils, and his eyeballs rolled a little. "He's got Jane in our room right now. Dead-bolted the door."

"Why are you telling me this?" James asked.

"I'm just trying to have a *goddamned* conversation!" Rafton shouted. He took a step toward the door. "Listen to me: You need a set of balls. You need to go out there and take her. It's what I've been trying to say. I've been trying to *help* you. But you spook like a girl." He moved back, close to James, his voice dropping conspiratorially: "How're the fingers anyways?"

"Healed," James said.

Rafton landed one drowsy, companionable arm on James's shoulder, and James grabbed Rafton's throat, cuffing the muscle.

"I don't want help," James said, gripping as hard as he could. Spit frothed in the corner of Rafton's mouth. His eyeballs bulged; a guttering sound came out of his mouth.

James squeezed till he could feel cords and tendons bend like guitar strings beneath his fingers, Rafton's beating blood, the ribbed Habitrail of his windpipe.

A photographer had appeared in the hallway, a bearded man in jeans standing above Louise and Greg, pointing the barrel lens of a camera down at them. Louise held her head at an angle. "Seems hypocritical to me," she said. "India and Pakistan have nukes. We're not preparing to attack *them.*"

The flash went off. James, closing the door behind him, blinked it away. His hand ached, and his ears popped whenever he worked his jaw.

"That's James," said Greg. "The kid you were asking about."

The reporter looked up. "James Wolfe?" A copy of *MUN To-day* lay off her left knee.

Surprisingly easy to ignore her. James just turned his back and started down the hall toward Sam's room.

"Could I ask you a few questions?"

James shook his head without looking behind him.

"I wouldn't go in there," Greg called over to him cheerfully.

James raised his fist and knocked on the door hard. He could feel their eyes on him — the reporter's, Louise's, Greg's — so he stood up straight, lifting his shoulders and pushing them back.

A few seconds of nothing, then footsteps across the floor, and the door opened on its safety bar. Randy squinted through the gap, shielding his eyes from the hallway light, his bare chest a superhero spread of pink, thatched in the center with hair. He held a towel around his waist. On his grapefruit biceps, scrawled in smudged black Sharpie ink, four letters: JANE.

"Squid," he said.

"I need to talk to Jane," said James.

"She's not—" He hiked the towel up around his hips and glanced over his shoulder into the dim room. "Dude, listen."

"It doesn't matter," said James.

Randy put his face into the gap, and whispered, "That Rafton kid's a scrawny little pube."

"He's been trying to clue me in for months." James faked a smile. "Can you just tell her? Tell her the lobby?"

James waited on a yellow, scroll-armed sofa opposite the concierge desk — not comfortable, not secluded, not quiet, but the bar had signs posted everywhere: 21+ ONLY. Here, at least, he had a clear shot to the elevator bank.

The panels slid open and shut; delegates piled in and out. James spotted the reporter's dark hair, her narrow shoulders and bent neck. She was checking the screen of her cell phone, hurrying through the teenagers around her, making for the exit. James rotated away, staring at the bank of tourist brochures and counting backward from sixty, willing her to go past without seeing him. He wondered what her story would say, how incriminating it would be. At least she hadn't gotten anything out of him. At least there'd be no quotes from James Wolfe, no speaking up for his father, no trying to get him off the hook.

His hand still ached. He thought of Sam tottering around the room, making choking, wheezing sounds, collapsing on the bed. It had felt good to do that: something he'd wanted to do, something he should have done, a long time ago.

Here was Jane coming down the hallway from the elevators, close to the wall, trailing her fingers along the paint. She'd changed from her conference skirt and sweater, James noticed. She wore jeans that rode her hips, belted with a ribbon, and a purple fleece. Wool, fluffy socks, no shoes. Her hair in a ponytail.

"Hey, James," she said, standing in front of the couch, letting her eyes wander all over his expression. She kept her arms folded, cupping her elbows, and made no move to sit down.

"Hey, *Jane*," said James.

"What?"

"You're so formal."

She didn't get it, didn't hear the echo from many months ago. "Are you okay?"

"Yeah." He wanted to tell her about what he'd done to Sam, about his dad, about the CCDG and George Choe, but he couldn't with her staring down at him as if she were measuring the distance of a jump. He took quick glances at her face, her still, calculating eyes and tight mouth.

She smoothed the hair on the top of her head, pulled her ponytail taut.

"I wrote his papers for him in 250. Did he tell you?"

She nodded.

"He did?"

"He told me you tutored him." Jane sat. The couch was a two-seater, but Jane kept herself at the far end, kept inches of space between their legs.

James watched a pack of boys jam into the spinning doors, five or six in the wedge of glass. "Tutor doesn't really describe—"

She held up a hand. "I don't really care."

"I *wrote* his papers. He copied off my midterm and exam blue-book. Sam told me he got into Princeton. That's thanks to *me*. It doesn't bother you?"

"Should it?" She looked at him sharply and then shook her head, her eyes doing a slow, sad blink.

"He *cheated.* He pressured me into doing it."

"Really? Did he threaten you? Say he'd pound you if you didn't?"

"As a matter of fact."

Jane shook her head. "You don't have to do everything people ask you to."

"Thanks for the advice," said James. He wanted to tell her that she looked guilty, but she didn't, not really. More like relieved, her shoulders dropped, her back slumped into the cushion.

Jane's lips were plump and pale pink. James tried to imagine the inside of her mouth, its rough roof, her tongue, the taste of her spit. He tried to imagine how she smelled underneath that fleece, the raw milk scent of her skin.

A police siren sounded from the street. James's head jerked around. Rotating blue and red lights jeweled the window onto Sixth Avenue.

"I went through the past few months feeling depressed about my bad decisions," said Jane. "By my fucking up and letting peo-ple down. But Randy says don't feel guilty. He says guilt is stupid. He says look out for yourself and let other people look after them-selves. You can't trust other people to take care of you."

"He got that from me," James mumbled, still staring at the po-lice lights, at the cruisers approaching the hotel.

She frowned at her lap and nudged James's leg with a closed fist. "Can't we be friends?"

"I used to wonder why I didn't have more friends," said James, feeling the nudge, a warm spot just above his kneecap. He waited for it to cool down to nothing.

Jane let her head drop, her messy hair tangling down around her eyes.

"When did the thing start with Randy?" James asked, forcing his gaze off the police cars, two of them now, parked in the hotel turnaround, their lights splitting through the prism of lobby doors.

Jane didn't seem to notice. "December?"

James put some more distance between their legs on the sofa.

"I used to think I'd miss my mom forever," she went on. "I used to think I'd be thirty and crying at greeting card displays, wanting to throw up every Thanksgiving." She smiled at this, as though it meant something, as though it would mean anything to James, and lifted her chin.

Four uniformed police officers came through the revolving doors and marched up to the registration desk.

"I think my dad's done something stupid," James said, his eyes locked on their belts, their cuffs and service revolvers and squalling two-ways.

But she hadn't heard him. "Or Henry. I was so intense about him. Now I see him lurking around this place, trying to get me alone with him, and zilch. I think he's thrown off by Randy's size," she said.

The cops headed for the elevator bank.

After the Ritalin had been cleaned out of the fourteenth-floor rooms, the dealer-delegates from Northridge Davis High School cuffed and packed into cruisers, the rest of the pills impounded, Dyer called Greta and left a message. "There's been a drug bust in the hotel. Kids dealing Ritalin and OxyContin. The word is they're ending the conference early . . . tomorrow morning. Oh, and Wolfe and I are sharing a room. So no reason to come, if you were thinking of coming. Not that you were. You know what I mean."

Dyer then went to do a head count, to make sure no one was hopped up on anything. Chip, Liem, and James seemed in good shape, watching MTV. Down the hall, Randy and Greg took in *SportsCenter* from opposite beds; Sam lay buried under covers on the cot. "He's okay?" Dyer asked. Greg nodded at the TV screen; a home run clattered off outfield stands.

Dyer knocked on the girls' door and heard Louise: "We're here. We're in. We're fine."

In 1218, Dyer found Wolfe stretched on the second queen-sized bed. He wore his Harvard sweatshirt with the puckering letters, a pair of unbuttoned Levi's exposing snail-curl belly hair, and Gold Toe socks. He lay there dead-limbed, his neck skin sagging, eyebrows gray and wiry, a man at the end of a hard day's work. Dyer had been expecting to see him, but he still felt a shock that he was just lying there as though he had nothing to worry about. Wolfe half waved at him — more salute than wave — and Dyer said nothing.

CNN's feed of Japan Sea naval operations ran with the volume down. Wolfe watched with his fingers templed on his chest. "This is it," he said, lifting his chin toward the screen. "The start of the next war."

Dyer eased himself onto his bed. The satellite image on TV, a sun-splashed carrier deck and gunmetal sky hazing up into clouds, kept combusting with static.

"Did you talk to that reporter?" Wolfe asked.

Dyer nodded, rocking his head against the smooth wood of the headboard. The camera panned the carrier deck, revealing a grid of parked, wicked-looking aircraft, a single red eye flashing on top of each. The deck beneath their jointy legs and toylike wheels lay stenciled with yellow running lines. Then the camera panned again, east, to a distant, blurry ocean horizon — the sun in the lens, light shooting into the picture.

"I told you the press would be interested."

Dyer felt his lips twitch. "She came because of what happened," he said. "And she asked me if your friend George Choe had come to Britton."

Wolfe just nodded. "What did you say?"

"I told her to talk to you."

"And I told her to talk to the students. They're the story." Wolfe scratched the side of his neck.

"She told me the CCDG's being investigated by the FBI."

Wolfe waved his hand, unsurprised. "Choe has enemies in his

community who spread rumors about him. They want him to stop talking about North Korea, which he won't do. There's no investigation."

"She told me the man with the gun was from Choe's neighborhood."

Wolfe shrugged.

"He *shot* at us."

Wolfe let out a long, even breath, and murmured wearily: "He aimed high."

"Some kids were taken to the hospital." Dyer propped himself up on his elbows, his face flushed. "If you'd been there, you could have seen for yourself."

Wolfe nodded this time, slowly, almost regretfully, as if he wished he had been.

Dyer dropped himself back to the mattress and stared at the ceiling. He kicked off his shoes and unclasped his watch. He was too tired for this, for confrontation, and it wasn't the shooting he wanted to talk about. The bed pressed against his back; he wondered how he would get sleep. He slid open the drawer on the bedside table, threw the watch in, and shoved it shut.

Wolfe observed this curiously. "So," he said, "Senator Angus Fieldspar has been shotgunning my fundraising all year long. Telling his rich alumni buddies to hold off donations until I resign or am made to. Because I expelled his son for drinking."

"I'd rather not know anything about it," said Dyer as neutrally as he could.

"Because I demanded a strict interpretation of the disciplinary code. Because I wouldn't give the little prick probation. Henry said my headmaster days are numbered. You should have heard him."

Dyer reached across the bedside table and turned up the sound on the television remote. The jet engines pealed out of the speakers; aircraft engines burned red and flew off the deck.

"Are you bothered by something?" Wolfe asked loudly, over the noise. "You seem to be."

"Why are we sharing a room?"

"To save money. This place costs a fortune." Wolfe paused. "You were expecting privacy?"

Was that a tease about Greta? The thought infuriated him. Before Dyer could collect himself, he murmured, "I assume you and Greta were sleeping together this time last year." Dyer chewed his upper lip. He'd been too quiet to be heard above the volume of the TV, but, waiting to be sure, his gaze pinballed between the sprinkler heads on the stuccoed ceiling. He touched his neck, trying to tamp the hot blood coming into the face.

Wolfe's laugh was grunt-low, as if he'd taken a basketball to the stomach. He laughed again, almost a giggle, enjoying the moment as it lasted. He finally settled into a sigh. "She was going through a phase," he said.

Dyer's gaze dropped to the TV, to kinked boomerang profiles of planes lifting in the sky. Jet-fuel air fussed the focus, and static exploded across the screen.

"A nice memory," Wolfe said drowsily, snapping off the light. Dyer fumbled with the remote, hunting for the power button. In the darkness, while Wolfe shucked off his jeans and slid under his bed sheets, Dyer sucked down the room's dirty-sock air. Knowing what had happened, having it confirmed, was supposed to make him feel better. He felt much, much worse.

Henrietta Talbot's article, a short piece in the "National" section of the *Times,* appeared the next morning: "Students Defend North Korea after Shots Fired at UN." The article recapped the shooting, describing Lee Mi-Rang as a "postal worker from Queens with a history of mental disturbance." A boy, Nathan See, had been admitted to Mount Sinai with minor neck injuries. On Britton, Henrietta Talbot took a light, gently teasing tack:

> The North Korean regime is famous for brainwashing its citizens, and though the students of the Britton School Model UN team certainly seemed sound of mind Friday evening, a few expressed sympathy for the world's newest nuclear state.

"I don't think that guy was trying to shoot anyone," said Louise Hampton, a senior at the exclusive Massachusetts boarding school. "He probably just wanted to point out some totally relevant stuff. Like the fact that the U.S. has had nuclear weapons for years. Why can't North Korea have a few?"

And on the escalating crisis in the Sea of Japan, Greg Smile, another senior on the team, took a distinctly North Korean perspective: "The U.S. could have gone back to talks months ago, but they'd rather make accusations about terrorism and assassination attempts, and then stage these stupid exercises. It's like they *want* to go to war."

The story went on to give background on the conference, making no mention of the CCDG or George Choe. It ran beside a photo of Louise and Greg Smile confabbing on the floor of the hallway of the Crawford. Dyer made his way to Talbot's kicker:

"North Korea's got this rogue reputation . . . the self-reliance thing, the outlaw mentality, thumbing its nose at the U.S.," said Britton's faculty adviser Dyer Martin, a history teacher at the school. "Easy for a seventeen-year-old to understand."

Then he added with a smile, "Most just came here for the extra credit, the weekend in New York."

Dyer cooled his cheeks with the back of one hand. He hadn't slept until early that morning, his head stuffed under the pillow, trying to muffle Wolfe's snores — and the headmaster had been gone when Dyer woke up.

The conference was off. The IMUNI director had made the announcement at the faculty-only breakfast that morning: "Last night's drug incident has made it impossible to continue," the man told the gathering, his face drawn, bags under his eyes. Angry questions volleyed up from the tables, but Dyer was already making his way for the exit. *Okay!* That was it. He was done.

He'd read the *Times* in the lobby, then stumbled across Greg and Louise, buying coffee from a kiosk. "Cool," Greg said, when

Dyer showed him the story. Louise took it next, looked closely at the picture, and made a disgusted sound. "Photographer was a total amateur," she said.

Back upstairs, Dyer went room to room, telling his students to pack up, they were leaving. Sam Rafton didn't move in the bed, even when Dyer nudged his cot. He gave it a kick, and Rafton's head stirred. "Let's go," Dyer said.

They were all in the van by 11:00. There was some teasing about the *Times* (Randy pitched his voice high: "Some *totally* relevant stuff!" "Okay, jealous," said Louise), but many of the students were asleep before they even got out of the city. James sat up front, staring hard through the windshield. Dyer drove in silence, wondering where Wolfe had gone that morning and why Talbot hadn't written anything about the CCDG. He gripped the van's steering wheel with both hands and tried to move his thoughts to Greta. He needed to forget what Wolfe had said (*a nice memory*) before he saw her.

An accident on 95 kept them stuck in traffic all the way through Connecticut. The light had disappeared by the time they finally made it to campus. Dyer's limbs were sore, his vision shot. He didn't want to show up under Greta's window without taking a shower first; after the shower, he realized how exhausted he was. Plus there was no welcome-back message from her on his machine. He stared at his cordless phone, spun it on the floor, sensing for the first time that she'd never really considered coming to New York. He turned the ringer off and went to sleep.

There were whip cracks in his skull that night, startling him awake at 2:00, at 2:30, at 4:00. His eyes would open, and he'd be grabbing one side of the bed, hearing the echo, seeing the man pinned on the grass, seeing Nathan See strapped to the board. He had to stuff his head under a pillow to get back to sleep.

Sunday morning was bright and cold, and he met Greta on the steps to Commons. He'd hoped to catch her on her way in. She usually came to brunch by 9:00, when the dining rooms were quiet, before most of the students even woke. And here she was, sipping water from a plastic bottle, eyeing him over the rim.

"I heard about the shooting," she said. "Jesus."

Dyer hooked her arm, redirecting her from Commons. "Come on," he said. "I'll tell you everything."

"But I'm *hungry*," she said, nevertheless allowing herself to be steered away. They proceeded, businesslike, to Bailey, and slipped through the dormitory doors. Upstairs, inside his apartment, Dyer put his mouth on her neck and wedged a hand into the opening of her coat. He popped a button getting it off. He pushed her by the hips into the bedroom. The morning springtime light sheeted over her flushed skin as she pulled at his belt, unbuttoned his pants, let out a pair of quick breaths. Her mouth tasted minty, like toothpaste.

He worked her jeans slowly over her hips; she wiggled to help. They tipped heavily onto the bed. Dyer kicked his underwear off his foot, pushed her sweater up to her neck. She untangled herself from her bra, and Dyer hunted a year-old condom out of his drawer beside the bed. He was rushing, going too fast — but the sight of Greta's breasts, her small, rounded stomach, and the sloping well of her hip made his breath hard and shallow. He tore the packet with his teeth, got it on, and rolled on top, clumsily pushing his way inside her, the back of his neck tingling. Greta closed her eyes. "Easy," she said. Dyer tried to slow down, move gradually, but in seconds his limbs went stiff, his fingers splayed. He was coming. He let out another breath, ducked his head, appalled with himself.

"Oh fuck, sorry. Sorry."

She landed her fingertips on his back. "It's okay," she said.

"No, really. God."

Lightly, she traced circles. "Don't apologize."

He eased himself off of her, his heart still jumping in his chest. He turned on his side and gaped across the soft line of her body. He should say something here. What? "I thought about you all day yesterday," he blurted.

"Probably not all day."

"Seriously. Thought about you coming and us kicking Wolfe out of the room. Throwing a tie on the doorknob."

She looked at him, then past him, out the window.

Confirmed, Dyer thought. She hadn't intended to come; she hadn't seriously considered coming. And he'd sounded so hopeful in his message. He blushed again, just as violently, and sat up so she wouldn't see.

"Tell me about what happened," Greta said, putting a hand on his back. "It sounds scary."

Another hasty sentence: "Wolfe had something to do with it."

Dyer pushed himself off the bed. He snapped the condom off in the bathroom, then padded into the other room and gathered her coat off the floor, finding the brown button underneath his desk. There was a sewing kit in his sock drawer. Greta lay on her side, the sheet pinched in her armpit, her gaze fixed on him, her head neatly fitting the depression of his pillow, her eyelashes curled up. A gorgeous sight, but Dyer couldn't rid himself of the soggy weight from the night before — and the desire to tell her all about it. He settled into the bend of her body, and dragged a corner of the sheet into his naked lap. He sewed, securing the button tightly against the heavy wool. His fingers moved the needle. "He helped plan the shooting."

Greta rolled out from under the sheet. "Come on."

"I'm serious." He briefly told her about the conversation he'd had with Talbot: the CCDG, George Choe, the terrorist group they funded in Korea.

Greta cut him off before he was done. "Weren't people hurt?"

"A few kids. Could have been worse than it was."

Disgust crossed her face as she pulled her underwear over her hips and stood. Greta had solid arms, strong field-hockey arms, hard beneath a layer of flesh, and Dyer wanted to grab her there, above the elbow, haul her by the biceps back to bed.

But her jeans were on, zipped up and buttoned, and she'd found her bra.

"You know how serious he is," Dyer said. "How badly he wanted us to make a statement."

"The power of education," Greta said, sighing. "I *know.* I've heard all of that stuff. He's an idealist. But *please.*" She stood near the door to his room, safely away from the window that let out onto the road. She shot her arms through the straps of her bra, the creamy cotton cupping her breasts.

"He told me the guy aimed high. Like he was there—but he wasn't there."

"He wouldn't get someone to shoot at a bunch of kids. At James. It's a crazy idea."

Dyer knotted the thread and bit it.

Greta's voice was firm, her stare direct: "You're in shock or something. You're not making sense."

Dyer found his boxer shorts. He gave Greta her coat, the button loose on the wool. He hadn't sewn it well. "You certainly know him better than I do."

Their eyes met and held. Greta looked away first, blinking at the whipped sheets, the duvet on the floor, pillows flung around. "O-kay," she said, and came around the corner of the mattress, closing on him. "I see. It's jealousy. You're crazed with jealousy." She leaned in and kissed him. "I already told you. Britton's a lonely place," she said into his teeth, her eyes a Cyclops blur.

"Tell me what happened last spring."

"You shouldn't ask."

"Why not?"

"Because it's not polite. And because you don't really want to know."

After sign-in that evening, halfway through a glass of whiskey, Dyer started a letter to Tipton Pal. Nothing he intended to send, just a chance to put his thoughts down on paper, avoiding undue speculation, using measured tones. He started slowly, cautiously, reminding Tipton that they'd met in December. Reminding him about the Model UN team and the conference that weekend. He refilled his glass, and, feeling bolder, let one sentence ribbon out: "Wolfe specifically requested North Korea from the IMUNI administrators in order to attract press attention to the school." He then backed up, describing Wolfe's memo to the Model UN group and highlights of the conversation they'd had behind his house. Dyer finished his glass and poured a third. "I understand the Choson Coordination and Development Group may be the subject of an FBI investigation, and I believe Headmaster Wolfe is connected with their activities. Specifically, I suspect that Headmaster Wolfe's connection with this organization led to his knowledge of, and involvement with, Friday's shooting. The shooting spurred press interest in the Britton team, and statements about North Korea by a couple of the students appeared in Saturday's *New York Times.* I believe the CCDG, and by connection Headmaster Wolfe, engineered the shooting for these purposes."

He thought of Tipton's wrestler's swagger, his cast-iron handshake. This was just the kind of straight talk he'd want to hear. Dyer set the letter aside. He picked it up again, reread it. He *should* send it. Before he lost his nerve.

He found the business card Tipton had given him and addressed an envelope, sealed it inside. He finished his glass and threw on his coat. There was a blue mailbox just down the street on Reservoir. Outside, the moonlight was slanting in, and a moist, earthworm smell drifted out of the trees. Dyer dropped the letter in the box and had to stop himself from wrapping his arms around it in a celebratory hug. His head was full of Greta's curved back, her little gasps, the way she pulled at his belt, the sweet taste of her mouth. She was right about the question he'd asked. He didn't want to know any more than he already knew, and he wouldn't ask again. The letter was off. A valve inside him had opened. He was drained, lightweight, elated.

Passing the mailbox on his way to class Monday morning, Dyer checked the collection time: 7:00 A.M. Long gone. A few of his sentences came to him, and he put them out of his head.

The whiskey had kept the gunshots out of his sleep, but he taught through a dry mouth and headache. He took a lawn chair to IM softball in the afternoon, split up the teams, and announced that there was an honor-system ump today. He notched the chair back, pulled the brim of his hat down, and did nothing but call foul tips for Jerome Katt and Samantha Twiss. Neither looked as though they'd get a hit all term.

Happily, he didn't spot Wolfe that day — but he didn't see Greta either. She wasn't at Commons for dinner, though Chris was, picking through a salad, making notes on a portfolio of photos. "Dyer!" Chris said. "Back from the war zone. Tell me."

"Not much of a story," he mumbled.

"Did you see the guy with the gun?"

Dyer nodded. Again, his letter came back to him, and he shoved it out of his head. He told Chris that they should get a drink that night, then winced. He wanted to see Greta instead. No, no, he thought, reconsidering. This was right. He hadn't spent any time with Chris in weeks, and Greta might be avoiding him. Given his performance the previous morning, he could — should — try to take things slowly.

So that night, fifteen minutes after sign-in, he headed to Weiss and found Chris standing outside, waiting for him in the shadow thrown by the wall, a lit cigarette cupped in his hand. "Something's happened," Chris said.

Dyer moved out of the wash of sodium light. Usually voices spilled out of the windows at all hours, but tonight the dorm was quiet. The third-floor windows marking Sam Rafton and Cary Street's room were open, pairs of sneakers set on the outside sills, waves of blue and pink screen-saver light chasing across the ceiling inside the room.

"James Wolfe's been writing papers for Randy Holiday all year," he said, and took a drag out of his cupped hand. "In your class. He's helped him on the midterms and finals as well. Too late to do anything about it," he said, blowing smoke. "Sam Rafton has already gone to Lambert."

A nerve spasmed in Dyer's forehead.

Chris swept his hand, sending ash onto Dyer's shoe. "All of his papers. All year." Chris took another, harder drag. "Rafton's in the infirmary. Apparently someone bruised his throat pretty badly in a fight at the hotel in New York. Hurt his trachea. Maybe Randy?"

"Why Randy?"

"That would make going to Lambert retaliation."

Rafton had gotten into a fight with Randy? How had he missed it? "The doctor called you?"

Chris nodded. "Rafton's spending the night over there at Smith. Maybe he doesn't want to come back to Weiss. He's a popular kid, but he's ratted two guys out. You're not supposed to do that."

Dyer rubbed his face, pressing his eyebrows together, touching his throbbing forehead. "What kind of trouble are they in?"

Chris rested the back of his head against the brick and let his arm hang limp at his side. "No first warnings for cheating."

"Wolfe'll do something," said Dyer, trying to sound sure. He leaned back into the wall, shoulder to shoulder with Chris, and stared up into the dark eaves. The night sky was clear; Dyer followed the white smear of the Milky Way until it disappeared in the horizon's glow.

"I'm hoping there's minimal fallout," said Chris. "The guys went a little nuts after Henry Fieldspar was thrown out last year. Set a tribute fire in the shower stall, melted the curtain. James is an outsider, but still. I should keep an eye on things here."

Across the quad, spotlights lit the length of Peabody Hall's ground-floor arcade. One floor up, the CAMPAIGN BRITTON banner billowed fatly, the middle grommet hanging free of its tie. There were lights in the windows — cleaning staff, Dyer thought — but Wolfe's office was dark.

Chris elbowed Dyer. "Rick and I are fizzling. Same problem as last year. The distance sucks; I can't handle having him here. You think things are going to work out, and then they don't."

8

April

A FTERNOON LIGHT. Rosy sunset light. James had had enough. Standing on a chair, he pulled the green plastic shade down over the window. The spindle clicked free of its bracket, and the whole shade clattered down on the floor. James stepped off the chair, sat down, and rerolled the spindle. He fit the thing back on the brackets and started to draw the shade again carefully, slowly, gently . . . Click, clatter, slap. Standing on the chair, he leaned his forehead against the warm glass pane. He sniffed mildew in the window frame, a dingy smell of rot. Beneath him, through the glass, a Snickers wrapper skittered across the sod that had been laid the day before. New grass to mark the turn of the month, the start of spring.

Five days had passed since they'd returned from New York. That morning in his disciplinary James had told Dean Lambert about the cheating. He'd also admitted to choking Rafton in the hotel. Lambert's decision had been quick: James wouldn't be able to finish the term. He had to be out of the dorms by Sunday night.

"Cheating's the cardinal sin, I'm afraid," Lambert had said, watching him carefully, as if for tears.

But tears had been far off. James still had his hand around Rafton's neck, Adam's apple knobbing against his index finger, spit coming off the guy's lips, his face turning pink, then red. James could have killed him if he'd just held on another few seconds, a five-count, his grip tightening all the way. James readied himself to take Lambert's hand, look him in the eye, and say that he didn't care that they were throwing him out. That he'd be okay. But Lambert's hands had stayed at his sides, and James never got the chance.

James had come back to the dorm after the disciplinary to find the building empty, the guys in class. He'd closed his door with something like relief. The thing to do was to wait for his dad to show up. He'd expected to see him in his disciplinary; he expected to see him now, any minute. He *wanted* to see him.

The light had started slanting in, bathing the walls in a cheery rose. The shade was on the floor. He'd have to live with it—this hopeful light, this reminder that time was passing, that his father hadn't come, wasn't coming, and he needed to figure out what to do next, where he and his clothes and books should go. To Knoxville, maybe. Take the bus to Boston, get a flight. Warn his mom that he was coming. This was the most practical thinking he'd done in days.

James heard the phone ring down the hall, heard Cary Street shout, *"Lower!"* Eventually, by the eighth or ninth ring, someone answered it. There was an exchange James couldn't hear, then a heavy knocking at the door. "Bull," Cary said. "It's your mom. What do you want me to tell her?"

"Tell her I'll call her back."

"Let someone in, Wolfe. We'll show you what we did to Rafton's shit."

"I'm fine, Cary. Really."

"No you're not. You're potentially, like, suicidal." That was Brain Jones.

"Rafton's gone home for the weekend. Rat-cunt asshole's afraid to show his face. Which he should be."

"Wolfe, come on. Come to dinner. We'll eat like kings."

"I'm not hungry," said James.

"They're gonna let you graduate, right?" There was a juicy slap of skin. "What? I can't ask that?"

Cary again: "Really, Wolfe. Times of trouble call for fraternity."
No they don't. Times of trouble call for total gloom, absolute
black, a nothing place that could be anyplace, but James couldn't
stop the sunlight from trucking in, lighting all corners of his room.
In an hour or two, the sun would go down, but then there'd be the
curdled glow of floodlights. He wanted a sealed chamber, a cabin
on a cruise ship, below the water line.

"She said she really wants to talk to you, Bull. You want me to
hang up on her?"

James sighed. He rolled his forehead on the warm glass. The
rungs of the fire escape ladder threw slanting shadows against the
brick. "No. I'm coming."

Brain, Cary, and Buddy Juliver stood in the hall outside his
door. Brain wore fleece-lined duck boots and a pair of nylon gym
shorts; acne cream had made a scabby, flaky mess of his bare chest.
Buddy's wet hair—he washed it once every two weeks—sat like a
mop on his head. James moved through them without saying hello.
Someone patted his shoulder. He noticed—as he always did—the
coin-shaped bloodstains on the carpet by the stairs. He thought of
the piss-filled humidifier in his room back in the fall. He thought
of the shot Rafton had taken at him in IM soccer. He thought of
the hotel room at the Crawford, the way force had driven up inside him, leaping along his arm and into the cuff of his hand. Rafton had deserved it, and not because he had ordered the lacquering, broken James's nose, left beer bottles in his room—guys did
that stuff all the time. Because James had wanted to hurt him and
because it had felt good to do it. This was the lesson learned this
year, more important than any of his classwork: force built up inside you, and you let it out.

The receiver twisted gently on its silver cord, his mother waiting for him in the perforated plastic. James sat on the three-legged
stool and took the receiver in his hand. In years past he'd never
have done that to Rafton; he'd have talked himself into holding
back, into doing nothing.

"Hi, Mom."

"Oh, James."

James waited.

"Your father told me."

James hardened against his mother's soft, southern voice. So his dad knew what had happened to him. Which made it worse that he hadn't come to see him. And now his mother would try to make sense of everything: Rafton, Randy and the papers, the shooting, the speech, George Choe, the reporter, the things Jane had said.

"Did that boy force you to write his papers for him?" Caroline asked, the words gentle and slow, the tone forgiving. So easy to say yes, and be pitied, taken care of.

"He didn't force me," James said. His teeth were coated with a soft film; he realized he hadn't eaten anything all day.

"Then what happened?"

"Are you coming back to Cambridge?"

Caroline sighed. "James, if that's what this is about."

"It's not. It's really not."

"The house hasn't sold. I want to come down on the price, but your father won't."

Back at the Crawford, when the police came through the lobby, he'd seen them all moving back to Cambridge, his mom coming up from Knoxville, the family reassembling in crisis. He'd imagined them at the cherrywood counter in the kitchen, bags of groceries crowded together next to the sink, his mother with a yellow legal pad and a ballpoint, jotting down lawyers' names and numbers to call.

But the police had come for the Ritalin and the dealers from Northridge. Not his dad. His dad hadn't been accused of anything.

"If he forced you, you need to tell me, because that could make a difference."

"Randy didn't force me."

She pushed out a little breath. "Then why did you do it?" She clipped the last word, and James pictured her tight lips. Her bare fingers and the sharp points of her hair. "What were you thinking?"

James wound the receiver cord around his thumb and chewed on a ragged nail. His dad should have been waiting for him outside Lambert's. He should have been *in* the disciplinary, in another stiff-backed chair, sitting by his side.

"I want you to come to Knoxville," Caroline said.

This had been his idea already, the practical idea. In the fall he would have jumped. He would have been packed in minutes.

"Is Dennis still in the picture?"

"Dennis is still in the picture."

James bit off a piece of nail and spit it on the floor. "You know," he said, "that deploying nuclear weapons in the East Sea violates the Nuclear Non-Proliferation Treaty."

"James?"

"And that North Korea's nuclear test was a reaction to the presence of the Fuller-Reardon UAVs?"

She was silent.

"Now that North Korea's confirmed its nuclear arsenal, Japan and South Korea will feel like they have to start their own programs."

"You're angry at me," she said.

"Which will pull China in as well."

"Stop it."

He waited. "I think I'll live here with Dad," he said. "If colleges make me repeat a year, I'm sure I could go to Britton High or something. But who knows? They might still let me in."

He listened to the silence on the other end of the line, trying to gauge how angry he'd made her. But when she finally spoke, her voice was gentle. "So he hasn't told you."

"Told me what?"

"Your father's resigning. They're making him leave."

Dyer found a letter from Tipton Pal in his faculty box. A quick reply, Dyer thought, gingerly lifting the envelope. He'd sent his own

letter only on Monday. Inside, monogrammed notepaper, a handwritten message: "It's perhaps worth pointing out that collusion
with a suspected terrorist group is a libelous charge. The board
was unimpressed that you found time to cook up unsubstantiated
accusations while the students you were supposed to supervise
were buying drugs and choking each other."

Dyer thought of the still berm of Sam's body underneath
the hotel blanket. He thought of Sam passed out in the van. He
thought of James's set, serious face on the drive. He shouldn't
have missed those clues, and he wouldn't have, he told himself, if
he hadn't been obsessing about Greta.

"Your lack of judgment, responsibility, and understanding of
appropriate conduct have been duly noted by the trustees." New
paragraph: "And then there's the matter of cheating in your classroom."

A single initial sign-off. He folded the letter neatly and slipped
it into his satchel, trying to swallow, looking around the nearly
empty faculty lounge. Will Hemmer was across the room, stirring
sugar into his coffee. Dyer smiled and lifted a hand and thought,
Get to Blanton's office. Right away. He could tell him what to do,
and maybe help him save his job.

Blanton was in, his door open. When Dyer tapped it with his
knuckle, the teacher put down a student paper he'd been reading
and gestured at the slick leather chair. He took one look at Dyer's
strained face and offered him a glass of Dewar's. It was 3:00 P.M.,
and Dyer still had IM softball to coach, but he accepted.

Dyer handed over the letter. Blanton read it twice, chuckling
the second time through.

"Lucky boy," he said, pouring the viscous liquor into a smudged
glass. "Wolfe resigned this morning."

Breath shot out of Dyer's mouth.

"Surprised? According to you, he's a terrorist provocateur."

"Why did he resign?"

"Money. He funneled about fifty grand away from the school's
discretionary fund and won't say what it was for. The board likes
strict accounting."

Dyer sunk back into the chair and touched his forehead with one cool hand. Twin lines of amazement and relief braided down his neck.

"Better tell me what you put in your letter," Blanton said.

Dyer unloaded the gist of it: Henrietta Talbot had told him that the CCDG was under federal investigation for connections to terrorism, the man with the gun had delivered mail in the CCDG's Queens neighborhood, and Wolfe had been calling her for months, trying to get her to write a story on the Model UN team. He recited from memory the message on the gunman's flyers. "I didn't *cook up* any of this," Dyer said.

"You think Wolfe would team up with a terrorist organization to get a sarcastic article in the *Times*?"

"He didn't think it would be sarcastic," said Dyer, remembering, clearly now, his conversation with the headmaster over the woodpile. "He told me the press would get Britton notoriety. He called it the first step." Dyer was suddenly excited; he had to stop himself from pointing. "And weren't you the one who said he pals around with terrorists? That he has meetings at his house late at night? He was meeting with Choe. Planning this."

Blanton drummed his fingers on his blotter and threw Dyer a weary stare. "But why write a bloody letter to Tipton Pal? Why not come to me?"

"I didn't want Wolfe to get away with it," said Dyer.

"I wouldn't have let him," said Blanton.

Dyer finally sipped his whiskey, and the liquor barreled hotly down his throat. "The money he took, it must have gone to Choe."

"Unless he spent it on himself. Or a girlfriend."

Dyer shook his head. "Wolfe had something planned."

"Moot question, of course. Wolfe told the trustees he'd rather resign than explain. Said if they didn't trust him, he'd leave."

Dyer turned to the window and watched runoff drip from the eaves of Ramm Hall. The relief was all over him now, the tickle of it netting against his skin. He rubbed his fingertips numb on the steel grid of his watch.

"I saw the newspaper on Saturday, of course," Blanton said. "Nothing about the CC . . . Whatever. Nothing about a federal investigation."

"CCDG."

"And Louise and Greg sounded like idiots," said Blanton.

That stung a little. They hadn't, thought Dyer. They'd done what he'd taught them to do: embodied the pro–North Korean position. Only days before North Korea deployed twenty-five thousand troops to positions just north of the DMZ. The Department of Defense was talking about evacuation plans for Seoul. Suddenly the decision to hold the naval exercises was looking reckless. International editorials, compiled in the *Times,* blamed any ensuing bloodshed on U.S. brinkmanship. New polls showed that 63 percent of the U.S. public wanted the president to ratchet down the tension, to get back to the negotiating table with the North Koreans. So Louise and Greg were in step with world opinion. Dyer was sure Wolfe was disappointed by the article's slightly teasing tone. And yet, he must have been pleased with what had actually been said.

"The only problem with the article was what wasn't in it," said Dyer. "Wolfe planned that shooting. Sounds like he paid for it, too."

"Keep it to yourself, for Christ's sake. If Wolfe weren't leaving, you'd certainly be. Now, I'll go to bat for you with Tipton, but stay well clear of our headmaster in the meantime. Chances are Tipton didn't show him your letter. But you never know."

Dyer shifted uneasily in the deep leather chair. He *was* afraid of running into Wolfe. He'd taken a roundabout route to Blanton's office in Morrow Hall, slipping in the back and up the rear stairs.

Blanton lifted his glass and rocked back in his chair. The hinge let out a mournful squeak. "To your continued employment at Britton."

Dyer drank to that.

"And don't worry about the other thing. Plagiarism can be hard to catch for first-time teachers. Over time you develop an eye for it."

Dyer set his glass down. What was left of his good mood disappeared. He glanced at the glossy surface of the steamer trunk, blinding himself on the refracted sparkle of sunlight coming off the metal latch. "Is there anything I can do for James and Randy?"

"A week ago you could've told them to come clean. It might have helped."

James kept trying to get clear on what he was going to say to his father — and then kept telling himself to forget it. He should say whatever came to him. What did it matter now? He started packing; he sat on the edge of his bed staring at the floor; on the back wall of the closet he carved JW beneath his predecessor's initials: HF, PC, LT, and TJ. He kept hearing his father's voice: *I don't want you to think you can just come back if things get difficult.*

He lay down on his bed, listening to the quiet of the dorm around him. It was Friday night, still an hour or so before sign-in — and there was a DJ'ed dance in the gym across campus. Cary had tried to get him to go along, but the idea horrified him. He'd be the star attraction, or the circus freak: the expelled kid. Plus there were those old feelings: *Who would I talk to? I don't go to parties.* Now no one was around, and James wondered if he'd made the right decision. Maybe solitude wasn't the best thing. He looked out his window, and saw Highbury Estates' neat stands of willows, saw Dennis's heavy eyelid, saw the white, unblemished walls of his mother's house. She had already found a very good high school outside Knoxville where he could finish the year, and if colleges didn't take him, he could repeat his senior year in the fall. James said he'd think about it. She'd told him he'd make a mistake if he stayed with his father. "You need to think about your future," she'd said. "He can take care of himself."

James fell asleep. With the lights on, on top of his bed in his clothes, a shallow ditch of a nap that he rolled out of, hours later, sweaty, alert, and neck-sore, sure he'd just heard something in the room, a scrabbling, pitter-patter sound. A mouse, he thought, swinging his legs off the bed.

Then, more gravel clattered on the windowpane. *Oh,* James

thought, crossing the room and sliding the sill up. Three stories down, Jane was pulling herself onto to the first rung of the fire escape. She was dressed in a black long-sleeved shirt, black jeans, and a ski hat.

James sniffed his T-shirt and went to his duffel to find a fresh one. Pulling it on, he crossed back to the window and surveyed the view. No campus patrol cars in sight, but she was taking too long to climb up. It was just past midnight; no one in Weiss would be asleep yet — except maybe, if they were lucky, Mr. Nolan. James couldn't get into any more trouble, but Jane could.

Rung by rung she made her way. James held his breath until she was within arm's reach. He grabbed her cold hand and yanked her through the window headfirst, supporting her by the armpit, catching her in a hug as she tumbled off the sill. She was warm through her shirt, and a slick of sweat on her neck dampened his cheek; she must have run most of the way. James moved around her to close the window.

"Hi," she said, still catching her breath.

"You're insane," he whispered.

"I wanted to see you before you left," Jane said, and pulled off her ski cap; her hair was damp and matted. She shook one hand through it, checked herself in his mirror. "Ugh," she said.

"Did you take the Reservoir route?" James asked.

"It's the darkest. But shit, there's a lot of light around your dorm." She looked around the room, her gaze sweeping across the bare surface of his dresser and desk, lingering in each of the empty closets, their doors standing open, the hangers hanging cockeyed. "You're all packed up."

"The guys told me they're going to keep my room empty for the rest of the year in tribute. Nice of them to say, but I know Brain's going to be in here first thing Monday morning."

"'The guys.' Listen to you," she said. She pulled out his desk chair and sat, fanning herself, pushing up the sleeves of her shirt. "Can you open the window?"

So James did. He moved stiffly, listening for footsteps out in the hall. Footsteps would mean Nolan had seen her; there'd be a knock at his door. He waited for it, opening the window, feeling the draft on his face and neck.

"So you'll be gone by Monday?" she asked behind him.

James nodded, even though he still had to make the decision to go to Knoxville. It was *his* decision, not his mother's. That much was clear.

"Have you seen Randy?" James asked.

"No."

He hid his surprise, glancing at the floor. He himself had seen Randy only once that week, outside of Commons — big, rounded shoulders rolling inside his Britton windbreaker, his hands in his back pockets, a pale, blasted look on his downturned face. James hadn't gone to say hello. A mix of feelings turned inside him: anger, but also pity, more pity than he felt for himself. Colleges often forgave top candidates disciplinary mishaps, particularly given certain circumstances: a defenseless star student, preyed upon by a football player. But Princeton would certainly review Randy's admission and probably drop him.

By now Randy would have had his own disciplinary; he'd be gone soon. James would probably never see him again.

"You didn't say good-bye?" James asked Jane.

Jane shook her head without meeting his gaze.

"Neither did I."

She cleared her throat. A breeze pushed in through the open window, and Jane turned toward it, cooling her face.

All this time, James had been standing awkwardly in the middle of the room; he now crossed to his bed and sat. He was opposite Jane, his knee a few inches from hers.

"I heard your dad's resigning," Jane said.

"How?"

"Henry called and told me. He said something like 'Mission accomplished.' I told him he was a fucking idiot. 'Don't call me again,' I said."

James nodded at this. "I've been trying to get myself to go over to Dad's and see him. But it's hard for some reason." He felt foolish, as if he were ten years old. What was so hard about it?

"Of course it is," Jane said.

That released something in him: gratitude. James felt his body sag with it.

"I'll go over with you tomorrow," she said. "If you want."

"Thanks," he said.

Jane tipped her head and threaded her fingers in her hair. "What are you going to do?" she asked.

"I'm not sure yet. My mom wants me to move to Knoxville."

"What about schools?"

"I haven't heard yet." Admissions departments would reconsider his offers as well. She'd know this; he didn't have to say it. "You?"

"Got into Northwestern. It's my safety, near my dad," said Jane, still staring at the carpet. "Nothing yet from the big boys."

"I guess they're coming in a little late this year." The moment was awkward. A quiet settled, and he didn't know how to end it.

"You know I snuck out to see you once?" he finally asked.

Jane looked up with bloodshot eyes and grinned. "Yeah?"

"I climbed out that window, took the Reservoir route all the way to South Quad."

"When was this?"

"December something."

"What happened?"

James thought of the damp heat of Jane's neck, the way she'd fallen into his arms, coming through the window. Stray energy bolted around inside him. He'd been tired before the gravel hit the window, and now he was wide-awake. "I didn't know which window was yours."

Jane stared down at herself and picked something off her shirt. She rubbed her knees, wiggled the tip of her nose. James knew he was supposed to do something here, make a move toward her. She'd be expecting it. Should be easy, but he couldn't think how to get himself going.

"Can I come over there?" Jane asked, pointing to where James was sitting.

James nodded, and she sat a few inches away from him. She leaned back, lying flat on the bed. James lay down next to her, and together they stared at the ceiling, at the cracked paint, the browning star stickers and their now consoling message. Their breathing fell into step; their chests rose and sank together. James turned onto his side and laid his hand on her hip, on the place where they'd taken out the bone. She rolled toward him and James closed his eyes. He felt her breath on his face. Under the hem of her shirt, right at her waistline, James's fingers traced the smooth slug of her scar.

James woke to discover a note on a lined piece of scrap paper in his father's handwriting slipped under his door.

"Need some help loading a moving truck today. Can you bring two extra hands? 10 or so."

James balled up the paper and lobbed it toward the trash can by the desk. That was twice, counting the morning before Thanksgiving break, that his father had paid an early visit to Weiss, all the way up to the third floor and then down again, slipping out undetected. Euphoria from the long night with Jane kept him from feeling real annoyance, but he had to close his eyes and think of her hands touching his in the narrow bed, the quiet timbre of her voice in his ear to ward it off fully. She'd told him about losing her mother, that it had been the reason she'd come to Britton, to get away from her father: "But then I thought he was going to kill himself. I still have nightmares about that. And the worst part is that I don't know what it would change if he really did it. I feel less like his daughter every day." At this, James gripped her hard around her waist under her shirt, so hard she winced. "Sorry," he'd said, letting go. They'd kissed and held each other and dozed a little. She'd left at 4:00, the way she came in, through the window, James helping her onto the fire escape. Now, standing in his room, staring at the patch of floor where the note had been, he wondered what was wrong with his father. Was he afraid to see him? He'd never thought of his father as afraid of anything before. It was enough to get him moving.

He jogged to Smithson Way. The sky was like a blue stencil cut around the shingled roofs. The wet lawns, bare and muddy in patches, twinkled in the bright sun. His shirt was sticking to him by the time he showed up at his father's back door. He flattened his hand on the frame before opening it. Don't think, he told himself. Tell him you're angry at him. Tell him you're going to Knoxville, and this is good-bye forever.

Inside Wolfe was at the stove in his kitchen boiling water for coffee, wearing a thin white T-shirt stained yellow at the armpits and a pair of old gray wool pants belted with clothesline. He was barefoot, and his heels, James noticed, were waxy with calluses. James let himself in, let the screen door slap back into its frame.

Wolfe jerked upright at the sound. He turned, and James noticed the skin under his eyes was sagging even more than usual, and flint gray stubble had grown coarse and ragged on his throat.

"Startled me," he said.

"Where have you been?" James asked, pulling a chair out from the small table. But he didn't sit down.

Wolfe went to the refrigerator and took out a carton of milk. "Didn't your mother call you?" he asked, setting the milk beside the stove.

"She told me you're resigning."

"Indeed I am," Wolfe said, moving to the sink, lifting a coffee mug out of the basin, tipping dishwater out of it.

James took a deep breath, and said: "You know I've been kicked out." His father just looked at him and nodded. This was infuriating. "And you thought I could handle it?" James asked. "That I wouldn't want you to be around? You haven't said *anything* to me about it."

"You cheated. It's disappointing."

James dropped into his chair, stunned. "It's *disappointing*? You're *disappointed*?"

"The cheating is disappointing to me. I didn't expect that from you."

"I've been disappointed in you all year!" He nearly shouted this, skidding backward in his chair. "You don't even *talk* to me. I haven't seen you since the conference."

"You're a big boy, James," Wolfe said in a quiet voice.

A choking sound came out of James's throat.

"You're angry. That's good. Anger's useful."

"I saw you in the kitchen. Here in the middle of the night. In the winter. You were talking to that man, George Choe. You were talking about the shooting? You were planning it?"

Wolfe shook his head.

"No. You were. That's why you threw me out of this house. So you could plan this whole thing. I thought you didn't want me to see you with Ms. Salverton. But it was this conference, the shooting and the news story. And weren't we all going to Korea? What happened to that?"

Wolfe answered evenly, neutrally. "Choe disappeared with the money."

James stared at him a moment, then laughed.

"You find that funny?" Wolfe asked, his face starting to show strain, to crease with lines around his nose, the sides of his frowning mouth.

"What were we going to do there? Make some statement? Who'd care?"

"Many people. Me," said Wolfe quietly.

"You again," James said, and smiled. He was already out of this kitchen, moving across Smithson Way to Bachelor, to wake Jane and tell her that he was going to miss her. Tell her that she was the best thing about being at Britton. That last night had meant everything to him. And they would stay in touch. Maybe he would see her this summer. Then he was on the plane to Knoxville. Making the most of the only option left to him.

"It was important what we were doing," Wolfe said.

"But Choe took the money," James said.

Wolfe's lips went tight. He answered carefully: "I haven't heard from him."

"So it was all bullshit. A scam."

"You know it wasn't," said Wolfe. "You of all people. What was it you said?" But he didn't need any time to remember. " 'Our country has stood at the receiving end of Western aggression for decades. We'll meet intimidation and provocation with force.' It was a powerful speech. I was *incredibly* proud of you."

But this time his father's pride just ricocheted away. "And the guy with the gun is in jail?" James wondered aloud. "He won't confess that you put him up to it?"

"He doesn't know me, I don't know him."

"Well, that must have been important," James said, nearly spitting the words. "Considering he *shot* at us."

The kettle started to whistle, and Wolfe flipped off the burner.

James was breathing heavily. He wouldn't calm down. He didn't want to calm down.

"I need your help today, James," Wolfe said in an even quieter voice.

"I won't expect you to visit me in Knoxville."

Wolfe was silent.

"And I won't come to see you."

Wolfe blinked at this.

"What would be the point? What would we talk about?" James asked. He was thinking of Jane and her father. *I feel less like his daughter every day.* This was what happened. You grew up. You lost connection. James realized that he'd lost it many years ago, years before they'd come to Britton. There'd been those nights in his bedroom at Cambridge when James couldn't sleep, there'd been those Saturday mornings in his father's office, when it had been easy to be in the room with him. He'd been ten when his father left for China for the first time. It hadn't been easy since. And now he was nearly eighteen, his birthday in June.

"Well," Wolfe said, trying a breezy wave, but his fingers quivered a little. "I'll be in Cambridge, if you change your mind. So long as your mother doesn't sell the house out from under me. But I do need help getting this place . . ." He gestured around him.

"I won't," he said.

"*James,*" Wolfe said, with feeling. His forehead was deeply creased. "Come on." Steam billowed from the kettle, but Wolfe made no move to pick it off the burner and pour. "I can't do this by myself."

"I won't *visit,*" James said, standing and moving toward the door. Bachelor, James thought. Wake Jane up. Tell her how much he already missed her.

"You won't."

"But I'll help you pack. And I'll bring some friends," James said, glancing back but not really looking, just catching his father's drawn face in a blur. He let himself out of the kitchen, skipped down the steps, onto the damp grass, out the gate. Something like helium had blown through him. He bounded across the street.

Dyer and Greta stood on the far side of Smithson Way, on the path that led to the back entrance of Bachelor Hall. Across Smithson, the door to Wolfe's house was open and a moving truck sat parked at the curb, the side painted with an ocher landscape of cacti and mesas. *Arizona, the Adventure State,* slanting letters read. Two Weiss guys Dyer recognized as Brian Jones and Cary Street hopped off the loading dock at the back and headed for the house.

"He's really going," said Dyer, feeling the sunlight on his neck. He hadn't felt true warmth like that since the fall, and it lifted his spirits.

"I guess he is," said Greta, sounding pleased. Dyer was grateful for it. He wanted the reason they'd walked over from Saturday breakfast at Commons to be the mutual desire to see Wolfe leaving, the mutual understanding that this was good news for both of them. Dyer hadn't showered and could smell his night of sex and little sleep, a sour, standing-water smell, rising up out of his shirt. In the early hours of the morning, Greta had folded on top of him in bed, nestling her face in his neck, and murmured that he smelled like boiled peanuts; she'd eaten a whole bag once, she said, and made herself sick. This was when she was eleven and her family had driven down to Disney World.

Dyer had asked her if she was coming back the next year. "Sure," she said. "Aren't you?" He thought of the fall, of the next batch of students, classrooms full of them. The prospect had actually pleased him. He'd nodded. He *wanted* to do it all over again, get that fresh start in the fall, and now, thanks to Wolfe leaving, he'd have the chance. "Are you happy teaching?" he asked her. "Sure. I don't know if it's a career," she said. "But for now, sure. Are you?" He'd kissed her. "For now," he said.

They'd had sex three times that night, a record for Dyer. Twice Greta had run her hand over his waist, withdrawing it to a contented position under her head and had fallen asleep easily, within minutes. Dyer had laid his arm across her hip and pressed his chest into her back, just to confirm the tacky dried sweat on her skin and to feel the faint beat of her still-slowing heart.

Dyer had every reason to hope that tonight would be more of the same — and the night after that. He was almost sure that he was more than a phase Greta was going through. Pressing his teeth together, he watched James and Jane Hirsch emerge from the front door of Wolfe's house, each carrying a cardboard box. They made their way to the truck, and James hefted his box to the deck. He slid it in with his shoulder and took Jane's from her. She climbed the ramp into the truck and disappeared out of view. Cary and Brian came down the paved walk, holding a floor lamp, a low bookshelf, and a set of navy couch cushions between them.

Dyer heard James tell them, "Set those to the side. We still need to get heavy stuff in the back." He put his hands on his hips and looked around. Seeing Dyer and Greta, he waved.

Dyer waved back. "I should say something to James."

Greta nodded, and Dyer started across the street, then stopped and turned. "I've got a thing I've got to go to in May. In Richmond." He tried to think through what he was saying, but he was already forming the next sentence. "We could drive down together. You could come with me." Dyer's stance was awkward. His weight still tipped forward as he was crossing the street, but his neck was turned over his shoulder. He straightened out, relaxed his shoulders. "A ceremony thing," he said. "My mom's getting married."

Greta brought a hand to her mouth. "Hey. God. That's great news."

"We can talk about it later," Dyer said, turning. Too much, he thought, too fast. His impulses were working again, rushing things, putting pressure on her. He hadn't planned to ask her, and now he wished he hadn't.

Brian tossed a sofa cushion to Cary, who whipped James with it from the side. Jane came to the lip of the deck and kicked Cary in the back. Cary tried to snatch her foot. It looked like fighting, but they were smiling, having a good time.

"I'd love to go," Greta said into Dyer's ear, scratching the middle of his back. Dyer nodded and let his shoulder drift into hers —but he couldn't enjoy the moment. He was afraid to check her face for ambivalence or doubt. A little breeze ran down the street; Greta's blond hair fluttered in his peripheral vision.

"Bull, you want us to get the stuff upstairs?" Brian asked.

"I think there are still boxes in the kitchen," James said. James looked taller, broader, and his expression seemed less pensive, harder, more settled. Dyer wondered what was going on in the kid's head. He blamed him, surely. Right under his nose, James had been forced to cheat, and Dyer hadn't picked up on the signs.

James batted the sofa cushion, producing a cloud of dust, and set it on the deck of the truck.

Greta paused a moment longer, then passed Dyer. "I should go talk to him," she said, heading calmly and slowly across the street. She nodded at the students in and around the truck, headed down the walk, mounted the steps, and let herself in the house.

It took a moment for Dyer's vision to focus. He should have known she'd wanted a moment with Wolfe; he felt twice as foolish for asking her to Richmond. His stomach cramping, Dyer moved on uncertain feet across to the curb. Sparrows filled the trees with tuneless chirping. A bus zoomed by on Elson.

"I guess they're saying good-bye," James said to Dyer as he approached.

"It's not our business," said Dyer, trying to sound stern, but as soon as he'd said it he felt that he needed to say it again. He made himself remember the light pressure of her hand on his neck when he was kissing her. The sight of her body beneath him.

James turned and touched Jane's knee. He climbed up the ramp, and Jane pushed herself to her feet. Cary and Brian came out of the house with a suitcase, more boxes, and a coat tree. Dyer helped load everything in the truck, laying the couch cushions on top of boxes, fitting the coat tree behind a desk. The truck was almost full; Dyer could see a jumble of bookcases in the back, rolled rugs standing on end, and the aluminum-rimmed kitchen table he'd sat at with Wolfe for coffee after choson do. Behind it, partially shrouded in a sheet, Dyer spotted the portrait that had hung in the living room.

How long was she going to be in there? What did they have to say to each other?

"Dude, I think that's it," said Cary. "Except for the chair your dad's sitting in."

"He'll bring that out himself when he's ready," said James.

Cary and Brian dropped off the deck and found sunny spots on the grass. They sprawled, letting the sun bake their faces, arms, legs. James, Jane, and Dyer were left in the darkness of the truck's bay. James seemed to know Dyer wanted to talk to him, and lingered near, pulling on a bungee cord hanging from a hook inside the door, testing its strength. Dyer remembered finding the boy standing cold and confused in the middle of the night back in December. Now he had a solid stance, a level stare. He didn't look unhappy about what had happened to him.

Jane wandered down the ramp and sat on the curb, a discreet distance away, staring over at Bachelor. Dyer drew the cool dusty air of the truck down into his lungs. This was harder than he expected. "I'm sorry about the way things have gone. I feel like I should have done something."

James snapped the bungee, striking the side of the truck with a hollow bang.

"But you had no idea, right?" James asked, after the reverberations faded. "About Randy's papers? That I wrote them?"

Dyer shook his head. James seemed satisfied at that, squaring a stacked box labeled KITCHEN 3 OF 4. Dyer recognized James's neat capitals on the cardboard.

"Well, I'm sorry," Dyer said. "I really am."

"For what?" James asked, turning his stare on Jane and blinking rapidly as if she were shining a flashlight into his face. "It was up to me to stop it. And 250 was a good class. One of my favorites."

Dyer stared at him, then glanced away, uncomfortable with how grateful that made him. "I'm still sorry."

James shrugged and looked past Dyer: Wolfe and Greta had emerged from the house carrying an armchair between them. They'd been inside less than five minutes, Dyer thought. A quick "so long," nothing more. Dyer nearly skipped to the edge of the truck's deck with relief. The chair, which Dyer remembered from the living room, was big, nearly the size of a loveseat, with broad arms and thick cushions: too much for Greta, who struggled with her end, a taut, strained look on her face. Wolfe looked over his shoulder, his eyes bloodshot, his cheeks blown out. He tugged at his end, jerking the chair nearly out of Greta's hands. He was moving them at a rapid clip toward the truck.

Greta took staggering steps, her teeth clenched. Her hold on the chair was slipping.

Dyer dropped off the truck's deck and reached Greta in two big, loping steps. Wolfe barked at him, "She's got it," but Greta was nodding gratefully at Dyer. He nudged in at her shoulder and slid his fingers under the upholstered frame of the chair, easing the weight off her hands. The load pulled at his shoulders; the wood frame must have been made of oak. Greta was strong, but he wasn't surprised she'd been struggling. The thing weighed over two hundred pounds.

Wolfe sent Dyer a tight-jawed look and gave his end a hard tug, ripping the chair out of Dyer's hands. Dyer jumped clear as it fell. It made a woody crack on the paved walk.

"Oh shit," Dyer heard Brian say. He was up on one elbow.

"For *fuck's* sake, Dyer," Wolfe said. His breathing was shallow, whistling through his teeth. His end had fallen out of his hands as well, and now the armchair sat on the ground, dust clouding the sunlight around it. There was no obvious damage, but the cracking sound, like a bone breaking, had been unmistakable. Beneath his heavy brows, Wolfe's eyes were carbon black. He moved around the chair, bumping into it with his shin, speaking quietly, evenly, "She had it."

"She didn't," said Dyer.

In the distance, the carillon sounded a few chiming notes, the first Dyer had heard since the fall. Wolfe was close to him now, his gaze angled down, making the most of his inch of extra height. "What's the matter with you?"

Dyer felt the heat radiating through Wolfe's flannel shirt, a ripe smell to match his own. He held still.

Wolfe's hands formed fists at his sides. He bent his knees a fraction, and his head went motionless. Slowly, a calm worked down his face, loosening the lines in his forehead, softening his stare, evening and deepening his breath. His shoulders dropped. Dyer recognized the feet-apart, balled-fist stance.

The loping transition into Fighting Crane or Sweeping Hip Throw would be sudden, Dyer knew. Wolfe was lowering his center of gravity, letting his body unlock. He was discovering his peaceful center, gathering his energy. Wolfe blinked at Dyer. Wolfe bent his knees a fraction more. Both hands were at his sides, fists turned up. His face was serene.

"Dad," James said.

Dyer felt a cold space open inside his chest where Wolfe would hit him. He'd never taken a punch before. He closed his eyes and waited for the blow, expecting another sound like the chair striking the walk. A splintery crack, bone breaking like wood.

"*Dad,*" James said again. "Don't."

Dyer's eyes snapped open at the sound of James's voice. Wolfe glanced left, toward his son, and Dyer saw the opening — he stumbled backward, out of reach. Wolfe's fists unclenched, and he shifted his balance. Dyer had his own hands up, afraid Wolfe was going to lunge at him.

The headmaster's shoulders lifted and tightened inside his shirt. He took a step toward Dyer, then stopped himself from taking another. Out came a long, unsteady breath. He wiped his palm on the leg of his jeans. A foolish look crossed his face.

Dyer sneaked a glance over at Greta, whose eyes were round, her mouth slightly open at what she'd just seen.

The moment passed. Wolfe turned back to the chair and stared into the cushions. Finally, he lowered himself onto them, sliding his hands under his legs, his weight forward, his back hunched.

Wolfe warmed his face in the sun, then looked at Dyer. "You're not a serious person, you know that? You don't believe in anything. You just put yourself through the motions."

Dyer weathered this.

"You told my son I had something to do with the shooting," Wolfe continued, as if he had stated a settled fact.

Dyer was caught off-guard; surprise came into his face. "I didn't," he said. James looked startled too, his weight back on his heels, his eyes wide. There was recognition in his gaze — recognition and astonishment. Dyer turned back to Wolfe, feeling bolder, feeling that he could go further, say what he was thinking. "He must have figured it out on his own."

Cary, Brian, and Jane all turned flat stares on Wolfe. Greta was looking at him too.

Dyer felt slick sweat under his arms, along the sides of his chest. He remembered how good he'd felt writing that letter, how he'd thought he needed to give Wolfe just what he deserved. And he had, he supposed. Look at him now, hunched over in his broken chair, forearms on his knees, ousted from his job.

"I didn't tell him," Dyer said.

Wolfe shook this off and turned to James, who executed a half turn and took a step toward Jane.

"Well, look," Wolfe said to him. "You're fine. More than fine." He scrutinized James, his gaze lingering before he spoke. James was standing next to Jane now. She touched his back. "Healthy as an ox."

James flinched a little with embarrassment.

"What do you think?" Wolfe asked, still trying to get him to look over, patting the chair's arms, a forced smile on his face. "Worth saving? Or should we pitch it?"

James shrugged, turning to his father with a tight face. "Doesn't matter, I guess."

"Junk," Wolfe said. "I agree." He sighed and leaned back against the cushion. Wood splintered and snapped beneath his weight; the frame sagged, the upholstery let out a belch of dust.

May

D YER JAMMED the nozzle into the tank and squeezed the trigger; the gas pulsed through his palm. Buried in snow since January, the Honda had needed a jump to get out of the faculty lot, and air in the tires from the nearest gas station. Its brown paint was spackled with a yellow scrim of pollen and sticky patches of pinesap. On the New Jersey Turnpike, Dyer had thrown in one of the mix tapes from the collection in the glove compartment, and now Morrissey's mournful voice vibrated in the doors' shot speakers. Dyer couldn't name the song — but it had been a favorite for a stretch of high school. Dyer la-la-la'ed the refrain, too quietly for Greta to hear.

She sat angled out of the open passenger door, rolling her jeans over her pale ankles, unlacing her shoes, and dropping a pair of flip-flops onto the asphalt. "Was Alice pretty?" she asked.

Dyer pretended he'd missed the question, drawing in the gas fumes, drifting inside his head to the whiskey air of Thomas Blanton's office. As newly appointed interim headmaster, Blanton was keeping Dyer on. He'd have a punitive schedule in the fall: two sections of World History for lower-formers, two sections of History 180, the remedial American History class for the upper form — hard work, but also rote. Difficult to fuck up. It was a demotion, but one Dyer felt he deserved.

Beneath the watery relief at keeping his job sat a stone-hard fact — whatever Blanton wanted from him, he'd do. None of the other faculty would know about the letter. Blanton had convinced Tipton to put it in his confidential file. So here was another surrogate father to owe. Howard Phelps, Jim Simon, Edward Wolfe, and now Thomas Blanton: Dyer saw them standing in a line, Dyer passing by, head bowed, wanting each to lay a warm hand on his shoulder. The Koreans had a Confucian phrase: tiger father, dog son. Dyer worked the rhythm, the double syllables, the *tum-tum* of the end.

Dyer focused on the gas-station sunlight, the heat waving up off the pavement, the wandering guitars in the song.

"Did your mom like her?" Greta asked.

Dyer shrugged, then nodded.

Greta sucked on her lips and looked around. "Where are we? Delaware?"

Dyer heard the irritation in her voice. But his mother *had* liked Alice. It would be worse to lie about it. Dyer kept his eyes on the pump, willing it to click off. When did gas get so expensive? In high school, five bucks could get you through the weekend.

"She's wishing you were bringing Alice," said Greta.

"No, she's not. She's thrilled you're coming," said Dyer. Which was basically true. When he told his mother about Greta, she'd said she was happy that he had a date. Greta just frowned at him. They needed to get back on the highway, Dyer thought. There he'd recover the taut-stringed feeling of his drive east, through that lonesome sweep of prairie. The shudder of speed keeping second thoughts at bay. Dyer had no second thoughts about *that* particular decision. Dreaming up development ideas for empty properties in Southern California? He'd been kidding himself. He felt like a teacher now.

The pump clicked off.

"You get my source of stress," Greta said as they pulled back on 95 South. The traffic started to clog.

"You're wondering if you made the right decision."

"I don't think I did," said Greta.

Dyer palmed her knee. "Remember when you fell from the roof of Range? I climbed that tree on pure instinct. I didn't even think."

Greta nodded.

"Same thing with kissing you under the tree. There was no dilemma, no should-I, shouldn't-I? It felt like nothing at all. Like I'd known you for years," said Dyer.

"You're saying, Trust it."

"I've been telling myself to."

Greta leaned over and kissed him on the side of the neck. "I fell anyway. And we didn't speak for months."

Dyer stared at her, his eyes off the road, daring an accident. "Tell me your middle name."

"Pell. One ugly syllable. Greta Pell Salverton."

"It's not ugly at all."

Dyer and Greta pulled up to the house on Stuart Street after 10:00; there'd been nightmare traffic from the Beltway all the way to Fredericksburg, and both were worn out from staring at brake lights. Climbing the steps to the front door, Dyer felt none of the stress echo he anticipated. No images of his mother facedown on the flagstone walk.

Bethany and Mary Joyce ("the brides" Greta had started calling them) were at the Armory Hotel for the weekend, so Dyer and Greta had the house to themselves. He gave her a quick tour, then hauled both their weekend bags up the stairs. The bed in Dyer's room was a single, so they collapsed onto his mother's queen. They lay side by side, took their clothes off, and that was all. Asleep in seconds.

In the morning, after a shower, Dyer found Greta an iron and collected the paper from the front steps. He read the headlines while she got dressed. They were headed to the Armory early so that Dyer could sit with his mother for a half-hour or so before the ceremony. His mother had made the request before he left Britton, and Dyer had agreed, without deciding what he'd do with Greta during that time. Yesterday, stuck in traffic, this had seemed an insolvable problem. Now, rested and happy, Dyer didn't see the big deal. He could just bring Greta up to his mother's hotel room with him, get the introductions over with, and then relax.

Greta came down the stairs into the living room wearing a pale yellow dress, fitted at the waist and crisscrossed by a navy ribbon. Dyer tracked her down the stairs and into the slant of sunlight in the living room. She'd done something with her hair — something with a brush and blow dryer; it curled under gently above her shoulders. Her skin was like white flannel.

"Is there coffee?" she wanted to know.

"You're gorgeous," said Dyer, smoothing a hand down his tie.

Greta smiled at him and turned around.

Dyer came up out of his chair.

"You'll wrinkle it," Greta said as he reached for her hips.

Upstairs at the Armory, Dyer and Mary Joyce moved stiffly into a hug. She wore a light gray pantsuit; a strand of pearls stood out against her tan chest. As far as Dyer could tell, she wore no makeup, but the filaments of silver in her hair had been dyed to light brown highlights. She rubbed his arms as if to warm him up.

" 'Stepmother,' " Dyer said. "I'm trying it out."

"Mary or nothing," she said, giving him a smile. "Come in, come in."

"It's terrific to see you," said Dyer, coming through the hotel room door.

"Your drive must have been endless."

"It's nice to get away for a weekend. And I had company," said Dyer.

Mary nodded over his shoulder. "Did you leave her in the lobby?"

"As a matter of fact."

"You did?"

"Greta wanted to wait," he said. "She thought everyone would be more relaxed after the ceremony."

"Let's hope she's right," Mary said, leading them through a short hallway to the sitting room of the suite. "Your mom's having butterflies."

"Don't minimize it," said Bethany. She sat stiffly and upright in a wing-backed chair, the table beside her crowded with flowers and overflowing fruit baskets. Pins held her dark hair out of her face. Her hands, one cupped in the other, trembled in her lap. Dyer helped her out of her chair, lifting her from her skinny bird arms (she'd lost weight, he noticed). Her mouth was tight and unexpressive, but Dyer could imagine that was a smile, that slight curvature, that plumping of her cheeks.

"Where's Greta?" asked Bethany, carefully articulating the name.

"She's in the lobby."

Bethany's hands came up to jaw height, following tight loops and figure eights. She waved one at him. "Bring her up."

"Didn't you want to sit for a minute?" asked Dyer.

"No," said Bethany. "I'm tired of sitting." Mary let out a noisy sigh. She shook her head and left them alone, closing the bedroom door. Bethany clamped Dyer's forearm with one hand. "She's impatient with me."

"Is she?"

"You could ask her."

But she didn't want him to go. She tugged on his arm, and they started short laps around the room, passing the window that let out onto the Capitol green. Pacing a room like this relieved her stiffness, Dyer knew. A few hundred yards off, Robert E. Lee's bronze head was visible between branches of magnolia and oak.

"You seem nervous," said Dyer.

"I'm morbid," said Bethany. She wore a long raw silk skirt, which made a rustling sound as she walked. "The feeling came to me this morning."

"You think you're making a mistake?" Dyer whispered.

"No, no," said Bethany. "I don't know what I think."

They passed a sideboard with the hotel's leather binder, open to the room service menu, and a notepad with "GRETA SAL-VERTON" written in his mother's wobbly capitals.

"Do you see how much I'm shaking?" Bethany asked.

"Not really," said Dyer, thinking of the smooth turn Greta had made on the living room rug, her skirt belling out from her legs. "You look good, Mom. Great."

Bethany's hand tightened on Dyer's arm. She'd noticed the watch on his wrist. He'd gotten so used to wearing it, he hadn't thought to take the thing off. Embarrassed, and angry at himself, Dyer stared at the floor, at her slow-shuffling feet. He'd never told her about the watch, and he didn't want to answer any questions now. Perhaps Mary had explained what had been in that package from his father back in November—in any case, his mother had never asked. Dyer held his breath as she let her gaze linger on the watch's round, black face. When they passed the sideboard, Bethany looked away. She gestured at the notepad.

"Tell me you're not going to abandon her like you did Alice."

"Last I heard, Alice was dating the director of her film," said Dyer crisply.

"Good for her."

"I think you liked her more than I did."

"I liked that you weren't alone."

"Alice wasn't right for me. We wouldn't have lasted. And I'm with someone now."

Bethany's fingers dug into the muscle of his arm. "So why did you leave her in the lobby?"

"Christ. I'll get her right now." Dyer detached himself from his mother's hand. Bethany wobbled, and Dyer reached out to steady her. "I thought you wanted some time alone with me."

"I do," said Bethany. She softened her voice: "Can we walk?" Dyer nodded, extended his wrist.

Bethany glanced at the watch again. "I wrote your father," she said. "I told him about today."

"Is he coming?" Dyer asked.

She shook her head, grasped his arm, and took a few steps toward the window. "I wanted him to know I wasn't alone," said Bethany.

"You're squeezing me a little hard," said Dyer.

"He sent me a letter thanking me. He made some comment about our wedding night," said Bethany.

Dyer shielded himself with one hand.

"How he kept me up till dawn."

"Stop," said Dyer.

"I didn't want to hear it either. I think he was drunk when he wrote it," she said. She gripped him. "He wanted me to tell you hello."

"He said that in the letter?"

"He hoped you would come visit him."

"No chance."

"None at all?" said Bethany.

"He can come here. Come up to Britton. I'll show him around."

They stopped in front of the window. Starlings were streaming out of a thick oak across the street, a dense black stream, like smoke.

"Going might make you feel better."

"I feel fine," said Dyer through his teeth. "You're the one who's morbid."

The guests stood in an arc in a small banquet room on the ground floor of the hotel, lit by a bell-shaped chandelier. They were friends and ex-colleagues of Mary's, Dyer supposed. Possibly his mother's friends too. He'd been away from Richmond long enough not to know who her friends might be. Dyer kept touching Greta's waist or taking her hand. He appreciated the fact that she let him do this.

The retired judge Mary had asked to officiate, a short, bald man in a dark suit, came in and joined the group with a smile, his gaze moving around to each of the guests, lingering, nodding, gesturing them in tighter around him. Dyer stood close enough to Greta that their shoulders touched. Mary and Bethany came in next — no music, just Bethany clutching Mary's arm, shuffling her feet.

"Your mother looks lovely," Greta whispered to him.

"She looks like she's about to collapse," said Dyer. Bethany's face was pale, her mouth set in a frown.

"She'll be fine," said Greta.

The little group quieted; the judge welcomed them and thanked everyone for coming. He remarked on how lucky Bethany Martin and Mary Joyce were to have found each other, to forge a bond at this happy stage in their life.

Had they had sex? Don't think about it. Of course, Dyer told himself, picturing his mother's sex life with a man wouldn't have been any easier.

He kept me up till dawn. Dyer blinked, trying to focus on what the judge was saying.

"It is a bond forged out of love, honor, and respect," he said.

Dyer watched his mother's gaze connect with Mary's, watched her hands settle into stillness. A little color appeared in her cheeks.

Going might make you feel better.

But it wouldn't. He knew that.

The lines in Bethany's forehead smoothed; her mouth formed a sort of smile.

"You will share equally in the trials of the days to come," the judge said.

He had the summer. Two and a half months, and nothing keeping him in one place.

The judge asked Bethany to repeat after him. "Mary Joyce, I take you as my partner," he said.

Bethany said it back in a whisper.

"And offer all that I am in return."

"And offer all that I am in return," she said.

Greta squeezed his hand. Dyer lost the words. He was sailing across water, spotting palm trees on a white beach in the distance. He felt salt air in his face.

"I pledge to remember, every day of our partnership, why we united here."

Bethany hesitated for a moment, closing her eyes, creasing her brow, as if running the words through her head before repeating them back.

Dyer moved his feet to keep himself steady and planted. Greta looked up at him. He gripped her hand, closed his eyes. He wanted a shimmering nothing to rest his gaze on, but there it was, like the view through a telescope, a circle zooming in: waves on a blue ocean, a sail bellying with wind.